FLYING BLIND

AN EAST MEETS WESTERN

JODI PAYNE
BA TORTUGA

Flying Blind
Copyright © 2020 by Jodi Payne & BA Tortuga

Edited by LC Hinson

Cover illustration by AJ Corza
http://www.seeingstatic.com/
Cover content is for illustrative purposes only and any person depicted on the cover is a model.

ISBN: 978-1-951011-35-2

Print edition published by Tygerseye Publishing, LLC, July 2020
Printed in the USA

As always, to our wives.

FLYING BLIND

an
East Meets Western Novel
by Jodi Payne and BA Tortuga

Sometimes the best thing about living in New York is leaving it.

When January Bell takes a risk on a business trip to Denver and introduces himself to the hot as fire cowboy across the bar, he has no idea what he's in for. Hawk is like nobody he's ever met, and Jan finds he is intrigued enough to want more than just one night with the deceptively complex man.

Hawk Destry is working hard to wring every moment he can out of his bull riding career. He's used to beating the eight second clock, but a life-long degenerative disease is causing him to slowly lose his sight and he doesn't have a lot of years left in the sport.

None of that seems to matter, though, when Hawk meets January, who treats him like he's worth more off a bull than on one, and who's willing to work just as hard to be with him.

The two men have to deal with the distance, unexpected challenges when Hawk visits New York, family on both sides, and neither of them sees any of it coming. Eventually even Hawk's dangerous job is thrown into sharp relief when tragedy strikes. How will January and Hawk find their way when they're flying blind?

1

———

Sometimes the best thing about living in New York City was leaving it.

"What can I get you?" The hotel bartender was burly and handsome, with deep-set dark eyes under a heavy brow and an easy smile framed by a carefully trimmed beard.

January smiled at the man and slid a credit card across the bar. "Do you have Glenlivet?"

"Yessir, twelve okay?"

"That's fine. A double."

The bartender picked up his card and glanced at it. "Running a tab, Mister Bell?"

"Yes, thank you, uh..."

He got a friendly smile. "Alex."

January nodded. "Good to meet you, Alex."

"What brings you to Denver?" Alex pulled the bottle down from a high shelf and set a glass on the bar in front of him. "Convention? A wedding?"

He grinned and shook his head. It was a hotel bar and he was wearing one of his favorite suits. Either one of those things was a good bet. "Just a couple of business meetings."

He wasn't going to say much more, he didn't like to talk about his philanthropy. But his foundation was always searching for new opportunities and sometimes he had to travel to find them.

Alex poured him a generous double, put the cap on the bottle and left it within easy reach. Good call.

A pair of women waved to get Alex's attention and the bartender inclined his head. "Excuse me. We'll get busy here in a bit. Wave when you need me."

"Will do. Thank you." He swirled his whiskey and sniffed it, sighing as the rich, warm scent filled his nostrils, making his mouth water. The weather report was on the TV over the bar and he was surprised that despite the altitude, it wasn't much cooler in Denver than it was back home. Even so, the Mile High City was much more picturesque than the Big Apple tonight, snow and the remnants of twinkling lights from the holiday season.

January touched the glass to his lips, savoring the burn as that first jarring sip soaked into his tongue and slid down his throat, setting him tingling. They'd split up months ago, but this was only his second trip without Lucas and, although the bar was lively, he still felt lonely.

Or no.

Not so much lonely as alone.

He was bad at alone. He'd been both blessed and cursed with a strong, extroverted personality. He could talk to anyone, but he really did need someone to talk to, and his first glass of whiskey was always too quiet.

A raucous band pushed and bounced through the door —cowboy hats and jeans and an amazing array of sports tape and IcyHot and bruises.

"Yo, Alex!"

"Guys, Coors Light all around?"

"All but for Charlie here, man. He lost his fight with Railrunner." One of the cowboys bellied up to the bar, damn near blinding him with a wild, excited shit-eating grin. "Let's make him a virgin something frozen."

Cowboys. One more reason to love Denver.

"You got it." Alex set four silver cans on the bar. "One fakey Pina Colada, coming up."

January glanced at the cowboy over his glass. "Somebody is on the good drugs, huh?" This cowboy seemed pretty beat up too.

"Got his ass trampled in the dirt, yessir. Made his ride, though." God, that smile—part Dennis the Menace, part Mathew McConaughey.

Made his ride? Come on, Jan. You're a smart guy. The pieces were floating around but he wasn't putting them together. Injured cowboy, dirt, Denver.

Trampled. Did cowboys do MMA? January tilted his head, failing to get a look at the eyes shadowed by the man's hat, though he caught the bright blond hair well enough.

"Railrunner, huh? Son of a bitch." Alex peered over his shoulder at the group of men in hats as the blender whirred. "Is Charlie still on the roster for tomorrow? My girl got tickets for the show. I might have a little money on him." Alex grinned at the cowboy sheepishly. "Sorry."

Tickets.

"Sure he is, but you wasted your money. I'm in a solid third, and I'm taking the short-go and the event, you watch." The guy didn't seem to be worried in the least, or offended.

"It's no fun to go after the easy money." That was an obvious tease. "I guess I'll see how you do tomorrow, won't I?" Alex shut the blender off, poured the frozen mixture into a glass and set it on the bar. A couple of arms reached between January and the cowboy and pulled all the drinks off the bar, leaving one beer behind.

I'll take rodeo for five-hundred, Alex. "Bulls?"

"Oh, these crazy bastards are bull riders. Good guys, great tippers, but rowdy? Wow."

Wow was right. But they were just having fun, which was good by him. "I can't say I've ever met a bull rider."

"You want me to introduce you to Hawk there? He's hilarious. He's like talking to someone from a movie or something."

He did like the accent. The shoulders too, if he was honest. And the cowboy's ass, if he let himself go there.

And why not go there?

"Sure. I'd love that." He'd talked to celebrities before, even straight ones.

"I'll make the intros when he comes to grab his beer." Alex nodded to him, like he did this every day, which January supposed he did.

"Cool. Thanks." Well, that would never happen in New York. He sipped his drink, enjoying the warmth and watched the group of men out of the corner of his eye. So much testosterone standing in those boots. It was hot as hell.

Hawk did, in fact, come for his beer, nodding to Alex as his hand wrapped around it. "Charlie says you did good, man. Thanks."

"No problem. Hey, you met Mr. Bell here? He's in on business."

"I haven't." Hawk turned to him, eyes hidden behind thick, little round glasses, and held out one square, scarred up hand. "Hawk Destry, pleased to meet you."

It only took him a second to decide it wasn't worth the risk of getting his ass kicked, so when he shook Hawk's hand he was careful to keep it all business, despite the allure of that stubborn chin. "January Bell. Good to meet you too. Alex says you're a bull rider?"

"That's the rumor." Hawk climbed up on the barstool next to him, the man laughing at himself. "Some days I do better than others."

January grinned. "Didn't you say you had this one in the bag?"

"I sure did, and I stand by that. Assuming I get a good draw, my bull rope doesn't pop on me, and I keep riding like I have, I'm golden." Hawk chuckled and rolled his eyes dramatically. "Good thing I tend to ride good late in the season, huh?"

He wasn't sure how Hawk managed to pull off arrogance and self-awareness at the same time. It was fascinating. Maybe the smile kind of smoothed out the edges. Whatever it was, January liked it. "Your draw is what? The order you ride in?"

"The bull you ride. The order goes by ranking. Right now I'm sitting in third. We'll see if I can't improve it."

He'd love to have this cowboy in the bag. "Are any of these guys ahead of you right now?" He knew he was wasting his time, but January dared to lean in a little anyway and took a sip of his whiskey.

He swore he saw Hawk's nostrils flare, the man tuning into him. "Charlie is, but he's hurting bad." The words were a fascinating mixture of sympathy and complete lack of care. "Tell me about you, now. Here on business?"

"Yes. I've got a couple of meetings, then I head back to New York." He tossed out a bone. "Just three nights."

"New York, huh? I been there a couple times for events. It's huge and shiny. Lots of folks."

"It's both of those things. I love it, though the hustle

and the crowds can get a little much sometimes." Thankfully he had a little sanctuary on the Upper West Side with a view of the park. He spoiled himself, he knew. Even his suite at the hotel was a splurge. "Did you like it when you visited?"

"Sure did. I like seeing new stuff. My job keeps me on the road a lot, so it's a good thing." Was Hawk checking him out? Surely not. They didn't make gay cowboys, did they?

"I get away once a month or so. Even more in the summer if I can find an excuse. It's hot in the city. I like the mountains, even if I don't get there as often as I'd like. I have a great view from my suite though. The Rockies are beautiful with all the white." He turned on his stool and swept the hem of his suit jacket off his hip to give Hawk more to glance at, if in fact the cowboy was looking. "Do you drink scotch? This is a nice one."

"Is it?" That smile flashed again. "Let me buy us a round, then. See if our tastes mesh."

Oh ho. So cowboys do come in gay. Sweet.

January caught Hawk's arm as the man reached for his wallet, trying again to get a peek at Hawk's eyes. The glasses were adorably geeky, incongruous under the hat. "Let me, please."

There was a sizzling moment where the air between them burned, and it was blistering, dangerous, and sexual as hell. "Sounds like a plan."

"It does, doesn't it?" He let go of Hawk's arm and waved the bartender over. There was no reason to play games with the pull so strong and clear between them. "Alex? I'll take the bottle, and I'd like to close out my tab please."

Alex seemed a little confused but nodded and punched something into the register. "You got it."

January dipped his fingers into his inside jacket pocket,

pulled out a business card and a pen, and wrote his suite number on the back.

"Sign here, Mr. Bell. I hope everything is all right?"

"Just fine, thank you." He wrote in a generous tip and signed his name, then lifted the half-full bottle of whiskey off the bar and handed the business card to Hawk. "I look forward to seeing you again soon."

"Give me two shakes to finish my beer." Hawk lifted the bottle and saluted him before he headed over to his friends, moving slow and giving him a chance to see.

"Making new friends with a sh-uit, Hawk?" Charlie was slurring a bit, but between the bruised jaw and the drugs that wasn't surprising. "What is he, a sh-ponsor?"

Hawk looked back at him, winked, then turned back to the group, giving him a nice view at a tiny, perfectly framed ass. "He ain't with the tour, man. I thought maybe he was a fan. Y'all going to get Charlie here up to his bed?"

He was definitely a fan. Just not of the rodeo.

He left Hawk to finish his beer and make whatever exit he needed to make and took his bottle of scotch upstairs to his top-floor suite, where he poured himself another shot of liquid courage. He didn't feel guilty or awkward; those weren't things he had time for. But it had been a while since he'd quite so obviously let his dick do the thinking.

It wasn't long before a knock sounded on the door, shave and a haircut. Hell, even the knock was brash, bold. He set two glasses next to the bottle on the dresser and went to answer the door.

There was a cowboy at his door all right. Boots, hat, jeans, square shoulders, bravado and all. Something about the way Hawk was standing felt a little like a challenge.

"Hey. Come on in."

"Thanks for the invite. I appreciate it."

"It's... good to be appreciated." He'd heard a lot of pick-up lines, but that was a new one. He stepped aside to let Hawk enter, laughing gently as he closed and locked the door behind them. "Do you not get many invitations?"

"I've had a couple three. Just needed to make sure we understood what I came up for." Suddenly Hawk was right there, solid as a rock, one hand on his hip.

"Scotch?" January teased.

Jesus. Hawk was giving off enough heat to melt the city. And with that touch on his hip, whatever electricity had passed between them at the bar was back, only this time without the restraint of public eyes on them, January could do what he'd wanted to do then. He reached for Hawk's shirt and tugged it out of the well-worn Wranglers, slipping a hand under the hem to rest on warm skin and the hardest set of abs he'd ever felt. "Damn, cowboy."

"I live and die on core strength." Hawk found one of his nipples through his dress shirt, thumb dragging over his skin.

Nothing like finding one of his hottest hot spots on the first try. January hissed and leaned into the touch, fingers going to work on Hawk's shirt, buttons sliding open one by one from the bottom up. He inhaled deeply, the scent of hungry man making his balls ache. He reached up with both hands and touched the frame of Hawk's glasses, raising an eyebrow. "May I?"

"Sure. Put them somewhere safe." The stroking turned into a firm pinch.

His toes curled. That was fucking right. "Easy, I don't want to drop them." He took Hawk's glasses, folded them carefully and set them behind him on the dresser, right next to the bottle of scotch. Didn't get much safer than that. He bent a little, but he still couldn't get a look at those eyes, hiding under the brim of Hawk's hat.

He shrugged his jacket off catching it with one hand and tossing it over a chair.

"Where was I? Oh right. Here." He fanned his fingers out across those abs again. "Living and dying."

"Mmhmm." Hawk put his hat, brim up, on the end table, exposing a short-cropped mass of white curls, and light blue eyes that were almost crystalline. Impressive. And lovely.

He pushed the shirt off Hawk's shoulders and took a light, tentative kiss, wondering, asking. Not every man he'd known was into kissing a one-night stand. The answer was straightforward and direct—Hawk kissed him like he was storming a beach at Normandy.

Oh. Fuck yeah. It was so on.

He helped Hawk get the shirt off while they fought for tongue positions and with each other's buttons and zippers. He got his fingers under Hawk's waistband and cupped a smooth, hot ass cheek that was nearly as muscled as the cowboy's abs. Fuck, that was hot. He worked out, but January felt like a marshmallow next to this guy.

Hawk was like a marble statue come to life—chiseled and hard, but still burning with his need. Burning he understood. He shouldered Hawk toward the bed. "Sit." He gave Hawk a light shove to make his point and tugged the man's jeans over his hips.

"Let me get my boots, or I'll be caught at the ankle."

"Boots? Oh." He stepped out of the way and watched as Hawk wrestled with the boots and the denim. Huh. He'd file that under *things to know before fucking a cowboy*.

He kicked off his own shoes while Hawk dealt with footwear drama and tossed his shirt aside with them.

Hawk stripped down, showing off a heavy cock, icy pubes, and a set of feathers inked over his collarbones.

"I hadn't planned on bringing a stacked, sexy cowboy to my suite tonight, you know. I thought I'd be finishing another glass or two and watching a game on TV." He kicked everything aside and stood at a short distance, letting Hawk have an eyeful too. Hawk seemed so young, naked and blue eyed and without that hat. He felt a little old.

"Mmm, that would be a waste. Look at you. I could eat your happy ass alive."

He was a little more interested in Hawk's happy ass, frankly. He moved forward, the proximity making him burn and his fingers long to touch. Hawk's blond curls were baby soft as he ran his fingers through them and long enough to tug.

So he did. "How about my cock instead?"

"Oh, I do like a man that knows what he wants." Those icy eyes flashed up at him. "You going to get it up again and fuck me like I need?"

Wow. Those eyes. And talk about knowing what you wanted. "Not to worry. I'm only offering you a taste, cowboy. We had an understanding, I think."

"Only a taste, hmm? We'll see about that. I'm pretty damn good at what I do." Hawk cupped his balls, squeezing enough to bring him up on his toes.

Okay sure good whatever you want. He leaned into the touch. Something about this guy made him so ready to let go. But he had plans too.

"Humble. I've heard that about cowboys."

"Meek. Mild. Salt of the earth." Hawk understood how to unfasten another man's slacks.

"Four for four." He watched Hawk's scarred fingers work,

thinking they were surprisingly delicate for someone that spent most of their time with thousand-pound animals.

"You forgot hard as nails and twice as tough."

He sucked in a breath as his cock and the cool room air met. "Oh, now you're talking about me."

"Mmm, look at this fine bit of rope." Hawk measured him, base to tip, then did it again, lips opening to take his tip in.

January sighed and reminded himself to be patient, but his fingers made a fist in the cowboy's hair anyway, blond curls popping up between his knuckles. He knew without asking that Hawk would be more than ready for whatever he wanted to dish out, but he was still a gentleman despite all appearances at the moment.

First times and all, right?

Hawk cupped his balls, rolling them and making him gasp, even as Hawk's mouth dropped down and down, the blistering suction surrounding his prick.

"Mmm." All right, it seemed like Hawk did have something to brag about. January spread his feet wider and arched his hips forward, his eyes glued to that hungry mouth. Hawk went down on him like a Hoover, taking him in to the root and swallowing hard before moving back up to work his tip.

He closed his eyes to feel for a minute, enjoy Hawk's heat. Hawk's mouth was heaven- he could let the cowboy take him all the way like this for sure. Sometime, when he was with a lover he knew he'd see more than once, he would let himself indulge again. But he *wanted* Hawk. He wanted that strong, muscled body underneath him.

Soon. January shivered and groaned as Hawk swallowed, throat going tight around his prick. Maybe soon-ish.

In a minute.

First, he needed to enjoy what this cowboy could teach him about flying.

"Jesus." He opened his eyes again. "I'm going to fuck you so hard you'll still feel me when you win tomorrow night."

"Mmhmm..." The hum sent vibrations all the way through to his bones. Fuck, Hawk was too good at this.

Too Goddamn good, and he'd had a little scotch. "Enough." The word came out softer than he'd intended, raspy in his dry throat. He tried again, with more conviction. "I said a taste, cowboy. That's enough."

He tugged on Hawk's hair, and his cock popped out of Hawk's lips. They both groaned at the loss, with Hawk swaying on the mattress.

"That's it." He did appreciate a man that enjoyed giving head. "Crawl on up there and let me see that ass." It was a thing of beauty in blue jeans, and Hawk obviously knew it. January was looking forward to what the denim had been hiding.

Hawk crawled up to the head of the bed, pretty little ass swaying back and forth to tease the fuck out of him.

"Mm-mm." He reached across the bed to give one round cheek a love-tap, then slid out of his trousers. "Has anyone ever told you that you have a perfect ass?"

"Oh, flattery will so get you laid." Hawk knelt up tall, ass cheeks clenched tight.

"Proud of it, are you?" He knelt right behind Hawk, coaxing Hawk's knees open a little wider with his own, and slid his hands along the line of Hawk's hips until they met, stretching wide again across those killer abs.

"You know it." He could feel the way those muscles worked to keep them both upright.

He pressed close to Hawk's back, letting his cock nestle into the warm cleft of that fine ass, and tasted a scarred shoulder with his tongue. That earned him a soft moan, and Hawk rocked back, ass teasing the hell out of him.

"There's a little black bag next to your hat on the nightstand. Can you reach it?" So, he hadn't made plans, but he was prepared anyway. Nothing put a damper on a spontaneous tryst like stopping in the hotel gift shop for a rubber, or worse, discovering it was closed.

"You got it." Hawk settled deeper, thighs parted as he balanced and reached. Oh. Oh, that was the promise of pure sex. He slipped a hand through that inviting gap and cupped Hawk's balls. They were silky and heavy and filled his whole hand.

Even better, they were shaved, smooth as silk, making all sorts of promises, each one better than another. Something told him waxing wasn't cowboy standard issue. So intriguing, this man. A tangle of stereotypes and contradictions that Hawk simply owned, without shame or apology. It was sexy as hell.

"Tada!" Hawk straightened up, chuckling as he did. "That's a right obliques workout. I'll have to remember that."

"I know I won't forget it any time soon," he teased and unzipped the little pouch pulling out what he needed. "That was a truly memorable view."

Hawk put his hands on the wall behind the bed and arched, showing off shamelessly.

He swallowed hard. "Damn, Hawk." January slicked a couple of fingers and touched the cool lube to the cowboy's beautifully presented hole.

"Guy's got to know how to get what he needs."

"You don't have to beg me, cowboy. I'm all in." He slipped one finger inside, twisting it and circling the rim before adding a second.

Tight. He could only imagine that heat around his cock, working him. Milking him.

And Hawk was definitely focused and clear about what he needed. Jan was looking forward to blowing the cowboy's mind a little. "I'm so ready for you."

"Bring it on." Hawk was so fierce, so in control of what he wanted.

January moved in close and lined up, wondering for a second if it would be rude to remind the man to breathe. "We'll start easy." He hooked one hand around Hawk's hip and used his body weight to start to push inside, groaning as he met the natural resistance of Hawk's body.

He heard the soft, shaky exhale, the first hint of any vulnerability at all. The truth of it was beautiful though and it made him shiver, the chance to own a piece of the cowboy's swagger, even for an hour, giving him a thrill.

"I've got you." He bent over Hawk's back and rocked forward, sinking deeper into that incredibly tight heat. "Breathe. It's good."

"Yeah. Fucking A it is." Hawk leaned toward him, hips moving in a steady rhythm that threatened to steal his breath.

He worked with Hawk, picking up the cowboy's rhythm and taking it deeper, stronger. The way it built up on its own was so sweet, made him ache just right.

"Oh honey, like that. Just like that."

That was better. That sounded like need.

"Yeah." January focused on Hawk, his own need slowly building. "You're going to lose your mind before I'm done with you."

"Promises, promises." Hawk gripped him, squeezing hard enough to steal his breath.

"Fuck," he managed to bite out, followed by a deep

grunt. Hawk was way too fucking together. He reached under and caught the cowboy's thick prick in one hand, gripping it tight.

January felt that response, all around his cock, and the soft grunt that he got from Hawk proved that he had the cowboy's attention.

"Hot." He stroked hard several times before letting go and taking hold of Hawk's narrow hips with both hands instead. He picked up the pace and drove in deep, moving beyond Hawk's direction and taking them where he wanted to be.

Hawk reached down with one hand, pumping himself hard. With the couple of brain cells not busy, January managed to be impressed with Hawk's balance.

That was the end of rational. He hauled back on Hawk's hips. The sound of their bodies coming together over and over filled the room along with their rough breathing. He was determined to hold out for Hawk. but that sweet ass clung to him, hot and tight, and it took all his concentration.

"Come on. Harder. So fucking close." The words weren't a plea; they were a demand.

"Pushy fucking cowboy."

He set his jaw, stared down the back of Hawk's damp, blond head and thrust hard enough to send both of them rocking toward the headboard.

That was it. That earned him a cry, but nothing coherent at all.

So there.

January took a breath and focused on Hawk, dishing out more of the same until Hawk gave up trying to counter him. The cowboy melted around him, the heat increasing as Hawk gave in.

It was hard to resist the draw of Hawk's shining skin and

tired muscle; he could lick the man all over. And he might, later. At the moment his body was screaming to let go, and it was all he could do to keep up his nearly savage pace.

Hawk's shout echoed as he shot, every pulse of pleasure echoing around his prick.

"Yes!" *Oh sweet fuck yes.* He fought through the tight grip around his hungry prick and took the last of what he needed—a handful of quick, shallow thrusts—and followed the cowboy over with a long, relieved groan.

Hawk slumped toward the wall, panting hard under him. It felt good, knowing he gave Hawk what he needed.

He shivered as he pulled away to ditch the condom, then he got a little of that taste he wanted, dropping kisses across the cowboy's back. "Lie down with me. Stay a while." He'd never kicked anyone out. People left and he got that, but he liked it if they stayed.

"Yeah? I can do that." Hawk exhaled, settling down, turning toward him.

Score. He was happy to hold that body for a while. He extended an arm, inviting Hawk to move in closer. "You good? Okay?"

"Better than. I may have lost a few brain cells with that orgasm."

He huffed, a weak laugh about all he could manage. "Well, they're happily somewhere with mine. That was great." He inhaled as Hawk settled in, more intrigued by the cowboy's scent than he should be. He was truthfully more intrigued by Hawk in general than he should be.

Cowboy. Seriously, he'd had the orgasm of the year with a rodeo cowboy in Denver.

"Nap? Stay as long as you want. The suite comes with a killer breakfast." He wanted Hawk to stay, and not because it was more food than he could possibly eat alone.

"Does it come with a round two?"

Oh. Heck, yeah. He wanted that too. "Are you kidding? That's hours from now. We'll be on three by then at least, don't you think? Four?"

"Oh, I do like how you think." Hawk snuggled right in with a moan.

He circled his arm over Hawk's shoulders. "I'm told I snore a little," he teased, talking through a huge yawn.

"I've been rooming with cowboys for fifteen years, honey. You could be the Latvian chain saw drill team and I could rest."

He laughed, or thought he did. He tried anyway. And January fell asleep with an arm full of studly, irresistible cowboy.

2

———

Hawk's ass ached in the best possible way, and he thought his balls might never recover.

It was amazing.

Go him for reading that scenario right and finding what he fucking needed without getting his ass kicked. Not that that was bad, honestly, just way more of a challenge.

He watched January sleep, the man nowhere near the snorer of some he'd slept with. January. What a fucking cool name. Seriously. Not as ironic as naming a kid Hawk that was damn near blind as a bat, already. That gave his momma about a zillion irony points.

January's dark hair stood out against the bright white pillows and pointed in every direction, not a bit of the neatly combed look and perfectly straight part left after round two.

On the nightstand, January's phone lit up and went dark, lit up and went dark again with the ringer off like the man didn't give a damn. And it seemed like January could afford not to.

He grinned and shook his head. He'd turned his off on

the way up, with the hope that he needed to save battery. He'd have to charge up in the locker room.

January licked his lips and tucked him closer, eyes staying closed. "I know you're awake. Your breathing is different." Such a soft voice, as if breaking the silence was a bad idea.

"I was watching you." He was committing the hot bastard to memory. He needed jack off material.

January grinned and stretched. "See anything you like?"

"You know it." He took it all in, reaching out to trace all those interesting lines and hollows.

January's eyes blinked open and found him. "Good. Me too. You're built like a tank, man. A hot little tank. I'm glad our tangle was friendly, pretty sure you could kick my ass."

"I'm a friendly cowboy. Almost timid." He did his best to keep a straight face.

"Oh yes, timid. We'll add that to humble, meek, mild..." January rolled up on one side to face him. "You're an angel."

"You know my secrets now..." He reached out and tweaked one nipple, teasing outrageously.

"Mmm." January took his hand and flattened it, and curious fingers reached up to play with his hair. "Surely you have more interesting secrets. Give me enough time, I'll figure them out."

Yeah, he held his secrets pretty close, but it might be fun to watch January try to ferret them out.

There was a friendly knock at the door. "Oh. Angel. Go let breakfast in, will you?"

"I can do that." He sat up, blinking hard. "Glasses?"

"I sat them down next to the scotch." January pointed in the direction of the TV.

"Cool. Coming!" Fuck. He headed that direction,

tripping over his jeans on the way. At least he found the jeans. He tugged them on, fumbling around for his glasses.

January appeared beside him all of a sudden, placed his glasses in his hand, and gave him a light chuck on the shoulder before walking away. "I'm gonna take the world's fastest shower. Cool? You help yourself."

"Thanks." He got the table in, then he poured himself a cup of coffee. He found his socks and tugged on his shirt. Should he go? Maybe. He had morning breath, and he didn't know if quick shower was New York for 'get on, man'.

It also didn't turn out to be too fast a shower. January wasn't going to win any contests that was for sure. But he was pink-skinned and clean-shaved when he came back from the bathroom, towel wrapped around his hips and sporting that perfect hair. And he didn't seem upset to find Hawk still there.

"Did you eat? You want a shower? Oh. Coffee."

"Nah, I'll shower in my own room, honey, put on work clothes and all." He finished his cup. He'd catch a ride in with Garrett and Little Ben, cover his two bulls, and pick up his buckle. It was a plan.

"Suit yourself." January pulled on black boxer-briefs, then started lifting off the room service plate covers and setting them aside. "There's eggs, bacon, pancakes... come on over and eat something."

"I don't suppose there's a spare toothbrush in the bathroom, honey?"

"Yep. You get spoiled in these suites. Toothbrushes, deodorant, all kinds of stuff in a little basket. Help yourself." January was totally casual about it, all 'help yourself' like Hawk was a real guest and went on putting a plate together for himself.

"Thanks, honey. I've got dragon mouth." And he was hoping for another kiss.

He toodled into the big bathroom, did his business, and gave himself a whore's bath before he brushed his teeth. Lord have mercy. He was going to soak in the tub for an hour before he rode.

January had the curtains open and was sitting with his plate at a little table near it texting like his thumbs were on fire. The view out the window was amazing—the darkness of the city, a swath of green, and a ton of blue sky between them and the mountains.

"Thanks for letting me borrow your bathroom." He stole a bite of bacon and another cup of coffee. He turned his phone on, unsurprised that he didn't hear any texts. The guys would all be sleeping it off.

"Anytime." January glanced up from his phone. "Not a breakfast person?"

He blinked. Obviously this guy didn't understand how many calories were in pancakes. "I love breakfast. I love food. I love paying my bills and riding more."

He kept himself on a strict diet during the season. It was the only way to ride—be lean and strong and stay healthy. He knew himself—that five pounds from eating some eggs and pancakes would unbalance his happy ass.

January seemed surprised. "Surely you work hard enough to burn off breakfast. Do bull riders have a weight requirement, like jockeys do?"

"Nah, not officially, but you got to figure, I learned to ride when I was fourteen. I weighed eighty pounds. I weigh more than that now, but my balance was set then. Every extra pound is a problem." And work hard? Shit, he worked for a couple minutes a weekend, to be honest. Otherwise he was in the air or at his folks.

"It's hard to grow into a sport. That happens to all kinds of athletes." January nodded and got up to cover up the food. "I'll move this. Nothing worse than staring at food you can't eat."

"No stress. I'm used to it. I got a big family. Six brothers. All bulldoggers." Six bulldoggers, their wives, sixteen grandkids—Momma was super good about providing egg white omelets on demand.

"Six brothers? Good lord." January pushed the cart off to one wall. "What does a bulldogger do?"

He blinked. He'd never had anyone ask. "Um. Well, they're rodeo guys—not roughstock, but ropers. Big old boys that tackle steers from horseback, throw them on the ground and tie their feet. And they're timed."

"Big guys that throw themselves off perfectly good horses." January grinned. "Ranch skills, I know, but wow. I like all my limbs intact."

"What's the fun in that?" He could tease, because he, at least, had all his fingers.

"None." January laughed. "There's no fun in that at all. I'm absolutely chickenshit. But at least there's a good chance I'll be in one piece if you need me."

"Rodeoing is a lifestyle, I think. Good money, if you're good at it. You get to go places." *You burn out quick, and you get to retire before you lose everything.*

"High risk, high reward? I'm more of a stock market junkie than an adrenaline junkie. But I definitely appreciate the hard work. It looks damn good on you."

"Thanks. You busy today? I can get you into the show, if you want." He didn't figure that it would work, but it was worth asking.

January smiled and leaned back in his chair, watching Hawk closely. "Are you inviting me to come watch you ride, angel? Because that's awfully close to saying you want to see me again."

Oh, for fuck's sake. "I am. You're welcome to come or not. And if you want to fuck again, I'm in. I'm here until tomorrow morning." He pulled out his wallet and found the plain white card with his cell number on it. "This is me."

"And you have mine." January stood and walked over to him, took the card in one hand and his jaw in the other and kissed him.

Fuck, that felt good. He opened and pushed up, letting January feel how much he wanted more, another night before they went their separate ways.

January's kiss was all heat and promise and left them both breathless. "I... If I didn't have a meeting in a half an hour I'd... If you arrange a ticket for me, I'll be there."

"It'll be at will call. Doors open at two, event starts at two thirty or so." Oh, he wanted a piece of that. Again. Now.

He'd jack off to that kiss in the tub.

"I might be a little late. When do you ride?"

"I'll ride first in around three thirty and then the short-go at five-ish." If he was lucky, as he tended to be.

"I'll make that for sure. Dinner and that scotch after?" January smoothed a hand over his chest. "Here... if you like."

"Sounds perfect. I'll be here with bells on." Hell, he'd even buy, especially if he won.

January fussed over him, finger combing his hair and smoothing his eyebrows. "I hope your friend is up to riding. He seemed pretty high last night."

"Charlie has been stoned since the last broken vertebrae, man. It's his natural state of being. I'll check-in on him before I get a bath." That was sweet as fuck. He liked that.

January shook his head and he finally got a good look at

the man's eyes. Blue. A dark, dark blue. "Be careful out there."

"That's the plan. Two rounds. Eight seconds. Big check." Up. Down. Payday.

"Oh that's all?" January gave him another quick kiss and stepped away, then pulled another fancy suit out of the closet and laid it on the bed. "I love that confidence. You're going to kill it."

"You know it." He buttoned his shirt and smoothed his curls. "All right, man. See you after. I'll leave you a ticket."

"Looking forward to it." January caught him by the arm on his way by. "Thank you." Hawk was pretty sure that was about more than the ticket.

"Ditto. I'm riding sore today. It'll be something else." He winked and headed out. Time to work.

He'd think about a different kind of hard ride after.

3

January had been born into money. That was a fact. His family was loaded. He'd been raised swimming in it, and he got everything he wanted and more than he could ever ask for, too. He'd been told all kinds of stories about how it was honest money, that his grandfather had emigrated to the states with a little and made a fortune out of it.

When he didn't get into the Ivy League like his siblings, he hadn't been invited to join the family business, so he'd had to figure out a future for himself that didn't involve sitting on his money. He made a couple of wise investments with it—well, lucky investments that had seemed wise at the time—so he was earning money of his own. But he wasn't working too hard for it, so he'd decided to start a foundation and give some away.

Yeah, he knew it was thumbing his nose at his father to a certain degree, but how honest was money if you didn't use some of it to make the world better?

"Uh... I'm going to the rodeo?" It probably would have been a good idea to ask Hawk the name of the venue; he felt like an idiot, but his cab driver didn't even bat an eye and pulled away from the curb.

Okay then.

His meeting was interesting, and he was going to have to give their discussion some thought. It needed his attention, but he was having trouble focusing. He was distracted by the delicious ache in his thighs, the little bit of stiffness in his back, and the pale blue eyes that kept looking back at him every time he closed his own.

That had been one hell of a night. He was feeling smug enough to brag so he pulled out his phone.

There were already two photos from Jax—a doughnut made up to be a single-serve strawberry shortcake, and a gorgeous loaf of brown bread.

His stomach growled. He hadn't eaten much breakfast after Hawk told him about his diet. It seemed mean to stuff his face while Hawk nibbled on a piece of bacon.

January glanced at his watch. New York was two hours ahead so Jax was probably at the gym. He texted anyway.

Oh those look good. But I win. I had a cowboy last night.

Like yippee-kai-yay? He could see Jax's pierced eyebrow lifting.

Like bull rider. Shit, I didn't get his last name, or you could probably google him. He got a phone number though. Ha.

*Was it a good ride? *waggles eyebrows**

Oh, funny.

Let's say he tried very hard to buck me off. Good time to call you? He had at least five minutes to chat before he got to the rodeo venue.

His phone rang almost immediately, Jax's face bobbing up on his phone. When he answered, he heard, "Are you popping cherries on the locals?"

He laughed loud enough his cabbie glanced at him in

the rearview. "No. Jesus. This guy knew what he wanted and apparently felt like I was capable. He wore me out."

"I didn't think that was possible," Jax teased. "I mean, damn! So, did you at least get his number this time?"

"Don't tell anyone, I have a reputation to look after." Jax. Talk about hard to keep up with. January was glad they'd never actually gone that far. "I did get his number, and a ticket to see him compete tonight. I'm on my way there now. Is that wild or what? I'm going to the rodeo."

"You. The rodeo. Man, I want proof. I want pictures." Jax cackled for him, the sound like a big bird.

"I'll get some! He has a great hat and everything, like a real cowboy. Not like a New Yorker in a hat. This one's worn in. Jax, he has this amazing accent. I think he's from Texas." He wondered whether Hawk rode in those glasses, or maybe athletic glasses? He seemed pretty seriously nearsighted.

"No shit? A Texan? Do they make gay Texans?"

"Yes!" January laughed because he'd thought the same thing. "And apparently cowboys come in gay too. Or bi. Or whatever, I'm not picky." He had good luck though. Because Texan cowboys definitely came in hot, as advertised. And the way Hawk took him, this particular cowboy was needing in the worst way.

"Well, obviously this guy isn't either. He's fucking around with you..." Jax managed not to laugh for about two seconds, maybe.

"See? You better lay off the piercings, asshole. That's the metal poisoning I warned you about talking."

"One day it'll draw Mr. Right in, you see?"

"Let's hope it works better than an expensive suit. That hasn't brought me much luck."

The cab stopped and he swiped his card through the

reader and punched in a tip, then gave the cabbie a wave for a thank you as he climbed out.

"I'm here." And he stood out like a sore thumb. "In a fucking business suit."

"Well, buy you a cowboy hat and you can pretend to be an oilman."

January kind of felt like pretending to be anything in this crowd was a bad idea. Except straight. He should probably pretend that. "I think I'll skip the hat. Hey, I better run, I'm already late. It's been good bragging to you."

"I expect pictures, man. I mean it."

The tickets at will call were marked VIP, which felt pretty cool, and when he showed it to the usher, a pretty little girl wearing a hat, boots, and very little else, lead him right down to the front to where there was a mass of cattle and cowboys and pyrotechnic shit, right in front of him.

Cool.

All right. VIP. He'd own the suit like he belonged there. He took his seat, nodding to the young woman in the seat next to him. "Hey. Where are we in the program? Did I miss the bulls?"

"They're running late—some problem with the cameras, so you're in luck. They're about to start." She offered him a wide smile. "I'm Nicole Jeffers, Danny Jeffers' wife. Are you family?"

"No. No, I'm in town on business and I met Hawk Destry in the hotel bar last night. We got to talking and he offered to get me a ticket." That was all true, right? Mostly. "I actually know next to nothing about rodeo."

"This isn't rodeo, honey. It's bullriding." She winked and laughed like she was telling him a joke.

"Well, I sat next to the right person. I've learned something already." He smiled back. "Glad I didn't miss it."

He looked into the group of cowboys, trying to spot the one he was there to see.

"I am too. The bulls are ready to go today. Did you say you were Hawk's friend? He's down there talking to Charlie and Houston. He won't ride for a few, but he'll be up on champion row."

"He seemed to think so." January spotted Hawk now that she pointed the man out and was instantly captivated by the cowboy's swagger. The way he was standing, the set of his shoulders... and January got to have that in his bed again tonight. His balls ached thinking about it.

"If he rides, he's got it by the numbers. He's going to have to go down in the well if anyone else is going to have a chance." It was like she was speaking another language.

He laughed, glancing over at her. "Cool. I don't know what that means, but you let me know if that happens." Whatever it was, he doubted it would happen. He liked Hawk's confidence, he believed it. And from the way Nicole was talking, it was earned. "Which one is your husband?"

"See the hot little redhead with the great smile and the broke free arm?" She pointed at a young kid with a huge cast and a shit-eating grin. "He's my baby daddy."

January thought the kid looked more like a goofy little redhead, but he was adorable all the same. He didn't seem a day over twelve though. "Congratulations. Is he going to ride with that arm?"

"Yes, sir. He bucked off yesterday, but he rode Friday, so he could still make the short-go." She shot him a smile. "And I can tell we're going to be friends, so you'd best tell me your name."

"I'm sorry, I'm terrible about that." He offered a hand to shake. "I'm January Bell. I'm from New York."

"Wow." Her eyes lit up, excitement obvious in them.

"Danny says it's too big of a place for me to go, even with the tour and him and all. Is it amazing? Do you get to see the Thanksgiving balloons and all?"

"They're something to see for sure." He didn't dare say that he avoided the parade at all costs and watched on TV like everyone else because he didn't want to hurt her feelings. "I love New York. It's big, Danny's right, but it's not scary once you get to know it a little." He reached into his breast pocket and pulled out a business card. "In case you and Danny ever want a tour."

"Oh, thanks. We'll see. Danny worries about me and this little one." She patted her stomach. "I'd sure like to go sometime. I want to see the lights. I've been to Dallas, Houston, Austin, Oklahoma City, and now here."

"It's his job to worry, so let him." He winked at her and was ready to ask baby questions but he was interrupted by a big commotion as the event finally got underway. "Oh. Cool. It's starting."

He was probably more excited than he should be at his age, but what the hell? How often was he going to get to see this? And from these amazing seats, too. He pulled out his phone and snapped a couple of pictures of cowboys and livestock and fired one off to Jax with, *it's starting.*

The lights went off, and the pyrotechnics started. It was a huge production—fire, banging, music, all the cowboys introduced. All the cowboys but the one he wanted. What the hell?

He leaned over to ask where Hawk was when Nicole beamed at him. "Hawk's fixin' to be featured. One day it'll be my guy up there as last year's champ."

Sure as anything, there was Hawk standing up on this huge walkway above the chutes, a spotlight on him, hat off as he waved.

Whoa.

He grinned and applauded, cheering along with everyone else. He couldn't claim that was his cowboy up there but part of him wanted to, and that was a strange truth he decided not to examine right then. He probably shouldn't ever examine it at all. But Hawk looked like a million bucks up there, and if he was last year's champion, he probably was. He took a few more pictures for Jax.

"Wow. I had no idea."

"He's going to the Finals this year too, I have no doubt. He wins this event, he's in." Nicole kept chattering to him about numbers and rankings and events and rules, but he watched Hawk and the careful way he made it down out of the rafters, so to speak. He didn't have his glasses on.

That answered his question, didn't it? Apparently you didn't need to see very far to stay on the back of a bull. That made sense though, it had to be about feel too, right?

He felt his phone vibrate but he waited until Hawk was out of sight before he glanced at it.

Nice. Which one is yours?

His. Damn. He sent off one of the pics of Hawk in the spotlight. *Last year's champion. Who knew?*

Of course you'd pick the champ. Niiiiiiiice.

He snickered at the text. That was him. Champ-magnet.

He looked up as people started cheering again.

"Bullfighters," Nicole said helpfully.

"Bullfighters?"

"You'll see." She beamed at another lady, one with three little ones and a baby on her shoulder. "That's Ben's wife. He's the bullfighter in the orange. Nice guy. Aussie."

He gave the woman a nod. "Ben's a busy man." He almost asked her if she needed help. "Okay what's next?"

"Tim O'Roarke's fixin' to ride. You hold on and learn."

A gate flew open and a man and bull leaped out, the crowd cheering wildly for a few seconds and then groaning as he was slammed to the ground. Nicole put a zero on a piece of paper.

January winced. That looked like it hurt. The bullfighters got O'Roarke out of the way and distracted the bull, and their titles made much more sense. "Are you keeping score?"

"Yeah. This is the daysheet. Lots of people keep track. Me, I'm doing it for Danny." Nicole opened his program for him, showing him the piece of paper slipped inside. "Here's yours."

He pulled the sheet out and glanced at it, but he was much more interested in what was going on behind that big gate. There were cowboys all around it helping the next rider, the bullfighters were watching closely, and the next thing he knew the gate swung open again.

It was a while before someone managed to stay on for a full eight seconds but there was never a dull moment.

Every so often the clown would come out, make a few jokes, give some shit away, and they'd start up again.

"Danny's up next, then Charlie and Hawk. It's going to be a great section!" Nicole bounced next to him. "Are you so excited?"

He laughed, because her energy was contagious, and because yeah, he was pretty excited. He was going to cheer loud for Danny, it was the least he could do. It felt like everyone around him was buzzing, and he wanted... he needed to see Hawk ride. "I am. And I couldn't have sat next to anyone better for this."

Danny, then Charlie, then Hawk... so it wasn't going to be long before her Danny was up in that spotlight, was it?

"Okay, there he is. Nate's pulling his rope. C'mon, baby!

Ride!" She grabbed his hand as they announced Danny, and then January watched the redhead nod on the big screen.

The gate swung open and the crowd went wild. Nicole screamed as Danny held on, casted arm held high in the air.

"Come on! Come on, baby! Ride that bull!" She stared like she was willing him to stick. "Don't you go down in the well! Sit up! Correct! Yes!" She grabbed him as the buzzer sounded. "Did you see that?"

He threw an arm around her shoulder and gave her a squeeze. "I saw it! He was amazing. Wow." It *was* amazing. His heart was pounding, he could feel that victory in the stands. The kid even managed to land and get clear of the bull without involving his broken hand. "I bet you're proud, huh? He did great."

"Eighty-eight five! That works." She waved as the guy jumped on the gate and blew her a kiss.

"Love you, girl!"

"Love you, baby! Good ride!"

Okay, that was sweet.

He imagined Hawk climbing up on the rail and blowing him a kiss and almost burst out laughing.

"So Charlie next?"

She frowned, staring down into the chutes. "It's supposed—looks like Hawk's loading up. I wonder if Charlie turned out?"

"Turned out?" He looked toward the chute sharply, not wanting to miss a second of Hawk's ride. Hawk was focused and looked like one of the guys off to one side was giving him a pep-talk.

"He decided not to ride. Maybe Dr. Bonner said no. There's no telling."

Hawk's face was serious, jaw set, clenching on the big screen.

Concentration was a good look on Hawk. "All right, cowboy." He leaned forward, eyes on the gate.

"This is Booger. He spins to the left, good for Hawk. He's a quick spinner, steady bucker."

Every time Natalie opened her mouth the sport got more complicated. But of course the bull would matter; for some reason it hadn't even occurred to him. "Good for Hawk, huh? Good."

"Yeah, good for—" The gate opened, and Nicole bellowed like a trucker. "Go, Hawk! Ride cowboy!"

Well, why not? He was here for Hawk after all. He cupped his hands around his mouth and shouted, "You got this, Hawk! Hang on!" Wow. Look at the cowboy go.

"Five. Six. Seven. He's gonna do it!"

And when the buzzer sounded, Hawk threw himself off and ran for the fences.

"Yeah!" He shouted. "Nice ride, cowboy!" He gave Nicole's knee a squeeze. "He did it. He looked amazing." Now that he'd seen a champion ride, he understood much better what he'd been watching earlier.

"He's the best. If he can stay healthy, nothing can stop him."

Hawk hopped down and disappeared behind the fencing. January could make out the hat as it waded into a sea of others. "So what happens now? Are they done?" He looked at Nicole. "And Danny must have done pretty well too, right?"

"There's the short-go. That's when the top ten ride. Hawk's on the top. Danny's number eight. They'll regrade the arena floor, let the guys rest. Hawk will ride last." She shot him a grin. "At least he's in the money, right?"

That he understood, and he grinned right back, then

winked. "At least. I was thinking I'd go get a snack and maybe a beer. Would you like anything? Is baby hungry?"

"These are the VIP seats. See that set up down there? It's for us. There's burgers, hot dogs, nachos, ice cream. You can get free Cokes and beers for two dollars. I'd love an ice cream sandwich, if you're going."

Whoa. VIP indeed. "Sure thing." He stood and set his program on his seat. An ice cream sandwich was easy. He might even have a hot dog. In his suit. At the rodeo. This was somehow so surreal. "I'll be right back."

He waded into the small crowd and put a hotdog and the ice cream on a plate, scooped up a bottle of water and got in the short line to buy himself a beer.

He was, indeed, the only man in slacks, but there were a number of men in western-cut jackets and a ton of jewelry —bolo ties, thick gold nugget rings, heavy watches. Everyone was laughing and friendly to him, though, acting as if he belonged there as much as anyone.

"Beer please?" He asked when it was his turn and put cash on the bar.

"Yessir."

He waited and put a dollar in the tip jar. "Hey, do you happen to know why Charlie turned out?"

One of the men milling around sighed. "Rumor is that he got out here this morning to warm-up, bent over, and passed right out. Doc pulled him."

"Damn." He shook his head. "Thanks, man." Well, that didn't sound good. He tucked the bottle of water in his pocket, pulled his beer off the bar and went back up into the stands.

Nicole was chatting away with some of the other people in the stands and eagerly introduced him around. Most everyone was either family or older Denver families that attended the rodeo regularly.

Once they got back to their seats, he handed her the slightly melted ice cream and the bottle of water. "So, Charlie passed out during warm-ups, and they said the doctor pulled him from the line-up."

"Oh man. Does his traveling partner know?"

"Traveling partner?" A strange expression that even seemed strange the way she said it. He shrugged. "I don't know. I didn't know to ask about a traveling partner."

"No worries. I know Ben. I'll have Danny ask." She pinked and worked on her ice cream sandwich.

He took a bite of his hotdog and washed it down with his beer thoughtfully. "So... do a lot of the guys have traveling partners?"

"Sure. They're on the road a lot. Lots of them have them until they get married, or when we can't come." She wouldn't quite meet his eyes. "It's super common."

"Ah. I thought maybe it might be code." He glanced at her, then took a sip of his beer. He was pretty sure he was reading her right. "I imagine some guys have to be careful?"

"Always. It's *important*." Okay, that was crystal clear.

"Say no more." In that case he certainly did hope Charlie's traveling partner knew. He gave her knee a pat. "How is your ice cream?"

"So good. I love ice cream anyway, but now? Damn." She relaxed now that discussion was over, smiling again. "How's your beer?"

"Hits the spot. I'm having a good time. This is fun." There was a commotion as things got started again.

The short-go went fast—the bulls seemed faster, scarier, and the cowboys were falling off, left and right. He found himself on the edge of his seat, beer empty, eyes glued to the ring. "Is that Danny?"

"Yep. Come on, baby. Ride for us. Please. We need a ride." Her gaze was burning.

"He's got this." Hopefully. But the pregnant lady needed the boost, he could do that. He stared hard at the bull rider in the chute, as if that would help.

Maybe it would.

Danny dipped his head, and the bull spun out, kicking mud and slinging snot. The cowboy held on, that casted hand up in the air.

"Six, seven..." Nicole whispered "Please, baby."

When the buzzer sounded, Danny was still solidly on that bull's back.

"Eight! He did it!" January was so excited anyone would have thought it was his husband. "Woo!"

"You did it, baby! Good job!" Nicole bounced, her entire expression lit up, so excited. Then she blinked. "Watch out! Run, Danny. Run hard!"

Danny didn't even hesitate. He sprinted to the closest fence and pulled himself up.

"Damn." That was close. The bullfighters jumped in as Danny made the fence and drew the animal's attention, and January was reminded that it wasn't really over until the bull was under control. This one seemed pretty pissed that Danny had bested him.

"He hears me. Everywhere." Nicole sat hard. "God, that never gets less scary."

"I can only imagine." These kids seemed so young. Well, most of them. "That's a big risk he takes every time he's up there. But I guess... he's good. And he's got you out here looking out for him, right?"

Hawk wasn't as young, and he didn't think the cowboy had family watching.

"He does." She nodded and sighed. "He's on top, at least for now."

"He's on top with a broken wrist. I'd call that kicking ass. If you'll excuse my French." Two more riders were up and down in the span of their short conversation.

"He's a stud. That poor wrist is nothing but Silly Putty and screws."

He wasn't going to pretend to understand, but he appreciated the athleticism and he really enjoyed watching. "Is that... looks like Hawk is up next."

Give 'em hell, cowboy.

"It is. I'm kinda hoping he goes down so Danny takes the event, but he won't. He's amazing when he's healthy. The best."

He was firmly in Hawk's corner, but he wouldn't say so. She had every right to want her husband to win, and Danny rode really well and would deserve it—if not for Hawk.

The look of concentration on Hawk's face as he got settled was sexy as hell and January caught himself licking his lips.

He wanted to feel that around his cock again. He wanted to see it when Hawk shattered with need.

Hawk nodded, and then the bull came out, the sound of hooves on the gate enough to bring him to his feet. The bull was a wild thing, and January didn't think about the eight seconds or the buzzer or anything but the way Hawk's arm bulged, how the fight between man and bull was going on and he'd never seen anything like it.

"Fuck. Look at him ride." Nicole's voice was awed.

The buzzer sounded, and Hawk tugged on his bull rope, a look of panic on his face for a half second before he pulled harder and went flying, landing with a thud on the dirt.

Time bent, making the next few terrifying seconds feel like forever as the bull twisted and kicked out, huge hooves passing right over Hawk's head. Then one of the bullfighters grabbed Hawk's vest and tossed him toward the fences—tossed *Hawk*, solid and strong as he was—and after a scramble the bull was headed off the dirt.

"Jesus." January let out a huge breath, eyes still glued to Hawk.

The crowd roared and confetti guns went off, pieces of paper covering them.

"Jesus. Ninety-two-point-eight? Go Hawk." Nicole sounded stunned.

Hawk waved to the crowd, hat up in his hand. Then the clown led him to the front for a buckle and a check.

He applauded for a minute, then offered Nicole his hand and a smile. "It was very nice to meet you. I appreciate your patience with a clueless New Yorker. I wish Danny best of luck with the rest of the tour."

"It was great to meet you, Mister January! I hope you get to come to more events. You do, you can sit with me."

So sweet.

"I wouldn't sit anywhere else." That was the truth. Not only was she kind, but she was safe, and like she said, that was important. "Congrats again on the baby."

He wondered if people did the backstage thing at bullriding the way they did on Broadway. He wasn't going to stop and find out though, the only celebrity he wanted was the one meeting him back at his hotel room.

The champ, coming off a big win. January figured the cowboy would be coming in hot, and he was looking forward to it.

4

——————

"So you won?" Momma asked, knowing the answer because they watched the live stream. "You looked good. Daddy says you were even spurring."

"I did. How're y'all?"

"Good. Good. You coming home tonight? Grainger or Bryan say they can fetch you from the airport, either one."

"I'm going to spend a couple days in Denver, Momma. I'm thinking about staying here and flying straight to Dallas for the big event next weekend. Enjoy the mountains." Enjoy January.

"Son, are you sure? That's a whole week." Lord have mercy, he was twenty-eight goddamn years old, a millionaire, and able to take a hit from a bull. He could hang out in a hotel on his own.

"I'll be fine, Momma. Y'all all coming to Dallas?" He knew they would. Not one of them had escaped Caddo Mills and he didn't reckon any of them ever would.

"Every one of us. You'll have the biggest cheering section known to man."

Goodie.

"Sounds great, Momma. Okay, I'm filthy and fixin' to take a bath. I'll call you."

They did their "I love yous" and "goodbyes", and then he texted January from the tub, because he'd lied a little bit, and he was already clean and now he was soaking his bones.

Howdy, stud

Well hello there, Champ. He could almost hear January's smooth voice. *Thanks for the ticket. I enjoyed watching you kick everyone's ass.*

He grinned and took a picture of his toes barely above the waterline, sent it. Not as dangerous as a dick pic, but proof he was naked.

Oh, that's not fair. When do I get to tell you in person how fucking hot you are on the back of a bull? The picture he got in return was January's suit jacket and tie lying on a tidy king size bed.

I can be dry and dressed in 10. He could be bent over January's bed in twelve, if he hurried.

No need to dress. Or knock.

Be right there.

He hauled his ass out of the tub, dried off, and threw on sweats and a T-shirt, a pair of flip-flops and his glasses. Then he took the elevator up a floor, finding the door propped open with the lock.

"Hey, stranger." He pushed the door open and moved the lock.

January looked up from pouring whiskey, met him as he came in the door, and pressed a glass into his hand. "That was less than ten minutes. I'm flattered."

"I didn't put on my tighty-whities." He raised his glass. "Cheers."

"Cheers." January clinked glasses with him and pulled

him into the room. "I gather you rode well. A lovely lady named Nicole whose husband was giving you a run for your money assured me you were amazing. I was mostly incredibly turned on."

"I rode like a champ." That was his job, after all. "You liked that, did you? Watching all the cowboys with beef between their thighs?"

"No. Just watching you." January sipped his whiskey. "You did ride like a champ. You owned it up in that spotlight. You have a cocky swagger in the arena. I liked it all."

He took his sip of the whiskey, feeling the burn warm him, all the way up. "Mmm, cocky describes me to a T."

"I'd say you've earned it." January set his drink down and unbuttoned his dress shirt. He pulled the hem free, and then worked more slowly on the cufflinks. January watched him with eyes so dark it was hard to tell they were blue if there wasn't good light. "I'm sure there are other things that describe you to a T."

"Things like sex on a stick?" He loved this—being playful, and January smelled like heaven, making his cock wake up and take notice.

"There's some truth in that." January set the cufflinks down and picked up the glass again, taking a sip of the whiskey. "I was thinking things like... tough as nails. Fearless." He got a sly grin. "Rich."

"A man should be good at his job, right?" He preened, even though he knew what January didn't. His money was in the sponsors, in the contracts, in the commercials and photo shoots and shit.

"Oh." January reached up with both hands, still balancing the whiskey in one and removed his glasses. "And hot. Had I said hot? Sexy?" January put everything down on the bedside table. "Tight. Really fucking tight."

"Mmhmm. All those crunches tightening things up." Everything went soft and easy. Well, not everything. Some of his bits were hard as Chinese algebra.

January pressed a hot palm against his jaw. "How about a kiss, cowboy?"

"Hell yeah." Hawk leaned into the touch and reached out, finding skin and drawing January in. He lifted his face and went up on tiptoe, bringing their lips together. Oh. Nice.

"Mmm." There was instant heat between them, like there had been the night before, but January's kiss went deeper—still hungry but more patient. That suited him to the bone, because he'd ridden twice and that last one had slammed him to the ground. Patient and deep worked.

January's hand tucked up under his T-shirt and slid over his skin, tracing and exploring his muscle. "I bet you're tired."

"I bet I can be tired tomorrow, stud." He didn't have a lot of chances to do this; he wasn't about to give it up.

"Works for me." January smiled, hovering an inch from his lips, then lifted his shirt off over his head. "I'm not tired."

"No?" He stretched up, rocking side-to-side, showing off a little. "You lit up for me, honey?"

"Like the Empire State Building. Look at you." January lifted his glass from his fingers and put it down, then a hand slid under his waistband and grabbed hold of his ass. "You feel good."

"I want you to make me feel fucking amazing." He wanted to fly like he got bucked off up to the goddamn moon.

January inhaled sharply, chest filling. "I can do that."

The next moment he was off his feet, and then flat on his back on the big king bed. Oh, fuck yes. He did like that.

"Good thing I know how to land, huh?" He spread wide, letting January look his fill.

"Mm. Nice. Good thing I know how to ride." January tossed his trousers, leaned on the bed, and ran both hands up the inside of his thighs. "Really nice."

His legs drew up, his knees bending like someone had pushed a button. "God, your hands are warm."

"You want me, cowboy? You look like you want me." January replaced his fingers with a hot tongue, drawing a line down toward his balls.

"Oh sweet fuck." His head fell back, any lingering aches and pains fading away. This was better than any hot bath.

That earned him a dark chuckle. January's fingers curled around his shaft and that tongue bathed him, balls first, then reaching to the very tip of his cock. He realized he was holding his breath when the room began to spin, and he sucked in a deep, deep lungful of air right as January's tongue touched his slit.

"Fuck!"

"Yeah." January's tongue burrowed deep, then circled around and did it again.

Christ, he wasn't sure whether to buck up or roll his hips or grab his knees or scream. Maybe all of the above.

Or he could blink and try to focus on this amazing son of a bitch.

January seemed determined to keep him guessing. Fingers stroked him, and that tongue teased and tasted, and every time he thought he caught a rhythm, it would change. His cock would slide down January's throat, or January would abandon it altogether to nip and lick and bite at his thighs.

"Jesus..." He tried to turn over, move, but January's hands held him where he was, and he let it happen, because it felt so fucking fine.

He finally got a breath when January stopped to find a rubber. "Feeling good, angel?"

"Shit, good ain't—good ain't even close." He felt like he was riding already, like he was balanced right there on the edge.

"I agree. You ready for me then?" January didn't wait for him to answer, just moved over him again and a cool slippery finger pressed slowly inside him. "I want you. I want you like you wanted that win."

"Fuck me. I want every goddamn inch of you." He wasn't a bit shy, and he loved that January wasn't either.

"Fuck." January groaned and the finger disappeared, replaced quickly with sweet pressure and the thick head of January's cock. January caught him under one knee and bent it up, dark eyes meeting his. "Right here."

He nodded and bore down, his lips parting with the pure frigging bliss of letting that heavy cock split him wide.

January hissed and let go of his knee, groaning and arching over him. The sound was full of clear and shameless need, and when their hips met it was followed by a hard, hungry kiss.

Hawk met January head on, both of them fighting together to find the right angle, the right touch, the best rhythm.

Finding it didn't take long.

"Hawk." January exhaled heavily, thrusts strong and even as they shifted into a backroad gear. "Fuck, you feel good."

He hoped so. He was so full he could feel January

tickling his tonsils with his cock, and his balls ached perfectly every time January pushed in.

January caught his leaking cock up in a hot palm and stroked hard. He could feel the man's eyes on him, watching him move, watching him breathe, and then that thumb was back, exploring his slit, spreading the sticky few drops it found around.

He groaned and reached down, wrapping his fingers around January's, encouraging the touch to go deeper, harder, and set him on fire.

"Like this, cowboy? Is this how you like it?" He thought he heard January's voice break, a little crack in the control. Just enough that he knew he could drive the man out his mind too.

He answered by squeezing January with his ass, with his fingers. Fuck yes. He needed it, like this.

January must have gotten whatever he needed too, because he grunted and his hips went a little wild before finding their rhythm again. And then January was on a mission. The hand around his cock moved fast, fist tight as it worked him.

"Yes!" The single word burst out of him, hard with his need. That was what he wanted. Just like that.

"Yes," January echoed, voice raw and honest, eyes focused on Hawk, hips pumping and fist flying. Even the air in the room was electric.

His eyes rolled back, the weight in his balls overwhelming for an endless second before he shot, his fucking bones rattling madly with the power of it.

January made a strangled sound and left him with his own hand around his cock. Big hands landed hard on either side of his shoulders, and since he was wider and taller, January was all Hawk could see. It was only a few more seconds before January shook and went still, exhaling hot breath across his chest. "Fuck."

"Yeah. Yeah, man." He fought to get the words out, to make sense.

January's damp forehead landed heavily on his chest, and the room filled with heavy breathing and satisfied moans and they each tried to catch their breath. Every so often January would drop a kiss on his sternum or a little higher, finally making it as far as his chin before flopping like a stone onto the bed beside him.

"Christ." January laughed weakly. "You're a workout and a half."

"Better than the treadmill," he managed, or at least he hoped that was what he said.

"Hell yeah." January's fingers tangled with his. "Fuck the gym."

Hawk started to chuckle, the laughter filling him right on up.

January laughed with him, rolled to face him, hooked an arm over his chest and pulled him in. "Short nap. Then I want that mouth of yours. What do you say?"

"I'm in. I'll suck you until you scream."

"Mm. I can't wait. I'm keeping you up all night. You'll have to sleep on the plane home tomorrow."

"Ha. I'm staying the week. I'm going to hang out until the next event."

"You're... why did I think you were leaving in the morning? Well, I don't head back to New York until Tuesday. So I guess that gets us tomorrow."

"If you got no plans. I'm not a stalker or nothing."

January snorted. "I have a late afternoon meeting. Three o'clock. It'll go until about five, I think. Those are my plans. Plus, who doesn't like a stalker that wants in your pants?"

"I'm intending to send out my laundry." And possibly have an egg white omelet and a chicken breast.

"Ooh. Fancy. Well, if I'm not encroaching on your laundry fantasies, I'd love to have you as my guest for breakfast, lunch, and dinner." January was teasing, but the kiss he got on his forehead seemed sincere.

"Mmm—You forgot late night blowjobs." Hawk stole a hard kiss.

January broke the kiss and grinned at him. "How could I do that?" They kissed again, want already simmering under the surface. "This has been a very worthwhile trip to Denver."

"I've never enjoyed the city more, swear to God." And he like Denver a lot.

"Well sure. You're on top, that's what Nicole said. On top in the arena, but I like you underneath me here."

"This ain't for money, darlin'. Not even a little." This was pure need.

"You haven't run off with my wallet yet, so I guess I believe you." January yawned and stretched long, back popping. Hawk reached out, dragging one hand along January's spine. He knew about having a sore back.

"Mm." January arched into his touch. "It's shifty. I don't mind flying, but I hate airplanes. I'll need to see my chiropractor when I get back to New York."

"Turn over." He knew a ton about massage. They all did. He could so help.

"Thank you, but you don't have to." It was a weak protest, January rolled right over.

There was lotion on the bedside table, and he slicked his hands. He had this. He could make January remember him, no question.

In fact, that felt like one hell of a plan.

5

One would think giving away money would be easy, but it wasn't. It was a lot more responsibility than January had realized he was signing on for when he started his foundation. Everybody wanted money.

He needed a beer.

Fortunately, he had a date, so a beer was definitely in the plan.

Listen to him. A date. It wasn't a *date*; it was meeting with his weekend man of the minute. Not that he wouldn't be more than happy to have Hawk on his arm the next time he ran into Lucas. Wouldn't that be great? *Hey, Lucas, meet my way hotter-than-you-are bull riding hunk of a date from Texas.*

Shit, he'd love every second of that. Hawk could flatten that arrogant gym-jock Lucas was fucking with a look.

Grinning at his imagined revenge, January pulled his phone out of his pocket and texted the hunk himself.

I'm headed for the restaurant you texted me, I'll meet you at the bar. I'll be the hot guy in the expensive suit. That seemed worth mentioning. They hadn't seen each other with clothes on all day.

It took a second and then he got, *I'm in the black hat, the black boots. You need a beer?*

Whatever you're having, Champ. Be there in ten. He liked Hawk in a hat almost as much as he liked the cowboy naked.

Denver was fucking cold in January, but he liked the city a lot. It was busy, but people were friendly, and no one out here had made any jokes about his name. It happened almost daily back home. There was plenty to look at as he walked from his meeting to the restaurant, collar turned up high and hands stuffed into his pockets.

He found the place and pulled open the door. That had been a good stretch of the legs, but he was glad to get indoors finally. He took a big breath of warm air, shaking off some of the cold as he looked around for the man in the black hat.

Hawk was at the bar, laughing at something the bartender said, the heavy glasses glinting in the light. He looked amazing—that ass in those jeans? Fuck, that was heaven. The jeans, the boots, the way Hawk leaned on the bar like he'd held up a hundred of them in his day. January was going to miss that sight when he got back to New York.

He decided he'd better go say hello. He couldn't stand here and ogle all night. Could he?

"Is that beer for me?" He pulled out a stool and sat on it, wiggling the life back into his frozen toes.

"It is." Hawk smiled for him, eyes looking over his shoulder before fastening on him. "How was your meeting?"

He glanced briefly over his shoulder to see what he was missing, but there was an empty stool behind him. "I don't know. I have to think about it. They're good people, I don't know if we're a good fit." Maybe it was a trick of Hawk's glasses. That was a pretty serious prescription. "How was your laundry?" He teased. "Did the pick-up go smoothly?"

"It did. I even managed to fill out that tiny slip of paper. Crazy. You impressed?"

"So proud of you." He held up his beer, admiring Hawk's rough look and bright eyes that managed to make themselves seen despite the glasses. "Cheers."

"Cheers." Hawk held up his glass with a grin. "You about ready to get us a table?"

"I can do that. Any preference?" The place was full but not busy, but you could tell from the look of it that a Saturday night could be insane. "Maybe one of the booths back there? I can ask."

"Works for me. I like to sit down to eat. That's damn important."

"You're a smart-ass, cowboy." He made his way over to the hostess and asked her for a booth, and he and Hawk were seated quickly. January picked up his menu. "So... a lettuce leaf and a rice cake for the bull rider?"

"Rice cakes have carbs." Hawk's grin was wide and easy. "Broiled chicken breast and broccoli. Supper of champions."

"Hey, it could be worse, you have a beer." He closed the menu and set it down. "I'll have the same."

"You sure, darlin'? I won't rag you for eating what you want. When I'm on break, I eat everything I want— pancakes and biscuits and pizza." There was an easiness to Hawk, a self-awareness that was so refreshing.

"I'm sure."

Call me "darlin'" again.

He liked how it sounded—both the accent, and how easily it rolled off Hawk's tongue.

"I'm here for you and the beer. And dessert is already ordered." It was sitting across the table from him.

"Mmhmm, and I'm high-protein, all the way. Not keto, though. I got no body-fat."

"You're high-strung and tightly packed, like a thoroughbred." Like a pint-sized Roman god. Jupiter maybe, bringing the thunder.

Hawk blinked and blushed for him, ducking his head for a second, before offering him a grin. "Thank you."

"I'd ask why you ride, but anyone can see you were born for it. It looks terrifying from where I'm sitting but so does the giant slalom and I like to watch that too." Some people needed that adrenaline thing. He respected that. He didn't get it at all, not in the least, but he didn't have to. He could enjoy it.

"When you're my size in a rodeo family, you ride roughstock. I've been riding since I was a kid." Hawk settled back into the booth, putting his hat on the seat beside him. "I don't even remember learning to ride horseback, but there's a picture of me and Momma riding fence when I was in a sling deal."

"Wow." He settled back too, not really realizing he was mirroring Hawk until he'd done it. He picked up his beer and took a sip. "So your whole family does rodeo? Rodeos? Is that a word?"

"Yeah. All my brothers are bulldoggers, Daddy's a team roper, Momma was a barrel racer. We're a rodeo family. Let me find you a picture." Hawk flipped through his phone, then showed January a picture of this vast family. Seven huge dark men, a tiny blonde lady, Hawk, and what had to be dozens of little ones. Jesus.

"Good lord. That's a whole lot of testosterone. Your poor mother." He pointed at the phone. "That's your dad?"

"It is. I'm the baby. Lucky number seven." Hawk chuckled softly, shook his head. "Daddy says he saw her ride and was in love. It took him a few months to convince her."

"That's lovely. This is an amazing picture." He pulled out his phone and looked for the very few pictures he had of his family. The one he found first was pretty good. "This was Christmas Eve two years ago. That's Mom and Dad, those are my brothers and my sister and her husband. I'm also the baby." And they all looked like Mom. His sister had two pristine and perfect children standing in front of her. "Neither of my brothers has children. Or... well, my eldest brother Sean does, but he's divorced and the kids are with their mother on Christmas usually."

"Yeah, that's always complicated as hell. My brothers have been pretty lucky that way. They don't tend toward divorce. Of course, they are all busy as hell with the ranches and the circuit and all those babies."

"Sean is a dick." He grinned and put his phone on the table. "He's Sean Junior and hasn't ever let any of us forget it."

Hawk shot him a wicked grin. "Dude—There are no juniors in my house. Daddy is Austin, and then there's Bryan, Canaan, Danny, Eagle, Foley, Grainger, and me. Momma called a stop before she got to Isaac."

"That—" He laughed, as amazed as he was amused. "That's incredible. That's... I mean, I guess it's better than one, two, three..." he couldn't stop giggling.

"Tell me about it. Although seven would be a rocking cool name..." Hawk hooted like a goofy bird, and suddenly he was young, silly, this naughty boy.

"I don't know, you might not want a name like that. January has its downsides." The teasing when he was growing up, and now the head tilts... "You mean like the month? Were you born in January? Hi, I'm November."

"Like Hawk with the huge glasses was easy. Talk about irony. So, why January? Do you have a middle name?"

"Oh God. Yes. It's Phillip." He snorted. He hated Phillip. *Hated* it. "Sean named me January. His birthday is January twentieth and my parents apparently thought it was 'so adorable'." He could hear his mother saying exactly that as she had a zillion times telling the story. "I guess it's better than Phillip as my first name... which was how it was going to be."

"You don't look like a Phillip. At all." Hawk managed not to laugh. "Or a Phil. My middle name is Anthony."

"Anthony. Who are you named after?" His beer was getting low and the server hadn't come by yet. He glanced over Hawk's shoulder to see if he could get someone's attention.

"San Antonio. Yes, the town."

He caught the waiter's eye, and the young man looked horrified, hurrying right over.

"Oh my god. I didn't see you."

Hawk jumped as the guy spoke, almost spilling his glass.

"Oh my god. I'm so sorry."

January chuckled. "It's all good. We'll have two more beers please." He pointed to Hawk. "And he's going to order for both of us."

"I want broiled chicken breast, broccoli, green salad with no croutons, cheese, ranch on the side." Hawk glanced at him. "You cool with that?"

"I'm not going to argue." January winked at him. It was fine. He didn't need a three-course meal. He wanted to sit somewhere and have a beer and talk to this gorgeous cowboy.

"He doesn't look like a bull rider," the server teased, talking to Hawk.

"He needs double the chicken. I'll steal bites." Hawk smiled at the server, but there was a little tension there. A hint of stiffness.

"Yes, sir, Mister Destry. I'm on it." The server hurried away.

He looked Hawk over and sighed. "Sorry. I forgot we're not in New York."

"We're good. No stress, darlin'. He startled the fire out of me."

"You have a pretty serious prescription. I imagine your peripheral vision isn't great, huh? What can you see without them?" He had to believe it wasn't much. Technology for glasses was pretty good. If they were thick, Hawk's eyes were bad.

"I am not one of those guys that leaves his glasses on the bedside table in the morning, for sure."

"Gotcha." That was interesting. He remembered Hawk couldn't find them that first morning in his suite. He took the last sip of his beer as the two new ones arrived. "So I heard the doc pulled Charlie out last minute yesterday. Is he done for the season?"

"Ben says he intends it to be. He texted me this morning. Charlie and him are heading home." Hawk shook his head, sighing softly. "I hope not. We already lost Sky. I'm starting to feel like the old man. It's early in the season, so only the good Lord knows."

Charlie's lover's name was Ben. He told himself to remember that, though he wasn't sure why. It seemed like they were worth remembering. "It's a rough sport. Who's Sky?"

"Skylar Cates. He was my biggest competition for a

while. He got in a wreck and retired. Went to live in Vermont with his husband."

Husband? Whoa.

He leaned forward, crossing his arms on the table. He gave Hawk a meaningful look. "So, Sky goes home to his husband, Charlie and Ben... you..." He left the statement open-ended, fishing for whatever Hawk wanted to say about that.

"I got a room at my folks' ranch. I'm not home much. I travel while I can."

He nodded, remembering Nicole's words. *It's important.* "How do you manage not to get your ass kicked?"

"I never make the first move, I don't play with other cowboys, and I take my hits." Okay, that was straightforward, solid.

"You may not make the first move, but you make your intentions known. I'm glad I decided to play with a cowboy."

"I'm having a ball, darlin'. You give a man what he needs."

"Yeah?" He searched Hawk's eyes, which were slightly distorted by the glasses and grinned. "What does a man need?"

Look at that blush. That was hot as hell.

"This man needs a good plugging. Connection. Laughing. Wild orgasms."

Hawk might be blushing, but he wasn't ashamed and that was sexy as fuck. Enough that it warmed him from his balls up. "So... check. Check. Check. And definitely check." January raised his glass to Hawk and took a sip.

Hawk nodded and grinned, lifting his glass as well. "Ticky boxes taken care of, supper ordered, beer refilled. Life is good."

Life was good, and it would be good all night. Life would

be okay when he got back to New York too, but he would have a hard time forgetting this cowboy. At least he had some great nights to jerk off to.

"Where do you go from Denver?"

"Dallas. Then home for two weeks, then it goes Orlando, Raleigh, Nashville, and then Connecticut, I think?" Hawk sighed and rolled his eyes. "My family is coming to Dallas en masse and following me to Orlando to do Disney."

"Wow. That's going to be quite a production." January laughed, leaning back as their food was delivered. "Have you done that before?"

"Oh yeah. Every other year or so. I love kids, and my family is....crazy, but kind." Hawk's fingers searched for the silverware. "I know that's strange, but true. We have fun."

"That's not strange, that's wonderful. I bet it's cool to have family you can hang out with. Mine's difficult. Tricky." He took a bite of his chicken, which, despite being broiled, was pretty tasty. "Dad is very impatient, especially with me. Sean is arrogant. Everything about my sister is perfect, which of course means nothing is right behind the scenes I'm sure. And David is a mouse. He and I get along fine, but he's scared of everything. And Mom..." He shrugged. Mom really was perfect.

"I'm sorry, darlin'. That sounds stressful. The worst I get is overprotective."

Okay. That was the absolute last thing he expected to hear.

"Overprotective of you? Why? Because you're the baby?"

Something January didn't understand passed across Hawk's expression, and then disappeared. "I'm sure that's part of it. They've always been that way."

"Well, they care anyway, right?" He could ask hard questions, but they were none of his business. They weren't lovers; they were weekend fuck-buddies. Hawk would go off traveling with his tour, and he would go back to being rooted in the city. He reached over and poked Hawk's shoulder. "Eat."

"Yeah, it smells damn good, doesn't it?" Hawk leaned forward to sniff. "I approve."

"It is good. Simple, and good." He watched Hawk eat, thinking if they were in the same place for more than five minutes he would like to get to know Hawk better. They were so different everywhere except in bed, he'd love to find out if there was anything else they had in common.

They were quiet while they ate, and it wasn't awkward at all. Lucas couldn't stand silence and had always tried to fill it. Talking incessantly about nothing. Just a lot of words.

"Would you like to walk back toward the hotel, have a coffee and chat after we eat?"

"Sure. I love coffee. Sometimes I can chat too." January popped the last bite of broccoli in his mouth. "How do you like your coffee?"

"Roasted hazelnut mocha latte is my please God I'm coming flavor, but I'll drink coffee in any form."

January snorted. "Your please God... I've never heard anyone say that before about coffee. Also, that is a much more complicated drink than I'd have pegged you for. Mine is a plain old latte. Almond milk is nice but not necessary, some cinnamon is good too. But yeah, if you pour it for me, I'll drink it."

"There's a coffee shop in my hometown—it's a drive through parked in the La Hacienda parking lot. That's Suzi's specialty."

"Yeah? Well, have one for me next time you're there." January put his fork down and swallowed his last bite with his beer.

"Will do." Hawk chuckled, and the sound was wry. "Too bad you're not a fan. Then I'd have a shot of seeing you again."

"Oh, I'm—" He started to reach for Hawk but pulled his hand back abruptly, horrified at the thought he might out the cowboy. He couldn't possibly live in the closet himself, but not everyone had his privilege. "I'm definitely a fan, Champ."

"Well, I'd love a shot to see you again after we leave Denver behind, darlin'."

Definitely. "So, I can keep in touch? I'd like that."

"Hell yes. I'm the texting king." Hawk dropped his voice. "I'll send you naughty things to get you through your workday."

"Oh ho." January was pleasantly surprised. Hawk didn't seem like the type. "I'll be sure to return the favor—give you a little extra swagger in the arena." Going back to the city didn't seem nearly as depressing as it had a bit ago.

"Remember, I'm at loose ends from Sunday night to Friday afternoon. I got time to tease."

"Shit, those are my busiest days of the week, Champ. But the good news is, maybe I can get out to see you ride on a weekend at some point." Their schedules were off, but did it matter if they weren't in the same place anyway?

And what was he doing? Was this a *Thing*? He'd just come off a *Thing*. Did he want another *Thing*? A long-distance *Thing*?

Damn. Drinks with Jax when he got back was a must.

"Anytime you feel the need, there'll be tickets for you at will call."

He wondered if Hawk meant that the way it sounded. Then he wondered if he was reading into it and completely misinterpreting what he was hearing. He still had no idea what he was doing or why this mattered so much to him—it had only been two days. Two high-adrenaline days, in and out of bed.

Oh.

Oh, okay, he got it now. He was fucking high.

"Thank you. I'll feel the need. I'm feeling it right now, in fact."

"The hotel has coffee on twenty-four-hour room service." And that offer was clear as crystal, wasn't it?

He felt a little bad for stepping on their nice walk back to the hotel. But not that bad. "Mochas have a lot of calories, right?" January raised his hand for the check.

"Tons. I intend to work off enough calories for that and pie, darlin'." That smile was pure evil. He loved it.

"I'm looking forward to that." He handed the server his credit card. "Apple a la mode. In bed."

"My treat. I'll feed you." Hawk waited until the waiter left. "Bite by bite while I'm riding your prick."

"Not gonna lie, Hawk. You make me hungry." He stood up and found his coat. "Can you hail a cab in Denver, or do I need to call a Lyft?"

"I got one at the hotel. Got the guy's number, hold up." Hawk's fingers flew on his phone. "He's going to be outside in five."

"Damn. It's good to be the Champ, huh?" January caught the server on their way out and signed the check with an inflated tip. Waiting out in the cold might be good, most of his nerves were on fire.

"Shit, that's knowing how to do it. I hate being stuck without a cab. Hate it."

"I like public transportation when I have the time. You get to know cities so much better that way. I don't bother with cabs in New York." There was a fair amount of high-profile in his work, he loved to blend in when he could.

"We went around in pods in New York. I think the league was trying to keep us from having bar fights." Hawk put on his hat. "You want to stand outside?"

"Yeah. It's... warm in here." He led the way, weaving through tables as they headed out. "Right?"

"Blistering, and it's fucking snowing, man. How amazing is that?"

His first thought was 'how romantic'. His second thought was 'what the hell is wrong with you, Jan?'

"Pretty," was what he said. He turned his collar up and stuffed his hands in his pockets, watching it come down in one of the streetlights.

"Yeah, you never know when you won't see it again, right?" Hawk had his face up to the sky.

"Where I'm from we see it fairly often in the winter. Somehow it's prettier here. It's coming down, huh?"

"It is. It's wild. When I was a little boy I thought it would feel like little bites on your skin."

"Sometimes a cold wind can feel that way." He thought about snow when he was a boy. Sleds and snowmen and... "I liked to make snow angels. You ever made a snow angel?"

"I have! My oldest brother married a girl from Steamboat Springs, so when I was ten we all went up to meet her people." Hawk's laugh was pure joy, not the slightest bit jaded somehow. "It was Christmastime, and the snow was up to an elephant's butt. I skied!"

"Awesome. I've never been." Hurtling down a hill wasn't his cup of tea. A car pulled up to the curb. "Is that us?"

"Is it cab number five-five-four-five?" At January's agreement, Hawk grinned. "It is. This is Norman. The best cabbie on the front range."

"Norman." He opened the door and held it for Hawk.

"Yep. It's good to know your people."

The cab ride was quiet, and if they'd cooled off at all in the snow, it didn't last long. It was the best kind of torture sitting a foot away from someone he wanted but couldn't touch. The anticipation made his palms sweat and his spine tingle.

Hawk played with his phone, and January's phone buzzed. *Hottest bastard alive. Need u.*

Really? He glanced sidelong at Hawk, trying to pretend like his balls hadn't drawn up so hard. *Gonna make you feel it.*

So ready. Want to be bow legged by tomorrow. Hawk's face didn't show a bit of what they were doing. Not a hint.

You won't be able to forget me. Which was only fair because it would be a while before he forgot Hawk for sure.

Hawk looked right at him, eyes serious as a heart attack. "I have absolutely no intention of that happening. At all."

Shit. He did his best to return the look. He didn't *intend* to either, but distance was hard and besides, they'd only just met. "Let's not make promises."

Hawk tilted his head, watching January for a long second like he was trying to memorize every inch. Then he nodded. "Fair enough. We're here."

Hawk paid the cabbie. "You working tomorrow, man?"

The guy nodded. "Just text."

"Rock on."

He didn't know Hawk well enough to read all of the silent looks the man gave him and this last one was no different. He probably hurt the cowboy's feelings. He climbed out of the cab and back into the snow. "There's time for that, you know? If things... go well."

"I hear you. No worries. No promises. No stress. Come on, darlin'. Let's go work off your dessert."

"All right, then." He'd take that at face value since he really didn't know any better, and focused on his evening. "This hot bastard has plans."

"Yeehaw!" Hawk winked at him, grinning as the valet held the door. "Let's go play."

6

Hawk was fucking tired. Man, give him bulls any day. His nieces and nephews were hooligans. And add Disney?

Fuck him.

Yeah, let his happy ass get trampled, for sure.

The family was heading home tomorrow, and then he could focus on his eight seconds. Momma was already crying and fussing, because he wasn't coming home for a month.

Lord have mercy.

You'd think he was broke dick or something.

Right now he was locked in his room with a beer. He'd talked to Mackey and Sky, to Parker and Ben and Charlie. Then he looked at his phone and pondered texting January.

He hadn't texted in Dallas. He'd sent one picture of Disney ears from here. No stalking. Hawk wasn't stupid. He knew himself. He wanted to fall in love. He wanted to have forever things, and he knew he was running out the clock. Still, that wasn't cool. This was fucking for January. That was it.

Happy stranger fucking.

Hey man. Good week? That was good. Solid. Safe.

Hey, Champ. No. It's been long and I'm working on getting hammered. You?

He sent a picture of his naked belly, his Miller Lite, and his open belt buckle. That was answer enough, right?

Looking good. Thinking about me? The picture he got in return was of the slightly dog-eared VIP ticket from the Denver show. *I've been thinking about you.*

You know it. Getting ready to get back to work. Lord yes, he'd been thinking hard. Wanting bad. Jacking off to the memory of Denver.

How did you do in Dallas? Did you survive Disney? Where are you headed? So many questions. A man that wasn't interested wouldn't bother to ask, would he?

Came in third. Disney was hell. Orlando through Sunday, then up to Raleigh. You having any snow?

Nope. Bitter cold though. Enough to freeze a Texan's balls off. You're riding in Orlando? Or having breakfast with Cinderella?

Fuck off. Did that Tuesday. I think she was stoned. He put his beer bottle on the table. *Riding tomorrow night so I can make pennies.*

You can do better than third. You're a stud. I'd give you a BJ for good luck if I was there.

He'd like that, wouldn't he? He wiggled and sighed, settling in the mattress. *Damn. I miss you worse now.*

That wasn't too far, was it?

There was no immediate response. The dead air before his phone finally rang probably felt longer than it was because it got him worrying, but sure enough, January's number and a goofy picture they'd taken in the hotel suite in Denver popped up on his screen.

"Hey, darlin'. How goes?" You interested in a little cowboy bod?

"Hey. I'm okay. This is easier than texting, right? And…" January cleared his throat. "I wanted to hear your voice."

"It's good to hear yours. Having a shit week, huh? You want me to come up there and beat something?"

"Well, it's not a shit week really. I've been off since this cowboy got under my skin in Denver and I don't know what to do about it. Got any advice?"

"You like Raleigh?" he chuckled. He was heading there Monday, would be there for a week, and occupying himself. He could stay with Ben and Charlie for Nashville, that would be easy.

"I have no idea, but I'll put it on my calendar." January sounded pleased. "That's two weeks or three?"

"I'm heading to Raleigh Monday, riding a week from tomorrow. Two weeks is Nashville. Three is Connecticut, then I have a weekend off." It was a weird schedule, but it worked out. They needed to please the fans and give the cowboys enough events to make points when they got hurt.

January jumped on that. "Oh, great. I'll see you in Raleigh a week from Friday then. Looking forward to those VIP hot dogs."

"I'll have your tickets at will call." He'd send all the details for hotel and everything in a text. He was so upgrading at the Marriott. "I'm a good use for airline miles."

"You are. I wish I was there right now. I'd put you to good use." January's voice dropped low.

Oh, he liked that. Hawk reached down, squeezed his package nice and hard. "Darlin', I have been Uncle Bird for a week. I need to be wanted."

"You know what I want? I want to get my hand around

that heavy cock. Just feel it in my hand. Give it a squeeze, I know you like that."

He swallowed and let those words heat him up. This was something new, something burning. "I wouldn't tell you no, darlin'. I would spread for you, no problem."

"Do it for me. Since I'm not there. Will you do that?" January spoke softly, but without hesitation.

Oh, sweet Jesus, didn't that leave a sudden hollow ache in the pit of his belly. He so would. He spread his legs, the act knocking a soft moan free. "Fuck, yes."

"That's it. You have it? Give that pretty cock a nice squeeze, angel. Let me hear how it feels."

Was he doing this? Hell yes he was. He unzipped and let his cock have some room, some air. He grabbed ahold and moaned, deep in his chest. "I could so suck you until you scream, darlin'. You move like you were born to it."

January sighed, and he heard the need in it. "Yeah. Love your mouth. Your tongue is tricky. Work your thumb over the head. I want to hear that sound you make."

January knew that? Already? "It is tender as fuck." He always worked it when he needed to get off. He stroked his slit, gathering the wetness that was growing there. His breath caught, and he sucked in air.

"There it is." January groaned, and breathed in deep. "Fuck, you're the hottest man I've ever known. Roll one of those tight nipples in your fingers, angel. Pinch it. God, I can't wait to have you again in Raleigh. We'll set the hotel on fire."

"Want to ride you until we come, darlin'." He did as January asked, and his eyes closed, January in his mind. "And then I'll do it again, take you until there's nothing more in my world."

"You can forget everything else right now, Hawk. Just

listen to my voice, believe that hand is mine stroking you right. Nice and tight, slow for a little while but not too long. You like it faster. I know. You feel me?"

"Fuck me..." Yeah, yeah, he felt it. He could sink right in, almost smell January right there with him.

"Nice and deep. Fuck." January's breath was loud through the phone. "We fit so well, don't we?"

"Like hand in a glove." And he knew from gloves. He strapped one on every weekend.

"You want me, baby? Tell me. Come on, let me hear you."

"I ache for you. Been riding my fingers, and it ain't right. You got what I need. Crave you." And he meant it. He could spend hours licking and exploring, making January moan.

"Yeah, my hand gets the job done but it's not you. Faster, angel. Harder, right? I want to make you come like I'm right there."

"Harder. Right." His teeth clenched, and his abs felt like rocks as he fucked his fist. "Darlin'." He wasn't sure what he was begging for, but he knew he needed January to give it to him.

"You can feel me now. Stiff cock deep inside that tight ass. Riding me the way I like it. *Fuck*. Just like you need."

"Fuck yes!" He dug his thumbnail into his slit, giving himself that zing, that sharp ache that he needed, his balls emptying in a teeth-chattering rush.

"Yes! So good." January grunted, moaned long and low, breath coming in short, quick pants. "Fuck, angel. Fuck, yes."

"I can almost smell you," he whispered. "Oh darlin', you're something else."

"I've missed you too." January took a deeper, steadier breath but his voice was still rough as he spoke. "I like things to make sense and we don't but... I swear I can taste your kisses in my dreams."

"Sometimes shit is what it is." His daddy had known Momma was the one. He knew he couldn't have a forever thing, but he could have a Mr. Right.

"I'm not complaining. Damn, Hawk. That was intense, huh? You feel good?"

"I feel like a million bucks. Shit, that was amazing." And he'd never done anything so hot. He hadn't been in his hotel room; he'd been flying somewhere with January.

"Dirty. I liked it." January's laugh sounded suitably worn out. "Don't tell Mickey Mouse."

"No. No, Mickey would send me to Disney jail." He had zero doubt there was a vast underground brig beneath the Pirates of the Caribbean ride. "It was worth it. So fucking worth it."

In fact, he couldn't stop smiling.

"We'll talk again soon. You have a good ride this weekend, Champ. You're going to kill it. I know it."

"I will. I'll ride my ass off so that I'm in good shape for Raleigh." He didn't want to wreck his booty call for an injury.

"Good. Goodnight, Hawk. Sleep well."

"Night darlin'. Have a better weekend." He hung up, because he could linger, but January was obviously ready to go. He lay there for a while, letting himself float before he got up to have a nice, long shower.

He had to get his mind in the middle. Tomorrow he was back to work, and he was going to ride like January was watching.

7

*I*t's Sunday, and you're a lazy asshole sitting around in your PJs. Pick up some beer and come over.

Jax liked to hide his head in the sand on Sundays, but January was going stir crazy knocking around his apartment alone. And he couldn't go out, he'd finally found Hawk's tour on cable and he was going to watch his hot cowboy lover ride.

Don't pretend you didn't see my text. I'll get us takeout.

Man, what kind of takeout?

Bingo. January had him. *Ramen?* The way to Jax's heart was with noodles.

Okay. Getting beer and dessert. Not getting dressed though. Right. Like Jax would go out and about in his Spongebob jammies.

Don't get arrested.

Dessert. Jax was talented. He was looking forward to dessert. He went into the kitchen and opened his iPad, pulling up his GrubHub app to place an order. *Ramen. Edamame. Mmm. Gyoza.* He was hungry.

He'd been going back and forth all morning about

whether he should tell Hawk he'd be watching. Would Hawk like that? Would it make him nervous? Would it turn the cowboy on?

It definitely got January's motor running.

What the hell.

I found the tour on TV. I'm going to sit back with a beer and watch you kick ass.

It didn't occur to him until after he'd hit send that he had no idea what the weekend rides had been like for Hawk. He was an idiot. Wouldn't that be on the internet somewhere? Surely there was a website.

He clicked Google and found the site for the league. Hawk had ridden Friday, bucked off Saturday, and was sitting in third coming into today. Not bad, he guessed.

Charlie was still marked as injured, and Danny had bucked off both nights before.

Poor Nicole. Danny had done so well in Denver, and she was hormonal. Not a great combination. Maybe he should be saying poor Danny.

That made him grin.

Ashton Cook was sitting in first. January remembered him… he was adorable and had such a baby face. He'd come in fourth or fifth when January saw him ride in Denver. But Parker Stephens, the cowboy listed in second place, must have been injured or not have done very well in Denver because January didn't recognize his name at all.

Okay, so third. Hawk could probably move up from third, right? And what did Nicole say about third? *At least he was in money.*

Every picture of Hawk was in dark glasses, unless he was riding, then he didn't wear any. Was he wearing contacts? Was he good without his glasses?

No. Hawk wasn't good without his glasses, he was blind

as the proverbial bat. Nearsighted in a big way. January noticed things; he liked details and that was one that was impossible to miss. So Hawk didn't want his thick glasses on camera. Maybe the dark glasses were prescription too.

January understood; part of the whole appeal was the look, right? It worked for him, didn't it? And Hawk had beautiful eyes, so it was nice to see them once in a while.

He went out to the living room and flopped onto the couch, turning up the volume on the TV to see if things had gotten started. It wasn't the same as being there, and he didn't have Nicole to guide him through it, but he did have more commentator chatter.

The cameraman was focusing on the chutes, on the cowboys milling around back there. Hawk was there, leaning and messing with his phone, dark glasses and hat shadowing his face.

Good. I pulled Boogerbear. It'll be a ride and a half.

Oh, boy. Was that a good thing or bad? *Wave at the camera, I see you.*

He smiled as Hawk grinned, one finger flicking that straw hat in an easy greeting. It felt surprisingly good, to know that was for him.

Handsome. Give Boogerbear hell. He could talk a cowboy up, right? Why not?

He ain't been ridden yet. We'll see.

Oh, Shit. *Like, ever? Or just this tour?*

Like ever. Cool huh?

Whoa. You're popping his cherry! Virgin bull. Jesus, that sounded terrifying. Wasn't it a thing to kind of know how the bull went? Nicole was telling him about how bulls usually went right or left or liked to jump out of the gate or whatever. A new bull must mean Hawk didn't know any of that. *Shit.*

Or he'll drive me into the dirt. We'll see. Hawk had a little smile on his face.

My money is on you, Champ. It was. Hawk had the cred to back up the swagger. His buzzer went off, which was either the food, or Jax. Either way he needed to answer it. *Take out delivery. Gotta run. I'm watching.*

Enjoy, darlin'.

Darlin'. January repeated it in his head. He did like that.

He hit the buzzer. He assumed it was Jax, but you never gave anyone on the other end of a blind buzzer the chance to lie. So he played dumb. "Hello?"

"Open the fucking door, man. I'm freezing out here."

He laughed and buzzed Jax in. He could have gone for an expensive building with a doorman, but this place was amazing, had great views from his high floor and an elevator, tons of room and light, a fireplace... that was what he wanted, not someone standing by the door making it look exclusive.

Poor Jax. He wasn't built for cold

He opened his door and waited as the elevator doors opened. "Hey, man. Happy Sunday."

Jax grinned at him, looking practically perfect in every way. Asshole. Good thing it was only skin deep. "Only for you, man. Only. Beer. Cupcakes."

He grabbed the beer and held the door. "This is not dressed? How long did you fuss with your hair to get the totally perfect messy look?"

"Shut up. You never know when you're going to meet Mr. Right. We're not all lucky enough to find a cowboy in a hotel bar. What did you tempt him with? Cowshit and Old Spice?"

"Scotch. And my business card with my room number on it." He'd felt pretty daring, but he'd gotten a strong vibe from Hawk. He'd be surprised for sure, but not the least bit concerned he'd read the cowboy wrong. He grinned at Jax. "You have to be an asshole, huh?"

"It's my job. So, we're watching rodeo? You'll have to point him out. Is he good in the sack?" Jax put his coat in the closet. "I brought salted caramel cupcakes. I know you like it salty."

"Oh, you're amazing. Were these for work? Or for you?" He set them down on the counter in the kitchen, pulled out two beers and put the rest in the fridge. "Yes, we're watching rodeo, it's the final day in Orlando." He handed Jax a beer. "And he *rides* well everywhere."

"I'm experimenting with a stout icing. Chef said fuck no. Too extreme. This is Corona instead."

Corona icing? Was that a real thing? "Sounds... daring." He left them for after they ate and went back into the living room. "I saw Hawk earlier. I'm sure they'll show him again in a minute. He's in Orlando. He got a bull that's never been ridden before. Can you believe that?"

"What does that mean? It's a new bull? Like a baby?" Jax plopped down on the sofa, sprawling happily. "So is he, like, famous?"

"I think it means a bull that hasn't been ridden on the tour before. Which is wild to me. They throw new bulls in. And he's..." January pulled out his phone and brought Hawk up on the league website and handed it to Jax. "He was last year's champion, and he's on track to do it again. He's definitely a name."

Jax looked at the picture, studying it. "He's tiny and cute. You're not worried about breaking him?"

"Wait until you see him. He could break *me*. Seriously, he's an athlete. He's strong and ripped and wow. He's muscle and bone, and that's all." So fucking hot, and the right size as far as he was concerned.

"No shit? That's actually cool." Jax pierced him with a stare. "You're into him, huh? Like deep."

He looked at Jax and sipped his beer. It was one thing to know he was, and something else to say it out loud. Jax knew all about Lucas, his cheating fuck of an ex, knew how broken up he'd been over it, and that relationship wasn't more than a couple of months cold.

So saying he was into a hot bull riding cowboy he'd met in a bar in Denver out loud was going to sound as ridiculous as it ought to be.

It wasn't. He wasn't completely sure what it was, but something about it was real.

He stared at his beer. "Yeah. I'm pretty into him."

"Cool." When January looked up, Jax shrugged. "What do you want me to say? You deserve a good love affair, man."

"I don't know. I guess I expected you to tell me I'm insane." Which he was, but that meant Hawk was too so... "Am I an asshole? Am I going to hurt him?"

"Why? Do you intend to? Are you going to be evil to him?"

"No. No I don't... of course not!" He sighed. "Of course not. But I don't know what we're... he's on the road, I'm here, he's in the closet like whoa and I'm definitely not. I'm not sure I can do this right. Is there a right?"

"He's an adult, right? Not some innocent virgin?"

Innocent virgin? His Hawk? Hawk needed fucking more than anyone he'd ever seen.

"He's neither a virgin nor innocent." January winked at Jax. "He knows exactly what he wants."

"Then have fun. Have a ton of sex." Jax shrugged. "It's

not like you're afraid of traveling. Go see weird rodeo cowboy shit."

Oh. Rodeo.

He looked over at the TV to find the event had started, so he grabbed the remote and turned up the volume. "Weird rodeo cowboy shit."

"Right? Who gets on the back of a bull on purpose? It's nuts!"

"It's an extreme sport, right? Adrenaline junkies or something. I don't know. Not me, that's for sure. But it's fun to watch. And I mean... cowboys in Wranglers? There's really no bad there." They watched a rider get tossed, land on one shoulder, and roll to his feet. "That had to hurt."

"Does it? I mean, was your guy covered in scars and bruises and shit, or is it like wrestling?"

He started to answer that question, but he stopped. Then started again. Then stopped. He tilted his head and grinned at Jax. "Yes."

"Yes. Yes, there are scars or yes, it's like wrestling?" Jax rolled his eyes. "Fucker."

"Yes there are scars and bruises and yes, it's like wrestling." He gave Jax a wide, cheesy grin. "Except I always get to be on top."

"Oh man. I know you like that, you toppy little bastard." Jax waggled his eyebrows. "I got to say, I'm surprised a bull rider would take it up the ass."

"Right? I actually thought man, who knew cowboys came in gay? But I made a coded overture and he picked it right up." He snorted and rolled his eyes. "Not everyone feels the need to roll over and show his belly like you do."

Jax pulled his sweater up and rolled his abs. "It's a great belly. I'm working on rolling a quarter up and down while having sex."

He stared at Jax and started to laugh. "If you can think about a goddamn quarter while fucking, you're doing something wrong."

"Right? Tell me all about it. After you point out your cowboy."

"Oh. Well, he was in third place, so he'll be riding in the last group. Let's see where we are." He took a long sip of his beer and turned to face the TV. "You know, eight seconds is a long time. It sounds like nothing, right? But watch these guys."

A cowboy named Huck—and who the hell named a kid Huck?—was riding, the clock slowly ticking. At a little over six seconds, the bull slammed up and Huck went down and then boom. Huck was on the dirt and the clowns were surrounding him.

"Damn. Six. So close." Part of him liked knowing what was going on in the arena right then, the way the crowd was holding a collective breath until the rider got back up. "Come on, cowboy, get up."

"Is he okay? God, is he bleeding?" Jax's eyes were huge.

"I didn't even see the bull hit him, did you? It must have been as he was going down. Damn." There had been some blood at the event he went to also, one kid was carried off the dirt. "Risky fucking sport."

And Hawk was riding a new bull. Great.

"I think his face hit the bull's head. I—whoa." Jax took a long drag of his beer. "This is intense. Cool, but intense."

"Oh when he shot up? Yeah, maybe. Shit there's the stretcher." Could he do this? Watch Hawk ride weekend after weekend and hope to hell he didn't end up like that Huck kid? "Damn," he said again. He didn't know what else to say.

Right about the time they loaded him up on the

stretcher, the cowboy waved to the crowd, and the crowd went wild.

"See folks? He's okay. Let him hear you while they take him to check him out." The announcer sounded too cheery, not a bit worried.

January imitated the announcer's voice. "See folks, he's bleeding profusely from the head but he's going to be *fine*." He laughed. "Oh. That's Hawk. See him loading up there? Straw hat." He was glued to the TV, watching Hawk climb over the fencing and straddle the bull. "That guy's big, huh? The bull I mean, not Hawk." Not Hawk, that bull made Hawk look tiny.

"He's teeny. He's going to ride that beast?"

God, he hoped so. He knew Hawk needed to make the ride.

"He's the champ. If anyone can, he can." January made himself feel confident by sounding confident. It was better than worrying, which wouldn't do Hawk any good. *You've got this, angel. I'm watching.*

"Folks, the champ is looking to ride Boogerbear. He's had no qualified rides in thirty outs, but Hawk's looking to be the first."

What was a qualified ride? What was an out? *Shit.* "Someone has to be first, right? That's all. Doesn't mean he's worse than any other bull, does it?" He had no idea. He didn't know what all that jargon meant.

"Dude, you're the one fucking a rodeo cowboy. Don't you know?"

He was going to beat Jax.

Hawk's jaw was set, the man slapping his gloved hand, pounding it closed around the bull rope. The bull was jumping and bucking in the chute, Hawk barely holding on.

By the time Hawk nodded, January was dizzy from not breathing.

Boogerbear leapt out of the gate, airborne before they'd even cleared it. "I'm going to throw up." He wasn't. He didn't like not knowing what was going to happen. Give him spoilers every time.

Hawk held on, eyes focused in front of him.

"That's the thing about Hawk, man," the announcer said. "He never looks off. Never."

The clock kept ticking and he willed Hawk to do it. Do it. Fucking ride.

The buzzer sounded, and the crowd erupted in cheers.

Hawk let go, and the bull bucked, sending him flying through the air, and the smack when Hawk slammed into the ground made him want to scream.

"Shit." Flew out of his seat. "Fuck." Hawk rolled, which was a good sign, he figured. And the bullfighters were right on their game, but *Jesus*. That landing looked like it hurt.

Hawk got to his feet and started running, but it was like the man didn't even see the bull, and he was running right to it.

"Where's he going?" Jax hollered, and January didn't know, but Hawk hit the stage in the center of the arena going full blast, rolling up on top of it.

"I don't—" January stared at the TV, horrified as he watched Hawk run the wrong direction. The wrong fucking direction. "He can't...Jesus." He couldn't see it. Hawk couldn't see the fence. That had to be it. "Shit."

"He's safe, right? He's standing with the clown guy?" Jax blinked as the announcer began to holler, confetti going everywhere.

"Ninety-five-six! Boogerbear has been ridden for a ninety-five-six!"

"Holy fuck." He collapsed back into his couch with a sigh. God, breathing felt good. "He's safe all right. And he's a fucking stud." And the champ could play off his run for center stage with a little swagger and a big smile now. "Holy fuck, Hawk."

"Is that cool? Is it good? What happened? Is it over?" Jax looked utterly confused. "Where's the ramen?"

"It's cool. I guess it's over? Confetti cannons kind of tell it all." He had his eyes on the champion cowboy all the bullfighters were escorting out of the arena. He wondered how much they knew. How much anyone knew.

The door buzzer went off as if Jax had summoned dinner. "And there's the ramen." He hopped up off the couch and buzzed the delivery guy in.

Before he made it up, a text came in from Hawk.

RODE HIM. MADE THE SHORT-GO.

Wait.

Wait. The short-go. Hawk had to ride again. Shit, he forgot about that. He wasn't sure he had the spoons to watch another ride.

I saw! That ride was amazing and your score was crazy. You're a stud, champ.

The answer that came back was a selfie, dirt coating his smiling cowboy.

That smile was the real deal, the cowboy looked absolutely exhilarated. *As hot and filthy as ever too. Do it again, baby. You're on fire. I'm watching.*

And he wanted to be there tonight, the one that was getting that passion, that adrenaline. He wanted to see it.

He'd have to wait for Raleigh. Impatiently. That was a long time to have a hard-on for someone. He'd call later. Yeah. That would work.

"Food!" He opened the door and took the bag from the

delivery guy, saying thank you before letting the door close. "Hawk texted me. It's not over. I forgot about the short-go. Come take this Jax, I'll get us set up to watch."

"What's a short-go?" Jax hopped up and took the bags from his hands and started unpacking at the table. "God, this smells good."

He cleared off the coffee table to make room while Jax put the food out. "It's a second round. Just the top scoring riders from the weekend. I guess they call it that because it's short? I don't know." Close enough to keep Jax happy. "So he won the day, and now he's trying to win the weekend."

"Wow. Complicated, huh? So do they get paid for each bull?"

"Honestly? I have no idea. I think only if they're in the top two or three? Hawk is last year's champion, so I guess he's made some money." He didn't ask about money. He didn't really care about money; he cared a lot more about getting into Hawk's Wranglers. He still didn't know how Hawk got into his head. "You want a fork?"

He ducked into the kitchen because he wanted one. And a real spoon too. He was feeling hungry, not fancy.

"Grab me a spoon too? I'm going to have to look this money thing up. What's his last name?"

"Uh—Destry. Hawk Destry."

"Right on. Thank God for phones."

"Forks and spoons, roll of paper towels, two more beers." January set everything out on the coffee table as he said it. "I honestly don't think I could function without the internet."

The station cut back from a commercial break and they were finishing cleaning up the arena as he sat down. The announcers started chatting and recapping the first round, and they cut to a replay of Hawk's ride. "Jesus, he's glued to that bull."

"He is, but dude, he was confused when he was thrown off. He almost ran into the bull."

"Landing on his shoulder probably rattled his cage. And Hawk's a little nearsighted."

Why was he passing it off to Jax as no big deal? It was a dangerous mistake and Hawk was more than a *little* nearsighted.

It was like he couldn't see the bull. Bulls were big.

"Yeah. He's really going to have to do it again?" Jax pulled his feet under him. "That's wild, man. Really wild."

"He is, and all the other riders that made the cut. What are you finding out?"

"So, he's worth about two and a half mil. He's won a season and a final event. They get money for showing up and signing autographs. The top eight in an event make money, but the top three make a lot more. And sponsors are where the real money is." Jax waggled his eyebrows at January. "This one website calls the Destrys 'rodeo royalty'."

January thought about the picture Hawk had showed him of his handful of enormous brothers. "Yeah, he said his mom and dad both did rodeo and all of his brothers too. It's crazy. I didn't know they were famous though. And I didn't know he was a millionaire."

It was kind of nice to be involved with someone that didn't need his money.

"He didn't say? That's vaguely cool, man."

"He said they were a rodeo family, that's all. Maybe he thought it was understood?" Maybe he thought it was nice to be with someone that didn't look at him like a celebrity. It was nice to be *you*.

He scooped some ramen and veggies out into a bowl and sat back. "It's starting."

"This thing is complicated as hell, man. No touching the

bull. No letting go. There's money and points and different levels." Jax put his phone down and got himself food. "So, where is your guy now? Second?"

"The bull gets points, that's what confuses me." For what? Being extra mean? "Hawk is..." He squinted at the TV. Nothing messed with him more than numbers and letters together. "It says second. Talk about pressure." He took a big bite of noodles. "Oh! I know that guy. His name is Danny. I sat next to his very pregnant wife. She was friendly, but I think they're both about nineteen."

"This isn't an old dude sport. Your guy is twenty-seven, and he's up there."

"That's what it looked like, yeah. Some sports are like that I guess. I feel like an old, old man." He'd only turned thirty. "He seems older." In some ways Hawk seemed older than January.

Danny had what seemed like a beautiful ride. The score seemed low, but he wasn't going to pretend he understood scoring. He was glad to see the kid make his eight.

Up and down, this short-go went fast. Danny had snuck up to fourth, and no one rode again and then Hawk was up again.

"So the worst he can do is second, right?"

"Yeah, because if they both fall off, they are where they are." And second wasn't bad, right?

Danny was adorable and ambitious, but there was no way Hawk was losing to a nineteen-year-old kid. January stared at the TV like he could send Hawk his confidence through the screen.

Hawk was on a huge white beast with one crooked horn, the bull snorting and rolling his eyes.

"Look at—whoa?"

The gate slammed open, the bull slinging snot. Hawk started sliding, leaning into spin.

"He's heading into the well, folks. Come on, Hawk! Put your mind in the middle!" The announcer sounded as stressed as he felt.

"Did he nod? Did you see him nod? Shit shit shit. No! Get up, baby. Pull up!" January was back on his feet again, hands on his head as he shouted at the TV.

The buzzer went off and Hawk slammed to the dirt, getting up and running for the fences. Red handkerchiefs went flying as a score of seventy-eight went up on the screens.

"That wasn't eight was it? What do the flags mean? Jax. Look up what the flags mean," Seventy-eight? God he wished he had a clue what was going on.

"Uh. Uh. Flags mean a re-ride? He can do it again for a higher score?" Jax stared at him. "Again?"

"Jesus. That would be three for the day. And that last one had to hurt. Did you see him all sideways?" He was watching, Hawk was talking to someone that was way too clean to be another rider. "Do most people ride again?"

"I don't know! Why are you standing up? Why am I yelling?"

January glanced at Jax. "Right. We're stressing this. I'll sit, you... talk quieter." He flopped on the couch. "This is awful. I mean, it's great, but it's awful."

"Maybe you should date a professional knitter." Jax stared at him. "Or a what's boring? An accountant?"

"A baker." He shot Jax a wink, teasing.

"God yes, but you and I had all the chemistry of oil and water. I love you dearly, but *damn*."

"Didn't I fall asleep during that BJ you tried to give me?"

Jax threw a noodle at him, hitting him in the chin. "The

deal was we would never speak of your lack of taste, butthead."

"Gross!" He pulled the noodle away and tossed it into the take-out bag. "*My* lack of taste? You don't appreciate caviar when you see it, my friend. I still like you okay, though."

He loved Jax. They'd become best friends in five minutes. Bizarre sort of odd couple best friends, but it worked for them.

"Dude. We missed the end. What happened?"

"What? *Fuck.* Where's the remote? Oh. This was the internet, I can't rewind." Shit. He reached for his phone. "Find it somewhere. Did he ride? I need to see it."

"Uh. Okay. Just a second. This website isn't the best on earth. Text your guy?"

"Working on it."

Hey, Champ. What happened? I have a friend here for dinner and we missed your re-ride.

It took forever for the text to drop. *Didn't take it. Took second.* A picture of Hawk with his shoulder and arm packed in ice appeared seconds later.

Shit. His first thought was how awful that looked and how much it had to hurt. That ride was Hawk's second dump on his shoulder in one night. But was it wrong that he was also disappointed? Second place was fantastic. And hell, Nicole had to be over the moon.

Second place is nothing to sneeze at, Champ. That bull was an asshole. Does that hurt?

He glanced up at Jax. "He's injured. He didn't take the re-ride. But he took second place, so..."

"That's still a lot of cash. Twenty K, man. He okay?"

Just getting the swelling down. No big. Got a bonus for the big ride from the contractor. Moved to number one in the world. Life is good.

No shit, really? Life does sound good. You're the hottest fucking cowboy on earth, you know that?

Wish you were here. Heading to Raleigh in the morning. Yay. Enjoy your friend.

Call me later. I'll give you something to think about until I get there. PS He's just a friend.

You got it. And good. Cheating isn't my thing.

It wasn't his either. Someone forgot to give Lucas that memo though. *His name is Jax, he's my best friend. He gives the world's worst BJs. I don't cheat, and I'd be a fool to anyway, with you on the other end of my line.*

Ha! You've met Charlie. He met Ben thru me. Gotta close my eyes a sec, darlin. Talk to you tonite.

TTYL Champ.

"Well, he's hurt. Bummer." He scooped up a couple of edamame and grinned at Jax. "But he moved up to number one in the world, so... I'm guessing he's pretty good with his night."

"Wow. Just wow, man. This was wild. We're going to have to plan a trip and go in person. Their Finals are in Vegas. I love Vegas." Jax dug into his noodles, finally. "God, that was cool."

"It was, right? It's a crazy sport. Thanks for coming over to watch with me, I might have lost my mind yelling at the TV alone." He had a feeling he'd be inviting Jax over to watch a lot.

Vegas, huh? Maybe he could find a cowboy for Jax. He laughed and shook his head, then glanced up at Jax. "I'll invite you to the next nail-biting short-go."

"Fair enough. So, you're going to see him next week?"

"I'm going down to Raleigh on Friday for the weekend."

Was it Friday yet? "Think good thoughts that his shoulder is better by then."

"Does he need that to give blowjobs?"

This time it was his turn to toss over an edamame, but Jax managed to catch it in his mouth. Asshole.

"If you were any good at them, you'd know." He laughed. "That was a good catch, man. I can't even be mad at you."

"Thanks. Good beans. Can I have another one?"

"Catch." He tossed one and Jax snatched it right of the air with his teeth. "Oh, good boy! Roll over and I'll throw you another."

"I will bite you, ass." Jax cackled. "Okay, so this was worth leaving the house. You win."

"See? Your little introverted heart loves me." Jax didn't do people. The guy had his reasons and that was fine, but there had to be more to life than cookie dough and the inside of Jax's tiny apartment. "You ready to try those cupcakes?"

"Totally." Jax uncurled and padded over to grab the oh-so perfectly frosted cupcakes. With gold sugar sprinkles.

Jax was right. This was absolutely worth it.

He cleaned up dinner while Jax dug through his kitchen for the fancy dessert plates his mother gave him.

Because something that pretty deserved better than paper.

8

———

"Where are y'all? I thought you were coming out?" Hawk wanted to introduce Charlie and Ben to January, maybe they could all have supper.

"No. We'll pick your happy ass up at the airport here, but Charlie's head is bothering him. Fucking migraines."

"Yeah. Yeah, that sucks. He gonna be okay?" There was a little dammit there, but a little more 'oh I'm going to get fucked' to take his place.

"He's fine. Just rattled. You know."

He did. He so knew.

"So, kiddo, last week..."

"Don't. It's fine." Hawk pushed his glasses up.

"Is it getting worse?"

It always was getting worse. The secret was not letting on. His folks knew, Charlie and Ben knew. He thought Skylar knew. That was it. No one else. He needed to ride. "Nope. It's good."

"Liar."

"Uh-huh. Gotta go. January's texting." Hopefully the hot bastard was here.

Landed, grabbed a cab, OMW to the hotel. See you there or not until tonight after?

I'm leaving here at 5. We got an hour or more. Enough to get January settled. Get a kiss. Touch.

Room number?

809. He'd been there since Monday and he approved. He'd soaked in ice, he'd watched porn, he'd napped for hours—it was fine.

I'll check-in and drop by. Can't wait to see you.

Soon, darlin. Not soon enough, but soon.

He made sure the room was decent, the cooler was filled with Miller Lite and grapes, and that there was a bottle of Glenlivet waiting.

When the knock finally came it was measured and calm, three steady raps. January looked good. No suit—just jeans, a thick cream-colored sweater, and a great big smile. "Hey, Champ."

"Hey, darlin'. Come on in. Stay a spell." So fucking handsome, his man. So solid.

"Thanks." January stepped in far enough for him to close the door. "Are you good? You look good."

"I'm solid as a rock." Hard as one, too, but it might be tacky to mention.

"Yeah? Cool." January reached for him slowly, the warm fingers that landed gently, tentatively, on his chest felt like a different question. "Cool."

"Missed you." He didn't have time right now for subtle. He pushed right into January's arms, going on tiptoe for a kiss.

"Yes. Missed you," January whispered on a breath. The fingers on his chest curled into a fist in his shirt and there was nothing subtle about the way January kissed him.

Fuck yes. A groan tore out of him, and he crawled up that big, fine body like he was meant to.

January leaned into him, pressured him back against the wall and broke the kiss off with a grin. "Like half an hour, huh? That's it?" January tore at his belt and got the buckle loose.

"Give or take. Yeah." He moved to January's ear, biting at the lobe. Lightning shot through him, and he felt so goddamn alive. "Need you like breathing."

That bite made January growl, the sound rumbling in the man's chest. "I'm right here." January pushed his jeans low on his hips and his cock fell right into eager fingers.

A second later, January was on his knees.

He bit his bottom lip hard enough to draw blood, the sight of January kneeling there pure fucking fantasy.

January kissed the base of his cock and inhaled deeply. "Fuck, you smell good." Then that clever tongue worked its way from there to the very tip. "Not going to tease."

"Thank God. I—" He shut his mouth. He was glad January was here. He wanted the man stupidly and for as often as he could have him.

"Mm." January took him right in with some sweet suction, stroking up from the root, lips and fingers meeting somewhere in the middle and moving back again.

"Oh God. Darlin', you're real." And so much better than any daydreams, any fantasies. Anything.

January let him go. "I'm real. Every inch of me. I'm going to show you how real after you ride tonight."

He stared down, eyes wide, heartbeat pattering. "I got your tickets."

"Thank you. I'm looking forward to watching your hot bod on the back of a bull." January took him down deep, all the way, and swallowed hard.

"Fuck!" He arched, hips rolling like he was bucking for a few desperate times before he shot like a virgin teenager.

January made a shocked sound but swallowed and licked and gentled him down off that cliff like they had all day. Like he mattered.

"Mm. That was something, angel." January stood, gracefully, stroked a hand over his cheek and kissed him.

"Sorry. Sorry, darlin'. I been thinking on you." And he was ramped up as all get out. "A lot."

"Mmm. Don't apologize. That was one hell of a compliment. Did that take the edge off for you a little? Mind in the middle and all of that?" January leaned close to his ear and whispered, "I've been thinking about you constantly."

"I been sitting in this hotel room with you on my mind for days," he admitted. It was stupid but it was true.

"We'll make the weekend count." January kissed his cheek. "We won't waste a minute of it."

He reached out, thumb tracing the heavy ridge of January's erection. "Sounds good to me."

He didn't intend to waste anything at all.

"Yes. Hungry for you." January rolled those narrow hips right into his hand, eyes going half-lidded.

"We have time." He worked January's belt open. "I can get you off so you can relax for the event."

"You think I can keep what I want to do to you tonight off my mind for that long, huh?"

"Fuck, I hope not." He fished out January's cock and started petting, keeping his grip easy and loose.

January sucked in a breath. "You have amazing hands. Gentle, but a touch rough enough to feel right."

"They like you." He focused on finding a rhythm, firm and sure, listening for every one of January's cues.

January sighed and curled a hand around the back of his neck, hips starting to rock in time. "Good. Fuck." He knew when he had it right. January wasn't shy, or hard to read.

"When we get back, I want you to fuck me in the shower. I want to feel every inch of this fat prick slamming into me." There was something about January that made him need, made him starved for every word, every reaction.

January's groan was rich and hungry. "Anything you want, angel. I can give you anything you need."

"I know. I'm a lucky son of a bitch." The luckiest. And he didn't feel that way, every day.

"Little more, baby. Just... harder." January's head fell back as he tightened his grip. "I've been craving you all... fuck. All week. Gonna..."

"Come on." He worked the slick tip with his thumb. "Show me, darlin'. I need it."

January lifted his head and looked Hawk right in the eyes, holding that stare as he shot, gasping and slicking Hawk's hand.

"Fuck, you're fine." He blinked hard, wanting to remember this, to see it.

"I feel that way with you." January didn't look away even as they both leaned in for a hard kiss.

Hawk groaned, telling himself not to get all ramped up before he had to go sign autographs. It was a fool's errand, though, because that kiss tasted like both of them, together.

"You ready to ride cowboy?" January stepped back and tucked himself back into his jeans.

"I am. I got one I've ridden five times tonight. Should be okay." No promises, but it should be okay.

"Beats one no one has ridden. Although that didn't go too badly for you." January chuckled and smoothed out Hawk's shirt while he did up his belt.

"Hell no. That rocked." Twenty-five-thousand bonus, man. It felt good. It felt damn good for an eight-second ride.

"So, am I pretending to sleep in my hotel room or are you pretending to sleep in yours?" January grinned. "And do I wait for you after or meet you back here?"

"You can sleep here with me, and I get us a car picking us up. So wait for me after the event, huh?" He felt brave as fuck, flaunting January around.

"Are you sure? Nicole said... I don't want to cause you any trouble. I mean, I get it."

"I'm not going to kiss you in front of my sponsors, but I'm allowed to have friends, and who's in my hotel room is my business." It wasn't that easy, he knew that. They had to watch themselves at the event, in the car, in public. This was fucking North Carolina, after all.

January gave him the side-eye but nodded. "I'll look for you after. Tickets at will-call?"

"Yeah, because I wasn't sure we'd meet here at the room." He started hunting the room keys, hands sliding over the flat surfaces. "If you're uncomfortable, you can meet me here. I understand. It's a risk."

Where were those keys?

"I'm not. I would kiss you on every corner between here and there if you wanted me to." January's hand settled on his back. "What are you looking for, baby?"

"The room keys. They're in an envelope. I have one for you."

"A little white envelope?" January reached around him, and he felt them slide under his fingers.

"There they are. Thanks." He pulled one of the keys out and put it in the slot in his wallet for room keys, then handed the envelope to January.

"Thanks. I'm going to change and bring my bag down here then I guess. And I'll see you at the show. Good ride."

"Thank you, sir. I'm looking forward to a new event." He took January's hand and brought it to his mouth for a kiss. "See you in a few hours."

"You'll hear me. I'll be the loud one calling your name." January squeezed his hand and took a few steps back before letting go. "Bye." He stopped at the door for a second before letting it close behind him.

Lord have mercy. He had never wanted to get an event over so fast. He wanted to ride a totally different beast.

For way more than one go-round.

First though, work. Dammit.

9

When January showed up at will call for his tickets he felt less like a stranger in a strange land and more like the newbie fan he was. His jeans were Levis and his baseball cap said NYU, but he knew what the daysheet was this time and he knew he could get a beer after he found his seat.

He was early this time, so he got to mill around a little bit on his way to his seat. He checked out the merchandise booth and thought about picking up a T-shirt for Jax and a new cap for himself at some point over the weekend.

It seemed like a different energy in Raleigh than Denver, but he couldn't quite put his finger on why. He was every bit as excited as he'd been in Denver though, maybe more now that he knew what to expect.

Or maybe it was because he knew his thing with a hot bull rider was more than a weekend tryst. He was invested now.

He took a selfie with a cardboard version of Hawk that was part of a sponsorship display and sent it to Jax with a text.

He's not this tall in real life.

The photoshop version of Hawk was pretty funny actually—they'd beefed up his shoulders a little, whitened his teeth, cleaned up his boots and given him at least six inches in height. You couldn't forget how tall, or not, a man was once you'd kissed him.

Also, he could be wrong, but he was pretty sure championship buckles didn't say "Red Bull."

There were cowboys everywhere, as well as the fans and girls in tiny leather shorts offering Jack Daniels stickers and looking for emails.

No thank you. Now, were there some boys in tiny leather shorts...

Beer. Find his seat, give Nicole a hug, get a beer. January could hear a little commotion in the arena, so he figured he better get moving so he went in search of the VIP bar first.

This bar offered Jack and Coke as well as beer, and there was pulled pork and sausages to munch on. He could get used to this.

He took a picture of the spread and one of his Jack and Coke—because why not, right?—sent those to Jax too, and went to find his seat. He'd eat during a break later.

There were lots of people hanging out and chatting in the aisles, so it took him a minute to find his seat. Not that there was a bad one. He scanned the VIP section looking for Nicole, he was hoping to run into her to congratulate her on Danny's first place last weekend.

He took his seat and watched the milling cowboys below him, seeing how many he could name.

He saw familiar faces, he thought, but the one he wanted to see was with Parker Williams and a dark-haired cowboy he didn't recognize.

Hawk looked so damn happy. Serious, focused, but

relaxed and easygoing. And probably half-blind without his glasses.

That had been something today, Hawk feeling around on the dresser for the key cards like an actual blind man. It was a good thing Hawk was experienced and smart, or January would worry a lot more than he did.

He glanced up at the jumbotron screen where they were showing footage and commercials and sipped his drink, as relaxed and happy as Hawk.

A man sat beside him, giving him a friendly nod as he settled with a drink.

He nodded back and raised his glass. "I figured if they're serving something fancier than beer I should go for it."

"Absolutely. I thought exactly the same thing. Cheers. I'm Beckett."

He "clinked" his plastic cup with Beckett's and grinned. "January."

"It's late February now I think."

January shook his head. "It is. But my name is January."

"Oh! Damn. I'm sorry. You must get that a lot, huh?"

"You have no idea." Really he didn't.

"Sorry. January, got it. Who are you here for?" Beckett sipped his drink and leaned back in his chair. The guy looked exactly like he belonged here, like he'd done this a hundred times.

"I'm a friend of Hawk's." January pointed down to where Hawk was still chatting with the guys, assuming being honest was a bad idea.

"No shit? I'm with Sky."

"Sky...?"

Beckett laughed. "You're new to this, huh?"

He didn't blush, but he cringed a little. He'd missed something big. "I guess I should know Sky?"

"He's a past champion, retired last year. We travel a lot now, get around as much as we can."

"Oh! Well, congrats. That's great." Oh! Damn, that was the rider with the husband that Hawk had mentioned in Denver. Right. Whoa.

Beckett laughed again and swirled his drink. "It is. We're promoting his invitational. It's up near our place in Vermont. Hawk's on the list."

"Yeah? I've been to Vermont a couple of times." Mostly to sip spiked cocoa in a hot tub and watch other people risk their necks skiing. "Sky runs an event? When is it?"

"In the spring." Beckett gave him a wide grin. "So, you're not a local. Where did you two meet?"

"Oh, no. I'm from New York. I ran into him when I was out in Denver on business a few weeks ago. He gave me some tickets to watch him ride and I'm hooked." By the balls. It would be embarrassing if he didn't think Hawk felt the same way.

"Hooked, huh?"

What did that look mean?

"It's a great sport. Scary as hell, gets your heart pumping, but it's fun."

"Uh-huh."

Jesus. This guy was sizing him up. He'd better shut his mouth. He sipped his drink, hiding in it.

"Sky will come in and out. He's supposed to sit and watch, but he can't help but pull rope and hold vests." Beckett rolled his eyes. "So long as he stays out of the damn chute."

"It must be good luck to have a champ do that for you, right?" It wasn't his thing, but he tried to understand it. Adrenaline was addicting. For him, adrenaline anywhere outside the bedroom was entirely unnecessary.

"Maybe some guys think so. That's not why he does it. You can't take the rodeo out of the cowboy."

He frowned. "Guess that makes it hard to retire."

"I had to lose him in damn near every way possible for it to happen."

Oh. Well how about that? Beckett and Sky were obviously not in the closet, because Beckett wasn't shying away from their relationship at all. He should have guessed... to this point, everyone that he caught Hawk talking to was into men. "Shit." He looked at Beckett. "That doesn't sound like a good omen." That statement was as risky as he was going to get.

"It's a young man's game, right?" Beckett laughed wryly, smiling at an older lady walking up with a glass of soda and a plate of chips. "Miss Vera? Let me help you. You sitting up with us?"

"One down from you, dear-heart. How's Vermont? Parker says your man damn near killed him on the snowmobile."

See? Adrenaline. It was nuts.

"I'm pretty sure Parker is plenty capable of trying to kill himself on a snowmobile without my husband's help." Beckett took her chips for her and she put her drink in a cupholder before sitting down.

"You know it. Asshole cowboys." She laughed like that was the most natural, normal thing on earth.

"You got that right, Miss Vera. Are you comfy?" Beckett handed her chips to her. "Can I get you anything else? Parker's riding in the last bunch. He's having a decent season."

"Well, now that Sky is retired, sure. We have to hope Hawk and Charlie have a few bad weeks, right?" She winked over at Beckett.

Wait. Was Charlie riding? Hawk made it sound like he was out for a while.

"You know I am one hundred percent in your grandson's corner, Miss Vera." Beckett looked at January. "Sorry, Parker's practically family."

"Beckett Adler. You didn't introduce me to your friend."

Beckett sat up like she'd pulled on his ear. "Oh! January, this is Miss Vera. She is Parker's grandmother. Miss Vera, this is January, the name, not the month, and he is here to watch Hawk ride."

January stood up and offered his hand. "Pleased to meet you, Miss Vera."

"Aren't you a lovely looking man. I don't suppose you're single and looking for a sugar mama?"

Vera was a live wire and he loved it. "I'm afraid I'm spoken for. But if that changes, I will be sure to look you up."

"Oh, honey. I could turn you inside out. Just ask the bullfighters."

Beckett was trying so hard not to laugh the man was turning purple.

He leaned forward, looking shocked. "Miss Vera. *All* of them?"

"Well, Mackey's always got an excuse to say no, but a gal can dream, right?"

"I dream constantly." January winked at her. The lights dimmed and the spots did a ballyhoo. "Oh, here we go."

A hand landed on his shoulder as he leaned back, and Nicole smiled at him. She was one row behind. He gave her a big smile and shouted "Congrats!" over the music.

"The baby will be at the Finals!"

He gave her a thumbs up and squeezed her hand. It was

too crazy to try to talk right now he'd make a big deal about Danny later.

Hawk was going to be up there on the top of the chutes, the spotlight on him, soon. So fucking sexy. And this time he was ready with his camera. He loved all the theatrics of the introductions. The fireworks, the music, the flashing shit on the jumbotron. It was like a circus for grownups. So much fun. He could get hooked on this rodeo thing.

The introductions went on and on, but his guy—he was the champion. He stood on the top of the chutes.

January cheered like mad and caught a couple of pictures on his phone, but really he wanted to look, take it in. How often could he say he'd been so close to so much talent and skill? To someone so brave? To something so brilliant? Hawk shined up there. And he had every ounce of January's respect for it.

That didn't mean bull riders weren't crazy. He respected the crazy.

Hawk stood up there, dark glasses on, waving to the crowd when his name was announced.

Beckett leaned over toward him. "He's looking good."

"Damn good." He licked his lips before remembering he ought to be more circumspect and leaned back in his chair to sip his drink. *Damn, cowboy.* He couldn't wait to get Hawk alone.

Beckett didn't look at him but patted his knee and then went back to cheering.

Okay. So, cool. Right. Married gay cowboys. Now he was starting to wonder if cowboys came in straight.

He supposed it was like anything else—like called to like. If there were safe pockets, the gay guys found them and stayed there where they were welcome and likely to find friends. That made January happy, that these men had like-minded friends.

It made him less worried about Hawk too.

He pulled out his daysheet and had a look. "Did Miss Vera say Charlie was riding today?"

"He's on the roster, but he's not here. Sky says he's not feeling great. Hawk would know best. They're good friends."

"Okay. I thought Hawk said he was out for a while." He'd ask for some details later.

The very first rider out of the gate had an amazing ride, got a solid score, and the crowd went nuts. January was pretty excited too. "That's the way to start a show, huh?"

"Not bad. Not bad at all." Beckett nodded and then turned to grin at Nicole. "Do you know if it's a girl or a boy yet?"

"Danny wants to be surprised. My mom doesn't."

"Danny wins." January nodded. "And speaking of winning... he was on fire in Orlando, huh? I watched from New York."

"He was! I mean, Hawk had the ride of the night, but I get to go to the Finals!"

"I know he was really happy for you both." Hawk had taken number one in the world, so he'd made a good call all around.

"Oooh. Ouch." Beckett hissed and shook his head.

January looked out at the arena. He'd missed that ride but the kid in the dirt was out cold. "What happened?"

"Bad landing." Off the kid went. One crazy score, one stretcher. This was going to be a hell of a night.

It went like that the whole evening, and it went fast—three ninety-point rides, two Sport Medicine visits, a bunch of bad jokes from the clown, and then Hawk was loading up.

Hawk was focused, a cowboy he didn't know holding his vest and talking hard, mouth going and going.

"Is that your Sky?" He'd only seen the cowboy from the back.

"It is. Hawk needs to be talked to. He counts on it." Beckett arched an eyebrow. "Hot, huh?"

January grinned. "Sky? He's a catch." He didn't look at Sky for long though; he wanted to watch Hawk's every move. Hawk punched his fingers down around the rope and settled.

Any second now.

Hawk took a breath and nodded, the bull spinning out, heels kicking up high. The crowd gasped, but Hawk wasn't worried. January could read it in the lines of his lover's shoulders.

Hawk said he knew this bull, and as far as January could see, it showed. January relaxed too, and admired Hawk's strength and balance. He really was quite an athlete.

As soon as the buzzer sounded, Hawk hopped off, running for the fence.

In the right direction. *Right on, Champ.*

"That was an easy night. I wonder how they'll score him? He made it look pretty easy." Beckett pulled his pen out, waiting for the score.

"That's bad?"

"Only if the judges score the bull low."

He looked at the screen, then at Hawk, and wondered if Hawk could see it.

Hawk never even looked up when the eighty-two popped up on the big screen. He waved all around and walked toward the chutes, then let himself out.

"Well, he's healthy for tomorrow, right?" Beckett stood up. "You want to come with me?"

"Where are you going?"

"To get Sky."

"Oh." He stood too. "Sure. Yeah."

"Are you here tomorrow, January?" Nicole asked. "Maybe you want to have lunch with us?"

He smiled at Nicole and gave her a hug. "That sounds great. I don't fly home until after the short-go on Sunday. You want my cell? Or do you and Danny know how to reach Hawk?"

"We'll text Hawk. Have a good one." She winked at him. "Night, y'all."

"You're waiting here for Parker, right Miss Vera?" Beckett took her hand and held it.

"Yes. Like always, I sit tight. I'll see you boys tomorrow night."

"Goodnight." January nodded. This was nice. Everyone was so friendly. Like a huge, weird family that only met in hotels.

"Hawk mentioned he got you two a Town Car and offered us a ride back to the hotel. I hope that's all right?" Beckett asked.

"Of course." He smiled at Beckett. "It looked like Sky stayed out of the chute."

"He did. He's earned his reward for the night." Beckett winked over.

He nodded, knowingly. "Gotta give a champ what he needs, right?"

"Rewards are important when you're asking a rodeo cowboy not to leap in." Beckett shrugged, and a hint of sadness crossed his face. "He had a bad wreck. One of the worst."

Oh. Shit. "That sucks, I'm sorry. That's why he retired?"

Beckett looked at him meaningfully. "That's what it took."

He held Beckett's eyes, and Beckett kept up a hard stare. He sighed finally and looked out at the arena. "I hear you."

"Good. It's something they all have to deal with, the top tier. Sky! Up here."

"Hey! I've been sent to fetch y'all. Hawk's got us a limo." Skylar gave January a quicksilver grin. "Hey. Skylar Cates. You must be January. Hawk said."

"That's me." January shook Skylar's hand. "Good to meet you."

He followed Skylar and Beckett through a throng of riders their families, and out a side door. Waiting there was his cowboy, all in one piece and leaning against a dark car in the cold. He stuck his hands in his pockets to keep himself from reaching for Hawk.

"Nice ride. You hardly even look dusty, Champ."

"That one was a breeze. They want me riding the easy ones and staying back off the ninety-pointers." Hawk shrugged, the lights reflecting off the dark glasses and hiding his eyes. "Y'all ready? Chris here had a limo that wasn't being used. I thought it would be fun."

"Let's do it." January opened the door for Skylar and Beckett. "Climb in."

"Is there wine? I love a limo with wine." Beckett climbed in first and held a hand out, which Skylar took and relied on to leverage down into the car.

"It's fully stocked, sirs, and we can take the scenic route to the hotel, if you'd like." The dude driving the car was the size of a Mack truck with a booming voice to match.

"Do you think we should take the scenic route, Champ?" January had no idea how he was supposed to conduct himself with all these people around; that was up to Hawk.

But he knew he wanted to kiss that cowboy. If this were a cab in New York, he wouldn't hesitate.

He really enjoyed the rodeo. He really hated never knowing for sure what was expected of him.

"Take the long way around, man." Hawk smiled at Sky, who put the privacy window up. As soon as they were 'alone,' Hawk reached for him. "Beck and Sky are family, like Charlie and Ben."

"I'd figured that out, I didn't know what you wanted them to know about me." He put an arm over Hawk's shoulders and scooted closer. "But now that they know..."

January went in for a kiss, and Hawk met him more than halfway, almost sliding into his lap.

Yeah. That was exactly how he felt too. Hawk smelled like honest sweat and tasted wild, and he loved it.

"Hawk Destry, you horndog." Beckett's laugh was low, husky, like he knew a wicked secret.

January grinned against Hawk's lips but didn't give up the kiss. If it was true about Hawk, it was true about him after all.

"Let the man have his sugar. Come here and kiss me like we were dating." Skylar was laughing at them, but obviously Hawk didn't care, because the kiss went deeper.

"You're trying to make me feel old." But they went quiet after that.

Everywhere he touched Hawk was burning up. There was no question where they were headed, but he backed off slowly, figuring they should take their time getting there with Skylar and Beckett in the car. He pulled back two inches, enough to see Hawk's eyes, and slid his lover's dark glasses off so he could do it. "You want a beer, baby?"

"Yeah." Hawk blinked at him, owlish and adorable, and his lover tilted his head, trying to focus before Hawk moved and his lips slid over January's jaw, the whisper tickling his ear. "I want you, darlin'. I need you like breathing."

The words felt like a touch, maybe better because he knew they were truthful. He turned and sank back in the seat, letting Hawk nudge and nuzzle all he liked.

"Beckett, can you reach the beer?"

Beckett and Skylar had been together a long time. January could tell by the way they were sitting so easy together, without the urgency he and Hawk felt with only a weekend to share and everything so new.

"I can. You want some wine, Stud?"

"Mmhmm. I do. I'll pour, you give the boys their beers."

Beckett and Skylar moved around the little limo bar like they'd done it a hundred times. He'd been in a few limos, but he was never the one in charge of that bar. That was usually his dad or Sean.

He clinked beer bottles with Hawk. "So... Nicole invited us to lunch tomorrow with her and Danny. I accepted, I felt like it was rude not to."

"She's a sweetheart, and Danny's a hoot. You'll like him. He thinks she hung the moon or held the ladder for the guy who did." Hawk took a swig. "To riding good."

"To riding good." All of them held their glasses up for that one.

"January told me he picked you up in a bar." Beckett teased.

He laughed. "I said no such thing. I said we *met* at a bar."

"Semantics." Beckett shrugged, but Skylar punched him in the arm and looked at January.

"He's a lawyer. He damn well knows better."

"Ow! Well, either way, this was a booty call, huh?" That grin was for Hawk.

"This was a necessary stress relief moment, I'll have you

know. You've gotten spoiled having him home every night." Hawk never looked away from January, those blue eyes twinkling.

"It was totally a booty call." January winked. "The second night wasn't though. I think it was already an affair by then."

He sipped his beer. He liked Hawk's friends, and he didn't fail to notice how comfortable Hawk was around them. He noticed a lot about people; that was in his nature. He could tell Beckett was worried about Skylar in the chutes, even though the man seemed relaxed. He knew Skylar's hip was pretty sore right now by the way he was sitting.

And he knew Hawk was ready for him by the look in those crystal blue eyes.

"Yep. I've had a shit ton of booty calls. Not so many affairs," Hawk confessed, and Skylar chuckled.

"It's the Yankee thing. They're interesting."

January and Beckett both laughed, and he nodded at Skylar. "We are. We are very interesting. And you bull riders are—"

"Hot. We know."

"It's not really them, it's the hats." Beckett gave Skylar a wink.

"Bullshit, it's the Wrangler butts." Hawk made him laugh; the words were so sure.

"Oh. It is the Wrangler butts. Though I think I prefer them out of the Wranglers. The chaps are a nice touch too. Like a leather picture frame around all the good stuff. Damn."

Beckett snorted. "Okay, don't feed Sky's ego, I've got enough bull rider on my hands tonight already."

"Beckett's getting old if Sky's too much for him now,"

Hawk teased, and Sky popped Hawk's thigh.

Beckett laughed. "Old for a bull rider, but in my prime for other contact sports."

"Lord, y'all." Sky looked at January. "Are you here all weekend? I hope so. You need to see Hawk on a bull that isn't so bored."

"Yeah, I don't head back to New York until after the short-go on Sunday." And he planned to spend every damn minute Hawk wasn't working tied to the man's hip.

"Oh, excellent. Should we plan supper somewhere away from the fans tomorrow night? Somewhere with meat?" Sky grinned Hawk's direction. "I'll eat your portion of dessert."

"Fuck off. Aren't you a little pudgy for that?"

Beckett kicked Hawk in the shin "Who are you calling pudgy, *Tiny*?"

"You're jealous because you're twice my size, gigantor."

There was a moment of quiet, then they all cracked up, the car rocking with their laughter.

The car stopped and January squinted out the window. "Hotel. I'll have to find my best behavior for a whole five minutes."

"Right. Bummer. Chris has been paid, and he'll be back to take us to the event at five tomorrow." Hawk finished his beer. "Let's go, y'all."

"Look at you, Mister Champ in a Limo." January appreciated that Hawk wanted to shepherd him around in style... and away from the fans. He climbed out and tucked his coat around him on the sidewalk. "Is it supposed be cold in Raleigh?"

"I think it goes back and forth—sometimes warm, sometimes cold. Always humid, though."

The lobby was full of cowboys and fans, Stetsons and

boots as far as the eye could see. They lost track of Skylar and Beckett in the crowd.

"Hey, Hawk," a young lady in the tiniest pair of shorts on earth came bouncing over. "Are you coming to the after-party?"

"We'll see. Got to get the dirt off me first. Have fun."

"Isn't she cold?" January asked as they ducked around people, headed for the elevators.

"Hmm?" Hawk pushed the button for up.

"Didn't you see those shorts?" He didn't think about that question until it was out of his mouth.

"Didn't notice. I was busy thinking about something else."

Right. He'd let that one go.

"I'm thinking about something else too." January stood alongside Hawk, hands in his pockets to remind him to keep them to himself. He was sure that anyone who was paying attention would be able to sense the heat building between them, so he kept a little distance.

It wasn't easy though, when what he wanted more than anything right now was no distance between them at all.

"Then we're on the same page. Eight floors and a hallway between us and heaven."

"Stupid hallway." He glanced over at Hawk with a knowing grin.

"Stupid busy elevators." The doors opened up and a ton of people stepped out, all dressed in their finery.

"Hawk! You're going the wrong way!" Someone called out. Hawk gave them a wave and they got on the elevator with about ten other people.

"They're all dressed up for the party?"

"They are. The after-party. Music, booze, dancing." Hawk waggled his eyebrows, eyes hidden behind the dark glasses again. "I got to jump in the shower before I leave the room."

Or be jumped in the shower. He'd promised. "I'm not a big party person."

"No. It's loud and drunks think they're funnier than they are."

2. 3... They stopped on four. And five. Jesus, they were on the longest fucking elevator ride in history. They skipped six and stopped on seven, and he was so eager he headed for the door, but Hawk pulled him back. "Oops."

"Watch the pretty lights on the wall. Those tell us where we are." The words were a tease, but they sounded like Hawk had heard them for years somehow.

"Ha. Wishful thinking." He sighed as the doors closed.

On eight, he followed Hawk off the elevator and down the hall, staying two steps behind, but never letting Hawk forget he was there. He could see the tension in the cowboy's shoulders and the carefully measured steps of those dusty boots.

Hawk's hand was steady as he unlocked the door, and he reached back to pull January in.

Okay, he'd been good. Now he was so done with pretending. January closed the door a little too hard and turned the lock, then went after Hawk, grabbing his shirt with both hands and pushing the cowboy into the wall.

"Mmm, hello, darlin'." Those words in that drawl made his eyes cross.

"Champ." He took a kiss, a hard one. He'd been waiting too long for it to go easy. They'd warmed up a little in the limo, and now he needed Hawk, full on.

He worked the buttons on Hawk's shirt open then tugged on his belt. "What do you need, cowboy? Huh? Tell me." He got Hawk's belt open and went for the jeans.

"I want you to fuck me. I want to get slick with you in the shower. I want to suck you off. Then I want to do it again." Okay, that was clear.

Clear right down to his balls. Clear enough to make him groan.

He slipped a hand into Hawk's fly and squeezed. "Go start the shower."

Hawk took off the glasses and his hat, then his boots and belt before disappearing into the bathroom. The water came on, the steam starting up soon after.

He liked that little scramble, liked that it was all for him. January stripped and left his clothing on the dresser, pulled his little black nightstand bag out of his suitcase and followed Hawk into the steamy bathroom.

Hawk was already in the shower, the scent of soap heavy on the air.

January pulled a little foil package out of this bag and opened the shower door. He'd planned to walk right in, but the view was so stunning he had to stop to admire. All that muscle and all that water... it was better than the best fantasy. "Look at you, cowboy. You're a sight."

Hawk turned to face him, cock full and hard, curving up toward that perfect six-pack. "I figured I'd lather myself up for you."

January's fingers itched for that slippery skin and he stepped in, set the condom down on a ledge, and pulled the shower door closed behind him. "How thoughtful." He started with Hawk's shoulders and worked his way slowly down to the small of Hawk's back. His cowboy was built like a Mack truck, no fat, pure muscle, ass you could bounce a quarter off.

He touched it all, finally getting a hand around Hawk's

prick, feeling the weight in his hand. "This ride is going to be way more interesting than that bull."

"Longer than eight seconds, hell of a get off, and I get a re-ride if I'm lucky." Hawk wiggled his ass, pushing into January's fingers.

"You can have as many as you like. All you have to do is ask, and it doesn't have to be nicely." He grabbed that condom again and rolled it on. What was he waiting for? He knew what they both needed. "Spread a little for me, baby."

"Anything." God, how hot was it that Hawk meant it?

And how hot did the cowboy look right now, ass presented and all laid out for him to take. "Jesus." He braced a hand on Hawk's hip, then guided himself inside, moving slowly, adjusting as Hawk did.

"Been needing you, darlin'." Hawk groaned, taking him, inch by inch, wrapping him in that tight, fiery heat.

"It's been driving me crazy that I couldn't reach for you." He had Hawk now though, and he wasn't going to waste it. They understood each other and were long past being polite. January rocked forward and hauled back on Hawk's hips, Seating himself deep and tight. "Fuck, yeah."

"Need this like breathing." Hawk's body milked him, ass rippling around him.

He didn't have one bit of subtle in him. Not a hint of shame. He wanted more than needed, and he knew Hawk wouldn't deny him. His gaze was fastened on Hawk's slippery skin, the natural tan, the plentiful scars. Nothing like anyone he'd been with before.

Hawk hummed and stretched up for him, crawling up along the tile. Oh, he felt that, all along his cock. It made him moan and try to go deeper, as if that were possible. Hawk was already offering everything.

January pressed up close to Hawk's back, wrapping both arms around Hawk's solid chest. "You feel so good."

"So glad you're here. In me." Hawk leaned back hard, body working to ride him.

He was pretty fucking glad too. "Fuck, angel." January slid a hand down over those hard abs and scritched his fingers through rough curls before measuring Hawk's cock with a tight fist from root to tip. His lips dropped open as he could feel the effect his touch had on Hawk, all around him.

The pace got away from him, both of them rocking faster, working hard with a purpose, filling the bathroom with filthy sounds that echoed off the tile. He breathed hard in Hawk's ear as he chased the cowboy to the finish line.

"Fixin' to..." Hawk grunted, the sound a clear warning.

"Yeah. Go." He was so close he was gritting his teeth. He plunged his thumb through that sweet slit deep enough to burn a little.

Heat poured over his hand, hotter than the water, hotter than anything right then.

Beautiful.

He thought it. He tried to say it out loud, but he couldn't get a breath to speak. Hawk tensed and shook and that was more than enough. January took a few quick, shallow strokes, then drove in deep, cock pumping inside Hawk as he came.

He kept his arms around Hawk, holding on tight as the hot water poured down over them and the steamy air filled his lungs.

"Damn, darlin'. I been waiting on that for days."

"Yeah." January nodded against Hawk's shoulder, still catching his breath. "Something about you, Champ. I can't keep my mind or my hands off you."

"That's okay with me." Hawk chuckled softly. "Damn, I feel fine."

"Mmm. Good." He let go reluctantly and ducked his head under the water to shower off and give Hawk some room to move. He felt great too. He knew he would, that was why he came. "Shampoo. Got it."

That *was* why he'd come. Right? It was a five-hundred-mile booty call.

Right?

"You hungry, darlin'? Was Beckett good to you in the stands?" Hawk turned to watch him with a smug little smile on his face.

"Yes. Beckett, Miss Vera, Nicole. I have a regular crew now." He was good with being watched and he played it up a little washing the shampoo out of his hair.

Hawk's fingers started following the trails of suds, exploring him, focused on him in a way he'd never felt before.

"You want to order dinner? Have a drink with me?" He followed Hawk's fingers with his eyes.

"I got you whiskey." Hawk closed his eyes, and it fascinated him, the way Hawk's face relaxed, all of the sudden.

"Easier to see with your eyes closed?"

"Huh?"

January hadn't meant to say it out loud, but as long as he had... "Is it easier to see what you want to see with your eyes closed? It looks like it is."

"It's easier to focus, yeah. My eyes are tired."

He covered one of Hawk's hands with his. "Your eyesight is pretty bad." It wasn't a question; he'd been looking for an opening for the conversation and finally found one.

"It's nothing to envy, for sure. Thank goodness for glasses."

"It doesn't bother you when you ride?" He kissed Hawk's neck as he reached to shut the water off. He wasn't trying to ruin the moment, he was so curious.

"You don't need to focus while you're spinning, and my glasses are expensive, so I don't risk them."

"I don't blame you." He grabbed a couple of towels and put one in Hawk's hands. "What do you do when you land though?"

"Run. Usually, I run." Hawk scrubbed his face dry, then wrapped the towel around his waist. "Do I look weird on the big screen?"

"Weird? How do you mean weird? You look like you got tossed off a bull, seems accurate." He grinned and kissed the top of Hawk's shoulder, then wrapped the towel around his body too.

"Good deal." Hawk nodded like that was that. "Last thing I need is the powers that be stressing me."

Oh, now he understood. "You look hot as hell on the screen. Your smile reads. Your confidence reads. You're fine." January figured the "powers that be" probably didn't care what Hawk looked like on screen as long as he was riding like a champ and pulling in the cash. "You know where you really look good? Up in that fucking spotlight. You look like a hot, bull riding god."

"That's my job. Bull riding god." Hawk laughed and grabbed him, dancing him around, offering him happy, playful kisses.

"And you do it so well." He let Hawk twirl him, laughing when he had to bend and contort to get under the bull rider's arm. He stopped near the scotch. "I lead next time. Is that for me?"

"It is. I remembered it was your brand."

January blinked at Hawk, surprised to find he was touched by that gesture. "Thank you. Can I pour you some?"

"Please. Just a bit. I haven't eaten yet today, except that beer. I'll be drunk as a skunk."

"Order some dinner, angel. I'll have whatever you're having." He could handle a slightly buzzed Hawk. No problem. He flipped over two glasses he found near the coffee pot and poured them each a couple of fingers worth. Enough to sip for a while.

"Good deal. They've got a decent grilled chicken boob with broccoli and a side salad. I'll get you a piece of cherry pie for after and steal a bite."

He'd never suspected how hard these guys dieted, how they worked to stay tiny.

Chicken boob. He laughed and brought a glass to Hawk, then sat on the little sofa near the window. "Sounds good to me." He could go for cherry pie. But he'd go easy, because this was a working weekend for Hawk. January could have his fill of food at the events if he got hungry.

"Me too." Hawk dialed and ordered, naked and unashamed, a pattern of healing bruises right along his rib cage.

"Those from Orlando?" January pointed with the hand holding his glass and then took a sip. Oh. Perfect." He didn't remark often on the scars and the bruises. Hawk had plenty, but it had to get annoying being asked over and over.

"Yeah. I hit the shark tank hard. It was sore as a boil for a couple three days."

The shark... "Is that the stage thing in the middle of the arena? I saw that. Jax and I saw you... uh. Run for it. Right before all the confetti cannons went off." Jax thought Hawk had run the wrong way. He was hoping it was on purpose.

"Yeah, on the big ride. I slammed into it and rattled my chickens."

"Ouch. Cheers to hot, studly, bruises." He held out his glass.

"You know it. Bruises are like tattoos with better stories." Hawk tipped his glass, nodded.

"I get remarkably few." He shook his head. He was boring as hell. "How was your family time? Did they get to see you ride?"

"They were there for the Saturday event, then they flew home. My momma prefers to watch on the TV so she can hide her eyes. She's overprotective of me."

"Well, I saw that picture. You are kind of the runt of the litter." He pulled Hawk down on the couch with him. "And you do regularly try to kill yourself on a bull."

"Everyone's got a talent. That's mine."

"It definitely is. Moms are like that." Even his. She didn't get much chance to show it, but he knew. "Has it always been like that? Does it bother you?"

"Ever since I was little, yeah. She's a mom with her little chick." Hawk rolled his eyes dramatically. "It wouldn't do any good for it to bug me, would it?"

"I don't know, at some point you get to be a grown man." Hawk raised an eyebrow at him, and he laughed. "Yeah, okay. Not so much with mom, I guess. Does she know... are you out at home?"

Nosy. Jesus, Jan. But he couldn't take it back now, could he?

Hawk cracked up—just hooting, and he wasn't sure what was so fucking funny. Once Hawk wound down, he wiped his eyes. "My folks are over the goddamn moon that I'm queer. Sixteen grandbabies right now. Two more on the way. They don't mind one bit."

"Ha!" He barked out a laugh. "That's it? It comes down to grandkids? The two-penis thing doesn't register, fewer grandkids to babysit, huh?" He chuckled. "What if you... do you want kids?"

It took longer than January would have thought for Hawk to answer. "I love kids, but I don't imagine I'll ever be a dad. No one needs more of me."

He stared at Hawk having absolutely no idea what to say. What did that mean? He couldn't fathom it, so went for the low-hanging fruit. "What? Because you're gay? That's bullshit."

"What? No. No, I mean, I guess it's way less fucking likely I'll put some random bun in an oven with guys, won't I?" Hawk seemed suddenly breathless, suddenly nervous.

Whoa. "No. That's not going to happen."

That didn't explain what Hawk meant by that remark at all. He'd walked into something touchy. January wouldn't say so out loud, but Hawk was a terrible liar. "I'm sorry. I didn't mean to upset you. Kids are a touchy subject, I know."

"You surprised me. Thinking about the future is scary, I guess. The idea of going home after I retire and sitting there for forty years is no bueno."

There were pieces to this Hawk puzzle he was not putting together, and if Hawk was going to keep lobbing bombs at him, he was going to have to volley. "Why do you have to sit at home for forty years?"

"Tell me about what you do for a living? I don't know anything about it."

He blinked at the sudden change of subject. Okay, Hawk drew a hard line. No more personal questions.

"I, uh." He rubbed his forehead and frowned, trying to shift gears despite the scotch on an empty stomach. "Sorry. I give my father's money away. And some of my own. I manage a charitable foundation."

"That's cool." Hawk swirled the booze in his glass. "Me? I don't have that. Like I don't have a plan after 'ride bulls until they make you stop'."

Oh. Oh! So that wasn't a slam the door? Was it?

"Okay, I get that, but Hawk..." January shifted and leaned closer. "What's stopping you from making one?"

Hawk frowned at him, like he'd asked his lover to solve quadratic equations. "You—what would I do?"

"Well..." What did cowboys do? "I don't know. What do you like to do? I mean, I'm probably the wrong person to ask, I haven't known you very long." And truthfully, he knew Hawk's backside better than his front.

Hawk laughed softly. "True that. What's your favorite TV show?"

"I don't really watch TV. I'm more of a binge guy. Jax and I binged the new season of *American Horror Story*. And sometimes he makes me watch that British... uh. *Great British Bake Off*, I think? That show is crazy." And then he'd work and Jax would steal the remote and watch porn.

"Cool. Do you like to bake?" Hawk seemed more than happy to listen.

"No. No, that's Jax. That's what he does. He makes amazing things. I'm his guinea pig." He patted his stomach. "It's a tough job. As in not at all. He's really talented."

"That's cool." Hawk patted January's stomach too. "How did y'all meet?"

"Oh, God. That's a story." He settled in to tell the short version, which he'd never been able to make all that short. "We met at a club. This was right before I met my ex, so I was single, and Jax was this adorable guy looking lost at the bar. So you know what I was thinking, that's how we met, right?" He sipped his scotch and went on. "Turned out he'd had a hell of a day. He'd decided to have a shot of something, but he didn't know what to buy, so I bought him—"

January pointed to his glass. "What else right? We each had a shot and then hit the dance floor—he's not a bad dancer, by the way—but the next thing I know, he passes out on me. Just...*boom*. Like that. Flat out in my arms. I didn't even know his name yet."

"Oh Jesus. What did you do? You obviously did the right thing by him, because y'all are still friends."

January laughed, remembering how disoriented and confused Jax had been. "I rode with him to the ER and waited while they gave him fluids. He's not as young as he looks, but he did look really young that night, and I didn't want him to be alone so I took him home and tucked him into my guest room bed. He'd been awake for three days on a crunch job. He wasn't drunk, he was exhausted." Jax had been so embarrassed. He'd played it cool and made brunch and a lot of coffee the next day. That had been their first Netflix binge weekend.

"You're a good guy." Hawk nodded, like he'd made a decision. "I like that. That's a great story."

"Jax tells it better. He throws in all kinds of anecdotes about lights swirling and thinking he was dead in Heaven. And he'll tell you he had a wicked headache and my eggs made him hurl. He's better at stories."

They really shouldn't be as close as they were, they couldn't be more different, but somehow they met in the middle really well. And honestly, they both *needed* a friend, someone to call bullshit once in a while.

"I hear that. Charlie's the storyteller for us. He is the master of no shit, there I was."

"So were you and Charlie a thing once? Or just friends?"

"Me and Charlie? Nah. A hand job between friends on the road, sure, but it wasn't no thing." Hawk's grin was goofy and fond, and January knew that look. It was the one he had when he talked about Jax. "You never met Ben, I can tell. Charlie's never once looked at a man like he does at Ben. Ben was a country singer—hot as hell, sex on a stick. We saw him play the rodeo and then, bam, that was it. Charlie was hooked through the balls. Took him a whole year to land his fish, but now? Shit, now they're married and everything."

"Good for you introducing them. It's hard to meet people. Good people, I mean. How long ago was that? Maybe I'll be able to do the same for Jax eventually. He's a little bit... he's a bit of a homebody." Sometimes January thought Jax would be perfectly happy baking and never leaving home.

"Yeah? That's cool. There are folks in my hometown that have never been north of the Red River. Lots of them, really."

"Oh, no. When I say homebody, I mean he doesn't venture out of his *apartment* if he's not working somewhere. I often have to bribe him with food or movies." In his defense, Jax did work a lot.

Hawk nodded. "That's why I'm out and about. I want to see all I can before I go home."

"You have time off after Connecticut right? I'm an excellent tour guide. You should come."

Okay, he'd invited Hawk to stay with him. Was that good? Did he mean it? That was totally not planned.

January looked at his scotch. Was room service slow tonight?

"I'd love that. You look at your plans when you get home,

and if you really got time you can tell me when and where to show up. You know me. I ain't got plans unless I'm riding." Hawk stood up and pulled a pair of pajama pants out of the dresser. He tugged them on and threw on a T-shirt that said Jeep Naked. "I can hear that cart com—"

A knock sounded and Hawk answered, keeping January's still naked body hidden by the door.

"I'll get it in, man. No worries. Have a good one."

"Time to put on more than a towel, huh?" January got up, grinning because yeah, the scotch was making him pleasantly muzzy, and pulled on sweats. "You've spent a few nights in hotels, huh? Good ears."

"Spent a lifetime in them, darlin'. I started riding at seventeen without my folks. Literally ran away, got my PRCA card, and it took Momma and Daddy three months to find me." Hawk pulled in the cart, then tripped over his shoes by the bed, going down in a heap.

"Shit!" He hurried to Hawk and pushed the cart away. "Hawk?"

Hawk's laughter cut his worry in half and then in half again. "Lord have mercy. Good thing my butt got in between the floor and my brain."

"Jesus." He chuckled and reached a hand down to help Hawk up. "Careful of that butt. I like it."

"No worries, darlin'. It's hit the ground a thousand and twelve times. It's part of my job, eating dirt." Hawk bumped shoulders with him and lifted his face for a kiss.

"I love the way you say 'darlin'." He happily took the offer and kissed Hawk just to kiss him. Just because he liked it, and not because he wanted more. Well, not yet. More of Hawk was definitely on his agenda.

Hawk cuddled right in, one hand hot as a brand against his waist, willing to stay close and love on him.

January hummed, surprised that Hawk had a cuddle in him. Hawk was tough and a demanding lover. He was starting to see that some of the bravado was covering, or maybe even protecting, a softer side the cowboy hadn't let him see too much of yet.

He pulled Hawk against him, running a hand under the T-shirt and exploring the uneven terrain of skin. "You're okay?"

"Right as rain, darlin'. I'm happy as a pig in shit to be here with you."

"That's pretty happy." He tucked the hand on Hawk's back down into the waistband of Hawk's pajama pants. "So should we eat?" January kissed along Hawk's jaw, under his ear and down the side of Hawk's neck. "Or let it wait?"

Hawk went up on tiptoe, rocking toward him. "Damn, darlin'."

Mmm. Hot spot.

"Does that give you a little zing, angel? Right there?" He went after the spot with his tongue and nibbled with his teeth.

"Little bit. Lord have mercy, that lights me up like you flipped a switch." That was magic, that husky need threaded through Hawk's voice.

Maybe the cowboy had other switches. He pushed his other hand under the shirt and circled a nipple, rolled the little bud with his fingers, tugged on it with finger and thumb.

He could feel it against his lips, the little hiccup, the way Hawk paused, body and soul, to feel him.

Oh. Oh, dinner could wait. Hawk had him curious now... was this new? Was that possible? He pushed Hawk's shirt up and tugged it off so he could see... so Hawk could too. He used both hands, eyes watching Hawk's face.

"Mmm. Hungry?" Hawk's icy blue eyes were burning, watching him.

"You want me to stop?" He didn't.

"No. I was hoping that look was for me, darlin'."

"You know it is." He tugged again, and he saw Hawk's teeth dig into his bottom lip. Bingo.

He moved them slowly toward Hawk's bed, buzzing a little and wanting to find more of those spots, wanting to short Hawk out. "I think I have a lot more to learn about you, angel."

"I'd love to have you try and find every single thing." Hawk's fingers pushed in his sweats and eased them down.

"I'm going to try." He stepped out of his sweats and kicked them aside, returning the favor and tugging Hawk's pajamas down. "If you're not on the back of a bull, I like you best like this."

"Bare naked and needing you? I can do that, darlin'." Hawk stretched out, unashamed, as proud as he could be.

He started with what was in easy reach, fingers going after Hawk's foot, thumbs massaging into the sole. "Yes. like this."

"Oh, darlin'." Hawk's toes curled, and he sat up halfway, abs rolling before he rolled back down to the mattress.

"Sensitive, hm?" He smiled, pleased. "These spend a lot of time in boots."

"You know it. I felt that in my butt cheeks."

January took his time, working his fingers over Hawk's heel, ankle, and up his calf, stopping to draw a finger through a scar. "Ouch. Do these all have stories you remember? Or do they all blend together after a while?"

"Six of one, half dozen of the other. That was when a bull stepped on me and separated my calf." Hawk turned his leg over. "That's where they cut me open and sewed me up."

"Hmm. Sounds... painful." He bent and kissed both spots, then moved higher, fingers exploring Hawk's muscled thigh, visiting scars and tracing ridges.

And teasing, of course. This was foreplay after all. He was curious and interested, but slow torture was really the point.

Hawk was hard as a rock, cock leaking heavily, but he never pushed January and waited, finally relaxing back and closing his eyes. That relaxed Hawk's face, eased the tension in a huge way.

"Just feel, baby. Like in the shower. This is for you to enjoy." He got to where his fingers could brush Hawk's balls and retreated, repeating the same attention on Hawk's other leg, learning patterns and tracing muscle that mirrored Hawk's other thigh.

He was warm, aroused, but not nearly as needy as Hawk by the time his fingers reached the cowboy's hips again. And he hadn't even touched anything higher yet. Rather than climb over, January moved around to Hawk's side and brushed a hand over tight abs.

Hawk moaned, the sound full-bodied and rich. "That's good. You touch me like you want to."

"Believe it. I do." He circled a deep scar below Hawk's ribcage. "Appendix?" Somehow he doubted it.

"We were jumping fences when we were kids, and I missed. Danny and Grainger carried me home with a piece of rebar stuck in me."

"Jesus. That's a hell of a miss." He kissed it. "ER and the whole thing?"

"You should have seen it all. Momma had my two big brothers hold the rebar in the back of the truck while she drove. It was a mess."

"Was that the first time you almost died?" January was only half-kidding.

"Nope. It was the second."

He snorted. "Okay. And what are you up to now? Oh. Here's another one." This one wasn't as deep, but it was long. He kissed that too, from one end to the other.

"I've been chasing death since the day I was born, darlin'." Hawk stretched long as he could, offering him everything.

"We all have, you're running faster than most." He found a nipple again, this time with his tongue. "I'm trying to slow you down for a while."

That tiny nub drew up hard, begging for his attention. Oh, wasn't that pretty? "You're making me feel like I'm flying. Never had a guy do that to me."

"You've been missing out. There's so much more to sex than fucking." He chuckled and moved to the other nipple, which was already begging for his attention. "Not that I don't love fucking."

"You make me want it all, darlin'. I'm on fire, and it's good."

"I love the things you say." Just so honest and real.

He wanted to know how on fire. January reached for Hawk's hungry cock and touched it, fingers ghosting across the head, drawing lightly down the shaft.

Hawk hissed, one leg drawing up like he'd pushed a button. He closed his teeth around the little nub that had been under his tongue, pinching as he started to stroke.

"Oh fuck. Slow down. It's too fucking good to lose."

"Mmm." He loosened his grip and let his fingers fall to one side and rest on Hawk's hip. "I'm in no hurry, angel." He moved his lips up and over Hawk's collarbone. "You can tell me what you like, I'll do it."

"I like how you touch, full stop. I reckon I've never felt so much from a man. Ever." Hawk reached up, hands sliding on his face, the touch delicate and careful.

"Touch is the best part." He took Hawk's hand and kissed the palm, wrist, then Hawk's lips softly.

"It's everything." Hawk's hand slid down along his side, the touch pushing in, petting him good and hard.

January leaned into it, finger circling that lovely, hard cock again, this time stroking slowly, enough to keep Hawk floating.

"I swear to God, darlin', I feel like I'm fixin' to shake apart."

"I hope you do. Just let yourself feel everything." He didn't let himself think, he stayed focused on Hawk, enjoyed his own buzz, let this be their own little bubble for now. He'd think later. This felt too good.

"You're something else. I ain't no virgin, but you make me feel like I'm brand new at all this."

He understood that Hawk came from a world where men got off. They'd started off that way too. "You've never had a lover, I guess?"

"Fuck-buddies, mostly. A couple of blowjob friends that were missing their girlfriends. You know how it goes." Hawk opened his eyes with a serious look. "I'm not bitching. Appreciating you."

"I asked the question." He smiled at Hawk. "Don't you worry, I'm feeling appreciated."

"I am too. And no, no lovers. Not until you."

He didn't know if they were really there yet, but he couldn't say for sure where they were. Lovers was a stretch if it took an airplane to go to bed together. But sometime in the last few minutes this stopped being that five-hundred-mile booty call. Their connection ran deeper than that now.

"Then maybe you *are* brand new at this." He rolled up and over Hawk so they could rub a little, feel each other.

"Maybe." Hawk wrapped strong hands around his ass, thumbs working his lower back. That sent lightning down his legs and made his eyes cross.

"That feels good. Your hands." He arched and found a nipple again with his teeth, the pinch a little harder than before, testing.

Hawk sucked in a breath, chest pushing right up into his lips even as those strong fingers squeezed and dragged them together.

He had to let go to gasp, shocked by how Hawk made his need to strong and so sudden. "Fuck." He dragged his tongue higher to Hawk's shoulder and pressed his face into Hawk's neck. "Jesus, baby."

"Make me ache, darlin'. Make me need you in my bones." Hawk groaned and tugged his ass. "Come up here and fuck my mouth."

His cock screamed *yes please* and he started to move, but he managed to slow down. "You sure?"

"I want to taste you. I know you want to fuck my lips."

He'd been a good boy, now he was allowed to be a bad one. "Fuck, yeah." January crawled toward the headboard, letting Hawk guide him, and shoved a couple of pillows aside. Hawk's hands stayed plastered to his ass, bringing him up to parted lips, a hungry, wet mouth.

He pushed right in, carefully but without hesitation. "Oh God." Hawk's tongue burned against his skin.

Hawk shocked him with deep-throating him, swallowing hard around his cock, over and over, before letting him back out. "I like to suck, darlin'."

He nodded. Someone had stolen all the air in the room and his brain was shorting out. "Jesus," he croaked, sucking in a harsh breath. All he wanted was more of that. "Jesus, Fuck."

"Take what you need." The words were sure, confident— almost was confident as the hands that pulled him back into heaven.

He started in easy but it didn't take him long to find the right angle, the right depth and as soon as he did he took Hawk at his word and went for it, ass clenching and his abs going tight as he plunged into that amazing heat over and over again. The expression on Hawk's face read as pure bliss, that tongue working him, throat clenching and squeezing on every push in.

This wasn't going to last long so he paid attention to everything Hawk was doing as his climax twisted and swirled inside him and settled into his balls. "Hawk! Close."

Hawk groaned and dragged him in deep, swallowing around him, over and over, throat working around the tip of his cock.

Oh God. He didn't know what to do. His hips jerked and his hands flailed and grasped at the headboard, everything completely involuntary including how hard he came, balls pumping as he filled Hawk's throat with spunk.

He felt Hawk's hands on him as he tried to breathe through a fog of hormones and aftershocks, his blood roaring in his ears.

January blinked down, fighting to clear his vision, desperate to see Hawk's face, but each soft lick made him dizzy. He decided he'd better lie down before he fell down. He moved slowly, stiffly, as if he'd aged twenty years, finally getting himself settled alongside Hawk with a rough groan.

Hawk curled around him, holding him like he was something precious.

"Damn, angel." January sighed, fingers exploring

whatever they could reach. "I think you took my brain with that too."

"You'll get it back, I promise." Hawk kissed his forehead.

"Maybe I don't want it back." He laughed gently, fingers hunting for the cowboy's lovely cock. "Maybe I want you to join me."

Hawk's prick was hard as diamonds, bobbing in his fingers. That was lovely. Just lovely.

"I feel you, baby." He tightened his fingers and gave it a couple of quick, hard jerks.

Hawk rolled, fucking his fist, pushing right into his touch.

He kept a firm grip and added his other hand, watching Hawk's face intently. "Beautiful."

"Don't stop, darlin'. I need you, bad."

"Keep calling me darlin' and I'll do anything you want." He was pretty sure that was true too.

"The name suits you." Hawk begged a kiss, those hips still moving, still driving that heavy cock into his fingers.

It was the easiest thing in the world to give it, he'd never wanted to kiss anyone more. He made it strong, giving Hawk an anchor, something to focus on.

Those light blue eyes fastened on him, looking at him, into him, and he could feel Hawk's cock swelling, filling his hands. Close. His lover was right there.

"Come on, angel," he whispered, barely a breath away from Hawk's lips. "Fly."

Hawk's gasp heralded the heat that splashed over his fingers. That was what he wanted. That pure pleasure.

He kissed Hawk between the harsh breaths, staying close and present as his lover trembled. "Beautiful, baby. So good."

"Fuck yes. So good, darlin'. Thank you."

"Mmm. Any time, cowboy. Any damn time." Hawk made him feel invincible. Maybe even better, Hawk made him feel important. It had been a while since he felt like he really *mattered* to a lover.

Hawk kissed his jaw, soft and sweet, and cuddled in. They needed to eat, but this seemed more important, both of them together, and he was more than happy to hold onto this moment. "I didn't mean to distract you from dinner, but I'm not sorry I did."

"It'll eat fine. I ain't worried one bit."

Neither was he. Not even a little. His appetite was satisfied. For now.

10

Hawk ordered breakfast on the TV, his belly gnawing on his backbone. He'd taken the supper out uneaten when he got up, saving back the waters and the cherry pie, because that was some congealed damn shit.

So he got him an egg white omelet with all the veg, a breakfast of eggs, bacon, and pancakes for January, and three pots of coffee. Then he went to sit and watch the light come up in the world.

January was still out cold, face down in bed and half-covered by the sheets. That perfect hair was an incredible mess and January had grown an impressive shadow on his face overnight. Hawk had felt it when he woke up.

He scrubbed his hand over his face, feeling the stubble. Maybe he'd grow a beard. He liked that idea—a long, shaggy beard. Though maybe January wasn't the shaggy type. He supposed that mattered. He'd never discussed that kind of thing with anyone but his momma before.

The sun came up slowly. The sky was dim, and it felt like the day was going to be pretty gray. Breakfast arrived, the loud knock on the door making January groan and roll over.

"Shh. It's okay, darlin'." He needed that coffee and something to shut his belly up.

"Is that coffee?" January mumbled at him as he rolled the cart into the room. "Oh. I smell bacon."

"I got you eggs, bacon, and pancakes." He searched out the cups, making sure they were turned the right side up before he hunted the coffee pot. "I got three orders of coffee."

"You'd think we didn't sleep." January stretched in the sheets and sat up. "Good morning. It's early."

"It is. We got all day. I got peckish." And Thursday evening was a ways off now.

"Peckish? I'm starving." January scrubbed fingers through that dark hair. "Is it going to rain?"

"Sure feels like it, doesn't it?" He poured two cups of coffee. "Coffee?"

"Yes, please. Look at us, all relaxed talking about the weather over coffee. So domestic." January's voice sounded deep and rough.

"We could talk about blowjobs instead." He was easy, but he was going to have to eat first.

"Jesus, baby. I could talk about that last one for days. You have a gift." He caught January's smile once he got close enough to hand over a cup of coffee.

"I do enjoy sucking you, darlin'." He went to pour his cup out. "I do indeed."

"Well, I won't stand in your way." January laughed. "I definitely want you to enjoy yourself."

His phone lit up with a text, and a second later another, vibrating loudly on the bedside table.

"That's you."

"Oh, thanks." He fumbled with it. "Siri, who's messaging me?"

"Charlie."

"Oh lord." He shook his head. "God knows what he wants."

He looked at his texts, holding the phone close.

The first text read, *You up?* and the second one said, *or am I interrupting?* followed by an eggplant emoji, a wink, a bunch of bunnies and a thumbs up

Srsly? I was talking BJs. He shook his head. "The dipshit heard about you. I wanted to surprise him Sunday night."

January snorted. "He's probably still surprised."

Sky called last night. Says you hooked yourself a Yankee and you're reeling him in.

He's gorgeous. I'm keeping him a while. He'd keep the son of a bitch as long as he could.

Right on, Bird! Is he keeping you? Does he know what a bull is? You got a picture?

I don't. Not yet. He snorted and shook his head. Asshole. Hawk adored him. "He wants to know if you know what a bull is."

"Sure. Tell him it's that thing you ride when you're not riding me." January leaned back against the headboard sounding smug as hell.

Get one. I need to see him.

I will. Promise. Will tell all Sunday night. Fair?

Oh ho! I am interrupting. Good! Get back to your man. See you Sunday. That was followed by another string of stupid emojis.

He put his phone down and got back to his coffee. "He wants pictures."

"Okay, let's get a selfie later. When I have clothes on, and I've combed this crazy hair." January got out of bed, crossed to the food cart and poured a second cup of coffee buck naked.

"That's more than fair." He grabbed the lids off the food. "Smells great, doesn't it?"

He was so getting pancakes the first morning he was on break.

January's stomach growled, sounding almost angry. "Damn. I think they might have heard that down the hall. Better hand me a plate, please."

"Sure. You want the pancakes or the other?"

January grinned at him. "Will you hold it against me if I have some of both?"

"Darlin', I got them both for you. I have an omelet." Silly man. He didn't have to starve his lover. He knew better. He felt around and found his food, praying he didn't knock anything over.

"Fork." January put it in his hand. "Have a seat, I'll bring your coffee over."

"Thanks. It all smells great, doesn't it?" He was a huge fan of maple syrup, when it got right down to it.

"Just going to find my sweatpants." January set his coffee down for him and wandered away. "What's in your figure-friendly omelet?"

"Veggies. I fight that eight pounds with all I am during the season. Then I give myself through Christmas, but the day after through the start of the season, I'm back to it." He had been a kid when he'd started riding, and his balance on the bull was best when he forced himself to be the same size as he'd been at fifteen.

"You know that's insane, right? You must burn a gazillion calories as built as you are. The whole pro-athlete thing is crazy to me. But I guess if it was easy, everyone would do it." January sat with him. "I'm a professional bacon eater."

"If I liked working out more, I could eat more," he teased, although the whole idea was a lie. Muscle weighed a lot, and he didn't ride with strength. His whole game was balance.

"That's true of all of us. I'll try not to gloat. Thanks for ordering for me." As fast as January was putting breakfast away, he wasn't going to have to look at it for long anyway. "It's really good."

"Excellent." His was fine—well cooked, not greasy. It wasn't Momma's, but no one's was. That was how it worked.

"When you come to New York, you have to save some calories for Jax's desserts. Just a bite at least. Actually, half of it is how gorgeous they are. He's like an artist with that stuff."

"I can totally do that. I'm looking forward to it." He wanted to go so that he knew where January lived, whether the man slept in a king-sized bed or a full, like him. Whether the place was modern or cozy.

"Good. Me too. You'll be the first houseguest I've had that wasn't family. Well, except for Jax, but he's more family than my family, you know?"

"I do. I have folks that I can stay with and we're family, soul-deep." He stayed with Ben and Charlie, he stayed with Mackey, he'd stayed with Sky in his trailer a bunch.

January nodded. "So lunch should be fun today. Nicole and I will eat everything you and Danny don't. She said she's due right before the Finals? When is that?"

"October. Right around Halloween. We have two and a half months off." And it was mostly okay. Sometimes it sucked to be at the house with the parents, spinning his wheels.

"That long? You must be exhausted by then."

"Yeah, I'm totally ready to get out of the house by the end of January." Oh, the end of January. He liked January's end...

"I hear that. I don't go home in January if I can help it. I'll stay for Christmas for a few days and that's it. Jax and I do Thanksgiving at my place with whatever stragglers are around. He calls it Ragamuffin Turkey Day. We have the weirdest group sometimes." January swallowed down a bite with a sip of coffee. "Last year we had an investment banker, two actors and a cab driver."

"That's too cool. We have the family." Hell, he was still at the damn kids' table. Last year he'd stayed in the front room with Daddy and dozed most of the day.

"Well your family is a whole lot of company. Do they all get along mostly?"

"For the most part, yeah. They all work together, the boys. They travel together. They all live in the same town. They'd better." He was the one on the outside for all sorts of reasons. He was little, he couldn't rope, he'd been born premature and broken.

"And you just... don't?" The look on January's face was hard to see, but that sounded like real concern in his voice.

"I can't." And January had to know that. Maybe he didn't know the extent of how bad his eyes were or how bad they would get, but he had to see his glasses, how tiny he was, how he was on the outside of a line of brothers that were carbon copies.

Hell, he didn't even know how he was going to survive retirement.

"I'm sorry. I get it though, I can't either. But look at you, you're the Champ. That's nothing to sneeze at, right?"

"I am. I'm the best in the world." And he would do it again, God willing and the creek don't rise. He would ride until he got hurt bad enough he couldn't do it no more.

"The best in the world. I guess I can ride those coattails."

January laughed. "I could tell my dad that. Hey, dad. I'm fucking the best bull rider in the world."

"Are you and your dad not friendly?" He thought Yankees were all liberal and gay-friendly and shit.

"We're civil. We're not friends. It was pretty clear when I was young that I wasn't going to keep up with my brothers. I don't get along with Sean much better, but really, nobody does. Mark and Penny and I are good though. Mom and I are good." January shrugged. "I'm not the smallest in the family, but I didn't fit the mold either."

"I'm sorry. My people treat me good. Hell, Momma would live in my back pocket if I'd let her."

"I got that impression. My mom is all about her grandkids now, but she likes hearing from me and she calls. Penny calls about my nephew Logan sometimes. He's got dyslexia too. She gets frustrated and needs to talk to someone that gets it."

"So, can you read? Is that rude to ask?" Was it rude to ask when the guy had had his dick in Hawk's ass a few hours ago?

"It might be rude to ask a stranger, but I'm not one. Yes, I can read. I've got some tricks and if I take it slow I do okay. I don't read for fun, though, because it's not really fun. I like audio books a lot." January refilled their coffee. "Logan's got much more support in school than I did, but it's still tough for him sometimes."

Lord, he got that. He could read the big print on his phone, but books? No. "I love audio books. I've used them when you had to have the CDs still."

January grinned, wide enough even he couldn't mistake it. "Oh, me too. I'd put headphones on so no one would know I was listening to books, not music. They had them at my library."

"I ordered mine from the big library in Austin. You can get the books for the blind whenever you want. You request them."

The words fell out of his mouth before he could stop them.

"Oh yeah? That's cool."

Dammit. Did that really mean cool, or was January being kind? Did he hear hesitation?

"So... are you considered legally blind, then? Or is your eyesight just... bad?"

"I was born legally blind. No one knows, at the league, I mean." Just his family, and his best friends—Sky and Ben and Charlie.

Well, and now January.

"God. I can't imagine putting my legally blind son on the back of a bull. No wonder your mother is overprotective." January moved to sit closer. "I'd say you could have told me, but if no one knows..."

"No one. Outside of my family, there are literally two people I've told, besides you." He reached out. "I was premature, and the cord was around my throat. It damaged my eyes and helped me be short."

January took his hand and pulled it in. "I foresee audio books in our future. Do you like horror? I started a great one on the plane."

"I do. I love it. Douglas Clegg is good. I have like more than a hundred on my Audible account." He moved and ended up in January's lap. "This cool?"

"I love it. How well can you see me with those glasses? Honestly?"

"I know you have dark hair and eyes. I know that you have amazing cheekbones."

January reached for his glasses. "May I?" Without

waiting for an answer, careful fingers took his glasses off. "You have beautiful eyes. But why don't you close them? Like you did in the shower. And then tell me how well you see me."

"Yeah?" He closed his eyes and reached for January, feeling the relaxation deep in his spine, the constant tension easing. January's chin was square and strong, the stubble against his fingers making him laugh.

"Shut up," January tried to sound grumpy, but he knew when he was being teased. "It's a lazy morning. I'll shave eventually."

"I like it. Texture." He traced the full bottom lip, letting his fingers stretch up over those amazing cheekbones.

January caught the end of Hawk's thumb between his teeth and circled the end with his tongue. "Gotcha."

He gasped, his eyes flying open as he fought to focus. Fuck, that was hot.

"Hmm." January laughed and kissed his hand. "Surprise?"

"A good one." He leaned their foreheads together, breathing with January. "Did you know?"

"I wondered. I notice things. I don't think most people do, but I had a reason to pay attention."

"You did. You're the only one that even wondered. I fake it really well." And he knew it.

"Lots of practice. The dark glasses are a nice touch." January took a quick kiss. "Would they retire you if they knew?"

"They'd fire my ass. I might lose my card. I can't afford that, you know?" He didn't have a plan. He didn't know how to do anything but rodeo. He'd never learned anything else. Hell, he'd been homeschooled. He only knew what he knew.

"Shit, Hawk. That's... kind of scary." January sighed and huffed a short laugh a second later. "I'm starting to sympathize with your mom."

"Yeah. One day I'll have that big accident, and I'll go home. She'll get tired of me quick." He joked, but God, that idea hurt.

"You'll figure it out." January tugged him closer. "I didn't mean to get so heavy. I'm trying to... we're learning things about each other. You're still the Champ. You're going to ride like one tonight, I know it. And I'm really glad I came. Still. If anything's changed it's for the better."

"Yeah. I'm—We have a shitton to learn. We only get to do that once." And he loved getting to explore with Jan. He — "Can I call you Jan? Is that cool or no?"

"Yes. Lots of people do. My family, some colleagues..." Jan snorted. "Four syllables are a mouthful."

"Well, darlin', in my mouth, it might be twelve syllables." He'd see how it worked out, like everything else.

"Seriously. It might! I heard someone at the show last night make 'shit' into four. That was impressive." Jan leaned close to his ear. "Save your mouth for other things."

That felt fucking amazing, made him feel like a class A stud. "Mmm, you liked that, fucking my mouth last night. It was blistering."

"I did. Liked it might not be strong enough. You were incredible. And full disclosure since you're resting your eyes... I think you made me blush now." Jan took his hand and touched it to a warm cheek.

"Mmm, good. You're damn fine, aren't you?" He loved this, talking, touching, breathing together and being.

"I don't know, I think I'm okay. I'm not a sexy cowboy, but I do all right."

Bullshit. His January was delicious. "You're so fine. You make me hard as nails."

"Mmm. Well, that's a compliment I'll take." Jan rocked him, and dumped him gently onto the couch. "I'm trying to decide what I want most right now, more bacon or more you."

"Have your bacon. I'm not going anywhere." He laughed at his hungry man, hunting his coffee cup.

"Bacon it is." Jan gave him back his glasses. "The bacon will get cold. You're always hot. You want a warm-up on your coffee?"

"I do. Thanks." God, he could get used to this fast. He shouldn't. It wasn't a safe, reasonable thing, but that wasn't really his jam.

He wanted January. Hopefully he could keep riding and keep the man interested.

11

Charlie was waiting at the kiss and cry section of the airport, and a hot coffee was pressed into his hand. "Hey, Bird."

"Hey buddy, how goes?" Hawk was sore as fuck after hitting a horn with his right shoulder last night. He'd ridden three of four, but he was hurting good and bruised down deep.

"It goes. Ben's got the guest room ready for you. I told him we'd pick up supper and bring it home. He's been cleaning all goddamn day, expecting your happy ass."

"Fuck off. He loves me. You're jealous." Hawk made himself cackle. Damn, he was funny.

"I promise you, I am *not*." Charlie chuckled and bumped shoulders with him—his left, thank fuck. "You have a bag to wait on?"

"Yeah. I got my gear and my clothes. You ready to ride Friday?"

"Sure. I'm always ready. It's Doc that's a pain in the ass." He followed Charlie toward baggage claim. "I'm glad you can't see so good. Seems like everybody I meet tells me I look like death warmed up."

"Fuck off." Dammit. "Your head still?"

Charlie ought to be better by now.

"On and off, you know? The headache never goes away but today it's good. Yesterday Ben wouldn't let me drive. Asshole." Charlie put a hand out to stop him. "This is us."

"Thanks. I've got the same old bag as always." His shit was black with a reflective white strip sewn on. They glowed in the lights.

"Looks like a skunk and smells worse. Got it."

"Ha ha. Remember, asshole. I knew you before your fucking balls dropped." He started laughing, feeling for the stopper in the coffee cup before inhaling deep. "Oh, hazelnut. You rock, man. Thank you."

"You're welcome. I may be an asshole, but I know coffee is important." The warning buzzer went off, loud and sudden. "Jesus. I hate that sound. Scares my pants off every damn time. My fucking head did not need that."

"Doc x-ray your brain?" Folks didn't have headaches for weeks, did they? There was something weird as fuck about this whole thing.

"Oh yeah. If you can test it, I done it. So sick of— Oh, I see your big one, it rolled off the belt." Charlie stepped away.

He didn't push in; Charlie could fetch it and carry until he could take over.

"Just the two?" Charlie was back in a couple of minutes and set the suitcase and his gear bag down by his feet.

"Yessir. Two's enough. Thanks." He handed Charlie the coffee and grabbed his gear. "Raleigh was a decent event."

"Any time you walk out with some money is a good

event, right? Ben said you took a hit yesterday. And Danny made a run at it. Sorry I missed it. You good?"

"Horn got me. It ain't no thing. I'm still at the top of the leaderboard." He knew what was important. He needed to be healthy and in the top three at the Finals. Then he'd do it.

He followed Charlie through the crowd and outside, glad that it wasn't the kind of winter here that they'd had in Denver. "Hang on Ben is texting. Toss your stuff in." Charlie pulled out his phone.

"You're caught through the balls." Lucky bastard.

He got his shit loaded in the bed and climbed in the truck, leaning back and closing his eyes for a second, relaxing.

"Siri, text darlin." He waited for her and then said, "Hey, darlin. Made it. Hope you have a good trip home. Call me when you have time. Send."

Charlie climbed in a second later. "Ben was checking up on me. He says hey, and to hurry home, he's hungry. My bottomless pit. What do you want to eat?"

"What do I want? I want a fucking triple cheese bacon burger. But I'll go with a grilled chicken sandwich from wherever fast food."

"Yeah. Me too." Charlie pulled out of the space and started to drive. "So. How was the *rest* of your weekend?"

Hawk felt the grin spread across his face. "Oh man. So good. So fucking good. He does it for me. All the way."

"Yeah? You're talking *all* the way?" He could hear the smile in Charlie's voice. "For real?"

"I told him about my eyes." That was as real as he got.

Charlie's touched his knee, giving it a quick rub. "Damn, honey. I'm happy for you. Wow. You met him in Denver?"

"I did. I picked him up in a bar. You remember? I think the bartender was Alex?"

"Maybe? Dude, I don't remember Denver. I was high as a kite on meds."

"You were adorable. You drank a lot of smoothies." That he understood. He'd lost an entire event once with a head injury. Those hooves hurt.

"Totally worth forgetting. So tell me about him. That was a great picture. He's hot and you look happy."

"He's from New York, he works for a charity, he's hot as fuck, and he likes bull riding." And Hawk intended to keep him a while.

"New York, huh?" There was definitely some concern in Charlie's tone this time. "You ever been? Not exactly the traveling companion type, I guess."

"He's thinking about inviting me up after Connecticut. I want to know about his place and all. He met Sky and them. I think Sky liked him okay." Everyone had liked January so far. He wasn't sure what Momma was going to think.

"Only thing that really matters is he's good to you. You need the stick by you type. Like Ben is for me." Charlie laughed as they pulled into a drive-thru. "Look at me, I've got you married already."

"Yeah, you know I wouldn't do that to someone I liked." He didn't intend to fuck with someone's life, long term. He didn't have a future. He had right now.

"Yeah, I hear you. I'm happy you have somebody, though. I hope I get to meet him. Chicken, right?" Charlie rolled down his window and ordered two grilled chicken sandwiches and a couple of side salads for them, and a big cheeseburger and fries for Ben.

"Tell 'em no mayo and lots and lots of pickles." He

chuckled softly. "I'll have you meet him at the next event he shows up at. He's real busy with his work."

"How could I forget the extra pickles?" Charlie snorted and added to the order, they drove up to the pick-up window. "Ben thinks I should retire. He wants me to live with him on his ranch. This last knock on the head – it was hard."

"He loves you. Y'all got money, music, great sex—why not?" It wasn't like Charlie couldn't run cattle, and hell, Ben's place was filled with hot and cold running musicians.

"Dammit, Hawk. You're s'posed to say, 'Naw, man. You have a couple good years left in you.'" It was hard to tell whether Charlie was joking or not. The food arrived and he was handed bags.

"If you still love it, ride. If you don't, you got a lover, a home, a life—take it and run. You got a future."

"We'll see. It's not a thing to worry about unless Doc clears me anyway. I'm here, right?" Charlie pulled back out onto the road. "That food smells good. Let's get it home to Ben."

"Sounds like a plan, cowboy. We got plans for the week?"

"You mean besides checking in with your momma and your new man, Bird?" Lord have mercy, Charlie was a shit and a half.

"I'll totally send dick pics."

"I don't need pics, I've seen it. I hope he's appreciative." Charlie laughed and turned down a bumpy road.

"Butthead. Can't y'all grade this damn road?" He never laughed with no one the way he did with Charlie.

"Can't you quit bitching, princess? I swear to God, every damn time."

"Just because y'all sit with your thumbs up your butts

waiting for someone to tell you what to do..." He didn't bother to hide his grin, but he fought his laughter.

"Yeah, okay, momma's boy. That man of yours good with you telling him what to do too?" Charlie was good at a straight face, but he could hear the laughter underneath it.

"Oh yeah. He's got fuck me harder, faster darlin', and touch me there down pat." Hawk couldn't hold it; he cracked up.

They laughed until Charlie parked the truck. "I'm glad you're here, Bird. Oh, look. It's the worrywart."

Ben came out of the house and gave a wave from the porch.

"I do love y'all's porch. It's so cool." Huge and covered with fans and rockers and tables for a cold drink.

"It doesn't suck. I'll get the food." Charlie slid out of the truck, and Ben was there in an instant, reaching for the bags of food.

"You okay? That took a while."

"Yes, baby. Hawk and I were talking. I got this."

Ben stuck his hands in his pockets and backed off. "Hey, Hawk. How was your flight?"

"It was fine. Come here and hug me, man." They might be fighting with each other, but they weren't fighting with him.

"Hell, yeah." Ben's smile was wide enough even he could see it. He got a big hug, typical Ben, swallowing him up. "Good to have you here. Come on in." Ben shouldered his gear bag.

"I'm glad to be here, man. I've missed hanging with y'all bad." They all trundled up the stairs and into the big, bright house. He loved it here—it was full of light and music, laughter and joy.

"You want to put your things in your room? We'll get

dinner on the table." He knew which room was his; it was at the other end of the hall from theirs and it had its own bathroom. It never mattered who else might be visiting, he always got spoiled with that room.

"Thank you. I'll be out in five." He needed to recycle his coffee and wash his face. He wasn't gone long, and by the time he got back Ben had his arms around Charlie and everything seemed right.

"Do you want a beer, Bird? Or is that too much?" Charlie leaned against Ben, happy as could be.

"God, yes. You want me to fetch them?" He knew where the beer cooler lived.

"Sure, thanks." Charlie hummed at Ben. "Come on, baby, let's sit."

He went to the fancy-assed beer fridge and grabbed three brews, popping their tops. He brought them to the table, letting Charlie and Ben take theirs before he took his place at the table.

"We'll cook tomorrow, but tonight we thought you'd appreciate a little quick comfort food and an early bedtime. I have some guys coming to the house tomorrow to play so Charlie will keep you out of trouble. I was thinking maybe the zoo one day this week." Ben unwrapped his food as he talked and tore open a hundred little ketchup packets for his fries.

"Sounds good. I'm easy as the flowers in May." He wanted to be somewhere he was wanted.

"Ben says you're the best houseguest because you're not a guest at all. You act like you're home." Charlie picked up his beer and took a sip.

"Hey, Charlie showed me the picture of your Yankee. Handsome."

"He's gorgeous, right? He's a stud." Hawk was so proud

he ached. "He's a good guy. Hung out with Sky's man and Danny's wife."

"Beck likes him." Ben nodded. "He called to catch up. Word got around quick."

Charlie chuckled. "So quick."

"He does stand out in the crowd, a little." Lord have mercy, it was good to have a somebody to brag about.

"Just a little."

"God, it's nice to have someone to talk about besides Parker and his latest toy."

Ben laughed and shook his head. "Parker."

"One day he'll find someone besides Beckett that turns him inside out." At least that was everyone's assumption. Who the fuck knew?

"Spoken like a man who knows shit." Ben laughed and took a big bite out of his burger.

"That's me. Shit-Knowing Man." That amused the hell out of him, making him snort like a moose.

Ben chuckled softly before asking, "How's your momma? Did she have fun in Orlando?"

"Oh lord. You know she was in her element, being Granny and Momma and at Disney. She was happy as a pig in shit." She'd taken pictures of damn near everything, ridden every ride, and had the entire family's face painted – even Daddy and Bryan.

"I bet. Good for her."

Charlie touched Hawk's hand. "Ben's working on a new record."

"Charlie—" Ben tried to interrupt.

"It's almost done. It's really good."

"Dude, can I hear it? You know I love your stuff. It's so fucking rich." It was like what he imagined seeing super clear was like.

Ben's sigh was long-suffering. "Yeah. Almost done, as Charlie well knows, means recorded. But it's not polished. Just so you know."

"As Ben well knows," Charlie shot back. "What he means is he's such a perfectionist that all not polished means is he hasn't let his agent hear it yet."

"I'm not your agent. I'm rodeo trash. I need to hear it, man." Hawk wanted something new to love.

"All right. Any time." Ben sounded pleased. "I'd like to know what you think."

"You're gonna love it, Bird. It's gonna be big, I know it." Charlie leaned back in his chair. "Oof."

"Full, baby?"

"And tired I think." Charlie sure sounded it.

"Y'all don't have to entertain me. You know I can watch TV in my room." He'd been here again and again.

Ben took a deep, full breath. "See? That's exactly why I appreciate you. I've got some straightening up to do, but I think I'll tuck Charlie in at least."

"You don't have to tuck me in, baby." Charlie got up from the table. "I need to rest my eyes."

Ben stood up, too, and pulled Charlie in close. "You sure? I won't be long."

"I'll warm the bed up." Charlie and Ben kissed each other like he wasn't in the room.

Ben let Charlie go. "Love you, see you upstairs."

"Night, Bird. Think about what you want to do tomorrow."

Hawk took a hard hug, one he felt in his soul. "Will do. Night, you ugly bastard."

They all laughed, and then Hawk started to help clean up, gathering up paper and all. "I appreciate y'all letting me come and hang out, man. I'm tired of hotels."

Ben leaned in the kitchen doorway, letting him help and sipping beer. "You know you're always welcome. I'm glad you came, it's good for Charlie. He needs you here. He needs the distraction, you know?"

"Is it bad?" He didn't want it to be, didn't want to have to ask, but he needed to know. Whatever it was, they could fix it. Doc fixed them all, and if it meant no more riding, it did. Charlie had Ben. That was everything. But still, Hawk didn't want it to be bad. Charlie was as much a part of his life as his folks.

"Well, we're not sure how bad yet, but he can't ride. It's one too many hits to the head. Doc won't clear him. He has to retire." Ben's words were even and without emotion, like he'd disconnected from it. "If he rides again, he'll die. No question. We're not going public with it, but you're family."

"There's worse things than retiring." He felt a little like a hypocrite for saying it, but Charlie could do this. Help on the ranch, travel with Ben, hell, learn how to help Ben with his music. Charlie was smart. Charlie had a reason to fight. "I told him so."

Ben didn't do such a good job of covering his emotions this time, and his voice cracked. "Well, tell him again. Doc told him he's done. You want to be a friend, that's your job while you're here. Get him to hear it. I'll take care of him. He can be happy with me. Here."

"Hey. Hey, man. You know I will. He's my best bud. I love y'all like family." He went to Ben and hugged him tight. "I want him happy and healthy. I don't give a shit if he never covers a bull again."

Ben hugged him back, then leaned on him and sighed. "Thank you. I love that stubborn asshole. I get it, but it's time. It's time for us now."

"I got your back." He didn't know what else to say,

because that was the truth. He loved both of them to death and he wanted Charlie to be okay. Riding bulls was only forever if you died. Everyone knew that going in.

"I know." It must have been the right thing to say because Ben breathed in a huge breath and relaxed. "I'm so relieved you're here. We're going to have a good week. You can sit in on some of the session tomorrow if you want."

"I'd love to. Seriously. Can I get another guitar lesson?" He had a guitar that lived here, and Ben taught him some. He was getting a little good at it, even.

"Yeah, of course. Let's do it. You're my favorite student." Ben laughed. "Also my only student. Oh! Wait until you meet my new fiddler. He has crazy fingers."

"Yeah? I can't wait." That was better. That was the Ben he knew. Lord.

"You'll love him." Ben finished his beer, rinsed the bottle and dropped it in recycling. "Thanks for helping clean up. I'm going to turn in with Charlie. Help yourself to some of Momma Vera's cookies. She sent enough for the whole band."

"Thank you." He got himself a huge glass of water instead, heading into the bedroom to see if January had texted him back.

Which he had. Several times.

I can't believe we're flying in two different directions.

Thank you for a great weekend.

Landed. It's cold in New York.

Home. I hope you have a nice dinner with your friends. Call me later?

He texted back. *Is now good?*

Hey cowboy. Sure.

He dialed, and Jan picked up quickly. "Hey. All settled in?"

"Yeah. You get home okay?" *Can you talk to me a minute?* he thought. *Because Charlie's hurt and Ben's scared?*

"I did. It was an easy trip. I'm getting ready for my meeting in the morning."

"Am I bothering you?" Because he could turn on some music and doze.

"No. I wish you were here. I don't want to sleep by myself."

"I wish I was there too. I'm—" A little sick, and he wasn't even sure if he should be. "—missing your face."

"I probably shouldn't miss you as much as I do. It's something I'm going to have to learn to get used to, I guess."

"Yeah. I—" What was he supposed to say? January wasn't even sure that he wanted Hawk to come and visit, and he sure as shit couldn't afford to fly back and forth and get a New York hotel for the weeks. "I wish I was with you."

"We should... why didn't we talk about this?" Jan sighed in his ear. "We should have talked about this."

"Because we went from booty call to I want to spend my nights with you real fast." That was simple as pie. He'd picked a man up in a hotel bar and fell in love.

"I miss you already. Are we going to try to make this work?"

"Yes." He didn't need to think about the answer; he knew it. "You in?"

"Yeah. I'm in, baby." Jan laughed on the other end of the line. "I'm so in. Now what?"

"Well, now we have a week to decide what happens next, but I want to be with you as much as I can."

"You'll come here after you ride in Connecticut? Stay with me for the week? We can talk then. Figure it out." Jan sounded hopeful.

"God, yes. You tell me where to fly in, I'll be there by

Sunday for supper." He didn't want anything more. He wanted to be in January's arms, holding on, breathing together.

"Good. It's a plan. It feels better to know when I get to see you again. We'll have fun. I'll show you around."

"I'd like that. I went to New York a couple times, but it was the hotel and the arena." He'd been stressed as all get out by the noise and the speed of all of it. "I'm ready to explore with you."

"We'll explore. Outside some, inside some." Jan hummed softly. "A lot, I hope."

"I want to explore all of you, top to bottom. I want to know what your bed smells like."

"I want it to smell like you." Jan made an exasperated sound. "Jesus, Hawk. You have a job, I respect that, and I have my own too. But, how do people do this? I can travel sometimes, but not every weekend. This feels hard. Is it because it's new? Does it get easier?"

"I got no idea, but we'll figure it. You may hate having me in your space, darlin'. I sure hope not, but it might happen." And he would be honest, if only to himself. He had to learn where things lived, and he'd only ever done that alone or with Sky and Charlie.

"Are you kidding? Come. Be in my space. We'll be fine." Jan paused, the line going quiet, but only for a second. "So how are Charlie and Ben?"

"I think Charlie's hurt real bad, darlin'. He's talking about retiring." And that made his heart ache. First Sky, then Charlie.

"I'm sorry, Hawk. But it doesn't seem like a job a man can do forever."

"No. I guess it doesn't." So what was right? Hooking up with January for a little while until the career was over? Or what? Saying 'I love you, but I'm a man that hasn't planned for anything more than rodeoing'.

"Hey. He has Ben, baby. They'll figure it out."

"They so will. Ben's excited to have him around here at the ranch. Did you have supper?" *Was it good?*

"I ordered pizza. I was feeling lazy after my flight. That's another thing you have to save a few calories for when you visit. A slice of New York pizza. So good. This one had veggies all over it—mushrooms, olives, broccoli, onions, peppers."

"Never had broccoli on pizza. I'd sure try it, though." He was pretty adventurous, as far as food went. He liked neat flavors.

"It's good. Do you have plans for the week?"

"Tomorrow Ben's letting me listen in to a session. We're talking about going to the zoo. Ben's going to give me another guitar lesson. Charlie and me will play dominoes some. I'll help around here as much as I can. Normal shit."

"Sounds like fun. You have a home with them, huh? That's great. Beats sitting home with your mother." Jan laughed.

"Yes. Momma's amazing, but..." He had the room he had grown up in and that was all.

"But you're twelve at home. I know. Me too. You want to get off? A little x-rated lullaby? I bet you wouldn't do that in your mom's house."

"Well, that's the first place I jacked off, but no. Momma and Daddy's is not sexy. At all." He chuckled and settled back in the pillows. "God, darlin'. I wish you were here."

I wish you could be here and hold me for a second and lie to me, tell me Charlie is okay.

"Take your glasses off and close your eyes. We can pretend I am."

"Yeah. Next week this time, I'll be in your arms." He put his glasses on the bedside table and closed his eyes.

"Forget in my arms, you'll be underneath me."

"Oh..." Oh, that made his breath slide out of him in a soft sigh.

He loved that idea, that promise. He wanted to be right there.

"You make me need, angel. Every second I'm with you. Even thinking about you."

It was magic, the way January saw him. Magic and a little breathtaking. "I love that. You make me dizzy with how much I need you."

"Yeah? Are you dizzy now? Are you hard? Do you want to come for me, baby?"

"Not yet, but I'm getting there." He rubbed himself through his jeans, letting himself feel it. "What about you?"

"Yeah. Since you said you wanted to know what my bed smells like. I can picture you in it."

"Are you going to make me wear pajamas, darlin'?" He found himself smiling, and he wondered if January could hear that.

"Oh, yes." Jan snorted. "We'll have a pillow fight and watch *Ghostbusters,* and whisper so my dad thinks we're asleep."

"Ooh. I'll bring my Spiderman jammies and some oatmeal cookies."

"Maybe we should one night. Jax would love every second of it. He has *Stranger Things* PJs."

"I know how to slumber party, darlin'. You make popcorn and margaritas, and we'll be a sight." He liked that, Jan's playful side.

"Mm. Yes. I suppose if we have a whole week I can let

you put clothes on for a little while." Jan practically purred at him.

"Once. Just once, hmm?" Hawk shivered. January's voice had all these levels.

"Just once. And only for company. I like looking at you too much. Have you pulled that pretty cock out yet?"

He unzipped, licking his lips as his prick sprang free. "Uh-huh. I want you."

"I know. I can hear it. Go ahead and touch. Tell me what you're doing."

He let his breath out as he wrapped his hand around his prick. "I'm all hard for you, darlin'. I'm aching and my hand don't feel as fine as yours."

"It's smarter though, it knows what to do. What feels right." Jan grunted softly. "Mine can't come close to your mouth."

"Mmm, I love the way your dick fits in my mouth, darlin'. Love the way you fuck my lips."

"You had me out of my mind." He heard the familiar strain in Jan's voice and knew it was his doing.

He started stroking, strong and steady. "I loved the way you took me, and I could suck and touch."

God, he never said things like this, but he liked it. A lot.

"You felt like heaven. I loved watching your face after, stroking you, the way you wanted."

He whimpered, feeling every word. "I want you. I want you inside me."

"Soon, baby. We'll have each other soon. You sound hot, are you close?"

"Closer than I thought I was," he confessed.

Jan chuckled darkly. "There's nothing like your face when you come."

He shook his head. Lord, he could imagine how much a dork he was.

"I mean that. Your truth is beautiful." Jan moaned. "Fuck, yes. Don't go quiet on me now, baby. I need... another minute."

"I want you to take me on your bed. I want to know that I'm the one that messed up your sheets and took your cock."

"I'm going to wear you out. Make you ache for days."

"Swear it?" Hawk started tugging harder, rolling his fist over the tip. Fuck, he was dripping.

"Happily. I... I swear. *Fuck.*"

Oh, he knew that sound. The hiss, the low, long groan.

"Hell yeah. Yours. Fuck me." He slammed his hand over his mouth to shut himself up.

"Now, baby. I'm... now!"

He came hard, his bones rattling, and he swallowed his moans as best he could.

"Mmm." Jan panted, breath loud over the phone. "Listen to you."

"Thank you. I needed you." Not for the sex, although that had been good. No. He'd needed his lover just because.

"Yeah." Jan took a deep breath, one he could hear. He imagined Jan sinking into deep pillows. "I don't miss you any less. I feel better about missing you at all."

"I'll be in your arms this time next week. Swear to God." He had the sinking suspicion by then, he'd be desperate for January.

"I'll be waiting for you. And not patiently. Get some rest, baby, you had a long day."

"You too. Can I call tomorrow night, or are you busy?"

"You can call any time you like. I want to hear from you."

"Cool. You sleep well, darlin'. You holler if you need me.

I'll have my phone right here." And he'd answer, no question.

"I will." He knew Jan's pause was deliberate, but he didn't know what it meant. "Goodnight, Hawk."

"Goodnight, darlin'. Dream good dreams." He hung up, feeling like he could breathe.

Thank God.

12

"Drinking on a Wednesday?"

January looked up from the crossword puzzle he was failing at on his phone and into very familiar eyes.

That belonged to an asshole.

"Killing time." He wasn't really drinking. He'd been nursing his scotch for half an hour.

"You're looking good, Jan."

Get serious. He rolled his eyes.

"Mind if I sit?" Lucas pulled out a barstool and sat next to him.

"Would it matter if I said yes?" Apparently not.

Lucas raised a hand to call the bartender and ordered a beer. "How've you been?"

"I've been great." He was one more stupid question away from getting up and leaving. Except he was here first. And this was his bar before it was theirs.

"Yeah? Good. Keeping busy?" The bartender sat a beer in front of Lucas and Lucas took a huge gulp.

He tossed back the rest of his scotch and tapped his glass for refill. "What do you want, Lucas?"

"Nothing. I'm just talking, babe."

He turned on his barstool, blood going icy. "Don't. Don't call me that, don't try to make nice with me. Don't act like you didn't fuck me over."

Lucas held his eyes for a second then looked away. "Yeah, I'm sorry about that."

"Sure."

"Come on. I made a mistake, Jan. I'm sorry."

"Oh, now he's a mistake?" Lucas was so fucking predictable. "Wait, let me guess. He dumped you? You're not sorry. You're just sorry you're single again." As soon as the bartender was done pouring he picked up his glass and shot it back, then tapped his glass again.

"It was mutual." Lucas shook his head and sipped his beer again.

"You're a cheater, Luc. The first time might have been a mistake. The second was a pattern. Don't fucking insult me."

Lucas bristled. "You know, I came over here to—"

"To what? Patch things up? See if I'm still a sucker?" Jesus, they'd split up months ago but somehow, Lucas could still hurt him.

"Fuck, you don't have to be an asshole, Jan."

"Neither did you."

Those once beloved eyes flashed in irritation. "I don't know why I bother..."

"Me either. Finish your drink and get out of here." *Just go away.*

"You're determined to be alone, huh?" Lucas chugged the rest of his beer.

"I'm not alone. Not that it's any of your business." Shit, why did he say that? He shot back his next drink. This time the bartender refilled it without having to be asked.

"Oh!" Lucas set his glass down hard on the bar. "Wow.

Well, good for you, babe. Best of luck. I hope he has a strong stomach."

What the fuck was that supposed to mean? "Excuse me?"

"You're not easy to keep, Jan. You're a high maintenance pain in the ass."

"Fuck you. You were leaving, weren't you?"

"Yeah." Lucas tugged on the waist of his jacket and zipped it up. "I was." Lucas gave him one last look and stormed away.

No problem, I'll pick up your tab.

January watched over his shoulder as Lucas left the bar, then pushed the empty beer glass farther away and turned back to his drink. But it wasn't five seconds before he picked up his phone and texted Jax.

Mayday.

It didn't take a second for the 'where r u?' text to come in, and he knew Jax was already putting on his shoes.

The Torch. He pounded back shot number four. Now he was drinking on a Wednesday.

K Slow down on my way.

Jax was a good friend. A real good friend.

Another text came in, this one a picture of his lover, head down, playing an old guitar.

"Oh." Something about it was so beautiful it took his breath away. It made him want to call, but he couldn't now, not as buzzed going on drunk as he was.

In a loud bar, can't call. Great picture. I love it. I miss you, he texted instead. The text stopped there but his inner monologue didn't. *I had a fight with my ex and now I don't know what I'm doing.*

Miss you bad. 4 more nights. Can't wait.

Okay. Okay, that felt pretty damn good but... *but I don't know if I deserve you.* He didn't text that though.

Soon isn't soon enough. He texted back.

No shit on that. Call later?

Fair warning I am so not sober. Ooh. He didn't slur in text. Awesome.

You ok? And I got you—sober or fucked up.

Nope. He was not.

I'm good. Just out drinking. Nobody liked a lover that whined about their ex.

You be careful going home, darlin I worry about your bod.

I will lover. Jax will get me home. He's the best friend ever. It took him four tries to spell "friend" correctly. Fucking autocorrect.

Good deal. TTYL. Love you.

Whoa.

Whoa.

He tapped his glass again and the bartender refilled it.

He tried a bunch of different replies and finally just didn't. He loved Hawk... he was probably in love with Hawk too, but he sighed and swallowed back shot number five.

"Dude, what number are you on?" Jax's hand landed on his back, patting him firmly.

"Jesus, Jax!" He jumped, the touch and the loud voice startling him. "Five. I'm on five. I haven't lost count yet so I'm fine."

"What happened, honey? Did you and your bull rider fight?" Jax sat on the stool Lucas had vacated.

"No. No we're not fighting, he said 'love you'. That's not a fight. Lucas was a fight. The fucker." He bit his lips closed. That made no sense and he knew it.

"Lucas was here? Like he showed up here? And Hawk said he loved you?" Jax ordered a margarita, on the rocks, extra salt. "Are you having the biggest goddamn night in history?"

"Yes. All of that. Yes." He tapped his glass again but Jax stole it and ordered him a Coke instead. "You're mean."

"Yes, but you hate puking, so let's slow it down a little. Start with the bad. What did the fuckmonkey want?"

"His gym-bunny dumped him. He was sniffing around. Does he actually think I'm that stupid? Am I that stupid? Would I be that stupid if I didn't have Hawk?" That worried him. A lot.

"Nope, because you have the best best friend in explored space, and I would beat you and drown him." Jax tilted his head. "Were you tempted?"

"No. I wasn't. I have no interest." He took a sip of his Coke, the cold and the bubbles made him blink. "Am I high maintenance?"

"High maintenance? You like good whiskey and you like a decent suit, but if I remember right, you're damn good to your lovers."

He took a deep breath and let it out, nodding. If he took a lover, he was devoted. He knew this about himself. And Luc still managed to make him doubt. "Okay. So Luc is really an asshole. He can still make me feel like shit. He pushes my buttons. I hate it."

"Yeah, fuck him. He doesn't deserve even another goddamn thought." Jax sighed and sipped his drink. "I think it's that he duped you, man. You let him in and now you're embarrassed—which I so get, by the way—but we all have that fucking asshole that took us."

January stared at Jax. "Yeah." Wow. That was spot on. *Duped.* "Fool me twice shame on me, huh? You are so right." So right. Jax had a way of cutting right through the bullshit sometimes. He didn't give himself enough credit.

"So, the good stuff. Tell me about your cowboy. He's into you deep, huh?"

He nodded and took another sip of his Coke before he answered. "It seems like he is. And I think it might be mutual."

"And that's scary as fuck, but also so goddamn cool."

"I don't want to... be wrong about him. And if I'm right, I don't want to fuck this up because I think he's absolutely sincere."

"Do you think you're wrong about him?" Jax didn't sound too worried, more curious.

He looked into his Coke. "I didn't think I was wrong about Luc."

"Nope. But you were. Don't let that little fuck mess up the good parts. That would be stupid, and you're not stupid."

"I don't think I'm wrong. I don't think I'm stupid either. I do worry about my judgment sometimes; he travels for a living. Nearly every weekend, almost year-round."

"Think of all the cool shit you could go see."

Okay, that wasn't what he'd expected Jax to say.

"I hadn't thought about it that way." There were times he wondered why he and Jax had hit it off the way they had, and then there were nights like tonight when he wondered how he'd manage without his best friend. "I guess I could travel with him sometimes. It won't always work out but... and then he's not out of course, not on the circuit so I'd have to play it pretty cool."

But Beckett had done it. Ben had done it. He wouldn't be the first and he knew who to go to for advice.

"But there is family on the tour, right? I know you said you'd met some guys with Hawk." Jax shrugged, then leaned in closer. "Man, don't overthink this. You're young, you got money, and you've got someone that wants you. Enjoy him. Enjoy learning about his life. Teach him about yours. It doesn't work? It doesn't, but you've had fun. It does? You've made a great start."

"I overthink everything. It's like comfort food." He finished off his Coke. "You should be a relationship counselor or something." Why was this guy still single? Someone wonderful ought to snap Jax right up.

"I want you to be happy. I want to meet your man. I want to make sure he's decent." Jax waggled his eyebrows, so evil. "Maybe not too decent."

"He's decently indecent. I want your stamp of approval." January laughed, looped an arm around Jax's shoulders and hugged him, feeling more pleasantly buzzed and less desperately drunk. "Thank you."

Jax squeezed him, holding on for a long second. "Hey. We're friends. Family even. I'm here, on purpose even."

"On purpose. Because I sent you a distress signal. You left the house for me and everything." They were family really. "You want to come watch again this weekend?"

"God yes. I'll bring chocolate chip cookies and pizza. You provide beer." Jax grinned at him, and January could see his friend relax. Suddenly he understood how worried Jax had been.

"I'm sorry I worried you. Lucas really threw me. I appreciate that you rushed down here. I'll get us a cab and get you home."

"First, you're going to let me finish my drink and tell me all about Raleigh."

"Oh, Raleigh was perfect. The hotel was comfy, which was good because other than the arena, that was all I saw of it. I paid for a room a didn't use at all. Can I have a beer?"

"Sure. Have you eaten? You want to share something?" Jax lifted his hand for the bartender. "No sightseeing at all?"

"I could eat. And I saw everything I wanted to. I'm looking forward to seeing more of him next week when he comes to visit."

"Ooh! You two will be able to play for a whole week? Your dick's gonna get chafed." The words fell from Jax's lips as the bartender walked up.

"Beer, please?"

The bartender nodded. "This is a better vibe than the argument you had earlier, man. I'd keep this one."

"Oh, he's... we're not... how about nachos. Let's get a plate of nachos too."

"He's got a hottie of his own. A Texan. Someone's going to turn him inside out." Jax wasn't helping. "Extra jalapenos, please."

"Extra hot it is." The guy gave Jax a wink and went to get Jan his beer.

"Is this why you're a hermit? Because you do shit like this whenever we go out?"

"I am not a hermit. Hermits live in caves and wear bearskin and smell like dirty socks. I live in a one-bedroom apartment, wear Levis, and smell like Ivory soap." Jax glared at him. "And yes, absolutely."

"That's what I thought." Jax made him laugh, such a dork. "The bartender winked at you."

"Yeah. Bartenders love guys that order margaritas."

"Jax, you're not looking hard enough. You have to stay open-minded. Look at how I met Hawk. I wasn't looking, but I wasn't *not* looking either."

"Yeah. You know how it is."

He did, sort of. Jax had been coming off his bad breakup

when they'd met, and January thought he was stuck there in the process of mourning someone that didn't care.

"Yeah. I do. Do I need to start turning your own words back on you?" He bumped shoulders with Jax to take a little weight out of what he was saying, keep it playful. Jax really didn't like serious much.

"Some people aren't meant to be in love, honey. You, though? You, it looks good on."

"It feels good. I'm looking forward to when it happens to you." It broke his head to hear his friend talk that way, but he'd never found the words to change Jax's mind. It was going to take more than words anyway. "So. What did you bake over the weekend? Did you have clients?"

"I made like a zillion eclairs. They were good. Everybody loved them. Made two princess cakes too. People have rediscovered them."

"I have no clue what a princess cake is, but I could eat myself sick on eclairs." Especially Jax's eclairs.

"The green domed ones from the British Baking Show? They're very popular at the teenager birthday right now."

"Oh those! I remember those now." God, Jax had made him watch so many baking shows they were all kind of a blur. Jax had even made him watch the competitions... they would binge them sometimes and he was almost embarrassed by how invested he would get. "Make sure you keep a night open next week. Hawk and I are planning to invite you for a slumber party. PJs? 80s movies?"

"Oh, excellent. What's his favorite sweet, and I'll bring that." Jax beamed at the bartender when he brought the nachos. "Those smell amazing."

"Extra Jalapenos." The bartender set a small bowl down next to Jax's hand and smiled back.

Oh, come on Jax. He took the bull by the horns.

So to speak.

"Hey, there. What's your name? I'm January, this is my buddy, Jax."

"Ryan. I've seen you in here before, good to know names." Ryan shook his hand and then offered one to Jax.

"Hey there, Ryan." Jax turned another of those blinding smiles on the man. "Nice to meet you."

"And you. Jax is great name. Is it short for something?"

"Joaquim Alonso Xavier Martinez." Jax rolled his eyes dramatically.

Ryan blinked and nodded for a second. "That's amazing. Someone felt you were very important, huh? Jax it is."

January laughed because he'd never felt better about his own name as when Jax told someone the mouthful that belonged to him.

"Yeah. Jax suits me to the bone." Jax winked at Ryan. "Thanks for the extra spice. I appreciate it."

"Anytime. Give me a yell if you guys need refills." Ryan moved down the bar to another customer.

January sighed. *You can lead a horse to water...*

But you couldn't make him flirt.

"The nachos here are pretty tasty." He scooped up a bite and crunched it happily.

"Uh-huh." Jax glanced at the bartender. "Did I do okay with interested but not desperate?"

"He didn't say don't call me." Okay. So Jax was interested after all. "Maybe ask him something personal next time."

Or... He rethought that advice.

"Not like 'how big is your cick' personal though."

"It's important to know." Butter wouldn't melt in Jax's mouth.

"Sure. I mean, if that's your angle, you do you, bro." He didn't even crack a smile.

Jax did, though. He laughed and the happiness cracked right through and, in seconds, he was cackling along.

"Maybe we should skip boyfriends and do the *Odd Couple* thing on a beach somewhere. We could totally entertain each other."

Jax tilted his head. "If you're willing to give up on the cowboy, I'm not going anywhere. I'd totally be your Oscar."

He leaned closer and gave Jax a quick peck on the temple. "I'm not giving up on my cowboy. But if he gives up on me, we'll talk."

"Yeah. I'm voting that he keeps you forever and teaches you how to ride horses."

God, no. Him on a horse? Scary. Dangerous. "Do they come with training wheels?"

"I have no idea. Maybe you can ride behind him and rub a lot?" He was going to pinch Jax. Hard.

"If we skip the horse he doesn't need to teach me a damn thing." He grinned at Jax. "Yeehaw."

"Are you saving a horse, buddy?" That sent them into paroxysms of hysterical laughter.

"Having fun, gentlemen?" Ryan leaned on the bar near Jax. "Another round?"

Jax glanced at him, then at Ryan. "Do I need one?"

Ryan shot right back with, "Are you planning to hang out a while?"

January pulled up Curb on his phone, thinking maybe he'd be leaving alone.

"I might be, yeah. You brought me these nachos, didn't you?"

"All those peppers. Can't rush something so hot. Let me get you another."

Ryan reached for both glasses, but Jan reached out and covered his. "I'm good, thank you."

"Just one then." Ryan stepped away and January smiled at Jax. "So... I'm going to get myself a ride home."

"Are you sure? I won't leave you hanging." Jax worried so well.

"I am so sure. You were exactly what I needed, thank you. I'm going to go home and call a cowboy... assuming you're okay here?"

"I'll call if I find myself in a spot. Promise."

"I'll have my ringer on. I'm not working tomorrow. If this doesn't go as hoped and you need an out, I'm your man." He sent the request for a ride and stood up to pull on his coat.

"Hey, enjoy your cowboy call. I can't wait to meet him."

"I'll see you this weekend for bull riding and pizza." He gave Jax another quick hug. "Good luck."

"I got this."

Yeah, he wasn't so sure about that, but what was he supposed to say?

"Goodnight." He'd leave it at that. He stepped out into the winter air to find his ride.

13

Hawk knew when he loaded up that his mind wasn't in the middle. He knew it. Charlie wasn't acting right. The man was scattered and down with violent headaches. Charlie wasn't even here tonight. He was throwing up, and Ben was taking care of him.

"Pay attention, man." Pistol muttered. "This bastard is mean as hell."

"Sorry. Sorry. Right." Ride the bull. Ride the bull and get a ride back to Charlie's and take the guys Sprite and chicken soup.

That's all he had to do.

"On it." He got his rope set, HoneyBoo rocking in the chutes, slamming him back and forth, Pistol's hand hard on his vest.

"Jesus. Come on, they're counting you down."

"Fuckers." He didn't need the judges pushing him too. He nodded before the bastard settled in the chute. He needed out and done.

Hawk wanted to be back with the guys.

He wanted to be—

He saw HoneyBoo's head slam back almost in time to avoid the hit.

Almost.

He took the hit on his right side, and he could hear the snapping sound as bones broke. He always thought it was weird, how the sound happened before the hurting. Always. Fuck. He had about a breath before the ground was coming up at him, and he held his breath, knowing this was gonna suck.

14

———

I'm fine momma. Dont worry. Doc's getting me set up now and I'll have a car bring me back.

Hawk pondered throwing up again, but it would hurt his broken shoulder and rib more, so he decided to not. Instead, he called his January.

Please, don't be pissed, he thought. *I'm tired.*

"Hawk." Jan answered on half a ring. "Are you okay? I've been texting. I know you probably couldn't answer, but I was worried."

"Hey, darlin'. I tell you what, I'm ready to see you." And he needed a break.

Jan exhaled heavily into the phone. "It's good to hear your voice."

"Yeah. I wrecked. I miss you." He was starting to hurt, and to be honest, he was fixin' to lose his shit, especially when Momma texted with, *Are you flying home tomorrow?*

"I saw. Jax and I were watching. It looked bad, baby. I mean, I don't know what wreck doesn't look bad, I guess. But... how bad is it?"

"Broken shoulder, cracked rib—not bad. They've taped

me up, and I have my sling coming after the ice does its job."
Please tell me you still want me to come.

Jan hissed. "Bullshit. That's not bad? I'm going to wrap
you in bubble wrap when you get here. You can still fly?"

Oh, thank God. "I can. I fly out at five tomorrow, get in at
eight fifteen. We'll have supper together."

And then he'd figure out whether he was going to be
able to stay with Jan a couple of weeks or head home.

"What do you want to eat? Text me your flight
information so I can meet you at the airport. You're not
going to want to deal with bags with that shoulder. I'll have
a car waiting."

"Your favorite thing. Thank you for letting me come." *I'm
so fucking tired, darlin'. I'm hurting and Charlie's really sick. My
heart aches.*

"Shut up, cowboy. I'm not *letting* you come, I'm asking
you to get here fast. I miss you. And now I need to get my
hands on you and see for myself that you're okay." He could
hear the sincerity in Jan's voice, and that made it easier to
believe.

"I'm ready. You have no idea. I'm so ready." His voice
shook, and he cleared his throat.

"Hurts, I bet. I'm ready to see you too. I'll take good care
of you. Just try to breathe until you get here."

"I'll be okay. I'm going to be packing it in ice, but Doc
says I'm out for three to eight weeks."

"Fuck, that's a long time. I'm sorry." There was a
question there, that hung in the dead air on the line. They
were still so new he wasn't sure what to say next. January
saved him. "I know you'll probably want to see your folks
and maybe Ben and Charlie again, and that's cool, but you're
welcome here as long as you like."

"Right now I want to be with you, okay? I want to close

my eyes and be with you." It was needy and not very macho, but it was the truth, and that had to count for something.

"Yes. Okay. I want that too." Jan sighed. "I want that too."

"Tomorrow. I'm going to sleep at Charlie's tonight, sitting up in the recliner, and tomorrow? Your place. Your bed. In your arms." And he was so thankful.

"I can't wait. You get some rest, listen to the doctors. I'll be waiting for you, okay? Tomorrow."

"Yeah. Tomorrow." He took a deep breath. "Okay, I'm going to call Momma and let her fuss at me. You have a good night, and I'll see you."

"Goodnight, Hawk." January hesitated before hanging up.

"Love you," he whispered, before calling home. She'd feel better if she screamed, and he could close his eyes and ignore her.

He just wanted January.

It was all he needed. Well, that and some pain pills.

15

The first thing Jax did after January hung up the phone with Hawk was call him an asshole for not saying "I love you".

He told Jax he hadn't said it because he still didn't know for sure. Jax gave him a look but was kind enough not to call him out for what he was.

A liar.

He knew damn well he was in love and he'd been up most of the night feeling terrible for not saying it when it might have helped Hawk feel better. Lifted his spirits. Made him less anxious.

Fuck, he should have said it.

He should have told Hawk to switch to an earlier flight too. Hawk couldn't ride anyway, why be there? Why not get to New York sooner instead of both of them waiting all day long?

He understood how Hawk felt. He'd heard the emotion Hawk had been fighting on the phone. He wanted Hawk here too. If Hawk hadn't been spending time with Charlie and Ben, he probably would have flown in for the show.

He'd wanted to respect Hawk's time with his friends. He wanted to be patient. But he wasn't patient now, he was anxious and antsy and wanted to get his hands on his lover.

Instead of sleeping, he'd made himself busy—the dishes were done, the kitchen and bathrooms were clean, he'd vacuumed and remade his bed. He ran out to the market early and stocked his kitchen. Mid-morning, he finally gave up looking for things to do in the apartment to keep him busy, poured a cup of coffee, and stretched out on the couch to watch TV. Maybe he could take a short nap.

Of course, his phone rang as soon as he closed his eyes. Hawk. Oh, that was a voice he could use to hear. He picked right up.

"Good morning."

"Can I come early?" Hawk sounded wrecked. Utterly wrecked and near tears.

He sat up abruptly, heart starting to pound. "Of course. Where are you?"

"Airport. The ambulance came for Charlie, and they're doing a bunch of tests. I can't help here, so I'm in the way."

"Come as soon as—or... would you rather be there with Charlie? You want me to come to you?" He stood and picked up his coffee.

"No." That was sure, short. "Ben's folks are on the way, Charlie's momma and granny too. They don't need me here in the way, and they don't know. They wouldn't understand why I can't drive and all. I got on the ten a.m. flight. I'll be in at one your time."

He had a handful of questions about that, but none of them mattered right now. Hawk needed assurances, and less stress. "I'll be there. Keep it together, baby. You can lose it here."

"Thanks. I— Thank you."

Oh, his poor lover. Hawk sounded raw.

"Hawk. You've got this." It made him nervous as hell, but he wasn't about to miss the opportunity this time. "I love you."

"I love you too, darlin'. Don't worry on me. I got a first-class seat so I'm not squished."

Squished.

Hawk was a five-three, one-hundred-ten-pound cowboy. He could share a seat with someone and not be squished.

"I want to hear that in person." *Complete with the "darlin'".* "Be safe. I'll see you at the airport." Forget telling him not to worry. He probably worried more than Hawk's mother. It was practically a pastime.

"I'll be there with bells on. We're fixin' to board. I'll see you soon, huh?"

"Soon. I'll listen for the bells. Love you." That was easy as anything this time.

"Love you too. See you in a few. Bye, darlin'." The phone line went dead.

But he felt better.

He looked at his phone. Three hours. He could nap for two, and then take the train to Newark to meet his man.

16

Okay, so January slept for one hour only, and he got to the airport an hour early. He couldn't have slept any longer, he'd been paranoid about being late. But that gave him time to get a snack and buy coffees for the ride back in the car he'd arranged.

He and Hawk said almost nothing to each other on the ride to his apartment, but there hadn't been a sliver of daylight between them in the car. They had a lot to talk about, but it was all secondary to being together.

Jan shouldered Hawk's bag as the car pulled away and left them on the sidewalk, noting there was only one. "You left your gear in Nashville, huh?"

"I did. They're going to ship it when I know where I'm riding next." Hawk's lips twisted. "It won't be Connecticut for damn sure."

He grinned, holding the elevator doors for Hawk, who looked like he was hurting. That had to have been a long flight. "Well, not in an arena anyway."

"Nope. I'm going to enjoy being with you. Going to heal this stupid assed shoulder." Hawk looked around the elevator. "I never knew someone that lived in a place with an elevator. That's cool."

"My place will probably seem small to you since you're from the land of open spaces, but it's pretty big by New York standards." Hell, he could fit two of Jax's apartment into his. Maybe even three. Jax's place was tiny.

It wasn't a long ride to the fifth floor, which was the top floor in his building. He loved it because it got more light than a lot of shorter buildings did. "This is us. Hang a right, I'm at the end."

Hawk drew in tight, making himself smaller than normal.

"You okay?" He took Hawk's good hand. "It's down the hall."

"Yeah. I don't want to bump into anything. I been tenderized." Hawk held on tight. "It's good to see you."

"Right. I get it." He led Hawk to his door, making sure to keep close. The hall was totally interior and not very brightly lit, so he could understand it being tough for Hawk to navigate. He opened his door and held that too. "My place has a lot more light."

"Oh, I can tell that." Hawk's face lit up, and his lover relaxed visibly. "I'm so glad I'm here."

Jan closed the door, dropped Hawk's bag, pulling gently on the hand still in his. "Come sit. We can breathe and catch up."

"Sounds like a plan." Hawk let him lead him to the sofa and ease him down, trying hard not to jostle that poor arm.

"You good? Comfy? Can I get you something to drink?" Jan grabbed a couple of throw pillows so Hawk could prop up his arm.

"I'm fine as frog hair. I want to sit with you a minute, please."

"I've got all day, and you don't even have to say please."
He sat as close as he dared. "Just lean on me."

Hawk didn't hesitate at all, he leaned in, snuggled in
with a soft sigh. "Hey."

"Oh, this feels good. You feel good. Don't let me hurt
your shoulder though." He kissed Hawk's hair. He wanted to
know about the wreck. He wanted to know about Charlie.
But he wanted Hawk relaxed more, and he figured that
would all come out in time. "I really, really missed you."

"I missed your ass like all get out. I—I needed this bad."
Hawk sighed and leaned hard. "I needed you bad."

"Bad enough to be stuck with me for six weeks?" He was
joking, and not. "Surely there was a better way."

"Yeah. I should have stayed on." Hawk chuckled, the
sound warm, like it was an old joke Hawk had told over and
over again.

"It's all good. I'm not mad that I get to keep you." He
sighed, breathed in Hawk's scent, a little awed by the
strength of their connection.

"It's been a wild week. Sounds like yours might have
been crazy too, huh?"

"Crazy. Kind of. I had one bad night, but Jax rescued me.
I was a little fuzzy the next day, that's all." Fucking Lucas.
The asshole didn't even belong in this conversation.

"You okay, darlin'? You need me to beat someone for
you?"

"Maybe when you have both arms again." He snorted.
"Just an ex who wanted back in. I told him off. I think he
heard me. If he didn't, he's an idiot."

"Well, I can tell him next time. I can do better by you, no
question."

"Oh, no question. He cheated on me. Twice. If we ever
break up, it won't be because you cheated. I'm confident of

that." He blinked. He sounded a little angrier than he'd meant to. Fucking Lucas. "Sorry. I guess it still makes me angry."

Angry, for sure, but not upset. Not hurt. That was a big improvement.

"Seriously? What kind of stupid fuck would cheat on you?" Hawk's expression was bemused enough to make January smile.

"The kind you don't want to know. The kind *I* was stupid enough to give a second chance to. Fortunately for us, he blew it. This is much better." The vision of Hawk pummeling Lucas was almost worth wishing for. He added Jax shooting spitballs and that really made him smile.

"I would have found you anyway. It was fate." Didn't Hawk sound smug? That was his champ. Much better.

"Certainly feels that way, doesn't it? We owe that bartender in Denver a beer for introducing us."

"Next time we go, I will. You should come to the zoo there with me. It's amazing." Hawk petted his hand, slow and gentle.

He watched Hawk's fingers, enjoying the touch. "I love the zoo. We have one here, in the Bronx. It's fun."

"Rock on. Let's go. Later." Hawk exhaled again, relaxing deeper. Someone was letting go, and it was gratifying to see.

"Later. You want to give me your glasses, baby? You don't need them right now." Hawk would relax even more if he didn't have to worry about trying to see with his eyes.

"Yeah?" Hawk handed them over without hesitation and closed his eyes. "I like being here with you. It's the first time we've been alone, really."

"I guess it is. A hotel room isn't really private. This is home." He set the glasses on the end table where they'd be safe and flipped his hand over on Hawk's so he could touch for a while. "How's your shoulder?"

"Tender."

Tender. A broken shoulder, a broken rib—tender, he says.

"I'm not a cowboy. You can be real. If it fucking hurts, you can tell me it fucking hurts." He nuzzled Hawk's ear. "I'm the most pain-averse person you'll ever meet."

"It more throbs than anything. Like with my heartbeat." Hawk grinned, and the look was sheepish. "It's not the first time I've broke it. I hate the shoulder ones."

He had to laugh. "I had stitches once."

"Mmm. I know that scar. It's hot."

"Oh, yeah. Appendix surgery is *so* sexy."

"No, but the scar by your cute little belly button? Oh my God."

"My cute—what are you talking about?" *Cute little belly button?* He laughed. "Shut up."

"Your adorable wee navel? It does it for me, you know? It's sweet, a little haven in your fuzzy belly."

"Wait. You're serious? You have a belly button thing?" He was proud of his fuzz, but he'd never given a second thought to his belly button.

"I have a touch thing. That's somewhere to start, you know." Hawk petted his belly, then went back to holding his hand.

Hell yeah. That he knew. "Mmm. I like your touch thing. You can start anywhere you want."

"Good to know." Hawk's hand traveled north this time, circling one of his nipples.

He chuckled softly and curled his hand around Hawk's again. "Listen, broken bones boy. We should maybe take it easy for a few days."

"It's only little bones..." Hawk brought his hand up for a kiss.

"Every bone in your body is little, cowboy." He kissed those fingers happily, and went looking for more, tipping Hawk's face up to his.

Hawk kissed him gently, almost lazily, and January felt like here, with him, Hawk could breathe.

"Mmm." He was into a lazy kiss. It felt good to be able to bring Hawk some peace, but it was sad that Hawk didn't have that elsewhere too. On the road with his parents. He hoped it was better with Ben and Charlie, but even there Hawk was kind of a fifth wheel. "This is good."

"No shit on that, darlin'. I been waiting on this. You and me, together."

"The best part is we have time. You don't have to leave in two days." He didn't miss that sense of urgency, like everything was temporary. They didn't have to burn each other to the ground in forty-eight hours.

"No, but if you want me to leave, you say. I'm not here to make your life bad. I want to hang with you." Hawk grinned at him. "Love on you. Watch terrible TV and eat good pizza."

Leave? Hardly. "What if I want you to stay? Do I get to say that too?"

"Yeah, I think you do." Hawk nodded, the move clear, sure. "I never wanted someone to let me stay so bad."

"I guess that's what this love thing is about. I'm a little surprised to find it feels totally new to me. I thought I knew." This was so much bigger than anything he thought he'd had with Lucas. It was wild to think things probably wouldn't have worked out between them even if Lucas hadn't been a dick.

"No one on earth can have what you and me have right

now. This is something we're building up together. You and me." Hawk sounded about as awed as he felt.

He smiled. Hawk was right, and pretty damn articulate about it at that. "Is this a cowboy thing? Being so wise about love?"

"You know it. We have had country music teaching us since we were in the womb. Cowboys were meant to fall in love."

"I wouldn't have taken you for a romantic in Denver, Mr. 'Fuck me like I need'." He grinned. They'd both been burning that night.

"That ain't romance, darlin'?" Oh, that drawl was *thick*.

He dropped his voice deep. "I'm not complaining, angel. Trust me on that."

"Mmm. Damn, I like that." Hawk's eyelids went heavy, and he licked his lips. "You turn my crank but good."

"I'm sure you've heard this a hundred times from clueless Yankees, but I love your turn of phrase. Not as much as I love you, but it's definitely a turn-on." He took another kiss, trying to keep them on simmer for a while. He knew they were good in bed; he wanted a little more of what they were out of it.

"That's sweet as honey right there. So, tell me about here. Why did you rent? Buy? Whatever. Here. Why this place?"

"Rent. I rent because I want to be able to pick up and move whenever I want. And because I don't have to deal with it if something needs repair. And *here*... because I didn't want a doorman building and a lot of expensive extras, I wanted comfort and light and privacy." He could say he wanted to pick up and move all he liked but he'd been here for years and expected he'd be here for many more.

"That's cool. I like a place with lots of windows."

"It's not a great view of anything but the sky really. The street is pretty cool at night with the traffic lights and all, but it's a city view. Buildings and cars. I like it though. With your vision, you'll probably enjoy the view more at night than during the day, but the light is always good, even on a gray day." He drew a swirl through Hawk's hair with a finger. "I'll give you a tour around the place in a bit."

"Yeah, you'll have to show me where the restroom is at some point and where the glasses are so I can get a drink."

"You'll learn your way around." His place was an open floor plan in the front and the bedrooms were all off a hall down one side.

"I will. I'm a smart dog. I've learned a thousand hotel rooms and airports."

"How do you manage? Are airports tough?"

"Yeah, but everybody goes the same way, to baggage. I follow them, and I always hire a car. They show me where the bathrooms are and help me with my luggage."

"That's remarkable, really. I'm impressed. I think I might be intimidated by all of that in your shoes." Intimidated was putting it mildly. He really couldn't imagine what it was like at all. "So, did you want to watch the short-go?"

"Sure. I'm thinking Huck is good for this one. He's a mean bastard. Didn't used to be, but damn."

Jan picked up the remote and turned on the TV, finding the right channel easily—it was familiar now. He hadn't met Huck, but he'd heard about the guy. "He's been on the injured list, right? He's back?"

"Yeah. He takes lots of risks, takes lots of blows to the noggin."

Things were already underway, though Jan had no idea where they were in the program. They'd tuned in in time to see a rider get tossed but land neatly on his feet. Jan laughed. "Wow. He's saying, I meant to do that."

"Did he make the eight?" Hawk still had his eyes closed.

"Um... whoa. Yes. Just. It's... Chad somebody? You want your glasses, or should I narrate?" He laughed.

"Rick does a great job." Hawk smiled for him. "I know the patter. I listen a lot."

"Oh. Damn. It's the monster that broke your shoulder. Honeyboo, right?" The kid in the chute looked tiny and young.

"Yep. Aaron won't ride him. He's riding against his free arm."

"I have no idea what that means, I know he looks like he's a toothpick."

"Yeah. He's eighteen and still growing. Lucky bastard." Hawk shifted, and January heard a sharp intake of breath.

"Easy, baby." God, it was easy to forget how much pain Hawk was in, the cowboy didn't make a thing of it. "Do you need to move? Get some meds or anything? I can find them for you."

"I—I don't want to miss any time with you, darlin', but I think I need a pill to take the edge off."

And ice, he'd bet. He'd read that ice and rest was the only thing to do.

"You're not missing time with me, we have plenty." Jan shifted carefully from underneath Hawk and propped him up with more pillows. "Are the pills in your bag? I'll get them."

"Yeah. There's a packet of shit from the hospital. I haven't opened it yet."

"What? Are you kidding?" He would have been begging for painkillers by now. He pulled out a paper bag that sounded like it had pills in it and had a paper stapled to it.

"Found it." He started to hand it to Hawk and thought better of that, opened the bag and read the instructions himself. "Okay. So it says you can have two of these with lots of water every six hours."

He opened the bottle and poured two into Hawk's hand.

"Thanks, darlin'." The tough son of a bitch took them dry.

"I'm getting you water, baby. Those won't sit well in your stomach. You want a snack too?" He headed for the kitchen, around the counter that separated it from the living room.

Jesus, he sounded like a worried mother.

"I'm saving my calories, darlin'. You promised me pizza later. You have any milk?"

"Some. Is skim okay?" He could go for pizza. "Pizza later. Maybe you should get a nap first."

"Skim is perfect. Thank you. And Aaron didn't ride. He's young and just moved up. It'll take him a bit to figure it out."

"Who's up next?" He got a glass and pulled the milk from the fridge. "I want to see this Huck guy ride."

"They're still doing the third round. It'll happen in a few." Hawk cleared his throat and swallowed a groan. "Is it cool if I take off my boots?"

"Baby, make yourself at home. You can hang out in your undies if you want to." He came over with the milk and held it out to Hawk. "Milk. You want help with the boots?"

Hawk reached for it and missed. Not even close. So January put it in his lover's hand.

"Thank you. That's perfect." Hawk downed half the glass before he toed his boots off. "Where should I put them?"

He grinned. "Where do you put them in your house?"

"There's a spot near the front door." Hawk pinked, but smiled. "My daddy built a wooden box in his shop, years ago. That box was for my shoes, my boots. Everyone knows. My name's carved in it."

That sounded like such a parent thing. So sweet. "What a great idea." He picked up Hawk's boots. "I don't have a box, but I'll leave them by the door for you."

"Thank you. Be patient. I'll learn where things are soon, I swear to God." Hawk finished the milk, licking the white off the pale hint of mustache.

"I'm patient. And I love you." He took the glass from Hawk, and a quick kiss too. "Your boots look great by the door. Like you belong here. Which you do."

"Good deal." Hawk turned his face in January's direction. "No bruises?"

"Not on your handsome face." Jan headed back to the kitchen to ditch the glass and get Hawk some ice. "I haven't seen the rest of you yet." He'd bet money there were plenty under Hawk's shirt. Broken bones came with bruises, and a run-in like Hawk had had with Honeyboo had to have hurt.

"So long as you think they're hot, we're good." Hawk chuckled, the sound low and sexual. "I want you. I know that I'm supposed to be hurt and all, but I figured you ought to know. When I can, I'm going to turn you inside out."

He hummed and let that sink right into his balls. Damn, that felt good. "We're not stupid. I can get you off without hurting that shoulder." He brought a couple of ice packs he found in his freezer and a big zipper-bag of ice over. "I'm going to help you get that shirt off, and ice you up."

"Yeah. It sucks, but I need it. The pressure from the plane is a bitch and a half." Hawk slipped off his sling and unbuttoned his shirt, and Christ. Look at that.

His lover was black and blue from collarbone to waist, ribs taped up, shoulder twice the size of the other one.

He winced in sympathy. "Jesus, Hawk." Jan immediately

started thinking about how to get Hawk a follow-up with his doctor, whether Hawk would need to rehab the shoulder... as if Hawk needed him to step in. Hawk didn't, of course, but it was reflex. He busied his hands instead, slowly and carefully working the shirt off Hawk's good arm, and then the bad one. "Are you going to be comfortable here? Would you rather be in bed?"

"I'll stay here. I haven't tried laying down yet. Slept in Charlie's recliner."

"I've got the Lazy-Boy, would that work better than the couch?" He pointed to his overstuffed recliner. "Jax sleeps in it a lot when he stays over." He didn't have a TV in the guest room and Jax liked to sleep with the TV on.

"Maybe, but I'll take a little hurt to sit with you, darlin'."

"Not that I don't want you to be totally comfortable, but I like that answer. We've had enough distance between us, right?" He helped Hawk get the sling back on and scooted back into his spot, letting Hawk show him where to put the ice.

"See? You get me. I need you. Just sitting and talking about nothing. Hell, I need to know things about you. Goofy things."

"Okay. Goofy... hm. I love peanut butter and jelly. Love it. I could eat it every day." That was the truth. "Lunch, midnight snack, second breakfast._" he laughed.

"What kind of jelly?" Hawk was beginning to blink slowly.

"Strawberry. I'll do grape in a pinch, but strawberry is what calls to me. It's one thing you can always count on being in my kitchen. Strawberry jelly, good peanut butter and soft bread." He stroked a hand over Hawk's good arm.

"Oh, that sounds good. Momma's fridge always has eggs, tortillas, and Dr Pepper."

"Is that what you drink? I'll have some delivered. I have eggs. We can talk about what you want in the fridge later when I have a pen and can make a list." He could feel a chill from the ice, but if Hawk could handle a little pain, he could handle a little cold.

"Diet and cherry, but yeah, that's my favorite kind of Coke. What's yours?"

"Coke is my favorite kind of *soda*." He added the emphasis to be silly, because the regional jokes about "pop" and "soda" and "Coke" were as old as the drinks were themselves. "Who's up now?" He watched the TV, not sure what was actually going on at the moment.

"Is it the short-go? I was busy learning about your strawberry obsession."

"I'm not obsessed. Much. How do I know if it's the short-go?" He squinted at the TV. "Oh. I think it must be, yes."

"How about fresh strawberries? Are those obsession-worthy?" Hawk giggled. Actually giggled.

"As fresh as you?" He gave Hawk a gentle squeeze. "Those are some good drugs, huh?"

"They take the edge off, yeah." He got a wink, a soft laugh. "If I get too stupid, tell me to shut up."

"It's kind of adorable. Is that Huck? He's huge. The bull I mean. Although Huck doesn't look as small as some."

"He rides with strength. He either does right or he sucks."

He laughed. "Kind of like you?"

"No. Butthead. I ride by balance. If I can stay healthy, I'm solid."

"Oh! I see what you mean. Be nice. I'm clueless still." He could tell when something looked good, and when something looked like it was going south. That was about all he knew about this sport. But he was learning. He'd learn everything for Hawk.

And speaking of going south. "Uh-oh."

"Come on, you bastard. Sit up." Hawk's muttering didn't seem to help because Huck hit the dirt and he was hooked on. Tied on. What the hell?

That couldn't be good. "Why doesn't he let go? Is he stuck? It's like he's caught." Could Hawk even see it?

"He's wrapped in his bull rope. Is he helping or is he out?"

"He's... helping. Or trying to. He's not out." He was getting yanked around though. The bull twisted, one of the bullfighters took a hit and Huck broke free. "Wait. Wait he's free. Oh, he's pissed. Damn. He threw his hat... punched the gate."

"The suits will snarl. They hate that shit." Hawk looked tickled as hell. "Maybe he broke his hand."

"I don't know. He stormed out. The bull fighters are all rolling their eyes. Didn't you say you thought he had this?" No wonder the guy was pissed. "Danny's loading up."

"Yeah? He must have ridden his ass off earlier today. I didn't have the little shit pegged for the short-go. Good on him!" Hawk's grin widened, eyes lit up. "Root for him to win, since I cain't."

"He's always on my short list. He looks totally focused too... nod... gate... oh, he looks good, Hawk."

"Mind in the middle, goofy little man. You got a baby coming." Hawk wasn't watching, but he was smiling, counting softly. "Six. Seven. Eight."

"And... whoa. He's off. He hit the dirt kind of hard but he's up. And he's smiling like a loon." And good for him. Good for Nicole too. He'd never met friendlier people.

"I imagine he looks like a monkey, somehow, with the way people talk about his grin."

Jan let that sink in a second. It was a wonder Hawk found his way anywhere. Somebody had to know more than they were saying. Or at least have guessed. "Nah. He's a handsome kid. His smile does kind of take over his face though. Blue eyes, red hair. Scar under his left eye." Not too big, but pretty deep.

Hawk nodded and stroked his fingers, one after the other. "He hit the gate on the way out. Bled like a bitch."

"I bet that hurt." Danny's score was high, and all Jan could think was with that strut, Nicole was so getting laid later. Although fucking and being pregnant sounded awkward at best.

"Danny got confetti. And I think it's over."

"Ninety-point ride. Go him. I bet he gets laid."

Ha! Great minds thought alike. "I was thinking the same thing. I think his dick led him out of the arena."

Jan shifted a little and readjusted Hawk's ice. "How are you feeling?"

"Fuzzy around the edges. So fucking glad to be here." Hawk looked like he was a kid in a candy store. "I'm *here*, darlin'. With you."

"You keep saying that. And I keep not being tired of hearing it. You want to catch a nap and then we'll talk about pizza?"

Did you want to check-in on Charlie?

He wanted to know what was going on. Hawk had sounded wrecked earlier. That could have been the pain and the lack of sleep... but Hawk wasn't bringing it up and he hated to admit it, but he didn't know his lover well enough yet to understand why.

"Yeah. Yeah, that sounds good. Can you—can we leave the TV on during our nap?"

"We can…I don't mind. But do you mind if I ask why?" He wasn't going to get to know Hawk on the level he really wanted to if he didn't start asking questions. Especially awkward ones.

"I'm stoned, and I don't know where anything is? It's scar —harder in the quiet."

He nodded, hearing what Hawk almost said more clearly than what his lover actually had. "Makes sense. Would you be better out here or in the bedroom? The bedroom has a TV too, and its own bath."

"Do you mind? I could totally take a bathroom break." Hawk's cheeks were almost maroon. "I'm sorry. I hate being weird."

Well, shit. "I'm sorry. I didn't mean to embarrass you. It's not weird to need a little help, baby." He helped Hawk sit up and took all the ice packs. "Let me put these in the kitchen."

His phone vibrated on the kitchen counter as he closed the freezer. He found a selfie of Danny and Nicole grinning.

Danny did it! Sending love to Hawk.

We saw! He owned that bull. Congrats. Hawk made it to NY fine.

He went back to the couch to help Hawk up. "Danny and Nicole send love."

"Yeah? They're good kids, and he's on fire."

He liked that—how Hawk was happy for Danny, not so competitive that he resented Danny's success.

"You're a good man, Hawk." Hawk got to his feet with less help than Jan thought he would need, and they started for the bedroom. "I have a ton of pillows, so we can prop you up."

"I'm a cowboy, darlin', but I'm tickled as a pig in shit that you think I'm decent." Hawk leaned hard. "Lord, these pills."

"I've got you. Just take it slow. You want your glasses?" He scooped them up.

"Thanks." Hawk took them back and put them on. "Do you like your bedroom?"

Did he like his bedroom? What an odd question.

"Yes. But it's going to be so much better with you in it. The wall behind the bed is exposed brick, and the one with the window in it is too, but that's painted white. The other walls are gray. It's not as bright as the rest of the apartment, so I made it kind of moody." It was tighter than the rest of the apartment too. His bed was big, his dresser was long... there was more to navigate in here. "Come on in."

"That's cool, on the brick." Hawk reached out, fingers trailing on the edge of his dresser.

Jan tested to see how much detail Hawk really needed. Or wanted. "The bathroom door is about two feet past the end of the dresser."

"Okay. I'll be out in a few." Hawk trailed along the dresser, then took the corner to the wall. From there he found the bathroom door and slipped inside.

There was silence for a long time before January heard the sound of a toilet flush. Then there was a loud crashing sound, and the unmistakable sound of someone falling.

"Hawk!" *Fuck fuck.* "I'm coming in." *Fuck.* Jan bolted for the door and opened it.

Hawk was sitting on the floor, arm drawn in, looking horrified and pale, glasses crooked on his face. "Oh my God. I'm so sorry. The shower door was open. Did I break it? I swear I'll pay to have it fixed."

"Fuck the shower door. Are you okay?" He took Hawk's glasses off and looked at them, then sat them up on the counter. They were okay at least. "How did you land? Did you hit your head? Is your shoulder...?"

Jesus, he was fussing like Hawk was a four-year-old and he didn't care.

"Embarrassed. A little queasy." Hawk felt for the door with a shaking hand and closed it. "I'm sorry."

They were going to have to talk. But one thing at a time. Some of it was the meds, surely. "Let's get you off the floor and into bed."

"Right." Hawk reached up for him. "Haul my ass up?"

It took them some time to get Hawk to his feet, but after that, January basically carried his lover to bed and propped him up with a bunch of pillows to support his back and his arm. "Do you want more ice?"

The bathroom doesn't have a window, it needs more light. Maybe a motion-sensing switch. Hang up the bathmat, clear the counter...

Or maybe climb into bed with Hawk and hold him.

"No, darlin'. Come nap with me. I'll stop taking the pills. I knew better. Just come settle and relax." Hawk held one hand out to him.

"Yeah." He took a second and pulled off his sweater, then climbed up to the headboard and got comfortable. "You should take them, and let me help. You're going to have to let me help."

"Shh. I want you to want me here. I don't want to be a problem. I want good pizza." Hawk snuggled right in.

"Yes. Because you only get pizza if you ask absolutely nothing of me." He sighed. "Hawk. I want you here. If I wasn't ready to have all of you, I wouldn't have invited you."

"I'm sorry, darlin'. I'm wore. My everything. I didn't want you to think I didn't want to be here with you." Hawk leaned in. "I need to be here with you."

"You belong right here. So rest for now, and later we'll talk about how to make being here work for both of us. Good?" He'd prefer Hawk not to be so broken, but his lover's sight was something he'd accepted when he let Hawk into his heart. He had to understand everything.

"I love you." The words were low, but he heard them, loud and clear.

And remarkable.

"I love you, baby." He reached for the remote and turned the TV on.

17

*I*s *he ok?*
    It took forever for Ben to answer. *Hes home. Sleeping. UOK?*

Hawk sighed and nodded, like Ben could notice. He was. He was here with January. He wanted to be here. *Good. Just got up from a nap.*

And he needed something to drink.

January was sleeping, snoring softly, so Hawk maneuvered his way up. He felt his way along the bed to the dresser, the dresser to the door, the door to the hallway. Okay. Rock on. He eased his way down the hall, exploring the edges of paintings and door frames. It didn't take too long to find the opening to the kitchen.

Bingo.

Charlie never slept during the day. Not even when he was sick.

In the kitchen, he went slow, knowing his glass had to be somewhere. When he found it in the sink, he got himself a glass of water, feeling like he'd accomplished something.

His phone buzzed and he asked who it was, and it was

Momma. He didn't want to argue with her anymore. He was a grown man. He wanted to be here.

It buzzed again. And again. Needling him like Momma would. Trying to make him feel guilty for letting it ring.

"Hey, Momma."

"Don't you ignore me, son."

"I was napping, Momma. That's all. What you need?" He knew what she needed. She needed him home where she could know he was safe.

"When are you coming home?"

"Oh, Momma. I don't know. I've got a few weeks off. I'm hanging out here with January." He deserved this time. He deserved a chance to see if he could hope to be something that wasn't sitting in the bedroom he'd always lived in.

"Baby, New York? Seriously? Aren't you scared?"

Fucking terrified, but he'd gotten used to that. "Nope. January's got a nice place. We're going to go sightseeing soon."

"And what are you going to do when he's at work and you can't do anything?"

Same thing he did in hotels. Watch TV, nap, and learn this space. "Don't be nasty. This is an adventure."

"Don't talk like that, son. We're all set up for you here. You're not made for that kind of adventure."

"I'm a bull rider. Adventure is what I live for." He shook his head. "Love you, Momma. I got to go."

He hung up and turned his phone off. He didn't want to deal with this shit anymore. She was a momma. She worried. He got that. But he was a man. A man had to make his way in the world.

"Hawk? Hawk!" January called, sounding closer the second time, an urgency in his voice. "Oh. Hey. I... uh.

Thirsty, huh? You found the... good." Jan let out a heavy sigh.

"I did. I was fixin' to discover what all was in the fridge." He grinned, trying to chill everything out. "You have a good nap?"

"Yeah. I didn't sleep last night." Jan rested warm hands on his hips and kissed him. "You?"

"I did. I needed a rest." He needed to breathe and float, even if he hadn't slept.

"Sorry I shouted, I... I'm going to get better at this. I'm going to make some coffee, would you like some?"

"I'd love some. Can I help?" *Show me things, darlin', please.*

"Yes. Why don't you do it. Um. Okay you found the sink. So... it goes sink, coffee maker, fridge. The coffee is one of those pod things. They're all... oh. Well they're in a jar thing right now. I should get a sorter."

"That would be cool, if you have different types, huh?" The fridge was huge, so he found the coffeemaker easily. He'd used a Keurig before, so he got the lid to the water open, found two pods. "Do these work?"

"Yep. Those are plain old dark roast. Work for you? I'd get a nice coffee maker but honestly, I like Starbucks and there's one on the corner. I use it as an excuse to get out of the apartment."

"Cool. It works fine. Coffee cups?" He leaned against January for a moment, enjoying the warmth. Oh, that was nice on his shoulder.

Jan nosed his hair, ran fingers down his side. "Right over the coffee maker, and there's a cup measure in there too that's the right size to fill the tank if it's empty."

"Good deal." He ought to stand up, but it felt so good to lean. It felt so fucking good to be right here.

Jan wasn't rushing him off, either. "There's a mug up there, it's heavy and kind of rough around the bottom. My nephew made it for me, and I love it, but it leaks so don't use it." Jan laughed. "I like that it's there. I like seeing it."

"Oh, that's cool. I have one at home that my oldest niece painted at one of them paint your own pottery deals." Shania had been so proud of herself, so proud of her work.

"I bet it's pretty. How old is she?" Jan kept touching, light caresses, fingers dragging over his skin.

"Seventeen, now. She's fixin' to graduate. She wants to go to TWU." He was proud of her, damn proud. Hell, the whole family was.

"Oh, good for her. College wasn't really my friend. It wasn't so much the reading as the exams and the research." Jan took a step, moving them together toward the counter, and reached up for a mug while he was talking. "I did eventually graduate, but from a small local college and it took me six years, summers and everything. They were great there though, I got lots of help."

"We are all homeschooled. One of my brothers wanted to try college, but they were too busy rodeoing." He'd never even considered college, but he really hadn't considered living beyond retirement, to be honest.

"Well your mom did a good job. You're a smart one." Jan put a mug in his hand. "Put that on the ledge thing and the brew button is right on top. It's a triangle."

He got things going, listening to the bubbling of the water. He knew this part. It was the sound of every modern, not too fancy hotel room.

Jan rested their heads together. "I want you to get around easily and feel comfortable, so you ask when you want to know where something is or need help and I'll show you. I don't mind at all. I don't mind doing things for you either. Okay?"

"I've haven't had to learn a place with someone else with me in a long, long time." Maybe since he could see a lot better than he did now. "It's a little...shit, I want to be the hottest, most macho bastard you've ever seen."

"Oh, baby." A growl rumbled in Jan's chest. He heard it, and he could feel it against his back. "You are the hottest, most macho bastard on the *planet*. Even better, you're *my* hot bastard."

"Kiss me?" He lifted his chin, not looking for hot sex, but something way more rare—care.

Jan turned him without a word, held his face in both hands and kissed him—deep and gentle—like he *mattered*.

He needed this—a few breaths of being someone normal, another rodeo cowboy in love. Just another guy in a huge city holding his man.

"How was that?" Jan took his fingers and touched them to smiling lips.

"Just what I needed, darlin'." He explored, tracing the curve of January's smile, fingertips catching on the tiny hairs of Jan's mustache stubble.

"Scratchy. Doesn't take me long." Jan turned and rubbed a scratchy chin along his fingers. "Finish the coffee. I'll call in some pizza."

"It's hot. I'm excited about the pizza." He found another mug, replaced pods, started another cup. "Where's the trash?"

"Oh it's... okay. If you're facing the coffee maker and you turn all the way around, it's to the left of the island... maybe, three feet away?" Jan stepped away, giving him room.

Turn around. Find the island. Take four normal-sized steps. "Here?"

He'd hunt around, but garbage. Ew.

"Close, it's got a foot thing to open it... step your left foot forward."

"Oh cool." The lid clanged, he found it, and dumped the pod in, then he threw the other one away and got his mug.

Now, the living room was out and to the left. The sofa was to the right then. "Is there a coffee table, darlin'?"

"Yes. It's square. Knee height. Glass top. It's between the couch and the TV."

Okay, that sounded like he had to be crazy careful because he had no way to see the edge of that. He found the sofa and stayed right there, moving with tiny steps.

"You can't see it at all, huh? You're fine, take another step toward me." Jan took his hand as he got close and bent with him so he could feel the table.

"You ever put a T-shirt over your face and tried to look through it? That's sort of my sight right now." It got worse as the nerves calcified. Eventually, it would be all over.

"That's a lot worse than you make it seem most of the time. That's impressive." Jan sat, coffee mug clinking onto the glass-top table. "And it's been like that your whole life?"

"I had the cord around my neck when I was born, so it's always been a thing. It's getting worse, slowly, but it's steady enough that I do okay." He toodled along, best he could.

"Okay. You'll be fine here in a few days I'm sure. You need to learn your way around. Do you want your glasses? Or ice for your shoulder, or meds or anything?"

"I'm good. So, what do you usually do on a Sunday night?" He was usually coming in to somewhere—either home or a hotel or a friend's. His life was totally different from most rodeo cowboys because he wasn't getting in his truck or his trailer.

"Jax and I hang out on Sundays. We watch baking shows

mostly, but lately we've been watching this hot cowboy ride bulls." Jan laughed. "Jax gets all wound up. It's pretty funny."

"I can't wait to meet him." He sounded like an important part of January's life, and everyone needed a great friend.

God knew he had one. He sure hoped Charlie got better in a hurry. Mainly for Ben, but for him too.

"Have you heard about Charlie's surgery? Is he out?"

"They didn't do it. They sent him home, and he's sleeping. Ben says he goes back in Monday." He wrapped his hands around his coffee cup so he had something to hold onto. Saying it out loud made it sound so much worse.

Jan's hand rested on his knee. "Did Ben say why not?"

"He didn't say." Hawk hadn't asked, either. He didn't want to make anything worse. "I'm sure—"

What? What was he sure of? Charlie never took naps. Charlie always answered the phone.

"Everyone is probably tired. Maybe call again tomorrow." The hand on his thigh got heavier and Jan leaned close. "Is it hard not to be there?"

"No. No, all the family is on the way. Everyone's scared and tense. I didn't need to be there complicating the world, hurt and one-handed." He did know the house though.

"He's your best friend. Any time you want to go back, I'll go with you. We can stay out of the way stay in a hotel." Jan sighed. "I'm sure everything will be fine, but I wanted you to know—"

"Thank you. We might need to. He's important, right? Like the best friend I've ever had that wasn't my brother."

Jan nodded and took a second to reply. "Like Jax."

Yeah. Jan understood because Jan had a best friend too. And like Charlie, Jax wasn't anyone Hawk needed to be jealous of, he was Jan's family.

"Just like." He sighed and shook his head. "We've all

known cowboys that had to retire because of injury, but I want him to feel better."

"He'll have his surgery, and then he will, right? He has to retire, but he has Ben and they'll be fine." Jan combed a hand through his hair. "He's lucky. He has Ben, family, you... he'll have a good life after he retires."

"Yeah. Yeah, he will. He'll work Ben's ranch, build it up. Enjoy the music." He didn't want to think about retiring. He wanted to die on the arena floor in a blaze of glory. It was so much better than the idea of sitting and waiting for things to happen at one of his brother's.

"Exactly. Now we have to figure your retirement out."

"Me? That's a hard thought, huh?" It was like January had heard him, seen his worry.

"I know. You told me you were worried about going home and sitting for forty years. I think you can probably do better than that." Jan sipped his coffee, the scent strong in his nose.

"Maybe. At least I—" He closed his mouth, because at least what? He rode bulls. That job led to two things—announcing or breeding bulls. Neither one of those were a thing for him. He needed to ride and make money.

"At least you...? How does the rest of that sentence go? Does it have my name in it?"

"The rest goes 'have saved most of my money'. I got no skills that anyone will pay for, but bull riding." He closed his eyes. "So, my retirement plans are sorta dim."

Dim.

Like super dim.

God, he was funny.

"Hm. I didn't hear my name." Jan leaned close and whispered, "Try one more time."

"Oh, darlin', I want to be someone you want to spend a long time with."

"That's better." Jan kissed his chin. "See? Your plans got less dim."

He wasn't sure about that, but it wasn't worth talking about. He wasn't retiring.

"Okay. What do you know you want to do while you're here? Is there something you know you'd like to visit? I want to do some sightseeing with you."

"Take me all the places you love to go, darlin'." He'd have to figure this out.

"What's on your list though? Empire State Building? Statue of Liberty? Times Square? We'll probably go to them all. We'll have to get out of the apartment, right? I'll try to teach you how to get around."

"I'll figure it out. I'm a smart dog. This is the biggest city I've tried in, but I can do it. No worries." He needed a little time.

"I'm not worried."

The door chimed and Jan gave his knee a pat. "Pizza. I'll get the door." Jan got up.

"Good deal." January didn't have to be worried. He could manage that, and whatever was left? Momma had worrying *down*.

He heard a buzzer and Jan opened the door. "There are paper plates in the middle drawer to the left of the sink."

"Okay." He stood up and headed to the kitchen, forcing himself to look calm and cool. He'd done this a thousand times—fake it 'til he made it. He wasn't stoned any more. Hell, he was about as clear as he could be, the pain smoothing everything out.

La la la end of sofa. La la la beginning of hall. Kitchen.

Oh, ow. Okay. Island. Fuck. Left of the sink and the second drawer. Who kept plates in a drawer?

"Oh, this smells so good. Did you find the plates okay?" Jan joined him in the kitchen along with the smell of melted cheese. "My stomach is growling now."

"I did. Smells amazing." He put two paper plates on the island. "You need anything else?"

"Maybe a beer? I keep them in the fridge door. I can get it, you're probably sick of me testing your sense of direction. You want one?"

"Yeah. I'll take it." It would take the edge off.

"You know where the garbage can was? If you face that and take a hard left you walk right into the kitchen table... maybe four steps. Have a seat, I'll bring dinner over." He heard Jan open the fridge.

He nodded and tried to remember where the garbage was. The garbage was away from all the windows, but that didn't help him now. He followed the island to the end, praying silently.

Please God, I'm tired. I'm real tired and worried and my arm hurts like a stone-cold bitch. I like this man, more than I ought, so please. Please. Let me figure it. Let me find this table without hurting myself or embarrassing either one of us. In Jesus's name. Amen.

He got an answer, but not one he was expecting. What he got was a hand, grasping his steady and sure, that led him to the table. "I've got you."

"Thank you." He thought about apologizing, but he didn't think that was what January needed to hear. "It smells so good."

"Beer. It's open." January set it down on the table. "I'll grab us pizza."

"I might have a whole piece." He chuckled at himself. He

was either starving or he never wanted to eat again, he wasn't sure.

Jan laughed and put a slice down in front of him. "I dare you."

Hawk cackled and nodded. "I can take that dare. I've been looking forward to this."

He waited for Jan to settle, and then he dug in, humming happily after the first bite.

"I'm giving you meds and tucking your cowboy butt back into bed after you eat."

"You are? Are you coming with me and fucking my lips?" In this, he felt like he was on equal ground. Seduction and happy sex was in his wheelhouse.

Jan shook his head. "No, baby. You look like death, and you need some rest. I'll snuggle though."

"I don't mind a good snuggle. Give me a day or two—I'll be all better." He was swaying a little, under the weight of the world.

"Uh-huh. I'm not in a rush. You have healing to do. If this is a long-haul kind of thing between us, then we have time to breathe. We need to get you healed right and back on a bull."

He nodded. Yeah. He needed to be back in three weeks, whether or not things were knit. He needed his ranking.

"I'll come. That first weekend you're back. I'll be there." Jan took a bite of his pizza. "Mmm."

"Sounds like a plan." He got a bite in, humming low in his chest. Oh, that was like greasy, gooey, spicy heaven.

"Good right? New York pizza is the best. What's your favorite back home?"

"Momma makes one that's breakfast sausage and onions." They didn't have delivery stuff where he was from. "It's spicy and rich. The crust though? This is like heaven."

"Mmm. It is. So what's Momma's specialty? When you go home, what does she make for you?"

"When I'm not dieting? She makes me pork chops and mashed potatoes with green beans and gravy. I love gravy."

"Sounds good. She can feed me any time. I'm going to grab another slice." Jan got up. "I'd offer you one but you're going to turn me down."

"Is there a little one? I didn't eat yesterday at all, so..."

"You're making me happy." Jan brought him a slice. "That's the smallest. It's okay if you don't finish it. Just have what you want."

"This is amazing. I could eat this every day." Every goddamn day until he was the size of a house.

"I admit it's a weakness. You'll have to try ramen while you're here, that's Jax's favorite. He can eat his body weight of the stuff. Which, granted, isn't much more than you probably, but still."

"Like noodles?" He liked ramen noodles. They were quick and he could do them himself, but it seemed like an odd choice for a favorite.

"Yeah, noodles. In a yummy Japanese broth with veggies and pork. It's good. It kind of feels like comfort food."

"I've had the ones with the chicken packet."

Jan chuckled. "Not quite the same thing. You'll see." Jan leaned back in his chair, beer in one hand. "That was really good. I haven't had pizza in a while."

"It was. Thank you. Do I need to give you some cash for my part or should I buy the next one?"

"Oh... you can get the next one, I guess. I wasn't... it's pizza." January set down the beer and scooped up their plates.

And now he'd twisted January all up. He reached out, pleased when he caught his lover's wrist. "Hey, honey, we've never been anywhere not a hotel. We got to figure out the bits and bobs of staying together."

January lifted his hand and kissed it. "I know. I'm sorry. That caught me off guard. I never thought about money, I wanted to buy you dinner. But you're right, we have things to work out, and a lot of it won't be easy-breezy like I'd like it to be."

"You did buy me the best pizza ever." He was full as a tick and so tired and happy and hurting and Lord have mercy, it didn't seem right that a man could feel so many things at once.

"Good. So make me happy and let me say this one was on me. We can keep score starting with the next one." January snorted, but was teasing him, he heard it in his lover's voice. "Your painkillers should love that beer. I think you should let yourself sleep as long as you like. When I thought you'd only be here for a week, I cleared my calendar so I'm not going anywhere. Tomorrow we can have a marathon of Oscar winners or something... eat popcorn and be judgmental."

"That sounds like a perfect day." He did okay with movies, and if he missed something, with Jan he could ask.

"Do people usually tell you what's going on, or do you guess?"

"Depends. If I'm home or at Charlie's, I ask. Otherwise I fake it if I can't figure it out. I'm pretty good, though." He leveraged himself up out of the chair. "Commercials are way harder to follow than shows or movies because they move so fast."

"I hate them. We can make out during the commercials." Jan caught his elbow. "I think I left your meds in the living room. Let me clean up in here, and then I'll go find them."

"Do you need help?" He hoped not, but he would do what he needed to.

"No, thanks. I'm going to wrap the pizza up. It'll take a second." He heard the foil and then Jan put the leftovers in the fridge. "Midnight snack."

"Yum. I'm in." He thought it might be worth it to sneak a piece actually. "Did you want to lounge on the sofa or the bed?"

"Wherever you're going to sleep better. Bed, you think? I'll get you some more ice too if you want." Jan pressed the bottle of painkillers into his hand. "How often do we need to rewrap your ribs? Does a doctor need to do it? I'll take you to mine." There was a pause and Jan laughed. "Sorry. I've been trying not to mother you, honest."

"It's kind of you. I'll have you tape me up after my shower tomorrow. I know enough to holler if they aren't stable." He grinned. He didn't intend to suffer with a collapsed lung if he didn't have to. Those hurt. "If I tell you I need a hospital, it'll be the truth."

"Okay, I won't nag. Probably. I'm clueless, I've never broken anything at all, let alone something big like a shoulder or ribs. I know you're going to be the tough cowboy, but it sounds awful to me."

"The shoulder's tender now, so it makes the rib easier to deal with. If I sneeze, I might lose my mind a little."

"Oh, man. No sneezing." Jan took him by the arm. "Bathroom, ditch the jeans, bed. Maybe a less than perfectly chaste kiss."

"I'd love that." Making out with January was toward the top of his list of favorite things to do.

Jan took time to help him get undressed, hands curious and warm as they moved over his skin. "Are you keeping the sling on? Or do you want to prop it up?"

"Can I have both?" The sling was on for at least a few weeks, and he knew it. Propping it would make snoozing easier for sure.

"You can have anything you want, lover." Jan purred and helped him into bed, made him take his pills, then started gathering pillows for him.

"Have I mentioned that I'm so happy to be here?" Like stupidly.

Jan stripped and climbed in next to him. "Yeah. A couple of times. I'm very happy myself. Have I mentioned how good you look in my bed?"

"Possibly, but you can absolutely tell me again."

"It's like a fantasy come true, to have someone as beautiful as you are in my bed." January snuck a quick kiss.

"Oh, doesn't that sound good." He had to smile, had to, because he felt that and he needed to. "Thank you, darlin'."

"I do like that smile, cowboy. Even when it's a little drunk on painkillers. It warms me right up." Jan turned the TV on and tuned in to some baking show. It was good of him to remember.

"You're good to me." He snuggled right in, going to split the difference between careful and remember I'm still sexy.

"Well, I love you. I hear that's what happens. You start being good to each other." Jan held him, so careful. "I don't know what you keep telling yourself in your head, but all I want is for you to heal. I want you to rest. Sleep as long as you need, don't worry about being a guest... you're not. You belong here. I want you to feel like you're home."

"You know, I've lived in the same room my whole life. I mean, the same room and a thousand hotel rooms." He settled in deeper. "I assumed I'd be sitting there forever."

"Believe me, I am as surprised and pleased as you are to have you here. I am not taking one second of it for granted."

He could hear Jan's heart beating strong under his ear. "I want to do this right."

"Me too. Can-can I ask you something?" Oh Jesus, Hawk. Shut up.

"Sure. Anything." Jan looked at him seriously. "What do you want to know?"

He closed his eyes, forcing himself to ask the question he didn't want to ask. "It's never going to get better. You know that, right? I mean, my eyes. They'll never get better, just worse. I'm not sure if I was clear about that, and I need to make sure you know."

Jan leaned in and took another kiss from him, this one slow as they traded breath. "I assumed they would get worse. It doesn't scare me, or worry me, as long as you're willing to accept my help."

"It scares me, a little, but..." Part of him was excited. Part of him was tickled shitless by the idea of not faking it one day, maybe learning Braille or getting a dog. He wanted to learn how to do things, but he couldn't. Not now.

"You'll have to retire." Jan went straight to the point there, didn't he?

It stung, but not as bad as he'd expected it to. "Eventually. Sooner than later—I'm not young anymore, I'm not seeing like I used to, and it's hard to lie all the time."

"Okay, angel. We know what eventually looks like. We don't have to worry it to death now, hm? Right now, you're hurt but you're having a great season, and you're still the Champ."

"I am. I got another Finals in me. I know it." He needed a couple weeks to heal up. "But right now, I'm going to learn about ramen and your favorite coffee shop and New York."

Jan smiled against his cheek. "No one said healing up

couldn't be fun too. Close your eyes. Rest up. I'm here now, and I'll be here for eventually too."

"I love you. When I retire, I'm going to eat one of them cake roll deals like on TV, I swear to God." He closed his eyes and listened. "I'm gonna eat two."

January's laughter wrapped around him, and he let the pain pill take him away.

18

Four days in and things were getting easier, Hawk was learning his way around the apartment, and January was learning what things he needed to do to make Hawk more comfortable. That glass coffee table needed to go, for one thing, to be replaced by something sturdy and dark enough to contrast with the lighter floor under it so Hawk could make it out.

He was glad he was really good with details too; he'd had to pay attention. He'd learned some crazy things in the last few days. Like, rule number one, *Don't Move Things*. Put the shampoo and body wash back in the same place and in the same order in the shower. Don't switch the cans of Dr Pepper and the beer in the fridge, or the OJ and the milk. Push chairs in. Nothing like pouring OJ on your cereal.

Some issues were more complicated though, and he was still trying to find the line between helping Hawk and being overbearing. But like Hawk said, it was all part of getting to know one another. He was trying to be patient.

But.

Or should he say *butt*.

Four days of living with a hot cowboy who was on the injured list was *killing* him. January could hardly walk by Hawk without visions of taking his lover on the couch, over the kitchen table, in the shower... and in his bed. The three nights since Hawk's arrival might actually have been even harder than the days.

Harder. Ha.

And what was the matter with him? Hawk needed to heal, and he knew the cowboy couldn't afford a setback. Personally, January thought he'd be fine if Hawk never rode again, but Hawk was an athlete and defined himself as a bull rider. It was important. And who was he kidding? He liked being the guy in the stands; he got off on being the guy that the Champion took home in a limo after a show. He might miss it when it was over, but for now, he was going to enjoy every second.

Fuck. That was not the train of thought he needed to be on.

"Darlin'? Can you come give me a hand, please?" Hawk didn't sound distressed, so January figured his cowboy had given up putting on his boots by himself. Finally.

He put his coffee mug down on the kitchen counter and made his way into the bedroom to see what was up. "You okay?"

January walked into the bedroom, blinking at the sight of his cowboy, naked and spread out on his bed, good hand working his cock. Oh. Oh, that was pretty.

He swallowed hard as he moved toward the bed. "Oh. I don't know if I should help you. You look like you've got this. Maybe I should let you handle it."

He had zero intention of not joining in; his mouth was already watering.

"No? You aren't feeling like rescuing me?" Hawk stroked

again, base to tip, showing off. "My poor needy cock? I haven't tasted you in days. I need you, darlin'."

"Days? It's been almost two whole weeks." He shucked his sweats, careful of his own prick, which was happy as fuck to be let out to play. He moved between Hawk's knees and bent to have a taste, bathing the head as Hawk stroked himself. "Mmm. Missed that."

"Yeah. I need you, darlin'. Sleeping so close and not being able to love on you is hell." Hawk stroked, finding him another clear drop to lap up.

"Fuck, yes. I was thinking exactly the same thing." He'd climbed out of bed before he could embarrass himself this morning. He covered Hawk's fingers with his own at first, then pushed his lover's hand away. "I got this."

"Mmm, sounds perfect, darlin'." Hawk spread wider, that sweet belly rippling.

"God, I want you." January slid one hand up over those abs and went hunting Hawk's balls with his tongue.

"I'm all yours. Lock, stock, and barrel." Hawk's voice got huskier and lower as January licked and touched.

"I like the sound of that." He tasted and teased. His mind and his cock were already five steps ahead, looking forward to taking Hawk's lips like he'd wanted to since the cowboy walked through his door.

"I need you, darlin'. Like breathing." Hawk groaned and pressed up with his hips, rocking in a careful, easy wave.

"Got you." January took Hawk slowly, an inch at a time, deeper into this mouth and toward his throat, tongue working up and down the shaft.

He slipped his hands under Hawk's ass and eased the sweet prick in deeper. January was addicted to the soft, hungry sounds each suck earned him.

He picked up the pace as he took Hawk in. Jan intended

to drive his cowboy wild, barely give Hawk time to breathe, and send him flying. He squeezed that perfect ass and held on.

Hawk grunted, one leg drawing up, muscles taut and hard. The heavy balls drew up, and he knew his cowboy was close.

He knew it wouldn't take long. Hell, he was halfway there himself and no one had touched him yet. He knew Hawk's low, understated sounds meant more than they seemed... such a stoic cowboy.

He hummed around the head and swallowed, then shifted one hand so he could press his thumb over Hawk's tight hole.

"Yes!" Oh, that was a lovely sound, honest and pure sex.

Yes. His own need flared, making him moan and a hungry heat spread through him. He pressed harder with his thumb, stretching that hole and showed Hawk's pretty cock no mercy, driving his tongue through the slit before taking it deep again.

"Fuck. Fuck me. Love. I need you. I'm fixin' to..." Incoherence was an amazing thing.

"Mmm." He hummed, knowing how that vibration felt, and pushed his thumb inside his lover fast and hard right up to the knuckle.

Hawk's body went rock hard, and the desperate cry heralded the wild orgasm, Hawk filling his lips with seed.

My stoic cowboy. God, he fucking loved that he could do this to Hawk. If it weren't for the promise of Hawk's mouth he'd have happily stroked off watching Hawk come down from that beautiful high.

But now he wanted. "Hawk."

Hawk grinned at him, the look wicked and sated all at

once, then crooked one finger at him in the universal come-hither gesture.

That look was everything. He may be a blur to Hawk right now, but he could see that sexy smile clearly.

Jan started to move but Hawk must have read his mind when he hesitated and directed him with a gesture to one side so he was clear of Hawk's broken shoulder. He had to grin, marveling at the way his lover had this all figured out like he'd done it before. Hawk probably had.

He caught his prick in one hand, exhaling heavily at his own touch, and tapped the head against Hawk's waiting lips. "So hot, cowboy." Even injured. Maybe even more because of it. He didn't stop to examine that thought, though, he simply enjoyed the view.

"All yours." The soft words seemed bigger, huge, because they were so quiet, so tender, almost like they weren't intended for his ears.

"Need you, angel." Jan combed his fingers through Hawk's hair and around to the back of his head, cradling it as he teased Hawk's lips open and pushed into his lover's mouth. The heat felt so good. "Oh. Oh, Fuck. Hawk."

Hawk's good hand wrapped around his ass cheek and pulled him in. That was pure hunger for him.

He rocked his hips, moving carefully as he got his balance and the angle just right. Hawk didn't seem to care if it was wrong or right and hauled on his ass, begging for more. His control wasn't going to hold out long if his lover kept that up. But that was probably Hawk's goal. Jesus. His lover was as hungry now as he had ever been.

Hawk pulled at him, head bobbing and letting him in, deeper and deeper.

He grunted and let go, knowing that Hawk could take it... and wanted it. He gripped the headboard hard with one hand as fire swirled in him and settled deep into his balls and took everything Hawk was offering, thrusting, cock sliding against a raspy, hungry tongue.

Hawk swallowed around him, throat squeezing the tip of his prick, the pressure threatening to blow the top of his head right off.

"Close. Fuck, baby." He said that, and babbled a bunch of other things, and didn't care if he sounded like he was out of his mind. He was. Every nerve tingled, his skin was on fire, and then suddenly he was shooting. It felt like all the oxygen had left the room. His vision tunneled and a freight train roared in his ears.

All the while Hawk swallowed and hummed, making the sensations go on and on.

He hung over Hawk until he stopped shaking, then shifted his weight and stretched out along Hawk's good side. "Wow."

"Mmm. So much better. I was fixin' to die from needing you." Hawk was a master snuggler.

He could handle a snuggle. God, that mouth. Hawk had wrung him out. "Yeah, I hear that. You were starting to make my mouth water like a cartoon steak."

"I was losing my mind. Thank you." Hawk cupped his cock, squeezed him gently. "Now I can be all logical and shit."

He laughed gently, feeling so much more relaxed. "No pressure."

"See, you understand. I needed that in a ridiculous way."

"Can I come give you a hand?" He snickered. "That was a good one. I was not saying no to that invitation. You looked delicious." Seriously, how did he land this cowboy? The man looked so good in his sheets.

"I thought you might take me up on it, since it was such a good offer."

"Best offer I've had in a long while." He threaded his fingers in between Hawk's. "So, now that you can think clearly, do you want to go out today? Are you feeling up to a little wandering?"

"Sounds like a great plan. I'm interested to explore, find out about your world." Hawk didn't even hesitate. He was lit up, face wreathed with smiles. "Me and my sling are ready to go. Well, once I cover my naked bod."

"Mmm. Hold off on that for another minute. I'm enjoying your naked bod." Like, a lot. "It's going to be cold out there. Do we need to get you warm stuff? I probably have scarves and gloves you can use."

"I have my good leather jacket with me, but I'd so take a scarf and a pair of gloves, especially for sling-hand here." Hawk wiggled his fingers playfully.

He laughed. "Poor chilly sling-hand. We'll get coffee and muffins or something on the way out. Surely you can eat something. Maybe one of those sous vide things with the egg whites?"

"I want you to get a bagel so I can try it! I'm in New York." Hawk's laugh was a thing of beauty.

"Excellent. There's a place across the street from Starbucks. My favorites are the everything bagels. I'll get one with a schmear and you can take bites." Now his mouth was watering. Everything bagel, hot coffee, hot lover. Perfect day. Maybe he'd text Jax too and see about the weekend.

"I'm so in. I have always wanted to know if bagels here are different. Always."

"Of course they are. They are better here than anywhere." Spoken like a true New Yorker. Pizza was better. Bagels were better. These things were facts. And those facts made his stomach growl, driving him out of bed. Again. He rolled and sat up. "Time to put something on that hot bod."

"Mmhmm. Jeans, undies, socks, boots, shirt. Bingo."

"Hat?" Jan took Hawk's hand and tugged it, giving him some help up.

"That's a given, darlin'. I have my gimme cap and my Stetson." Hawk got carefully to his feet.

"All right then. You good? You need any help?"

"I'll beg a hand with my shirt." Hawk's grin was irresistible; the twinkling eyes might not work well, but they were beautifully expressive.

"I might be looking forward to that." He dug out some jeans and a T-shirt, then went looking for a hoodie. Good coffee and a soft, fresh bagel sounded so good; his stomach was starting to growl at him.

Hawk managed to get his jeans and boots on, whistling like a little bird as he worked on getting dressed. January was learning that there was rarely silence in Hawk's world.

It made sense. His strongest sense was hearing; it was how he got his bearings and the only convenient way to entertain himself. Maybe Hawk's second life was in music. "How did you learn to whistle like that? I'm terrible. I'm lucky to stay on key."

"I had no idea. I've been doing it forever. Does it bug you?" Hawk ran his fingers through his hair, smoothing it out.

"No, I like it." He reached for Hawk and pretended to help, but really wanted to get his own fingers in Hawk's hair.

"Oh, that feels damn fine." Hawk hummed and leaned into his hands. "That's sweet."

"You have great hair. It's soft. I love that you're so tough and hard but soft and gentle too."

"I'm multilayered." Hawk chuckled softly. "Man, that makes my eyes cross. You have the best hands."

He leaned in, surprising Hawk with a kiss, then pulled away chuckling. "Shirt. Before we end up in bed all day." Not that that would suck. But they had all night too. "Oh, maybe I'll take you to my bar tonight."

"I have been known to enjoy a bar or two." Hawk eased off the sling, the bruises had gone from deep to ugly now, covering his lover's torso. "Help a guy out?"

"Yeah." He took the sling and helped with the rest of the Velcro, then slid the arm of Hawk's shirt on carefully. He brushed his thumb over one perky nipple on the way by. "Any excuse to get my hands on you."

"I can live with that. The way you need to touch. Especially the way you need to touch me."

"We're compatible that way, it's good." He got the shirt over Hawk's good arm and did up the buttons, then helped with the sling. So many fussy bits. "You look great."

"Thank you, darlin'. I feel pretty goddamn fabulous. And hungry. Let's do this thing."

He scooped up Hawk's glasses and put them in Hawk's hand. "Gloves... come on." He led the way back to the living room and opened the closet near the door. "Don't want your fingers to freeze."

"Nope." Hawk leaned close, nuzzling his jaw. "Because that would be achy on your nuts."

"No kidding. They're shriveling just thinking about it." He gave Hawk's ass a squeeze and reached for an extra scarf and some gloves.

"No shrivels. Is shrivels even a word?"

"Put those on, dork." He laughed and put his own scarf on, pulled on his coat and grabbed his keys. "Bagels, ho." Once they headed out the door, he locked up and took Hawk's hand for the walk down the hall to the elevator.

"You ain't worried about getting in trouble? It's a safe neighborhood?"

Oh, wow. Jan hadn't even thought to talk to Hawk about the city. He squeezed Hawk's hand. "Well, if you're worried, I took your hand because you had trouble seeing in this dark hallway the other day. But it's a safe city, mostly. I never worry. I don't want to make you uncomfortable though."

"I'm not worried. Don't want you to get in trouble, and I'm not in the best shape for a fistfight today. Maybe tomorrow." Hawk squeezed his fingers tight.

"We're good. Especially in the touristy places, you'll see. It's a whole different world here." He pulled Hawk onto the elevator and tucked an arm around his lover's waist. "Believe it or not, I can throw a punch or two if I have to." He didn't, usually. He avoided confrontation if he could. But he'd stand up for Hawk if he needed to.

As if he'd have to. Ha. Hawk could probably kick his ass and two others at the same time, even without perfect sight. It sounded impossible, but he believed it.

It was chilly on the sidewalk, but the sun was out, the morning bright and the sky blue. "It's a perfect city winter day, wow. Sun!"

"Man, you're built like a brick shit house. I bet you could tear somebody up." Hawk snuggled right into his side. "This is amazing. I do love me some sunshine."

"Me too. This is a great day." And it felt great having his arm around Hawk on his turf, in his town, on the way to his coffee shop. He could get used to this.

He was smiling as he got the door for Hawk and kept a hand on his lover's waist to steer him through the door and toward the short line counter.

"Oh, that is an amazing smell. Wow." Hawk lifted his head and inhaled deep.

"This place is like a second home. I'm here a lot, I like to sit over by the window and watch people walk by. I don't bring people here very often though... I don't have many overnight guests."

"I'm more than an overnight guest, darlin'. I'm your cowboy."

He felt those words in his chest. "Damn. Yes, you are. Ever kissed a man in public?"

"No, sir. Want to pop my cherry?" Hawk's smile could light the entire city.

"Damn right I do." He took Hawk's face in both hands and gave him a quick, hard kiss. He followed that with a slower one, then let Hawk go, smiling back. "Boom."

"Mmm, now that didn't hurt one little bit." Hawk's laugh had the people in the coffeeshop turning to look and stare.

"Where'd you find the cowboy, Jan?" Dana, one of the weekday morning baristas grinned at him from behind the counter.

"At the rodeo, where else?"

Dana laughed. "You're too much."

"Hawk, this is Dana. She makes the best coffee in the city."

"Hello, Miss Dana. Pleased to meet you." Hawk nodded and grinned at Dana. "Tell me what your absolutely favorite drink to make is."

Dana answered like she's been waiting all day for Hawk to ask. "I make a killer mocha. Just enough chocolate but not too sweet. Highly recommend an extra shot and a dash of whipped cream."

He laughed. It was possible that many calories would send Hawk into a coma.

"Oh lord. I wouldn't be able to eat for two days, maybe three. When I'm not in training, I'd love to try it." Hawk grinned. "How about a quad espresso?"

Dana laughed. "Well, all right, cowboy. One rocket to the moon coming right up." She didn't even ask what he wanted, went to make their coffees. Another young woman whose name he didn't know rang them up and he started to pay but hesitated to see if Hawk wanted to.

Hawk pulled out his wallet and handed over his credit card, a huge piece of tape at the bottom. There was a nice amount of cash in there too, all paper clipped together.

Maybe it was nosy to ask, but he was curious. "You have a system there, huh? In your wallet?"

"Yeah. The cash money is tagged—my folks or Charlie does that for me, the credit cards have different shapes cut in the tape. My ID has a notch cut out of it." Hawk shrugged and gave him a sheepish grin. "This way, if I panic, I got a system."

"I think it's brilliant. But hopefully, you don't need to panic." Was it weird that he was hoping the job Hawk's parents or Charlie did would fall to him? He wanted to be trusted that way, to be someone Hawk relied on.

"Yeah. I got a bunch of things I do to make it easier. Some you've seen. I bet it seems a little weird."

"I don't know. I've never seen anyone do that with their wallet. It's not weird really, it's clever. Coping skills are good. I'm surprised at the things I wouldn't have thought about."

"Thanks." Hawk took his coffee and added a Sweet n Low. "I do okay, I think. I have my shit together."

"You do." He took his latte and hung out close to Hawk. "I'm really impressed. You've totally got this. And I guess you have to, since you travel alone so much."

"Yeah." A hint of worry crossed Hawk's face, disappearing quickly.

That worry could mean anything, his lover was a worrier. But he was fairly sure Hawk wasn't about him. Just in case, he cupped Hawk's cheek and kissed the other one. "Less alone now. You ready for a couple of bites of my bagel?"

"I am!" Hawk pinked, one hand coming to rest against his belly, solid and heavy. "I like this random kisses thing. I like it a lot, darlin'."

"Me too. It's nice to have you close enough we can." He fussed with Hawk's scarf, tucking it in for no real reason except that he could, then left the coffee shop feeling in love. More than he'd ever been. He was so stupid happy there might as well be little birds singing around his head.

Thankfully there weren't, Hawk's cowboy hat was getting them enough attention. He was good with that, he felt like showing his man off a little.

They crossed the street and for the first time he noticed the warning chimes as the time counted down to zero. Jesus, a Manhattan crosswalk must be terrifying without being able to see. "You thought the coffee shop smelled good, wait until you get a sniff in here." He pulled open the door and ushered Hawk in ahead of him.

"I can't wait. I—Whoa. Oh, tell me everything."

He hummed happily. "Okay. There's a bakery case straight ahead with a gazillion bagels. Ready?" He read them off, like a radio announcer. "Plain, cinnamon raisin, asiago, blueberry, sesame, whole wheat, pumpernickel, chocolate chip, poppy seed, french toast, garlic, salt, marble, onion, sundried tomato, jalapeno..." He took an exaggerated breath. "And my personal favorite, the everything bagel."

"Oh, can we try all of them? I mean, since we have time?" Hawk looked like a cowboy in a candy store.

"Maybe I'll pick up a dozen on Sunday morning for Jax and we can have a taste test. We won't have time to try them all... you'll have to come back and visit me again." They stepped up to the counter and he ordered an everything with a light schmear.

Hawk waited for him, sipping his coffee, patient and quiet, paying attention to everything.

"Listening?" He pulled Hawk down to the pick-up counter to wait for their bagel. "You can get sandwiches here too. BLT on a bagel. Bagel, egg and bacon. Tuna bagel. Hot pastrami. I could eat here every meal."

"Cool. I have places like that all over the country. It's always so much to go back and have a favorite. It smells amazing."

"Next time I'm at a show take me to one." He grabbed the little brown bag with his bagel in it and hauled it out, slipping it partially out of the wrapper. "Okay. Open up, cowboy."

Hawk trusted him, lips parting, one hand sliding up his arm to steady them both.

Jan stuck the bagel in Hawk's mouth and held it steady. "It's chewy, bite hard." He had to giggle watching Hawk bite and rip at it with his teeth.

Hawk chewed hard, the strangest concentrated look on his face.

He took a bite for himself, the onion and poppy seeds and cream cheese making him happy. "Mmm. Well?"

"There's so many flavors—garlic, onion, cream cheese, little crunchy bits, and then the bread. I think I would like it with a big slice of tomato."

"Yeah. And have you ever had lox?"

Hawk tilted his head, obviously confused. "Like combination ones?"

Jan laughed. "No, baby. Lox is really thinly sliced raw salmon. It's salt-cured. You like fish? It's yummy."

"I like fish. I love baked haddock and fried anything. I like sushi too, but not in a restaurant. I don't like that at all."

"No?" *Where else do you have sushi?* "You make your own?"

"Shee-it, no. Can you imagine me going to Momma—who does not allow me to touch the stove, thank you—and asking her to make sushi?" Hawk's eyes were huge, then he grinned, and the look was wicked. "Close your eyes a second."

"Okay." He closed his eyes. "Why am I doing this?"

"Just for a second. Now imagine trying to eat little fally apart bits with all these different sauces with two *sticks*." The disgust in Hawk's voice proved there was a story there. "Like *that*."

Fally apart bits. Adorable. "Hmm. Sounds like a challenge to me." He grinned, teasing. It actually made a lot of sense. "You don't have to use the chopsticks, dork. Can I open my eyes now?"

"You can. And I love sushi in a hotel room. Assuming that some asshole friend doesn't put all the washatabi goo in the soy sauce. I like some, not all."

"Wasabi. Oh, this has to be a good story. Come on, let's walk and you can tell me." He dumped all the paper and took the bagel and his coffee. "Another bite?"

"Just one. It tastes good, but I'm trying to hold my glass and walk and chew and know your gorgeous ass is within reach."

"Rub your tummy and pat your head?" He waved the bagel under Hawk's nose.

"That's the secret to life, darlin'." Hawk took a bite, this one a lot more sure.

"I guess." He took Hawk's free hand and curled it around his arm, tucking the cowboy right up next to him. "All this sun, we need to be outside. Let's hit up Central Park, want to?"

"I'm all yours. Take me and show me things." So easy. So eager.

He started thinking, planning as they walked toward the subway. He ate his bagel and didn't talk much, Jan wanted Hawk to hear what he couldn't see. The lady walking her dog, the bicycle passing them headed uptown against traffic on Second Avenue. The random conversation and the car horns. He'd thought about this a lot before Hawk even arrived for a visit—how to help someone appreciate a city known for the view from high places and all the things to "see".

They could take a cab, but he thought stop and go traffic might be disorienting. On a train Hawk could count stops and listen to the announcements. Learn his way around a little.

Maybe.

Or maybe he was overthinking everything as usual.

"You okay, darlin'? You're thinking hard."

"I am. Okay and thinking hard. I'm taking you on the subway, so I was figuring out where I want to come up again. And giving you a chance to get to know the neighborhood." He steered them to the curb and stopped walking. "Want the last bite of bagel?"

"If you don't want it." Hawk bumped their shoulders together. "I've never been on a subway. How does it work?"

He popped that last bite into Hawk's mouth. "We're going to go down underground, get on a train that runs under the city and stops near the park, and come back up. Simple." He took Hawk's arm. "Are you okay with steps? There will be a handrail on your right."

"Cool!" Hawk tested the first step and then bebopped down the rest. Okay, so stairs were good. Actually, Hawk was lit up, eyes sparkling. "I am so ready. Me and Charlie decided not to try it. I'm going to so rub it in."

Charlie. Hawk hadn't offered any update. Maybe he'd ask later tonight.

He trotted down the stairs after Hawk and dug his MetroCard out of his wallet. "There's a turnstile. You have to slide a card to go through so, when you hear the little beep walk on through."

That was easier than the stairs. *Awesome.*

"Have you never been on a subway anywhere?"

"Nope. I been on a steam train, a gondola, lots of rollercoasters. This is new."

"This is nowhere near as exciting as any of those things." The train platform wasn't crowded at all and he kept Hawk back well behind the yellow line. "Just so you know, when the train comes in, it'll be moving pretty fast but we're three feet back so we're totally fine."

"Excellent. So do you sit down or stand? How far are we going? Is it expensive? Do they know how far you go?" There wasn't an ounce of fear, simply this wild, fierce curiosity.

"We'll sit if there are seats left, sometimes there are, sometimes not. We're only going two stops. Getting on at eighty-sixth and off at sixty-eighth. And it's not cheap, for sure."

"Eighty-six. Sixty-eight. So you use a credit card? You'll need to show me. Do they have, like an app where you can hear where you are? I don't know Braille or anything, because Momma didn't want anyone to know." Hawk's mind was sharp, engaged, and he loved it. This was why his cowboy was a champ.

He pulled his MetroCard back out and handed it to Hawk. "You buy that card and then you can refill it over and over. It's called a MetroCard. I have no idea if there is an app, let's look tonight. Sometimes you can hear the conductor say where you are, but that's not reliable."

He smiled. "Feel the wind? That's the train coming."

"Oh, that's something. So you put it in twice? The card?"

"I did. Once for you, when you went through, and then again for me. You swipe it through a reader. You can't feel the strip though... I wonder..."

"There's a corner missing. Did you do that?" Hawk handed him back his card.

"There's a what?" He flipped the card over in his fingers. "Huh. You know I never noticed? If I hold it like I'm going to swipe it... that corner is up and close to me. Oh cool." That was crazy. He'd honestly never even thought about it.

The train roared into the station, brakes squealing, breeze blowing his hair. He took Hawk's hand but didn't bother to say anything, he wouldn't be heard over all the noise.

Hawk held on, eyes wide and searching for lights and information.

There was something wonderful about experiencing the subway with someone who thought of it as different and new and didn't take for granted the way he usually did. It was the subway. But not to Hawk.

The train doors opened, and people crowded in with them. "No seats." He pulled Hawk over to a pole. "Hold on, cowboy. You should be good at this."

"Balance is my thing." Hawk held on with his good

hand, keeping his hurt shoulder drawn in and protected. "This is rocking cool."

"We'll see how you feel about it during rush hour." He laughed. "Who am I kidding? I avoid it during rush hour at all costs." The train moved along and picked up speed. Two stops was a short trip. That and a quick walk and they'd be where he wanted to take Hawk first.

"Where I grew up, rush hour was when school let out." Hawk chuckled and shook his head. "Did you grow up here?"

"Not in the city. Just north, in Westchester. My folks are still there." So was his sister and her family. And Sean had retreated home to Mom and Dad after the divorce. "We came here a lot though as kids."

"Westchester. Cool. I'll have to look it up on my phone."

"You can't miss it. It's pretty much right on top of Manhattan." The train stopped and the door opened, letting people off. "We're next. Shoulder okay?"

"So far so good." Like his stubborn cowboy would admit that something hurt.

At the next stop, he led Hawk off the train and up the stairs, back into the sunshine. "We have a little walk still. About seven or eight blocks to get where we're going."

"I am a champion walker. Truly champion." Hawk lifted his face toward the sun. "Lead the way."

"My Champ." He hooked their fingers together loosely as they walked. The sidewalks weren't busy over this way and they could walk and enjoy the day. They entered the park near the zoo, which was next on his list to show Hawk, but he had something else in mind first, so he walked right by it.

Hawk tilted his head, smiled. "Do you hear a carnival?"

He smiled, of course Hawk would have heard the

Calliope music. "Not a whole carnival, just a carousel." A carousel. Because wandering in the sunshine was nice, but he wanted Hawk to experience the park, even if his lover couldn't see it the way most people did.

"Like with the horses? Can we go see it?" Hawk's eyes moved constantly, searching wildly. No wonder Hawk wore dark glasses all the time. No one could miss that. "It's so green. I like it."

Of course they'd go see it. They were going to ride it. "It's greener in the summer. It's actually pretty gray comparatively right now except the evergreens. You should see it in the snow."

"Is that an invitation?"

"Yes. If it ever snows. This has been a weird winter. Not that you need an invitation." He tugged Hawk in close and kissed his temple. "You tell me you're coming and get on a plane."

"Thank you. One day I'll—" Hawk turned his head, following the shape of a man on a bicycle.

"Bicycle. You're good." He patted Hawk's arm. "One day you'll what?"

"Huh?" Hawk turned his face toward him, then looked around to watch another bicyclist.

Interesting. "Are you curious about the bikes or worried about them?"

"I like riding. It's been a while, but I enjoy it. They go fast here."

"Yeah. It's serious transportation here. And a bunch of them are messengers too, taking packages around the city, or food delivery. They're often working." He really couldn't count the number of times he'd almost had his toes run over by a bike messenger.

"Really? That's cool. That's really neat." Hawk grinned at

him, the expression bittersweet. "So where's the merry-go-round?"

"We're getting there. Can you make out the red and white building straight ahead? It's sort of striped. That's it. You ready to take a ride?"

"We can? Rock on. I bet I can last more than eight seconds." Hawk's laugh rang out, pure joy.

"I bet even I can!"

There was only a very short line and they got right in, but it was a little dark inside and even he was squinting a bit after being in the bright sun so he helped Hawk find the step up and steered them both to a pair of moving horses. "You want the ones that move, right? Not the stationary ones? They're boring."

He laughed. He didn't know about riding a real one, but he was brave enough for a carousel horse.

"Sounds like a plan." Hawk shot him an evil grin. "I do up and down real good."

He got behind Hawk and hummed. "Mmhmm. Get on up there, cowboy." *Keep it family friendly, Jan, this is a carousel.*

Hawk swung up like it was nothing, the motion as natural as breathing. It was more than a little fascinating, if he was honest.

"Show off." He climbed up on the one next to Hawk, which was up high, while Hawk's was low. "No fair, yours is lower. Look at me! I'm on a horse." He grinned as the music got louder.

Hawk grabbed his phone. "This deserves to be shared. Ride 'em cowboy!"

He grabbed both reins and leaned forward, trying to look like he was racing. "Yeehaw!" Jesus he was a dork. Fun, but a dork.

Hawk cackled at him. "Eight seconds, you can do it!"

"Not in a million years." He sat back laughing as the carousel started to move. "Here we go! You get a chance to be taller than me for a minute."

"Look, Gigantor, I *like* being a pocket cowboy!"

"Pocket cowboy!" He cracked up. "I'm glad you said it. You'd probably kick my ass if I'd said something like that first. Pocket cowboy. You're never going to live that down now." He was only like, five-foot-ten, most people didn't consider him tall.

"What? I so am. I grew up with all the bulldoggers. Beat them all in money by the time I was twenty-one. Tiny and stuck like a burr."

"You won't hear any complaints out of me, cowboy. You can climb into my pocket any day." He grabbed the pole with one hand and leaned back, kicking his feet out in front of him. "Wheee!"

Hawk videoed him, laughing and playing along, the happiness filling him up.

He waved at the phone and shook his head. He enjoyed the ride and enjoyed watching Hawk have some fun too. If not for the sling, you'd never know the man was hurting, because he was all smiles.

It was like magic—Hawk was his magical lover, and he couldn't stop smiling.

19

J anuary was sound asleep, having the snooze of a
sucked-off man. Hawk watched him for a few long
minutes, then got his phone and started dealing with
shit.

When are you coming home?

Momma's worried about you.

Charlie's doing a little better I think.

I swear to god, Bird. Make these assholes leave.

*It's not like you can survive out there, son. You need help. You
need family. NY is HUGE.*

Have you set up PT?

*Jesus, go home. Momma and Daddy are climbing up our
asses.*

God, his head hurt.

He needed an apartment. Maybe in Nashville? Or maybe
Dallas. No, not Dallas. Dallas wasn't enough room from his
folks. In Nashville folks knew him. Denver? It had an airport
and he could have a place to ask January to come to and
have a place to see.

Jesus.

He leaned forward, swallowing at the deep ache in his side. He'd overdone today, but January had taken time off work to see him. He wasn't going to waste it.

Hell, for a second there, he'd thought— Shit, it didn't matter what he thought. He was a moron.

He ignored Momma, Doc, and his brothers and sent Ben a yay and Charlie a, *Buck up, cowboy. Thinking about moving to Phoenix.*

Phoenix? Things not working out with your Yankee?

He's fab. Hawk was stupid in love. *I need a place where he can come visit me too. Got a big airport*

It's hot in Phoenix. Tell me about your week. How's the shoulder? When are you riding again? I was out of it when you got hurt.

Hurts pretty bad. It's cool here, but—I don't know how to get a place. Mommas losing her mind man. Like seriously. Going to take one more week off for sure.

There was a pause before Charlie replied. *Can you call me? Texting is kind of hard right now.*

Yeah.

He crawled out of bed, grabbed a Coke, and curled up on the couch with a blanket. He was good at being quiet.

As soon as he dialed, Charlie answered. "Bird."

"Hey, buddy. How you feeling?"

"Good. Better. Squinting at the damn phone gives me a headache." Charlie's voice sounded dry, rough. "So January is treating you well?"

"He's amazing. He keeps talking about the next time I visit." So he needed a place to go when he wasn't visiting Charlie or here. "I stay in my bedroom, man. I sleep in the same bed I've had since I was a little boy. I need a place to go when I'm not a visitor."

"Oh. You're not invited to stay, huh? Well, y'all are new.

He's not ready yet. You could have him here if you want, you're not a visitor here."

"Yeah. Yeah, but you got people there. Tons. Has your mom fed you biscuits every morning?" He couldn't pretend that he belonged there. His home was a ten by ten room that looked out over the pasture.

"Ben won't tell her to go home. I need everybody to go away now. I'm better I swear. I need some peace."

"You want I should call Ben in the morning?" He would, if only to hear what was really going on.

"Yeah. Call him. Thank you. But I want to talk about you. Tell me what's good."

"He is. He's amazing. I've had pizza and a bite of bagel." He loved a lot of the city. Some of it made him feel a little small, a little broken. "We went on a merry-go-round and on the subway—that was cool. Jan's got a neat apartment—it's big and bright and he has a lot of movies."

"You sound happy, Bird. It sounds real, huh?"

"It does. I am. But I can't be real, can I?" Hawk rubbed his forehead. "I need an apartment. Maybe a trailer house or something."

"Ask Ben. He's good at this stuff. He'll help. You should be real too."

"Yeah. Maybe he can." He needed somewhere with an airport, public transport to the airport, somewhere big enough to have groceries delivered, north enough folks wouldn't know him and where Momma wouldn't show up.

No big.

"I didn't want to move in with Ben at first." Charlie sighed. "I felt like that would be lazy or something you know? Like a cop out. I'd have nothing of my own. But. But I have him."

"You do, and he loves you, man." One day that would be

him and January. He knew that like he knew his name. Well, maybe. After he retired and got himself a dog and learned how to do all by himself.

"The feeling is mutual. Are you... are you getting around okay? Is it still scary up there?"

"A little. I think I could learn it, though. It's a matter of doing things a couple of times." A couple hundred times. He'd never been anywhere this big without Charlie.

"And January's cool with... did you tell him yet?"

"About my eyes? Yeah. I mean, I think so?" He sighed. "Not that I didn't tell him, but I think he's cool. I think he's a little wigged. I think he's more curious than anything."

He could almost hear Charlie nodding and see the shrug. "Sounds like he gets it. Cool. Curious is good, right?"

"Yeah. Just ready for the shoulder to heal so he can remember how blistering hot I am." He wrapped himself up tighter. "You feeling any better? The doctors think you're getting better?"

"Surgery went good. Yeah. The constant headache is gone, that's a big deal. Eyes are a little squinty sometimes, but I'm doing good."

"I know from squinty. You want me to come by before the next event? I can get a hotel room, maybe bring January, if he can."

"Sure. That'd be great. I'd love to meet January... see you. Yeah. That'd be good." He heard Ben's voice in the background, but not what was being said. "Oh. Ben says I have to try to sleep."

"Okay, buddy. Love you, huh? Sleep well."

"Yeah, Bird. Love you. Hug that man tight. Night."

"Night." He hung up and sat there, thoughts buzzing through his brain. Lord have mercy.

January on Ben's ranch. That was a hell of a thought. But

it sounded to him like Charlie wanted a visit. Maybe January would enjoy it if they stayed at a hotel. But that might hurt Ben's feelings.

"Baby? You okay?" Jan came out of the bedroom in a loose robe, bare feet slapping on the hardwood floor. "Shoulder? Can't sleep? I thought for sure I'd worn you out today."

"Hey, you. I didn't want to wake you or be a little bitch." He stood up. "You looked so sweet, snoozing there."

"Yeah, well. My brains needed rest to put themselves back together." Jan sat on the couch with him, fingers finding his thigh. "Bitch all you like. You need your meds?"

"I'm okay. Just—" Hurting. "—tender some."

He tried to lean in, but he was too goddamn sore.

"If you call that tender, I'd hate to see what you call actual pain. Go on, back to bed. I'll get ice and your meds." And just like that, Jan was fussing over him. "Do you need help getting up?"

"Give me your hand." He wasn't broken—well, a little, but only in two places. He hauled himself up and followed Jan to the bedroom.

"You did too much today. You should have said something sooner." The apartment was dark, but Jan got him to bed. "Why didn't you?"

"I wanted to play. I was having a ball with you." He wanted to keep up.

"You're here for a while, there's no hurry to do everything in one day." That sounded exactly like something Momma would say.

"Did I?" he teased, tickled as all get out. Silly, wonderful amazing man. "Did I do it all today?"

Jan snorted. "Shut up. I'm going to get ice. Though I'm

not sure you deserve it." Warm fingers squeezed his thigh and then disappeared.

"I so do! Just not around the balls. No balls and ice." That drew up things in a bad way.

"Ooh! That sounds like a dare!" January called from somewhere down the hall.

He sat and panted, letting his pain show a little because no one was there to see.

He could hear January in the kitchen digging in the ice bin in the freezer and opening and closing things. He didn't get much time; Jan was back quickly. He felt the chill from the ice packs Jan sat down on the bed next to him. "I'm guessing tomorrow you'll be sorry you didn't speak up, tough guy."

"I'll manage." He was a stud, and he needed January to know it. To believe it. "I'll breathe through it right?"

"Sure." Jan touched his face and kissed him gently. "And I'll be right here."

Hawk found himself sucking in a shaky little breath. He'd never felt so vulnerable, so exposed, and he didn't know how to deal with it. God, he hoped January did.

January breathed with him a second, then he got another quick kiss before his lover started packing him in ice. "Great day for a walk though, right? We don't get too many of those this time of year."

"It was a glorious day. I—God, it was a whole new thing. I love that. Seeing things with you."

"It was fun. You're a good sport. You're curious too, I like that about you. You trusted me. That felt good." Jan was getting good at placing the ice in the right places.

"Oh." He couldn't help the sound that escaped as the cold eased him, made his eyes cross.

"Mmm. Better?" He heard the rattle of his pill bottle. "Open up, Champ. I've got water here too."

"Better. Christ." Hawk opened up—although it had way less to do with his lips and more to do with his soul—and took what January offered.

"This will get better. We'll get you back up on your bulls. New York's not going anywhere; we have lots of time to explore." Jan tucked a blanket over his legs and another pillow behind his head. "Let the meds do what they do and rest, okay?"

Jan settled beside him and turned the TV on.

"Yeah. I reckon I ought to. We're good?"

Jan looked over at him so suddenly he could feel the bed move. "What? We're better than good. I think it's love." A warm hand slid down his hip and rested on his thigh.

"Yeah, darlin'. I think you're right." And he thought he would do damn near anything for this man. Damn near anything.

20

J an had been impressed with Hawk's ambition in the morning, but his cowboy barely made it out of bed. They'd listened to an audio book and Jan took a stab at talking Hawk through a movie. He'd done his best to keep the mood light and didn't try to be too ambitious himself so Hawk wouldn't feel bad, but he didn't feel like he'd done a very good job.

Hawk was in a lot of pain. A lot more than he wanted Jan to know about, but Jan had eyes that worked better than Hawk's did and could easily see the tight lips and the way Hawk would occasionally go pale when he moved wrong.

Jan still felt like he was walking on eggshells.

It had been a long day.

Jan had drugged Hawk up to the eyeballs and put the cowboy to bed an hour ago, but he couldn't sleep. He finally got up and padded barefoot through the dark into the kitchen in search of comfort food, which made him think of Jax. Maybe it wasn't too late to call. He decided to text first.

Hey. You up?

The response was gratifyingly quick. Weird bakers keeping crazy hours. *I am. How's your live-in?*

Good. I mean, he's hurt but we're good. Mostly good. Some of it's hard. But he and I are good. Oh God. Why did he send that? He wasn't sure if he needed coffee or scotch.

Call? Jax knew him, bone-deep, knew what he wrote between the lines.

"Yeah," he whispered. "Probably a good idea." He made the call, and opened up the fridge, squinting at the sudden, bright light.

"Hey, man. What's up?" Jax's voice was soft, like he was afraid Hawk would overhear him over the phone.

"I'm hungry. I'm standing here staring into my fridge." He sighed. "I hate not knowing what I want."

"You didn't— Oh, right. He doesn't eat. God, how do you deal?"

"It's not like I can't. He doesn't care. We overdid it yesterday, and we spent the day quietly, that's all." He pulled the milk out and closed the door. He'd have a bowl of Cheerios.

"Is he okay? Are you bored to death? Do you need an intervention, a scotch, a cupcake?" Fuck, Jax made him laugh.

"I always need a cupcake, but I've got Cheerios. And I'm not bored--he's amazing. He's hurting; he really did in his shoulder, and we're still taping his ribs. He needs some help, you know?" He poured his cereal. "Not that he wants it."

"Really? I'm surprised. If I was him, I'd be scared out of my mind. I wouldn't leave your side, man."

"Scared? Of what? The man rides bulls for a living, Jax. He's been hurt worse I'm sure." Hawk was macho was all; he didn't want to need help.

"I don't know. You don't think the city is huge? He's from

a teeny tiny town, right?"

Oh. The city. "Well, he seemed pretty comfortable yesterday but... yeah. Maybe you're right. He even has enough trouble with my glass-top coffee table. He can't see it."

"No shit? Did he hit his head or something?"

Shit. "No. He... Look, keep this to yourself, okay? But he's basically blind." Saying it didn't make it any easier to believe. It still seemed crazy.

"I—What? You mean? What?"

"Yeah. You heard right. And nobody knows. I don't know how he does it." But he could see how a big city could be pretty terrifying, even if Hawk did trust him.

There was a long silence. "You're serious? He can't see? Why doesn't he have a dog? A cane? How the hell does he ride bulls? Seriously?"

"Think about it Jax. They won't let him ride if they find out. He can't have a cane or anything." But he'd been thinking about that. About finding Hawk a service dog if the cowboy retired.

"Okay. I have so many questions. Like, one, did he hit his head? Does he travel with help? How long has this been going on? Has anyone taken him to a doctor?" Jax stopped and took a breath. "I need an eclair."

"Jesus, Jax." He could totally go for an eclair. Instead he put milk on his cereal. "He was born with a condition and it's slowly got worse as he grew up. Less slowly I guess, now. But no, he has some friends on the road, but he travels by himself."

And his mother called constantly. Like three times a day at least. But Jan wasn't going to tell all of Hawk's secrets. He wasn't even sure he had the right to tell this one.

"Jesus, talk about brass balls. I can't wait to meet him.

We've got to get him a dog. If you get a dog, I'll baby sit."

"I'm hoping he'll be on his feet tomorrow. Maybe you could come tomorrow night for dinner. But one thing at a time, man. I need him to believe in this a little more before we're talking about dogs. We've got some stuff to work through. I need to stop feeling like I'm tiptoeing around. We'll get there."

"He's not being a bitch to you, right? I mean, I won't have someone being a shit when you're good to them."

"God no. Not at all. He's amazing, Jax. He's so... real. But he's trying very hard not to be a bother. I feel like he thinks if he's too high maintenance I'm going to run. I'm trying as hard to tell him it's okay to need help."

He took a big bite of cereal and chewed it thoughtfully.

"That sounds like sort of normal relationship shit, honestly. How do you get what you need without being a dick? How do you give him what he needs without taking over? And vice-versa." Jax chuckled and January could see his smile. "That makes me feel good."

"That we're normally dysfunctional?" He laughed. "Excellent."

"Yep. Same shit every bull riding couple with a blindness thing and a foundation goes through."

He snorted. Jax was such a little shit. "It's nice to be so *normal*." He chuckled, but he heard Jax snort back a laugh and that was enough to get him laughing. "I can't wait for you to meet him. Will you bring dessert? I'll make him have a bite."

"God yes. What's his favorite, do you know?"

"Apple pie. With ice cream." It was the only dessert he'd seen Hawk eat and if Hawk was taking the calorie hit, it was probably a favorite. "Pretty sure."

"Apple pie a la mode is totally in my wheelhouse. I'll

bring you something chocolate." Jax's laugh made him smile. "I can't wait to talk to him, see for myself how cool he is."

"Not cool. *Hot*." He let himself be smug about that. Hawk was the sexiest man he'd ever had. "So hot."

"Right. Like you want me to notice that. Or is it you want me to notice and me jealous?"

"Jealous? Didn't you take that bartender home?"

"I did. He was dear. Sort of like fucking someone that was watching himself in the mirror."

He laughed. Poor Jax was so date-worthy but couldn't seem to catch a break. "Wait... was it Lucas in disguise?"

"A little nicer, less good in bed."

He hated to admit it, but Lucas had been pretty damn good in bed.

"I don't want you to be jealous. I want him to meet you because you're my best friend and you need to know each other." That was probably exactly as hokey as it sounded, but he didn't care. Truth was allowed to be sentimental.

"Cool. I'm excited, man. He sounds like a superhero, somehow. Huh." Jax stopped, trailed off until January cleared his throat.

"Jax?"

"Sorry. Sorry, I was thinking that it was cool, that he's finding something exciting to do. Learning you, learning the city—that seems to fit with his personality."

"It totally does. Maybe yesterday scared him a little, but he loved it too. I took him to the carousel, and we went to the zoo... I was trying to find things he didn't need to see— in the traditional way—to enjoy. I think he had a good time."

Hawk was brave. Willing to take risks. Basically the total opposite of Jan's careful and calculated safe life. How ironic.

But Hawk touched him like he was precious, and talked to him for hours, listened to him. Made him feel like he mattered.

"I want this to work." He sighed. "I really want this to work, Jax. That's what scares me."

"I don't blame you. Lucas hurt. Hawk, though, he seems different. You talk about him like he's special."

Lucas was work. Every day. Lucas had felt like something he had to live up to. Hawk appreciated him.

"He is. And I better get back to him. Thanks for letting me babble at you." He chuckled. "Hope the eclair was worth it."

"Always. Apple pie and ice cream will appear with me tomorrow."

"Come around six. I'm not sure what dinner will be yet, but we'll feed you something fabulous." He could cook, and Hawk could tell him stories. Sounded great to him.

"Fair deal. Call if you need me, okay. I'm here."

"Thanks. Don't work too hard. Night." He hung up and put his phone down nodding. Jax was the reality check he'd needed. He dumped all his dishes in the sink and went back to the bedroom to climb into bed with the hottest man on earth. His man.

Hawk was waiting for him, the man's expression relaxing when he heard January's steps.

"Hey. You're supposed to be sleeping." He scooted in carefully, as close as he dared.

"I was. I'm more floating right above the mattress." Hawk cuddled in.

"Mhm." He could handle a snuggle. Hawk was warm and relaxed. "That sounds like the pain meds. Sorry, I was hungry. I got some cereal and checked in with Jax."

"No worries. How's he?" Hawk petted him with clumsy

fingers, loving on him. The touch felt good, reassuring.

"He's good. He was making eclairs. I invited him for dinner. I hope that's okay. He's going to bring you an apple pie to have a bite of."

"Sounds great. I want to meet him. What are we making?" Hawk chuckled softly. "Eclairs. I never met no one that makes eclairs."

"I don't know, what should we make? I'll have to run out to the market probably for anything fresh. Fish? Chicken? Pasta? Have you got a preference?"

"I miss pasta. God, I could murder a plate of meatballs and spaghetti."

Oh, spaghetti. "Let's do that. I can cheat and get meatballs at the Italian market."

"One cheat meal can't hurt too bad, right?" Hawk twined their fingers together.

He smiled, loving the way their hands fit together. "I could grab zoodles and turkey meatballs. That's less cheaty."

"If I'm going to cheat, let me have the real thing." Hawk chuckled softly. "I'll run stairs if I have to."

He snorted. "I don't think you could run to the bathroom yet, Champ. But we'll work on that."

"Hey, I know where the bathroom is now!" Hawk waggled his eyebrows and they both cracked up, laughing hard.

He touched his forehead to Hawk's temple as their laughing turned into soft giggles. "Does the city scare you?" he whispered in Hawk's ear.

Hawk shrugged, the movement this tiny thing. "It's frightening and wonderful and exciting all at once. I worry about getting lost, but I can figure it out. I *will* figure it out."

"Do you really want to? I mean, could you live here?" He realized after he asked that question that it was much bigger than he'd meant it to be. But he thought he was okay with that.

Yeah, he was good with that.

"I don't know. Can I be like stupid and honest and forward and shit with you? I mean, right now?"

"Yeah. I'm the one asking hard questions in the middle of the night. I better be ready for the answers." Shit. Maybe he wasn't ready.

"I want to be with you. I want to live with you, on a 'I get to sleep with you all the time' way, but I know it's too soon and I've never lived alone. I still stay in the bedroom I grew up in at home." Hawk pinked, obviously embarrassed. "I don't think I can live here alone—it's so big, so different. I'm thinking about getting a place somewhere so you know I can live on my own, but it'd have to be somewhere easier to learn. Maybe Nashville. I don't know."

"Wow." That was a lot to process. He didn't want Hawk to worry, but he didn't know where to start with an answer either. He went for the low-hanging fruit. "Is there a rule about how soon in cowboy-land?"

"I don't think so. Folks do what they will. Is there one here?"

"Definitely not. New Yorkers do what they damn well please. I think we can let that worry go. Do you *want* to live alone?"

"No. I'm not scared to be alone—I am at hotels a lot, but I want— I like being with people. I grew up in a big family, work in a big group of men. I *want* to be with you." Hawk traced his fingers, one after the other.

Okay. Right. He got it now. He squeezed Hawk's fingers. "I want you to live here with me. You don't have anything to prove to me about what you're capable of, you're stronger and braver than I am."

"Yeah? You want me in your space?" Hawk's eyes searched his face, the fingers following right after, tracing his features. Jan loved that, because Hawk wasn't looking. He really wanted to know. To feel him.

"Well, I'd like to make it *our* space."

"I've never had that. I told myself I couldn't have it, but maybe I was wrong." Hawk scooted closer, more of their bodies touching.

"You were wrong, baby." He kissed Hawk's fingers and pulled them away from his face so he could find the cowboy's lips to kiss instead.

"I won't be a burden. I can learn damn near anything." Hawk's words sounded like a promise against his lips.

This man could never be a burden. But Jan knew he wasn't going to dispel years of worry in one night. He'd have to teach Hawk how to believe it. "I'm not asking for part of you, I'm asking for all of you. You're not a burden. You're mine."

"And you're mine, thank God. Gonna make you happy, darlin'. I'm gonna make your days good."

"As good as our nights?" He grinned, sliding a hand over Hawk's hard belly.

"Ain't nothing so good as that. We were made for loving on each other." Oh, exceptional answer.

"I do kind of feel that way, yes." If that was possible, it had to be true. "So have I made a New Yorker out of you?"

Hawk shook his head. "I'm a Texan, darlin', but one that wants to learn all the things this city has to teach him."

"Fair enough. You can teach me Texas too. And with all the traveling you do, home could be anywhere I guess."

"We can go anywhere—the beach, the mountains, everywhere. I'm a go-baby." Hawk made him smile—that raw courage that pushed him to ride bulls, to do things no matter what—that was so fucking attractive.

"We can. We should. Why the hell not?" Traveling he liked, though he tended to be the five-star type. He and Hawk together could probably pick places with fewer people in their business.

"That's right. You and me, causing trouble—we've never been swimming together, you know? Do you know how? I do. Momma was afraid the boys would drown me."

"I do know how. We'll put that on our to do list. I'm not worried about you drowning. I'm not worried about you at all." Well, that wasn't entirely true. He wasn't going to say he worried about the bulls, that was Hawk's passion, and the cowboy's bread and butter. Jan intended to be supportive and keep the doubts to himself.

"I can't tell you how fucking weird this is. I can't tell you what I thought, but now it's like there's more life after the bulls."

"We have all kinds of life after the bulls. Tons. Years together." He lifted Hawk's fingers back to his lips so his lover could feel him smile.

"Life after the bulls." Hawk looked stunned.

"Don't worry, we'll figure it out." God. What a weird and wonderful conversation. At a crazy hour. "You think you can sleep, Champ?"

"Long as I can stay here with you. Yeah."

"Oh, I'm not giving you a choice. We're going to wake up together every day we can."

Hawk kissed him, long and lazy, but without intent. Hawk simply loved on him, that was all either of them needed.

Long and lazy turned into slow and sleepy and he wasn't sure as he dozed off if they actually finished the kiss.

21

Hawk sat hard. They'd shopped, they'd gone out for coffee, they'd explored places by the apartment. Now he was exhausted as all get out, but happy?

Lord.

"That was a good day, huh?" And he was fixin' to get to meet Mr. Jax, too. That was important. That made things more real.

"It was. Are you feeling okay?" Jan appeared from the kitchen with two beers in one hand and a couple of bags of ice. "Beer."

"I'm getting better every day, darlin'. Thank you." He grabbed the beer with one hand and January with the other, stealing a kiss.

January kissed him back, grinning as he pulled away. "Back in the saddle in no time." Jan packed his shoulder with the ice. "How did you like that Italian market? Doesn't it smell great in there?"

"Oh my God. It was heaven. I swear, I want to learn how to cook all of it."

"I've got a great kitchen. Go for it." Jan's laugh was cut

short by the door buzzer. "Oh. That's Jax. I should have warned you he'd be early. He's always afraid he'll be late, so he shows up early." Jan hopped off the couch to get the door. "You sit tight, I'm gonna buzz him up."

Lord have mercy, he hoped this Jax guy liked him. He knew it was important.

"Hey. I'm kind of early..." A voice came over the intercom.

"What else is new? Come on up." The door buzzer sounded. "Oh. Champ. Let me get that ice." Jan scooped the bags off his shoulder and was back before the knock at the front door.

He sat up straight, the scent of apple pie the first thing he got. Cinnamon and sugar and all the good things. Damn.

"Hey!" He heard their bro-hug, the back slaps so familiar, and then the footsteps got closer. "Come in. Man, that smells good. Come meet my man. Hawk, this is my best friend and partner in crime, Jax. Jax, this is my boyfriend, lover, and personal pocket cowboy, Hawk."

Hawk stood and offered his hand. "Please to meetcha, Mister Jax." *You'd best like me, 'cause I'm not going nowhere.*

Jax took his hand. "Really good to meet you. I'm generally a hugger, but it looks like hugs might be out for now with that shoulder, huh? I'll take a raincheck. You have a hell of a grip, man."

"I have to hold on for a living." He eased up his grip. No hurting the pastry chef. That was tacky, and he'd been raised better. "Whatever you brought in smells like heaven."

Jax gave his hand a strangely affectionate squeeze, then let go. "Well a birdie told me you like apple pie, and I've made it my personal mission to make sure he never runs out of chocolate, so I brought both." Jax laughed. "It's really is good to finally meet you. Jan talks about you constantly."

"Oh, shut up. Give me that stuff. You want a beer?"

"Yes, please."

"Sit down, I'll bring it." Jan headed for the kitchen.

Jax leaned closer. "Constantly. Seriously."

"He's important." That was that. January was important to him, special. "Very important."

"He loves you. And he must be important if you're braving this crazy city for him."

"He's been an amazing tour guide. I'm having a ball." Was he braving it? Hawk thought he was busy learning everything.

"One beer. You can stop talking about me now." Jan sat beside him. "Unless it's good stuff, then you can keep talking."

"I don't want to talk about you." Jax snorted. "I want to hear about bull riding. We watched that crash. What goes through your mind when you know it's going south?"

"You try to figure out how to make the best of it. It's quick. The ride is quick, the crash is too. Recovery takes forever." And that was that. He didn't ponder the crashes too much because they happened or they didn't. The first ride after a bad crash? That he thought on a lot.

"Well, you had a lot of amazing rides before the crash. I'd never seen bull riding before Jan made me watch."

"I bribed him with ramen."

"He totally did."

He didn't get the ramen thing, but he nodded anyway. He'd figure it eventually. "Did we make y'all a fan?"

"Oh my God. I love it. I don't really know what I'm seeing but it looks terrifying."

Jan laughed. "He's been known to climb into my lap if it gets tense."

"Shut up. You yell at the TV."

"You yell at the bulls."

"Good thing there's an event this weekend. We should watch." Danny was on a roll. It might be a decent event. "I can answer all your questions."

"I'm so in. Uh. If I'm invited of course. I wouldn't invite myself over and bug you guys, you know. Sorry. Wait. What's for dinner?"

Hawk blinked, and Jan started laughing.

"You're invited. Spaghetti and meatballs with salad and garlic toast. I'm going to splurge."

"Ooh, meatballs. Did you get them from Lorenzo's down the street? That place is amazing."

"Yeah. It's the best reason in the world to be lazy and not cook. Hawk's going to make the garlic toast though."

"I'm sold. He's a keeper."

"I'm sure as shit going to try." The beer was cold and hoppy, and Hawk approved of the choice. Good beer was amazing. Bad beer was horse piss, meant to hit the ground.

"How's business, Jax?" Jan turned to Hawk. "Jax is an amazing baker. I'm surprised I don't weigh a thousand pounds being friends with him."

"You said. I'm waiting impatiently on retirement so I can taste test things." Hawk chuckled at himself, tickled at the thought. "Do you like it? Baking? I mean, you must, right?"

"Yeah. I love it. Everyone loves dessert, right? It's creative and it makes people happy. It can get crazy and exhausting sometimes and the hours make most people I know think I'm nuts but it's what I do."

"Sounds like hard work." Again it hit him—what was he supposed to do after he retired? What was he going to do with himself? Lord.

"So does riding bulls. At least I'm way less likely to break something. Jan says you've been riding forever."

"Over fifteen years." And his body was getting older, every day.

Jan gave his thigh a squeeze. "Come on, guys, Let's go get dinner together."

"Just point me and shoot me." Hawk stood, managing not to scrape himself on that damn glass table.

"Can you cook? I mean, Jan told me about..."

Hawk's cheeks went hot, and for a second, he didn't know what to say. He wasn't used to people knowing, he wasn't used to answering questions, and he didn't know what the fuck to do.

"He's a better cook than I am." Jan looped an arm around his waist.

Jax snorted and moved ahead of them into the kitchen. "Well, that's not saying much."

"I hope it's okay that I told him," Jan said quietly.

"No one ever has, that's all.' He didn't know. He'd been keeping this secret for his entire life.

"I know, baby. It's not a big deal to us."

Jax started in again. "Can you use a knife? How do you not burn yourself on the oven? Damn. How do you keep your ass on the bull?"

Jan sighed. "He means well I swear."

He heard a soft sigh, then, "I'm just curious. I'm sorry. I don't know anybody else who is blind."

"Me either." Hawk was never going to stop blushing. "I can feel if the stove is hot, you know. And I can use a knife. It's only that I'm real slow."

"I'm slow too. It's a good thing I'm a pastry chef and not a prep chef."

January touched his shoulder, right above the sling, and it sent electricity down his arm. "Jax, grab the bread out of the bag on the counter? I'm going to put the meatballs on and start the pasta."

"On it."

Jan put Hawk's hand on the center island and left his side.

"Bread, cutting board, bread knife..." Jax put a hand on his shoulder this time. The touch was light, cool, not like January's at all. "What else do you need? Garlic... butter?"

"Yep. Thank you, sir." He could cut bread and spread butter. Smashing garlic into butter? That was a 'speciality'.

"Cool. I got it."

He heard the rattle of a pasta box, the click of a gas stove lighting, a little friendly banter between Jax and January... they were all working, putting dinner together, like they'd done this before. Like it was normal.

He wondered what his folks would think about this, about whether they'd approve of this. He thought so. He hoped they understood he needed to be happy rather than safe.

"God, that garlic smells good." January stepped up behind him and kissed his nape. "Mmm. You too."

He leaned into the touch, luxuriating in the freedom to touch, to make food, to act like he was a normal man doing normal things. "You're warm. It feels so good."

"It does feel good. This is us, in our kitchen."

"Us. In our kitchen. I like that." He spread the butter mixture over the bread. It would go in last, but it was ready. "Bread's done."

"Awesome. What should we watch after dinner?"

"Are you a *Great British Bake Off* fan, Hawk?" Jax asked, and he chuckled.

"Not yet. I'm looking forward to learning." He listened to a lot of TV—mostly documentaries and crime shows.

"We'll start with that and see how it goes. Jax can narrate and describe all the wonderful and horrible things people make. You wouldn't believe some of it. I'll heckle."

"He doesn't understand patisserie..." Jax shot back.

So this was what citified gay men did instead of sports. Baking shows. It made him cackle.

"I don't try very hard honestly."

"I bet he knows a shitton more than he lets on." January liked to be clever. "Do I need to do anything else?"

"Yeah, you want to put plates on the table?"

Plates. They'd done that a couple of nights ago.

"No problem." And it mostly wasn't. He clanged the plates on the table, but he didn't hear any breakage, so that was fair.

"I've got silverware." Jax buzzed around him, light like a dancer, quiet on his feet.

"Good deal." Hawk imagined that Jax was like a big fairy —wings and all—this glorious, quick, bright light.

"Hey. How long before you can ride again? Is this hurting your Champion status?"

"I'm falling in the rankings, not bad. I'm at three now. Doc's got to clear me. I'm probably looking at three more weeks so. Maybe two. I'll have to see how the shoulder goes."

"Wow. Well, you and Jan will get to spend some time together. Like, without the craziness of the riding and travel. That's an upside."

"For me it is. I'm sure Hawk is itching to get back on his game." Meatballs. He smelled them before January passed him to set them on the table. "I put your bread in the oven, it'll be another minute. Why don't you guys sit?"

"I'll get our beers." Jax walk by him, but January stayed close another second.

"All good?"

"All good. We'll be heading to Anaheim and then Portland if I have the timing right. I like both the host hotels." They could have a ball, when you get right down to it. Maybe they could rent a car and drive up the coast, stop and see the ocean.

"Sounds great. I've never been to Anaheim."

"Beer for Hawk... beer for January... and mine." Jax sounded accomplished. "I think dinner can start now."

"Right. Pasta. And bread." January kissed his neck. "Sit you guys, I'll be right back."

"So did you choose pasta?" Jax asked, and he nodded.

"I'm a chicken breast and broccoli type when I'm riding, but if I was going to cheat, I wanted spaghetti and meatballs." He craved it, and he intended to have it.

"Best cheat ever. Wait until you try these meatballs. And the sauce... mmm. Or gravy? Are you Italian? I bet you're not Italian. I bet you call it sauce too."

"Yeah, gravy goes on meat—well, not chile gravy, that's for enchiladas. I'm German and Scottish, but I do love me some pasta." He thought he was keeping up with Jax's questions pretty good, although he should have asked if the noodles were long or short.

"Okay. Spaghetti and bread." The dishes went thump on the table. "I know you're cheating, Champ, but I kept the sauce and the meatballs separate so you could make decisions."

"Champ." Jax giggled, but it sounded genuinely joyful, not mocking. "He actually calls you Champ. That's adorable."

"That's me. Adorable as fuck." That was decent. He could tell what was what. Still, he needed to know about the noodles. He could have reached out, but Jax knew and

January would need to help him out sometimes. He rarely ordered anything not chicken breast and broccoli in public. "Are the noodles long or short, darlin'?"

January didn't miss a beat. "Oh, they're long. Do you prefer them short?"

"Short is easier, but I need to figure out how to eat them long. How do you do it?"

The silence was deafening, and his cheeks started to burn.

"If you're Jax, you wear most of it." January broke the silence with a joke.

"One time." Jax protested. "You drop a big fat meatball one time, and you never live it down."

"One time, sure. But that one time it rolled right over his chin, down his shirt and drew a big saucy line over his fly. Classic. I laughed so hard I had to get up from the table."

January moved around behind him. "I've never taught anyone to eat spaghetti. This should be interesting."

"Think of it as a challenge." *Come on, man, start out like you can hold out.* If this was forever, then January would have to teach him things that Momma hadn't. He was smart. He could figure it.

"For me, maybe. You'll get it."

"You gonna show him the cool spoon method or the boring one?"

"Are you kidding? I can't make the spoon thing work for myself, let alone teach it to someone."

"Yeah, me neither."

"Hm. Okay. Let me serve you some first." January moved around him, dishes clinking. "So, you twirl it onto the fork. Like... I don't know. Winding yarn around your fingers? Maybe if I do it first and you kind of feel what I'm doing that might work?"

"Sure. Let's do it." He thought this was harder on January than it was on him. He liked to learn shit. He'd been kept in a little bubble as a kid, and he wasn't living like that. He wanted to know everything.

"Okay, I've got the fork, yeah just like that." He felt January nod. He had pretty smart fingers and he focused on them, letting January show him how it worked. "So you put the fork into the pasta and twirl it like this."

"That's going to be a mouthful," Jax teased.

January laughed. "You shut up and eat. We have to start somewhere."

"Do you nibble on it, eat the whole fork at once?" He lifted Jan's fork, or was it his fork. The fork? "It smells good."

"Don't eat that whole bite at once, Hawk, you'll choke on it!" Jax sounded genuinely concerned.

January laughed. "Well, this is a big bite. But usually you put the whole thing in your mouth and—"

"And anything left over you slurp into your mouth as loud as possible!"

Hawk took the bite, managing to get the whole bite in, chewing happily. Oh, so good.

"Oh, you're a lucky man, Jan. He got that whole thing in—"

January cracked up.

He swallowed, let one eyebrow lift. "I guarantee you he's a very, very lucky man."

"You got that right. How's the pasta?"

"He's the color of the sauce, Hawk. In case you were wondering."

"Can we get back to work here?"

Hawk was laughing too hard to manage the fork the first time, but he got some on his fork on try two.

"You got it!" January gave his good shoulder a light

squeeze. "I guess the hard part is knowing where the pasta is so you don't twirl the placemat."

"If I do, push my fork over." That and warn him when the noodles were almost gone.

"I can do that. Thanks for being patient with me." January kissed his cheek. "Meatballs are at the top of the plate."

"Thank you." Okay. Okay, so that wasn't bad. He could do this.

Without a word, January moved from the end of the table to sit beside him. "So have you heard how Danny and Parker and all of them are doing on the road? Is everyone off this week?"

"It's a bye week, yeah. I heard from Danny —- he's rocking it and the baby's kicking up a storm."

"Excellent. Did they go to the beach? She said she was going to make him take her."

"Danny?" Jax asked. "Like the guy that won the day you wrecked?"

"Yeah." He grinned. "He's a neat kid, baby on the way. We've been friends a while." If he didn't have the championship, he wanted it to go to Danny.

"Cool."

"Hawk, this bread is amazing." January crunched on another bite.

"Right? It's perfect. Crunchy and garlicky and buttery and ohmygod."

He'd have to ask January if they should invite Jax to an event sometime, let him have the full experience.

"I usually go out if I want bread this good." January's fingers touched Hawk's gently pushing his fork back onto his plate.

"Bread is delicious evil. Tasty carbtastic evil." And he loved it.

"So, why the wild dieting, man?" Jax asked. "You're tiny."

"I ride by balance. I learned to ride when I was a kid and eighty pounds, so I try to stay as lean as I can."

"Balance. I guess that makes sense. Especially since you can't see. So wait. Why the glasses? Do they actually help?"

"They do. I wear dark ones in the arena. It's getting worse, so they're helping less, but they still do some good, yeah."

"I saw the dark ones on TV. They're pretty slick, and they make you look badass. I approve."

January bumped shoulders with him. "As do I."

"Thanks. The glare from the spotlights is something." And he had to be up there at the top of the chutes on that catwalk deal. The first time he'd done it, he'd damn near died.

"Jan says nobody knows, huh?" Jax's voice dropped as if they could be overheard. "That has to be hard to do. Secrets are hard. I mean, I can keep yours but my own? Hard sometimes."

"I never tell. I've told three people in my whole life— January, Charlie, and Sky. Charlie told Ben; Jan told you." And until he retired, that was that.

"Skyler and Beckett definitely know." January added. "But they're safe. And Nicole and Danny? Parker and... his mother, I've forgotten her name? You don't think somebody told them?"

"Miss Vera. Sky and Beck guessed early on, but I don't think Danny and the rest know. Maybe that I wear thick glasses, but not the scope of it." They couldn't. That was too many people. The only way this worked was if he could control who knew.

"Just seems hard. Charlie is your friend that's out for the season with the head thing? How is he?"

"I talked to him last night. He was—" Sick. Charlie had sounded a little off, tired, wrong. "Getting better. He hit his noggin but good."

"Those things take a long time to heal I guess. Hope he's back on his feet soon."

"Hey, you've got the twirly thing down, baby. Did you want more?"

"No. No, I have to eat my meatball and have pie." And he was suddenly tired, a touch overwhelmed by everything. Not enough to be evil, but enough that he wasn't terribly hungry anymore.

"You don't have to do anything." Jan's warm, firm hand rested on his thigh. "That's more food than you've eaten in days."

"Yeah, no worries. The pie will keep in the fridge or freeze or whatever."

"I wouldn't miss it. It smells too good to freeze." He took January's hand and held on. He wanted to do this right.

"Want me to cut that meatball for you? You don't want to end up in that song..."

"Oh!" Jax gasped. "I know that one! On top of spaghetti, all covered in cheese..."

"You remember the words?" January laughed.

"It's a gift."

They all had a long, hard laugh, and things eased up. Hawk ended up eating a bite of the meatballs—which were amazing, thank you very much—and feeling the knot of stress in his belly relax.

He mostly hung back as Jax and January cleared the dishes and picked on each other, but he wasn't left out at all.

January's affectionate touch was constant, every time his lover walked by or reached past him for something.

"Jax put the pie in to warm-up so our stomachs can settle a bit before we have some." Jan slipped an arm around his waist. "Do you want some coffee?"

"No, thank you. Can we go sit for a few? Hang out?" He was wearing out.

"Yeah, of course. Are you okay? You want your ice back?" Jan helped him settle into the couch.

"Nah, I want to sit." He wasn't a pussy; he was wearing down some.

"You want a snuggle." Jan sat close. "That's okay, me too."

"Where's your remote, Jan?" Jax moved so quietly he hadn't realized the man was in the room.

"Side table."

"Oh, Yup. Got it." The TV came on. "Let's see who's baking."

He leaned into his lover a little. "This okay, darlin'?"

"Better than." Jan took his hand. "Lean all you like."

This was the best part—the way that January was willing to touch and let him touch in the simplest of ways.

It wasn't long before the pie was ready. Jax told them both to sit tight and served them each a small slice with a scoop of ice cream.

"Jax, that was amazing," January said and leaned forward to put his plate down on the coffee table. "I'll try the chocolate tomorrow. I'm totally stuffed."

"It was amazing. Genuinely. Worth the calories." And that was the best praise he had.

"Yeah? I guess that's saying a lot coming from the tiniest cowboy on earth. Thank you."

January snorted. "You'd be surprised. I saw a couple even tinier. They look bigger on TV."

"It's the pure macho in us." He had no doubt.

"Pure macho. Mmm. I'm a fan." Jan picked up his fingers and kissed them, letting him feel the smile.

"No kidding," Jax agreed. "I think maybe I'm a fan too."

"We'll have to introduce you around. We're basically decent folks." He could think of a couple guys that would love Jax.

Jax laughed. "Oh, I'll never have a weekend off, but thank you. I get Sundays sometimes, but usually I'm baking and delivering."

"Jax likes to keep busy."

"I do. What would I do with myself otherwise? Busy is good."

"That's a shame. If the tour comes to the city again, I'll get you VIP seats for two, so you can see a live show."

"Yeah? Thanks. I'd love that. I really would." Jax got up. "I think I better run you guys. I have a ton to do in the morning."

"Yeah? Already?" January gave Hawk's knee a squeeze and then stood up.

"Thanks for having me over. Hawk, it was really good to meet you."

"Ditto. You'll come over to watch the next short-go?" He stood, rapping his shins on the table and held out one hand to shake.

Jax shook his hand. "I'd love to. Yes. Thanks."

"Cool. It'll be fun." January followed Jax to the door and saw him out. "Text me when you get home."

"I am not five."

"No. You're a New Yorker." January laughed. "Night, man."

"Night!" Jax voice was already down the hall. January closed and locked the door.

"That was cool. I liked him, and you can tell he adores you." That rocked for January, and it boded well for him.

"The feeling is mutual. He's a good friend. A real one. I'm glad you liked him. I know he liked you, plus you complimented his pie and that scores high." Jan sat with him again, fingers resting on his belly.

"It was the best—even better than Momma's." He leaned in with a soft sigh. "And supper was great. Sorry about the noodle lesson."

"Sorry for what?" January kissed him lightly. "Why?"

"I don't want to be an embarrassment, a stress." Momma needled him about that all the time, about how he was going to have to understand no one wanted to help him all the time.

"You're not. I actually thought it was kind of fun showing you. There's nothing to be ashamed of, and you can't embarrass me." Jan carded fingers through his hair. "You can't."

"You're a good teacher." God, that touch. It soothed him, all the way to the bone. "That's nice."

"People haven't touched you enough, Champ." January's fingers unbuttoned his shirt and slipped inside against his skin. "Not yet."

"I don't think there will ever be enough of you, darlin'. You're my own personal addiction." And that was the God's honest truth.

"All right. That sounds good to me." January shifted on the couch. "Bed? You look pretty tired."

"Let's sit here together, neck a little. I might doze off, but I'd like to be with you." He thought that was a grand idea, all the way.

"I think I can handle that." And to make that point,

January kissed him, just for the taste, but he recognized the heat simmering under it.

"Apple pie kisses." Hawk chuckled and stole a second kiss. "I like this."

"I do too. I feel like no one ever gets enough of this. The easy stuff, you know?"

"You know it. This is the part that I ache for." He could always get laid, but being touched? Being known? That was a whole new thing.

"I want you to have what you need, baby. Whether that's kisses or spaghetti lessons. I'm in. Okay? I'm all in."

"Be nice, darlin'," he teased. "Or I'll work you all in. All the way in deep."

January chuckled, breath warm against his cheek. "Oh, if that's a promise, I'm not going to be nice at all. No more Mister Nice Guy."

"Mmm, I swear to God, darlin'. I love the way you fill me up to the top." He couldn't stop grinning. Lord, he was happy.

"And I'm looking forward to when we can do that again. I'm being very patient and telling myself it's good for us. We met fucking. We're necking right now, remember?"

"We are. Necking, and imagining how you're going to fill me up." This was more fun than color TV.

"You know what you need?" Jan laughed. "Ice."

"Ice?" He went for innocent, but he had no idea if it would work.

"Wow. That was impressive. I bet your mom falls for that." January's fingers slid over his chest and ghosted over his bad shoulder, which hadn't had a touch like that in a while.

"Oh." January pulled away, and he shook his head. "No, darlin'. Please. Touch me. It's what I need."

January's fingers came right back, picking up where they left off. "I know you still hurt, and I know you're still tired, but this is getting better. I can see it. You have more energy, your color is better. You're moving around more."

"It is. I'm one hell of a healer. I hate being worthless to anyone, you know that." That touch echoed inside him. It wasn't a horny feeling. It was bigger, deeper. Somehow perfect.

"I do. But you're not worthless to me, even hurt. You're still my cowboy." January kissed him, following those words with physical truth.

He held on, luxuriating in their closeness. "Yours, darlin', and you're mine. You make me fucking happy."

"Necking. Necking happy. Fucking in a few more days."

Their laughter was easy and genuine. There was no pressure from Jan to be more than he was or more than he could be in that moment.

"I do love you." He made sure that every time he said it, he knew January heard how he meant it.

22

No matter how this weekend went, there were worse places to be than Anaheim in the spring. January had his sunglasses hooked over the collar of his T-shirt, he'd worn shorts on the plane and his Pearl Jam ball cap... he was ready for warmer weather and sunshine.

He should have been in a great mood as he hauled their suitcases off the carousel, and he honestly was trying to shake the worry, but he was anxious. He wasn't sure Hawk was ready for all of this. Still, it was time to be a hundred percent behind his man. Hawk didn't need his doubts. What Hawk needed was his confidence, his trust, and all the positive energy he had.

"This one is yours, cowboy." He needed to pay attention now. He was about to spend the next few days pretending Hawk wasn't blind and he was a friend.

Good thing it was love, right?

"Charlie shipped my gear to the hotel, so we're supposed to go down and find our car." Hawk moved through the airport pretty easily, really, the man looking relaxed and easy in his skin.

"Okay. I'm following you, Champ." They had a car? This was so weird. Hawk had made all the arrangements, so he was along for the ride. He couldn't remember the last time someone else handled his travel for him. Maybe his sister's destination wedding? Yeah, probably. That had been years ago.

There was a man standing with an iPad waiting immediately to the right of the elevator, and Hawk went right to him. "Hawk Destry."

"Excellent, sir. I'm Bill, I'll be your driver for the event."

"Nice to meet you, Bill. This is January. He'll be on our bill as well."

"Last name?"

"Bell."

Bill typed like mad with his thumbs on his iPad. "Very good. Both headed to the same hotel?"

"I... Yes?" He looked at Hawk.

"We are. We've got a suite. I don't know what the number is until check-in."

"This way." The driver took Hawk's suitcase but left him to carry his, which made him laugh.

We have a suite. "A suite. Fancy." And plausibly shareable without being too suspicious. Nice.

"Yeah. I like the idea of a bedroom and a sitting area, so I get them when I can."

He liked that idea too. Elbow room was never a bad thing.

They got into a black car, and he pulled out his phone. "Just want to let Jax know we landed." Not that Jax needed to know, but texting would keep him from stealing the kiss he really wanted. "He's going to watch on TV this weekend."

"He'll watch me crash and burn a couple of times." Hawk sounded like there was no question of that.

"You're still worth watching." Hawk had been working out. Crunches and hand weights, whatever he could do to rehab. Jan was a little awed at how much Hawk could pull off even sore. "And Jax is hooked on the sport in general, as you know."

The couple of events Jax had come over to watch with them on TV had been hilarious. Jax had become a total fan, and he was totally hooked on the insider info that Hawk had.

"You want anything on the way to the hotel? Food? Drug store? Coffee?" Hawk's hand landed on his leg.

He stared at that hand for a long moment before carefully covering it with his own. This was Hawk's world, Hawk's career, and he would follow Hawk's cues. The warmth of that hand was reassuring when he hadn't realized he needed that. "Coffee. But I bet I can get it there, right? We don't need to make a special stop. What were you thinking for dinner?"

"Oh, chicken breasts? Or maybe an egg white omelet?" Hawk rolled his eyes dramatically.

"Lettuce-wrapped air?" He squeezed Hawk's fingers and bounced them on his knee. "I meant eating in or out."

"Let's eat in tonight and then we'll go down for a beer after. Sound good?"

"Sounds great. We can relax for a while." Hawk could probably use it. "And if we don't get to the beer, that's okay too." He looked out the window taking in everything. This was totally unfamiliar country to him.

"Excellent. There's supposed to be a decent restaurant in the hotel with good choices close, plus a great bar off the lobby."

"You did your research, huh? Is this a different hotel

than where you usually stay?" *A great bar off the lobby.* He was liking this. Hawk seemed animated, happy to be back.

"I've been here once, but it's been redone. They gave us some great deals on the rooms, corporate said."

"That's cool."

Bill glanced at them in the rearview mirror, eyes meeting Jan's for a second. "The renovation was finished right before Christmas. The rooms are nice. The restaurant makes good burgers."

"Yeah? Thanks." He could do a burger.

"Almost there. You're right in time for check-in. There's usually a bit of line, but it moves."

Hawk grinned wide, in the general direction of the driver. "Good deal. Do I call you in the evenings Mr. Bill, if we need a ride?"

"You do. If I can't come out, I'll send my son, Bill Jr." Bill winked in the rearview. "I saw your name come up. We drove for you last year, and it was a good weekend, all around."

"Excellent." Hawk nodded once, as if to say that was that. "That's what I like to hear."

Well he wouldn't forget anyone's name anyway.

The car pulled up and he climbed out, looking around as he stretched his legs. It was a beautiful hotel, the wide drive was lined by palm trees, and the sky was bright blue. "Wow."

"Hooray, Southern California. I do love it out here." Hawk was beaming, so exciting.

He slipped Bill a tip once they got their suitcases. "I am so ready for this sun."

"Enjoy it." He got a business card in return and Bill was on his way.

"Doors are kind of diagonal to your right," Jan said,

thinking he was helping and then wondering if he should have kept his mouth shut. This was Hawk's show.

"Yeah, the big dark squares. I'm going to follow you in, okay?"

"Sure. I'll head for the front desk." Okay. Good. They'd figure this out.

He rolled his suitcase through the front doors and into a wide open, marbled lobby. "Everything is so shiny."

"Hawk! Man, good to see you!" Mackey the bullfighter came wandering up. "How's the shoulder? Do I need to watch it?"

Hawk chuckled, but nodded. "Doc'll probably let me ride, but I don't need to whack it again."

"No. No, let's keep you whole, son."

"Have I introduced you to January, Mack?"

"January Bell." How cool was this? He stuck out a hand to shake. "It's great to meet you. I love watching you out there."

"Well, thank you, sir. I appreciate it. Y'all come to my room around eight—we're celebrating Tommy's birthday with a little cake and a beer or two. Number 1102." The short man was stacked like a machine, the bright blue eyes seeming to see everything. Did Mackey know? It was hard to believe he didn't.

He wasn't going to make any assumptions. "Sounds great. I'm still on east coast time, but if I can stay awake that long I'd love to meet Tommy too. Thank you." He would. But Hawk had a big day and he'd rather his cowboy be rested and ready.

"We'll save seats for you. It should be small—folks are coming in and out."

Hawk's lips were twitching, the laughter barely held back.

"All right." He grinned, glancing between the two of them. "Okay, what am I missing?"

"He *so* lies. The old man lies. Small. Everyone will make their way over to have beer and cake and fuck with Tommy."

"Ah." These guys were like a big family, he should have known better. "Sounds like we might be there."

"We'll stop in, for a beer and a peek at the birthday boy." Hawk got up to the desk and started checking in, handling it easily and leaving him in a slowly growing crowd of rodeo people.

Someone shouted Mackey's name and he excused himself, leaving Jan there to handle the bags.

Not only was Hawk in a good mood, but he was standing straighter, moving easily. Jan wasn't sure if he actually felt better or was putting on a good show with all the fans and cowboys around. Either way, seeing Hawk looking healthy and confident was a lot more of a turn-on than was probably appropriate for a hotel lobby.

Hawk came to him, chuckling softly. "We're 1104. Next door to the bullfighters. Lord help us."

Oh boy. He grinned and shook his head. "So we might as well go to the party instead of listen to it, huh?"

"At least we don't have far to go." Hawk's grin was naughty as hell.

"I can appreciate a short trip home." He licked his lips. "Shall we go upstairs?"

"Fuck yeah. Let's go get settled."

This time January stepped ahead of Hawk and led the way to the elevators. One more thing they had figured out.

They headed up to eleven, Hawk humming softly under his breath.

The humming was back. Also a good sign. He was still a little worried about the ride, but it was amazing to feel his cowboy coming back. This was Hawk's comfort zone. This was where he knew things, and people. He was happy here and it showed.

"Eleven," he sang as the door opened.

"They said go left and we're the last door on the right." Hawk dragged his fingers along the hall, counting doors. "Are you looking forward to our drive up the coast? Seeing the ocean?"

"I am. I've been to the coast in the San Francisco area, but not down here. The terrain has got to be totally different. I love that you planned this out for us."

"You, me, a convertible and a week. I'm so in." Hawk did seem completely tickled, lit up inside.

"Eleven-oh-four." Jan put a hand on Hawk's chest to stop him and immediately pulled it back before someone could see. "Sorry."

"No worries." Hawk winked at him, opening the door and then handing him a key card. "For you."

"Thanks. This is... great. And kind of surreal."

They got in and the rooms were decent—good-sized, king bed, couch. It all worked. The view was fine, and January could stay here a few days.

"I'm going to explore the room a little."

"Sure. Um... we're in the sitting area. The bedroom is ahead to the left, the bathroom is right inside that door on the right. I'll take our suitcases into the bedroom." He left Hawk to learn his way around.

"They're going to be delivering my gear in an hour or so." Hawk walked the room, searched the bathroom, then went to open the curtains.

"Light. Good idea, let's let in the sun." Jan tossed his ball cap on the bed and wandered over. He'd been dying to get a hold of Hawk since they got off the plane. He stepped in close behind his lover and circled his arms around Hawk. "Privacy. Yay."

"Yes. Yay." Hawk leaned back into him, the sigh utterly pleased. "You approve of the hotel room, darlin'?"

"I do. I approve of the hotel room, Anaheim, the sky and the cowboy I'm holding onto." He tilted his head and kissed the side of Hawk's neck, under the ear.

"Mmm..." Oh, wasn't that a satisfied sound? Hawk tilted his head, offering him more skin. Hell, offering him everything.

"You've taken care of everything. I'm not used to that, I feel spoiled. Thank you." Jan traced the ridges of Hawk's abs through his shirt.

"I'm loving having someone to explore with. Having you here. Knowing that we can do this." Hawk's belly jerked and jumped under his fingers.

"We can definitely do this." He found the wide buckle of Hawk's belt and slid his fingers lower to rest over Hawk's fly. "We can do anything we want."

"We can. I'm ready to do anything we want, darlin'. I want to walk bow-leggedy tomorrow." Now that was clear. Enough his balls took notice, and his cock too, stretching to press against Hawk's back.

"Will that help you keep your ass in the saddle tomorrow?" Hawk wanted bow-legged, he could absolutely oblige.

"How did you guess?" Hawk turned and pushed into his arms, taking a hard kiss.

This was an unexpected surprise and he wasn't going to question it. He pulled Hawk in tight, tighter than he had in weeks, and took everything his lover wanted him to have.

He'd been good. He'd been patient. He'd been as

considerate as he knew how to be. But he didn't have to hold back anymore.

He wanted his cowboy.

"Darlin'. Darlin', please. I need your cock. I need to feel you spreading me wide."

"Fuck yeah. Gotta have you." Jan backed his lover into the window then dropped his hands to Hawk's belt and tugged it open.

"How? Over the arm of the sofa? Over the bed? Here against the wall?"

Jan laughed, and was pleased that it came out low and sexy. "Yes. But right here first." He spun Hawk around to face the window and went for his suitcase to dig out his little black bag. "If your shoulder can take it."

"I can take it. Hell, I need it." Hawk stripped off boots and jeans, leaving him with a tight shirt and nothing else.

He walked back slowly, taking in that incredible view. "Mmm. You put that beautiful blue sky to shame, angel." He got hold of one firm ass cheek and gave it a squeeze.

"Flatterer. I'm damn glad you think so." Hawk wiggled, the soft chuckles making his heart ache a little with the happiness there.

Fuck. That was every inch his hot cowboy.

He set the little bag down on the window ledge and pulled out what he needed. He wanted Hawk even more than their first time in Denver, and he'd never been so glad to see a rubber in his life. "Need you." So bad his hands were shaking as he rolled it on.

"Take me. I'm yours." Hawk pressed his hips back, the offer clear and undeniable.

"Lube." He slicked his fingers and leaned into Hawk's back, pressing them against his lover's hungry hole. "My cowboy."

"Yeah..." Hawk took him, rocking back, taking his fingers, inch by inch, swallowing him up.

Hawk was eager and it was a struggle to take his time and make sure his lover was ready for him. He listened to Hawk's soft grunts and told himself to have another minute of patience. Just a few more seconds.

Okay. He'd had enough.

He tugged his fingers away and stepped up close, one hand on Hawk's hip and the other guiding his prick into glorious tight heat.

"Oh god." His eyes went wide, and he groaned. "Yes."

"Fuck, that's still so good." One heavy hand braced against the window. "Love."

He pushed in deep, moving until their bodies pressed together. "Love. I've missed this. Missed you. Fuck." He had to move. He rocked back, and dove in again, his free hand reaching for Hawk's good shoulder to hold on. Hawk held him like a burning fist, the hot muscles working his prick.

He took what he wanted. They had forever to savor each other, but right now all they had was desperate need. He held onto Hawk for leverage, one shoulder and one hip, and didn't hold back.

"Yes." The single, bitten-out word came with a huge squeeze, a needy cry.

Fuck yeah. He grunted and hammered that spot, determined to drive Hawk out of his mind. The string of filthy thoughts that surfaced never made it past his lips; he didn't have enough air, or enough sense to form the words.

Hawk knew. He believed that whole-heartedly. Hawk heard him in his fucking soul.

"You," he grunted and paused long enough to slide the hand on his Hawk's hip around to his lover's swollen cock. "First."

"Uhn."

January wasn't sure if it was an agreement or an argument, but Hawk's cock leapt into his hand, eager for his touch.

His knowing fingers closed over the silky skin that covered hard heat and he moved again, taking Hawk with long, purposeful strokes. "Good, baby."

"G-good. Oh fuck. Fuck, darlin'—needed you so damn bad." Hawk moved like a piston, driving hard.

"Got you, angel." He spread his legs wider for balance and held on as Hawk did most of the work, thrusting deep every time the cowboy rocked back to take him, squeezing Hawk's dripping cock.

"Fixin' to..." Fuck, yes.

Just the words made his balls draw up hard and he gasped. "Yes. Do it, Champ. Give it up for me."

"For you!" Triumphant, Hawk shot hard, spunk coating his fingers, ass rippling around his cock.

"Jesus!" He choked on the word, went up on his toes, and humped in short bursts as Hawk drew his climax from him. He came hard, shuddering, lightheaded, and had no control over it at all. He fucking loved it.

January held Hawk up against the window, both of them shaking as they panted together.

He tucked his nose into that warm spot right behind Hawk's jaw where he could feel his lover swallow and smell the sweat in Hawk's damp hair, feeling like his chest might explode. "Love."

"Fuck yes. So much." Hawk sounded as blown as he was, and January loved it.

He nodded and pushed back. "Mmm. I remember you. You're that steaming hot cowboy I met at that bar." His voice was rough and dry, and he swallowed hard.

"Mmhmm. I got a bottle of whiskey being delivered around six. Two glasses."

Details. He loved that Hawk paid attention too. "So thoughtful. I think I love you even more—"

There was a heavy knock at the door. Jan blinked, and then remembered, stepping backward. "Your gear?"

"Fuck. Yeah. You got more clothes on than I do?"

He laughed as he zipped up, or tried to. He was worn out. "I was thinking that. Hang tight."

Jan ran his fingers through his hair and closed the bedroom door as he left the room. Timing was everything.

"Jesus this thing is heavy. Thanks." He grinned at the young bellhop and gave him a five-dollar bill from his pocket before closing the door. "What do you have in here, Champ?" He called as he made his way back to the bedroom. "Bricks?"

"Yep. I carry around bricks to put in my boots to keep me on the bull." Hawk came over to him, shaking his head. "God knows what Ben and Charlie put in there."

He set the bag on the floor and tucked his hands up under Hawk's T-shirt. "Do you want to be more naked or less right now?"

"More. We're here and alone. I vote happy nakedness."

"Me too." He lifted the shirt over Hawk's head and then tugged his own off tossing them both. "I am definitely happy."

"Lord, me too. I been needing that like breathing." Hawk stretched up tight, wiggling side-to-side.

"Shoulder okay?" He kicked off his sneakers and shoved his jeans and briefs down, adding yet more clothing to the mess on the floor.

"Stiff, a little tender, but better. Good enough, right?" Hawk carefully rolled it, and January saw the tiniest flinch.

"I think it held up pretty well. I might have to test it again later." Carefully. But there was no way he was keeping his hands off his cowboy all night. He took Hawk's hand. "Come to bed?"

"Yes, sir. We can roll around in cool sheets and nap. Post flying naps are the best."

"Post flying fucks are better." He pulled Hawk over and turned the bed down. "I want to hold you." A nap sounded perfect though, and then that scotch would arrive and they'd order dinner in...

Then his first cowboy party.

He felt like he ought to go buy a hat.

23

Hawk had never done this—never had a lover that he was able to hang out with. He wasn't stupid—he had to be crazy careful in public, but here with the guys that were family or friendly? He could be proud.

You riding 2nite? Charlie's text came in, making him smile.

Tomorrow. It's Thursday.

Ah. Shoulder good?

Sore, that's all. And Doc would approve him to ride. He knew it. *How u feeling?*

Tired.

Damn. *Rest. I'll call tomorrow after I ride.*

Fall off u mean.

Fuck off.

"What's funny?" Jan leaned over his shoulder, breath tinged with the scent of good scotch.

"Mmm, Charlie. He was checking in." Hawk couldn't wait to take January to Ben and Charlie's. Couldn't wait.

"How is he?" January kneaded his shoulders, fingers

working into his sore muscle carefully but purposefully. "And Ben?"

"Charlie says they're tired. We need to go see them soon. I'm worried about him some." That was the understatement of the century.

"Well, do you want to go on Sunday after the short-go? We can rearrange our week." Jan's thumb hit a nerve and he twitched his shoulder away reflexively. "Sorry. Sorry, baby."

"No. I want our week in the convertible, our drive up the coast, the Winchester Mystery house. Maybe week after next?" He was selfish, but he'd been wanting to do this—to go and be with a lover, no parents, nothing but them—forever.

"Any time you want. I know he's important to you." Jan settled beside him. "The Winchester house sounds so cool."

"I want to go to the beach, feel the waves. I want to be in a convertible with you, go to a weird diner." He needed it.

Even better, Jan was as into it as he was. "Monterey. Half Moon Bay. You, me and a Mustang."

"Yes." He turned to push into January's arms. "God yes. I'm so excited."

"I'm a good driv—" A whoop went up next door and the thump of the bull fighter's party music interrupted their conversation. Jan shook his head and laughed. "I guess it's party time!"

"It's going to be for a while." He cracked up, shaking his head. "I bet we call security tonight."

"Jesus, really? Are they that wild? I'm not sure I remember how to party anymore, but I'll give it a go."

"They're bullfighters. They only come in wild." He loved them, but they had stress.

Jan played with his hair, tugging lightly. "What does one wear to a cowboy party?"

"Jeans. You should totally wear jeans." He had to grin, had to. "Tight ones."

Jan laughed. "Really? You want all those cowboys ogling my butt?"

"They can ogle all they want. I get to touch." He wasn't a jealous man. He had January's heart, dammit.

"I hope I remember we're supposed to be just friends." Jan snorted. "I better not drink."

"We'll be fine. Mackey is family. We can't kiss up on each other, but we don't have to stay a yardstick apart." It was a balancing act, from what he could tell.

"Mackey? Huh. I would never have guessed." Jan started gathering up the clothes they'd left all over the bedroom floor.

"You don't think? I've known for a long time..." He guessed that Mackey had known about him. They tended to huddle together in rooms, in parties, at houses. There was a group of family and allies, and he loved them.

"I think I look at the guys you work with and assume they're straight. I shouldn't obviously, there's a handful of guys I've met already, but... I know you have to be careful and I don't want to make a mistake."

"We do, and we will." He wasn't going to stress it. He wasn't—he was pretending like he wasn't blind as a bat, and he was pretending he wasn't scared about his best bud retiring. Hell, he was pretending he wasn't scared about Momma showing up because he hadn't been answering her phone calls. This was way down the goddamn list.

Jan poured them each another finger of scotch and handed his glass to him. "I guess we should think about maybe eventually getting dressed."

"Yeah. We have to go over and make an appearance. I'm

warm and melty here, though." The whiskey was swirling in his veins and making things fuzzy.

"We can take our time and sip." Jan had to speak up a little to be heard over the ruckus next door, but still managed to sound husky. "I can tell you about how hot you were up against that window, and how even though I love you naked, I am looking forward to your ass in your Wranglers."

"Mmm, I felt like I was fixin' to explode, I needed you so bad." He wasn't sure if he had bedroom eyes, but he bet he did. He felt heavy and sensual, like even January's words were touching his skin.

"I guess you were saving that surprise for when we got here, huh?"

"It was a surprise I needed you?" He couldn't believe that.

"No, baby. That wasn't a surprise, it was that I could actually *have* you again. Finally."

"It's been a long few weeks, hasn't it?" The waiting had almost been worth it. Almost.

"It has. But it was for a good reason. I get to watch you ride again tomorrow." Jan nipped at his ear.

"And the day after that. And the day after that." This was a good game.

"Yeah, yeah. It's not going to get boring, Champ." Jan swallowed back the last of his drink and set the glass down. "Never a dull moment."

"No. That's why I'm in this game. That and I got no other skills." None.

"I don't like it when you say that. Of course you have other skills. You're smart. You learn quickly. Also, you give the best fucking head I've ever had." Jan chuckled.

"Ha! I'll take that, yessir." He rolled with amusement.

That would rock on his resume—champion bull rider, master at giving head, cute in jeans.

"I love you. Let's get dressed and crash this party so we can stumble home and go back to bed." Jan gave him a playful shove. "And I can put you to work."

"Yeah, yeah." He pulled on a pair of good Wranglers and his T-shirt, smoothing it over his abs as he tucked it in. He was already humming to the music, rocking side-to-side.

Jan dressed in those tight jeans he'd talked about, but he wasn't sure if it was for him or just to be a smart-ass. Didn't matter, he supposed, it was his smart-ass either way. The black T-shirt showed off Jan's sturdy shoulders, but the belt wasn't western, and neither were his lover's black sneakers. They said New York City, or maybe L.A., but definitely not rodeo.

It said that January was pretty and his, and he closed his eyes as he ran his hand over January's ass. Oh, that was fine.

"Mmm. You like these jeans, I know. And you look great. I like that shirt. I think you're going to blend in better than I do."

Of course he would. This was his family, his tribe, where he belonged. "You're going to do fine."

"Well, shall we find out?" The sound of laughter came through the wall from next door.

"Sounds like a plan." Hawk grabbed a key card and his wallet, because you never knew when you might end up in the back of a limo with a fifth of Crown and all your buddies. "Let's go play."

Jan got the door but let him lead this time, hanging out behind his shoulder. The party was louder in the hall, but also sounded a little less wild.

"Happy birthday, man!" Hawk grinned into the sea of

faces, waiting for Tommy to grab him up and swing him around, which Tommy did.

"Oy! You came to sing to me, did you? Mother, did you see? Hawk came and brought his friend."

Mackey chuckled. "I see. We'll all sing here in a bit."

"You know it. I'm next door, so our caterwauling won't matter." Hawk drew Jan up next to him. "This is Jan, y'all. This is his first rodeo party. Be kind."

Jan ducked his head and offered Tommy a hand. "Happy Birthday. Great to meet you. I'm a fan."

"Sorry, mate. I don't shake hands with strangers." Tommy grabbed Jan up too.

"Whoa." Jan stammered, laughing. "Okay, then."

Tommy set Jan back on his feet. "Somebody get this man a beer?"

January was whisked away by a couple of guys while Mackey found him a stool to perch on in the middle of all the action.

"How you feeling, man?" Danny asked. "You gonna ride?"

"I am. I can't have your skanky ass taking my title, can I?"

"My money is still on you this season, but I wouldn't count on next year if I was you. Still, Nicole was liking my paydays."

"I bet she was." He hooted, tickled as all get out. "How's she doing? That baby growing?"

"Every day!" Faces were usually a blur, but he could make out that smile no problem. "She's not much for parties right now. Well, not bullfighter parties anyway. She said to say hi, and she'd see you tomorrow."

"Good deal. Maybe she'll come to breakfast Saturday?" He did like her, and January was very fond.

"That sounds great." Danny leaned close. "It's a boy."

"Oh, another bull rider, huh? Congratulations!" He hugged Danny hard.

Danny laughed. "Thank you!"

"Did he tell you it's a boy? We've been taking bets on names." Neil, one of the veteran bullfighters poked him in his good arm. "I'm going with Danny Junior."

Danny snorted. "Nicole has ideas."

"Danny Junior, mark my words. Hey, Hawk. What do you hear from Charlie?"

"He's getting better, still real tired."

"He coming back?" Danny asked, and Hawk shook his head.

"I think he's ready to lay it down."

"Damn." Danny signed. "Wow."

"Doc didn't want to give details, but word is one too many hits to the head. Probably best. I miss him though, you tell him hey for me when you talk to him next?"

"Will do." He was going to Nashville, as soon as he could. Not this week, though. God forgive him, he couldn't wait to experience California.

A group in the back corner of the room started singing along—more like shouting along—to the Steve Miller Band, and he swore he recognized Jan's voice. As the song ended there was laughter and the clinking of beer bottles.

"Everybody likes that one!" Tommy shouted, headed his way. "Hawk, your friend here is all right."

"He's a good 'un. I intend to keep him around." That should be clear enough shouldn't it?

"Crikey! If that's how it is, then you need to teach him some country. He can sing." Tommy had his arm around Jan's shoulders.

Jan laughed. "I'm not sure that was singing, actually."

"You know your bloke there can sing, don't you?" Tommy told Jan. "He's like a wee bird."

"Shut up."

"Really?" Jan sounded way too interested.

"Indeed. Don't let him tell you otherwise."

"I know he can whistle like a bird. And he sent me a picture of him playing guitar, but I haven't heard him sing yet." Jan gave his knee a firm pat. "Why haven't I heard you sing?"

"I doodle." He wasn't a singer. Not like Ben. He was a shower superstar.

"Well you're going to doodle for me sometime."

Danny choked and nearly spit out his beer.

"Oops?" He could hear Jan's evil grin much better than he could see it.

The whole room burst out into wild, happy laughter, and Hawk joined in, even if his cheeks were on fire.

"While we're all laughing," Mackey shouted above the noise. "How old are you now, Tommy?"

"Oh, around ninety. Mother here is at least a hundred and ten, right?"

Mackey rolled his eyes, but bowed. "You know it!"

"Lord, that makes me a true dinosaur at least. Is there cake, Mackey? Who throws a birthday party without cake?" Neil coughed like the heavy smoker he was, covering it with his arm.

Jan moved closer. "I think I might have made an okay first impression."

"You did fine. We'll have a piece of cake when it gets here and then we can slip away." Hawk loved the way January smelled—it was a mixture of soap, whiskey, and sex.

"Perfect. So I can get another ride in before yours tomorrow."

"It's good practice," he whispered.

Jan gave his shoulder a squeeze, and the heat in his lover's fingers was a promise. "You know, I'm watching Mackey... I don't see it at all. And I'm usually pretty good with this stuff."

"I brought the cake, y'all!" Jack the safety man came in with a huge personality, filling the room.

"You are the man!" Mackey came up and took the cake. "You get a couple hundred candles?"

"Only a hundred. It's not your birthday yet."

"Fucker." Mackey blew Jack a kiss, and Hawk wondered if Jan saw it yet.

"Hawk!" Jack didn't know the meaning of the word gentle and pulled him into a hug. "Welcome back, man. You ready to ride?"

"You know it. You met January yet?"

"This your city man? He's pretty. Good pick."

"I am." Jan chuckled softly. "And actually, he's *my* cowboy."

"Oh ho! Listen to that." Jack thumped Hawk, almost gently. "Good job."

"It's good to meet you, Jack. I love watching you work." Jan and Jack shook hands, the gesture strong enough he could hear it when their hands met.

He liked that. Jack was the old guard—him and Mackey—and the approval was important as hell.

The lights went out, the candles on the cake the only glow in the room. "Everybody sing!"

The chorus of voices singing to Tommy was loud and joyous, even Jan joined in at the top of his lungs.

Tommy blew out the candles, and they all applauded, the beer and cakes flowing free. Lord, there were going to be some bloated guys tomorrow.

"We can share," Jan said as he accepted a plate. "A bite for you, two or three for me, hm? Ooh. I get to have those VIP hot dogs tomorrow."

"You do, unless they have some wild California veggie burger with avocado."

"What? They better not fuck with my hot dog." Jan laughed.

"I know how important hot dogs are to you, darlin'." He managed to keep a straight face.

"Oh, good one." Jan bumped shoulders with him. "Open up I have a big bite for you." He could smell the sweet frosting under his nose.

He let January feed him his bite, feeling utterly daring, wildly free.

"So... are Jack and Mackey...?"

"Friends with bennies." Jack was damn friendly. Crazy friendly. Wildly damn friendly.

Jan nodded. "I see it now. Mackey stands differently around him. Another bite?"

"No. No, one was enough." It was sweet and not worth the calories. "You can have it."

"I'm having this one more," Jan chuckled. "And then I want you to take me home with you."

"Sounds like a plan. We can have a dance." Strip down and rub together like they were made to.

"Great idea. Do we say goodbye or sneak out?" Jan took his beer. "I'll ditch these."

"We'll ease out. They're busy, you know? Partying. You and I have plans." Hawk stood and waved randomly. "See y'all tomorrow."

"Bye!" They were showered with shouts, but it died down quick.

"Nicely done."

"Thank you. How did you like your first cowboy party?" He pulled out the keycard and opened their door.

"It was like college only with more hats." Jan hustled him inside, one hand on his ass.

"And boots." He leaned into the touch, feeling that heat in his balls. "And fewer girls."

"There weren't many girls at my college parties. At least not ones interested in boys." Jan spun him, stole the hat off his head and kissed him, happy and heated.

Oh. Oh, right. They had gay parties. He'd never thought of that. He wrapped his arms around January and held on.

"Put some music on, cowboy, and let's have that dance." Jan let him go and took his glasses too. "When we go home next, I'll take you to a club."

"Yeah? I've never danced in public." He got his phone to play his 'happy' playlist, the music bouncy, something to rub to.

"Never?" Jan hooked an arm around his waist. It was nothing like a western dance hold, pulled him right in close.

"No. No one's ever asked." He hummed and pushed right in, fascinated by the hard lines of Jan's body.

"Well, I will ask. I am asking." Jan rocked him to one side and back again, holding him tight.

"You got my dances. All you want." He groaned and moved, trusting in Jan's arms.

Jan curled fingers around the back of his neck and touched their foreheads together. "This is nice. Just holding you. Just breathing you in."

Lord, January knew how to say the best things, words that settled in the pit of his belly and grew.

Jan rocked them again, belt buckles scraping together. "You don't have to see me. We don't even have to talk. You know? It feels good."

"It feels like heaven." He rested his cheek against Jan's chest, listening to the solid, steady thump of January's heart.

"Hang on." Jan reached back and tugged off his shirt so Hawk could rest against a bare chest instead. "Better."

They didn't talk for a while, they listened to the music and breathed, and Jan led Hawk around the suite like he knew what he was doing.

It was the closest thing to magic he'd ever known, and he had won the Finals. "Love."

"Mmhmm. Love you." Jan tugged Hawk's shirt from his jeans, and helped him get it off, then leaned down for a kiss. But before their lips met, Jan's hands smoothed over his chest, thumbs finding his nipples and brushing across them. His lips parted on a gasp, and he rocked up on his tiptoes, totally captured. "Every bit of you."

Jan kissed him and danced him toward the bedroom door. "Ditch the boots, Champ. I want to show you."

"On it." He loved that, that Jan knew about the challenges of jeans and boots.

Of course, Jan didn't make it easy. His lover tickled and groped him, touching and teasing and getting in his way. "Need some help, cowboy?"

"Butthead!" He couldn't stop laughing, the world warm and right, January's hands like little brands wherever they touched him.

"Careful, don't lose your balance. Oops!" Jan toppled them onto the bed, fingers fumbling at his belt.

"Two left feet?" he hooted. "Or is it four?"

Oh fuck, he was funny.

"Ha! Let's hope you do better tomorrow." Jan laughed. "These western buckles are so fucking easy."

"Easy access to the important bits." And he didn't need

his feet to ride except to spur. He wasn't expecting to ride. He was going for don't get hurt.

"You won't hear me arguing." Jan licked a warm line from his sternum to his belt, then tugged and shoved at his Wranglers.

Fuck, that tongue! He arched and twisted, trying to get more. It felt amazing, knowing that he could beg and push and Jan got it.

"I've got more for you, baby. Lots more." Jan got him bare and worked his own jeans down and off. "I'm going to taste every single inch of you."

"Making me crazy. Please, darlin'. All of me." He was babbling. *Babbling.*

"All of you." Jan lifted one leg and kissed the inside of his ankle, right on top of the bone and blew across the bottom of his foot, the cool air sliding between his toes.

His eyes went wide and he gasped, totally caught by that not-there touch. His balls drew up, his belly went hard, and his toes curled.

"Mmm. You need touching, Champ. Every bit of you deserves to be touched, loved." Jan didn't touch but licked and bit over his ankle and up his calf, then a curious tongue tickled the back of his knee.

"Tickles." Not enough to pull away, because it felt too good to move away.

"Not sorry." Jan put his leg down, knee bent out to the side and tasted the skin up the inside of his thigh toward his hip.

Oh fuck. That was sensitive as hell, with his nerves firing all the way up into his belly, high enough his nipples went hard.

"Mmm. Goosebumps?" The path Jan took from his hip,

over his belly button, across his ribs, was slow torture. "Good?"

"Better than. I am fucking flying." This was the whole world—riding well, spinning, and so fucking in love he hurt.

"Good." Jan's mouth closed over a nipple with a soft hum.

He had never considered that his nipples were for anything more than decoration, but Jan was teaching him otherwise.

There wasn't a part of him Jan couldn't make tingle.

His lover's cock pressed into his thigh, sliding and leaving a wet trail that cooled quickly. "Baby." Jan sighed and leaned up to kiss him.

"Yes." He didn't know what he was agreeing to, but he didn't care. It didn't matter. The answer was yes.

Jan's kiss was soft and sweet, the connection almost more mental than physical. It was beautiful but didn't last long. It built, growing hungry and impatient until they parted, both of them breathless. Jan took a deep breath, and Hawk barely had time to register the tension in it before Jan grabbed him by the hip and flipped him onto his belly.

He pulled his legs up under him, offering his ass, the line of his back, his hole. He got his arms under him, supporting his shoulder with the pillows.

"Fuck, look at you." Jan shocked him, smacking his ass hard enough to leave a mark, then drew a hot tongue over his hole.

"Jan!" He spread a little, his hips moving without his permission, like he was dancing with his lover again.

"Every bit, baby." One hand spread him wider and the other cupped and tugged on his balls, but that tongue didn't let up.

He began to babble, making promises that he meant,

deep in his soul. He'd never felt so exposed and so fucking protected at the same time. Never.

By the time Jan's cock replaced that tongue he was pretty sure he was begging for it. Or trying to.

"I'm going to make you scream, Champ."

"You-you're gonna try all right." God, he hoped so. He needed a good hard screaming orgasm.

"Is that a dare?" Jan grunted as his thick cock pushed in, sliding deep as they rocked into one another.

Electricity slammed up along his spine, sharp and bright enough to light the room, and his ass clenched. "Fuck yes."

"That's what I thought." Jan took Hawk hard but held back his weight, using Hawk's hips for balance as their bodies crashed together. Hawk was beginning to burn, his world tightening down to nothing but his aching hole, his heavy ballsac.

Jan bit out a string of hungry words, and Hawk heard the strain, the little crack in his lover's control. He might be headed for a meltdown, but he wasn't going to be alone.

"Fucking love you." He was fixin' to be shoved over that edge, and there wasn't a thing that could be done about it. Not a thing.

"Love you baby... so much. Fuck!" Jan's thrusts went suddenly short and shallow for a second, but he found control again and pulled back hard on Hawk's hips.

"Jan! Jan, fuck!" It wasn't a scream, but his need echoed through the room.

"Yeah." Jan sat back hard on his heels and pulled Hawk with him. "Ride, baby." Jan's fingers reached around his hip and gripped his cock, letting him slide through the firm, hot grip.

His back side on January's chest, and the angle of Jan's cock inside him changed, giving him something he'd never felt before. His eyes rolled back in his head, and he flew, forcing himself to hold back and ride.

"Beautiful, angel." His lover's voice felt like it was coming from everywhere and Jan's breath washed over his skin.

He opened his mouth to answer, but all that came out was a long moan that was pure need. All he needed was a single word, a push, anything.

"You ready, baby? You want it? Right now? Let it go." Jan's fist tightened around him and teeth clamped down hard on his good shoulder.

That was all she wrote. He shot so hard he lost himself. The only thing he knew was January, inside him, surrounding him.

"Shi—fuck!" That shout cut through the fog though, as Jan bucked under him, arms wrapping tight around his middle.

They slumped together, Jan careful of his shoulder, holding him as they hit the pillows.

"Fuck, baby. You okay? You good?" Jan asked, hot breath grazing his ear.

"Love you. Jesus. You—Wow." That was his best.

"Okay, then." Jan chuckled and curled around him. "Thank goodness for that party next door, huh? Drowned us right out."

"Mmhmm..." He'd bet he'd get ragged tomorrow. He didn't care.

"You're amazing, love. Beautiful. Hot as fuck." Jan spoke slowly, drowsily.

"You make me feel amazing. I didn't know that—" He didn't know things could be so overwhelming.

"Mmm. Well, I thought I did, but I didn't."

"Yeah." He snuggled right in with a happy sigh.

24

S how time.

Jan had done his job and made sure that Hawk was stoked and had a little swagger before they left the hotel. Hawk didn't seem nervous, but Jan was sure the nerves had to be there, even if Hawk fully expected to get dumped. It was still his lover's first time back.

Jan was doing his best not to seem worried at all, and he wasn't really, a little anxious for things to go well enough that Hawk could hold his head high.

"I could get used to these limo trips," he teased, resting a hand on Hawk's thigh. He could get used to nights like last night too. He felt like a fucking champion himself today.

"I've found that, lots of times, you can get a limo for the weekend about the same as cabbing it." Hawk rolled his shoulder, pushing it, testing it.

"You're solid, Champ." He felt like half the game was confidence, he wanted Hawk to have plenty.

"I am. The doc says I'm ready to ride." Hawk had gotten his check up this morning, had his approval.

"You've got this. I'll be yelling the loudest." Jan smiled at

Hawk, but the cowboy had sunglasses on, and it was hard to read his lover's expression.

"Just make sure I don't run into the camera cage again." Hawk snorted, and the sound turned into laughter.

"No problem. You'll hear me shouting 'Left, baby! Run left!'" He cracked up.

"I'll be keeping an ear out." Hawk hooted, knocking their shoulders together.

The limo pulled up outside the arena. Jan took Hawk's hand and squeezed his fingers. "Just ride your bull as best you can, and we'll skip the after-party tonight."

"You know I will. This is my job." Hawk leaned forward. "Pick us up after the event?"

"Yessir. I'm on it."

"Kick ass, Champ." Jan took Hawk's chin in his hand and gave his lover a quick hard kiss, then slid across the seat and opened the door.

They headed in through a side door, both of them slipping into a series of locker rooms.

The place went quiet when they walked in, everyone staring like they were fucking, right here in public, and Hawk tilted his head. "What? What's wrong?"

"Your family is here. All of them." One of the elder statesmen, Chris Walker, walked up, expression serious as a heart attack. "Your momma is *pissed*."

Jan blinked. "All of them?" What else was he going to say? He was looking forward to meeting the family? In his world he was always in the doghouse; he wasn't used to it being a big deal. But she must be quite a presence for everyone to stare like Hawk was in big trouble.

"All of them. Brothers. Wives. Kids. Folks. They have been here and they're waiting."

"Where?" Hawk rolled his eyes. "I want them to meet January."

"I'll take you."

Right, that was his cue. He stepped in behind Chris so Hawk could follow him. "She's upset, huh?"

"She's fucking furious at you, Bird. Like whoa."

"Yeah. I haven't been taking her calls."

Chris looked behind him. "Dude! She's your momma! You can't not take those calls. That's like, in the Bible!"

Jan snorted, trying hard to hide his laughter. He ghosted his mother all the time. "Sometimes you have to be wrong to be right."

"Sometimes you have to have a little space." Hawk didn't sound scared.

They turned a corner to a simple little hallway that was filled with huge men, tired women, at least a thousand children, and a tiny middle-aged woman who looked like his Hawk.

Except for the fire flashing in her eyes as she stood.

"Hawk Anthony Destry! What in the Sam Hill do you think you're up to? Not answering my calls? Not telling me how you were doing? Not coming home even once?"

"Now, Momma—"

"Don't you now, Momma me. I will personally put you over my knee. I was worried!"

Uh-oh. She'd pulled out the middle name trick. Hawk really was in trouble. He decided maybe he could be a distraction.

"Mrs. Destry?" He stepped right up with his best smile and took her hand in his, covering it with his other one. "I'm January Bell. It is such a pleasure to meet you. Hawk has told me so much about you, and all his brothers... wow. This is amazing."

"You're the reason for all this nonsense, are you? You're Mr. New York?"

"Momma, he has a name."

"Shut up, boy," she snapped.

"Guilty." He nodded. "I am from New York, and I'm also very fond of your son."

"And I appreciate that, but Hawk's got..."

"Momma—"

She actually stamped one flip flop on the ground. "Shut *up*, son. Hawk has responsibilities at home that he can't shirk."

"Momma!" Hawk snapped. "Jan knows."

Well. Jan glanced around at all the faces staring at him. Serious—and huge—brothers. *Damn.* He didn't stand a chance if he fucked this up.

He took a deep breath, gave the hand in his a gentle, meaningful squeeze and looked into Hawk's mother's eyes dead on. "Mrs. Destry. I've been helping to rehab his shoulder, teaching him to dance, and chasing down his glasses for a few weeks now. I'm in love with Hawk. After this weekend, we're taking a drive up the California coast, and I promise I won't let him drive."

There was a moment of heavy, intense silence, all those eyes staring at him, and then the man that had to be Hawk's father began to laugh, the sound loud and warm and merry.

Oh, thank goodness. Maybe he would survive this.

"Daddy, this is Jan. Jan, my father, Austin Destry. Momma, he's a good man." Hawk and his mother never stopped staring.

"Good to meet you." He shook Austin's hand, and pretended like everything was okay, whether it was or not. Confidence was key, right? But he kept one eye on Momma

Destry, because he realized now that all of Hawk's brothers were still as stone, waiting on her nod.

He started to wonder, only half jokingly, if he should be looking for the exit.

"Excellent to meet you. Let me introduce you to the boys." Austin began to point to the others who, barring facial hair length and color of their plaid shirts were carbon copies of each other. "Bryan, Canaan, Danny, Eagle, Foley, and Grainger. Then we have Lacey, Brittany, Bethany, Briony, Brianna, and Brandilyn."

What the hell was in the water in Texas? "Did you forget to change your name, Lacey?" He grinned at her.

"I'm one of triplets. Lacey, Lissa, and Leeanne. It's nice to be the outlier." She walked right up to him and held out one hand, blonde ponytail bouncing. "Our kids are Taylor, Austin Jr., and Kathleen."

Oh, he liked her. One of three was used to having to speak up to be heard. "Well, now there's two of us." He shook Lacey's hand. "Good to meet you."

She grinned at him, then stage-whispered. "Don't worry, man. The boys all knew he was queer as a three-dollar bill."

"Lace!" One of the brothers—Eagle, he thought—stepped up. "Girl, you cain't say that! What would your husband say?"

Jan laughed. He'd assumed they all knew; Hawk didn't bat an eye at introducing him. "She can. As long as no one's going to beat me up, she can. It's Eagle, right?" He offered his hand.

"Yes, sir. Pleased to meet you. Y'all really going to drive up the coast? That sounds fun."

Behind him he could hear Hawk and his mother beginning to argue.

"Yes, we..." Jan glanced over his shoulder at Hawk frowning. "We are. I should—"

"—damn it, Momma. I'm not worthless! I manage fine!"

"And when the riding is over?"

Hawk pulled back like he was stung. "Don't. Don't go there."

"Excuse me," Jan let go of Eagle's hand and went to Hawk. "Mrs. Destry. If you're concerned about Hawk's life after riding then you must think very little of me."

"I don't think about you at all. My son hasn't been bothered to introduce us." She stood up and got in his space. "And what kind of mother would I be if I wasn't concerned? I have been concerned for him from the second he was born blue and not breathing."

"Now, Charlene. Honey. You got to let the boy grow up. He's thirty years old." Austin muttered.

"Twenty-seven, Daddy. I'm the one that's thirty."

Oh boy.

"You're right. You're his mother, and I know Hawk loves and appreciates you." Jan let her have that, because she'd helped make Hawk the amazing man he was, and because it wouldn't prove Hawk's point to have him stepping in to say what his lover could say for himself.

"Y'all. Hawk's got to get to work. We can fight after the event." Bryan was the biggest, with the longest beard and a voice like a foghorn. "Work first. He's got a signing at the Carhartt booth."

Jan nodded and turned to Hawk. "Bryan's right. Time to work, Champ. Can I walk you over?"

"Yeah. I need a coffee. Momma, we'll deal. Y'all are at the host hotel?"

"Yes. Tonight." She turned to look at January, her eyes

flashing. "We'll meet in my rooms for supper so the babies can go to bed."

He wasn't saying yes or no to that, because it was up to Hawk. "It was a pleasure to meet you. Come on, baby. We need to find you coffee and a smile." He turned Hawk toward the door with a gentle touch on his lover's shoulder.

Hawk looked around, then went to his mom and hugged her. "I love you, Momma. Love y'all. Cheer for me."

"Always," Austin said. "You know we're on your side."

He followed Hawk out, silent until they were out of earshot. "Sorry, I wasn't much help."

"You did great. Eagle likes you already." Hawk was tense as hell, muscles like rocks that he could see under the cowboy's shirt.

"I'm a nice guy. They'll all like me eventually, even your mother. I'll win her over." He laughed, trying to lighten things up. "Let it go for now, Champ. Mind in the middle, right? You've got this."

"No. But it has to be done. Is there a place to get coffee?"

Jan stopped a cowboy walking past, asked where they could get coffee, and then led Hawk in that direction. "Breathe. Let it go."

His job now was to help Hawk concentrate on the bulls and not get hurt again. Part of him wanted to let Mrs. Destry have it for fucking with Hawk's headspace before a ride. If Jan knew better, she for sure ought to know better.

"She surprised me. She hates not being in control. Hates it. She wants me home and where she can keep tabs on me."

"Ironic, considering you're almost never home and regularly risk yourself in the arena. Shake it off. You're mine now."

"Yeah. And I like it." Hawk smiled, and Jan swore he could see his lover relax.

"Me too. My cowboy. Keep that smile, you have to go sign stuff." He'd walk Hawk over to the booth and then he'd... maybe he'd trade his coffee for a beer. Or something stronger.

"Thanks, darlin'. I'm damn glad you're here." Those easy words filled him up, and he liked this, feeling like he meant something, like someone honestly wanted him—not Joe Blow, but *him*.

Jan hung back and watched Hawk's confidence build as the Champ shook hands and talked with people. He tried to keep Charlene's words at bay, but they kept creeping in. *And when the riding is over?*

Well, it wasn't over. Not yet. Jan had time to make them all understand that Hawk would be fine.

But he so wanted to have words with her. He was going to have to watch himself or he'd make things worse instead of better.

Hawk wasn't worthless. Christ, the man did something ninety-nine percent of people couldn't, and he did it without all the help that many visually impaired people had—no dog, no assistive devices. Just his phone. Hawk lived on pure adrenaline and bravado.

And brains. Hawk was smart. Someone had convinced him—probably his own mother—that he couldn't function in the world on his own, but that was bullshit. And Jan thought Hawk was on his way to believing it. Hawk was more self-reliant and had more tricks for getting by than most people, and he'd figured them all out for himself.

Okay. The cowboy was good. It was time for him to find something to do with himself until show time. He finished the last sip of his coffee and tossed it. Maybe he'd go find himself a hot dog.

25

Hawk could imagine the vast swath his family made in the stands, with Momma on one side, Daddy next to her, then the guys, the kids, the ladies surrounding Jan.

Lord have mercy.

Chris, of course, was cracking up, telling him about the whole thing while he warmed up. "Your buddy looks like a Yankee in the center of Southern flowers."

Fuck a doodle goddamn doo. "Shut up. Is Momma glaring at him?"

"She hasn't looked his way at all, far as I can tell. It's like he's invisible."

"Daddy likes him."

"Your daddy is a good guy. You pulled Merman. He'll spin into your hand after a big jump out of the gate."

He nodded. He liked that. He might actually ride this one.

"She's probably nervous about you riding after your injury is all. Just do your thing, you'll be good."

The crowd started getting loud, reminding him of what he'd missed these last few weeks.

"Prob'ly." He didn't really care, if he was honest. He rolled forward, loosening up his hips, making sure his body remembered all this, knew what to do when he needed it to.

Thank God he could trust in that. His body had ridden bulls longer than it hadn't.

"Hey, man. Your clan is taking up half the arena." Danny walked up, laughing. "Jan looks like a twig next to Bryan."

"You know how it is. I'm the shrimp. You pulling my rope, man?" He was two rides away.

"Of course. Don't I always?"

Chris bumped shoulders with him. "You ready? This'll be cake."

"Up, down. Eight seconds of joy." He put his glasses in his bag and grabbed his rope. "Let's load up."

Merman was an easy loader, and he got himself ready to ride. Both Danny and Chris talked to him—not saying a thing that was important, filling the air with words that washed over him like white noise.

He heard his name announced, and as the cheer went up he pretended he could hear Jan shouting to him.

Hawk nodded and rode the first big jump out of the gate, but the second jump startled him, and the third one had him going ass over teakettle, tumbling in the air and disorienting the fuck out of him.

He heard Merman snort and it seemed pretty close but then he landed almost on his feet, strong arms catching him from behind and setting him upright. "Oy!" Tommy shouted over the crowd. "There you are, mate."

"Give me your hand, cowboy!" Chris's voice was clear as a bell and off to his left.

He reached up and they connected, Chris hauling him up and over.

"You see that, man? He was like a damn jumping bean."

"Hoppin' around like something stung him. Crazy. You okay?"

"Yeah. Yeah, that was sorta fun." He clapped Chris on the shoulder and went for his dark glasses. He would hang up here for a few, let Momma get her shit together.

"Right on. First one back is tough. You did fine. Just get through the weekend, right?"

"That's it. Do the rides. Don't get hurt." He leaned back against the chutes, listening to the conversations whipping around.

"I guess you have plans tonight with the family? Probably won't see you at the bar, huh?"

"No, Momma needs to ream my ass, yeah? It'll chill her out for a few months." She wasn't a bad person; she worried.

Chris snorted. "So did she bring the whole family as backup or did they come as a buffer?"

"Disneyland, man. *Disneyland*."

Chris cracked up. "Right! No wonder they only watch you ride here and in Orlando!" Chris kept on laughing and trying to talk. "Here I thought they were coming to watch your first ride back. Silly me."

"Yeah, they've seen a lot of first rides. That's nothing new. Mickey Mouse? That's important." And with all those kiddos, that was a big deal.

"So this was a convenient time for your momma to bawl you out, then."

"Chris! Parker's up!"

"Oh. Said I'd hold his vest. See you tomorrow, Champ." Chris chucked him on his good shoulder and jogged off.

"You cool, man?" Danny bumped shoulders with him.

"As a cucumber. You?" He was ready to go back to the hotel and breathe, maybe take a half hour nap before the drama ensued.

"Yeah. Good. Keeping my standing tonight since you got tossed off a pogo stick." Danny sounded somewhere between happy and worried. Or maybe both at once.

"Man, you know how it is the first ride after you get hurt, and that bull was a fucker. I was cool for two jumps, but no one could have held on for the third." He wasn't worried. This was how it worked.

"Oh, no way. Merman was on a roll." Danny started to stretch. "You sticking around to the end?"

"I doubt it. I like to slip out early, you know that." He liked to avoid the crowds, the traffic.

"Yeah. Well, good ride, man. Have a good night." Danny tipped his hat and took off to get ready to ride.

"Hey, Champ." Oh, that was Jan. Thank God. He wanted out of here.

"Darlin'. You ready to shuffle off?" He sure was. He wanted that nap.

"I'm so ready. My seating arrangements were a little awkward." Jan chuckled, not sounding stressed at all.

"Yeah, Chris said. The ladies were nice to you, right?" They all tended to be nice—Lacey was his favorite, but Bethany was a hoot, and Brit could drink like a cowboy.

"Oh, sure. Everybody that would speak to me was nice."

Dammit. "So that would be Lacey, Bethany, and Brandilyn?"

"Spot on. And anyone shorter and younger than you are... if they got away from their fathers." Jan was leading him out the back toward where the car would be.

"Ah. They're good kids, mostly. One or two may turn out to be serial killers." It was a matter of time.

"Austin Junior told me I looked like a nice man, so I managed to fool someone anyway."

"Well then, that's the important part. I'm dying for

some time in the bed before I deal with Momma again." He thought a naked nap with his man sounded like heaven.

"I'm all in." Jan put a steady hand on his back, fingers scritching discreetly. "Car's here."

"Let's go. You get your hot dog?"

They slid into the car, and Hawk closed his eyes against the threatening headache.

"I did. I even got to eat it before the Destry Hoarde descended on me." Jan rested a hand on his thigh, voice dropping, quiet and serious. "You got a little bounced around, huh? How did it feel?"

"Did I do a cartwheel in the air? That's what it felt like." He was fine. He'd landed right on his feet.

"Yeah, kind of. Sort of a sideways flip. Tommy had his eye on you the whole time. Mackey pulled the bull away, but you guys were pretty much nose to nose for a second. Had my heart beating for sure."

"It felt fun as hell. Like I was flying there a second."

January laughed. "Well. Cool. It probably would have been less fun if you'd landed differently, but as it was Tommy caught you like you'd done it on purpose."

He nodded, then knocked their shoulders together. He hated that his people had made this bad for Jan, had made his lover uncomfortable. "You okay? I'm sorry about the bad surprise."

"I'm fine. You told me you didn't think you'd stay on." Jan must have caught him shaking his head. "Oh, you mean your family? They're not a *bad* surprise. Maybe it's the arrogant New Yorker in me, but I'm not afraid of your mother. And I get it. I bet you're hard to let go of. I know I don't want to."

"She's overprotective. She has this weird-assed guilt

about me having a bad birth." It was ridiculous, but she was his Momma.

"Well, you turned out great, so we'll have to convince her she has nothing to feel guilty about." Jan shrugged. "It would help if your brothers weren't such cowards."

"They listen to Momma." Hell, they dated who she liked, married who she liked. He was pretty sure they only had missionary sex in the dark.

"Yeah, well. I respect that, but I don't have to. I'd like her to like me, but that's not my goal either. We'll see how dinner goes later. I'll try to be good. I can't make promises, but I'll try not to get my ass kicked."

"Well, you know me, darlin'. I respect her, but I got me a life of my own. And..." He stopped himself. This wasn't a discussion for a car with a stranger.

"And." January chuckled and nodded. "And I am really looking forward to getting back to the hotel."

"Yes. A nap." A nice long talk, he thought. Which worried him, that he wanted to discuss this whole thing, his heart, with Jan. He did though. He almost needed to.

The rest of the ride was quiet, but not lonely. Jan's hand stayed tucked loosely in his until the car pulled up outside the hotel. They were strictly friends in the lobby—Jan was pretty good at pretending after all—but he wasn't sure which of them was more relieved to close the door to their suite and turn the lock.

"Hey." He turned and held his arms open for a hug. He needed the contact.

"Mmm. Hey." Jan pulled him in, and the hug was familiar and comforting. "Champ."

"Darlin'." He inhaled, filling his lungs with the scent of his lover, the musk familiar and comforting now. "Hey."

"You want a shower, baby?" Jan kissed his jaw.

"Yeah, let's." Hot water, rubbing—there was no bad there.

"All *right*." Jan took his hat and his glasses, a strange ritual now, and then started right on his belt.

He returned the favor, opening Jan's fly, both of them working on getting naked. His fucking brain was filling up with things—worries and needs and hopes and shit. This wasn't like him. He didn't think all that much. Not normally.

Jan's fingers were happy and busy, even getting his boots off. "These need a shower more than you do."

"Shit, I need to retire them soon, but they fit so good."

"I'm not complaining, but they're staying out here in the main room tonight." Jan set them aside and tugged his jeans off. "Better. Ready?"

"I am. Thank God for hotel hot water, right?" He stole a quick kiss, laughing the whole time.

"Damn right." Jan pulled him along, started the water, and backed him into the shower. "Nice and big, glass doors, I like this hotel."

"I like that they have full-sized soap." He grabbed said soap and started making bubbles. Touching January like this was one of the rungs on the ladder to Heaven.

"Mmm. I like your hands." He got a hard kiss that he knew was a promise. "You have something on your mind. Something you didn't want to say in the car?" Jan tipped his head under the water.

"Yeah. Yeah, you know that I—I wasn't intending on living past retirement. I wanted to die on the arena dirt because the idea of sitting on Momma's porch for years and listening to them get older and older? I'd rather be dead. Now, I ain't got much of a plan, but I intend to make one, with you." Lord, he talked and talked.

Jan must have been thinking hard about it all because

his lover was quiet for a bit while working the shampoo into his hair. Jan rinsed it out for him too, scrubbing sure fingers across his scalp.

"I don't have a plan either. I wing it. I always have. But I want to make one with you too." Jan took the soap from him. "I have a question though, and I... it might be a hard one."

"Ask away. I ain't scairt." Whatever it was, it wasn't a rocking chair on Momma's front porch.

"Understand, I love what you do, okay? I'm proud of you. I want you to do it as long as you can... but..." Jan leaned into him. "How do you know how long that is? I don't like the idea of you dying out there."

"Not long." He wasn't stupid. He might have a couple years, if he was lucky. If he stayed healthy. If he rode the right bulls and the younger guys in better shape didn't take his title.

If he could manage to stay in love with the ride.

That was the hard part. He was beginning to figure out that he wasn't, not anymore. And he couldn't say so, not even hardly to himself.

"Okay. I guess it's hard to know for sure. But I know you heard me, and that's what's important." Jan's soapy hands slid over his skin, touching and soothing. "So when we walk out of your mother's hotel suite after dinner, what do you want the outcome to be?"

"I want her to know that I ain't coming home for good. Not tomorrow. Not next month. I got my Mr. Right and I intend to keep him."

"I'd like that too." Jan kissed him again, tongue sliding slowly along his.

He reached up and wrapped his arms around Jan's shoulders, stepping in and pushing up, breaking the bubbles between them.

Jan caught him up with one arm and braced the other on the shower wall behind him. "I love you. Fair warning, it's my job to make you happy, not your mother."

"I can live with that." In fact, he'd never thought that was a thing, not something in the realm of possibility. "I'm not my brothers."

January laughed. "No. You're half their size and twice as brave. And about fourteen times hotter."

"Only fourteen?" He cackled, tickled balls to bones. "I'll take it."

"Maybe more. I'm distracted." Jan kept that possessive arm around him. "We were making out, right? I think we were."

"We were loving on each other and telling each other our secrets." Hawk took another kiss, and another.

"I don't have any secrets." January said between his kisses. "I don't think. Just questions."

"So ask. I'll tell you the truth."

"Well," Jan reached past him and shut the water off, then climbed out and pressed a towel into his hands. "Do you really want to live in New York?"

"I don't know. I've never lived anywhere but home, but I want to learn. I want to try." It was big and scary, but that wasn't a bad thing.

"Okay." Jan pulled him out of the shower. "I can't promise my family is going to like you. They barely like me."

"I got lots of family. They ain't got to like me." He didn't care. He could bluster his way right through.

"I won't always be able to travel with you. I might have to go somewhere for work or be in the city..." Jan finished drying off and tucked the towel around his waist. "I hated those weeks we were apart. I won't let it go that long at least."

"Of course not. I wouldn't keep you from your work. I'm cool going and doing whenever. I was enjoying the idea of having a little vacation in between events." Surely Jan didn't think he was in this to having a traveling partner.

Jan took his hand. "I *want* to be where you, and I will be as much as possible. This vacation is going to be great. I'm looking forward to it, and it's not keeping me from anything."

"Good. I want to be. I want to have fun. Like as an us." It was all new, and it all felt shiny.

They headed for bed, and that naked nap he'd been looking forward to. "Me too. Hopefully you get through the weekend uninjured, and we'll be able to relax and explore together."

"Yeah, yeah, yeah. Don't jinx me, darlin'. I intend to stay whole." That was the goal, even more than making money.

"Oh, sorry. I didn't mean anything by that, I was talking. Ditch the towel, love, and get in bed with me."

"No worries." He draped the towel over a chair, and then slid into the bed, holding the sheets open for Jan.

"I like that view." Jan climbed in, giving off heat in the cool sheets. "What time do we have to be at your mother's?"

"She'll call. I'd say we have a couple of hours." He settled one cheek against Jan's chest.

Jan wrapped an arm over his shoulders. "This is the best part. Nothing we have to do. Nowhere else we need to be."

"Just us." Lord have mercy, this was fine. He was addicted to this, sleeping in Jan's arms.

Jan kissed his hair, nuzzled in. "You got back on that bull today, Champ. I'm proud of you. Won't be long before you're kicking ass again." Jan's voice was soft, relaxed.

"Yeah. Soon. Tomorrow. Right now, I need this. It was fun though, the cartwheel."

"That's what counts. Get some rest, I think we might need it to get through dinner." Jan's soft laugh stirred his hair and echoed in his ear.

"Shit, we're going to be glad we can sleep in tomorrow morning." Momma wasn't going to be easy.

"I plan to bring you back here and fuck you stupid... if that helps."

"It helps. It helps a lot." He grinned. "Shit, there's precious little that doesn't help..."

"That's definitely my take. Something for you to look forward to." Jan's hand slid down to his ass and rested there, fingers hot against his skin.

"I'm glad you're here. Hell, I'm glad you met my people." They were a huge part of him, and they were going to be there, forever. He loved them—and he was Uncle Bird, and there was no bad there.

"It'll work out. Get some rest for now, baby. I love you." The soothing tone and strong arms were hard to disobey.

"I love you, darlin'. Don't worry about Momma. I got your back."

"I am not worried about your mother. If I decide to worry, and I'm not, it will be about you. And don't tell me not to, that's my job."

Hawk chuckled. Silly, wonderful man. He adored the fine son of a bitch.

He closed his eyes and let himself breathe.

26

Jan stood behind Hawk's shoulder outside the Destry suite as Hawk rapped on the door. He'd dressed for dinner, more or less the way Hawk had, in jeans and a decent shirt, trying to at least look polite and respectful. He wondered how well he'd pull it off the rest of the evening.

"I love you," he whispered, and gave Hawk's ass a pat.

"I love you, darlin'. Open the damn door, Momma!" Hawk was wearing one hell of a frown, and he wasn't sure if Hawk even knew he was doing it.

Lacey—thank fuck—opened the door and he breathed a sigh. "Hey, Hawk, January. Come on in." She kissed Hawk's cheek. "Relax, little brother. You're scowling."

"Am I?" Hawk smiled for her. "How's the weather?"

"Partly cloudy, possible thunderstorms in the horizon."

"Well, the rainbow has arrived." Jan grinned at her.

Lacey laughed and took Hawk's arm. "Can I get y'all a beer?"

"Please. Jan?" Hawk smiled back at him.

"Yes, please." He wasn't sure about that smile, it was

partly genuine, and partly... something he couldn't read. But definitely forced.

"I'm on it. Momma's in the—"

"You're *late*, son."

Oh boy. Jan discreetly steered Hawk in her direction by the shoulder.

"Stop it, Momma. I'm not six. The elevators were slammed." Hawk managed to sound calm and not in the least bit stressed out.

Hawk's mother sighed and settled back into her chair. "You and your friend look nice."

"Thank you." Hawk leaned down and kissed her forehead. "I'm glad to see you."

"Are you?"

"Yes. I wanted you to meet January."

"And I have. Is he going to let you come home now?"

January laughed. "Mrs. Destry, I can't make Hawk stay in New York any more than you can make him go back to Texas."

"Momma, don't you think it's time for me to let you have my room back?" Hawk crouched down in front of her. "It's time. I'm ready. All the others were married long before me."

"All the others can see."

Jan blinked, words popping out before his better sense could stop them. "I'm sorry, how is that relevant?"

"What? You're going to take care of him? Cook for him? Do his laundry? You don't think that'll get old real quick? It's my job; I don't have a choice. You do."

Everyone was silent, staring, and Hawk was white as a ghost.

Oh, for... Okay. He picked up the gauntlet. "Um. *No*. He can do all of that for himself because he's a grown man. I mean, I'll take care of him if he gets hurt, but he can do his own fucking laundry."

"If you're superduper nice, I'll even do yours." Hawk came right back, proving the fine son of a bitch was used to keeping on his toes.

"You can't ride bulls forever. You have to understand that. This life will stop, son."

"Yep. That's a sure thing." Hawk stood up. "Are we going to order supper now that we've had our spat?"

"The burgers downstairs are amazing." Eagle moved in and sat next to Mrs. Destry. "What do you think, Momma? With onion rings?"

"Sounds fine." She looked furious, but Hawk met her with a mild expression, this empty refusal to let her get to him.

"Momma... may I call you 'Momma'?" Jan crouched in front of her. "I will take care of him to the extent that he needs me to, and not because I have to, but because I want to. I'll make sure we visit. I'll even make sure Hawk returns your phone calls once in a while. Have you ever been to New York? Maybe you'd like to visit sometime and see our apartment. See where Hawk and I live. We have room, and we'd be happy to have you. Think about it."

Her eyes went wide. "You wouldn't mind?"

"Well, you'd have to leave all the brothers at home. We don't have that much room. Two at a time." Hawk's drawl was thick as molasses.

She rolled her eyes. "You are a little ass, boy. You know that, right?"

That made him laugh. "He does, sadly. Can we call a truce? I'll even apologize for swearing."

"I'll take it under advisement. Come on and find a chair.

We're really all too many for a hotel. We rented a huge old house for Disney."

Hawk's lips twitched.

"Sounds like fun." Did that look mean Hawk wanted to go to Disney? Or was he annoyed he hadn't been invited? Jan stood. "I'll get us chairs, baby."

"Thank you." Hawk began to chuckle. "I knew, when all the guys were here, this was about Disney."

"It was about you, runt." Grainger, Hawk's next eldest brother, took the chair Jan was carrying and set it down near Momma for Hawk. "We dragged Momma this time. We wanted to cheer you back onto your feet."

Jan smiled. Hawk had told him Grainger hardly ever said a word to anybody about anything.

"Disney was a nice perk." Lacey pressed a beer into Hawk's hand. "How do you say no when you're right here?"

"And everyone wanted to meet your..." Eagle squinted at him. "What do we call you, Jan? Boyfriend?"

"That works. Boyfriend works." There were things he liked better—lover, partner—but he was happy with whatever the family was comfortable with. Jan stood next to Hawk with his beer and gave Hawk's shoulder a squeeze.

"Boyfriend. Partner. January works too." Hawk leaned into him—no hesitation, no shame—and damn, it felt fine.

"Chicken breast and broccoli for the bull rider. What are you having, January?" Eagle started taking orders.

Hawk, he knew, would probably not even finish the chicken, and would hold that beer for hours and hardly drink any of it. He tried to say he'd have the same, but Momma wouldn't hear of it, and he'd decided they'd argued enough for one weekend. He ended up with a bacon cheeseburger.

"Are you sick of chicken breasts and egg whites, man?"

One of the middle brothers—Canaan? Danny? He wasn't sure—slapped him on the back. 'I swear to God, Banty, I don't see how you can live like that. You don't eat enough to keep a tick alive."

Banty. That was funny. He wondered how many nicknames, and how much teasing Hawk had to endure growing up with this set of enormous brothers. "He eats enough to be a champion." Jan let himself sound proud because he was.

"I am. And I'm shooting for one more championship at least. Then I'll eat all the New York pizza I want." Hawk grinned and wiggled. "That is good shit, y'all."

Jan grinned, then laughed, probably louder than he should have but Hawk was so in the zone right now. Just a hundred percent the man he fell in love with.

"There's no Disney up there, huh?" That was one of the wives... he was going to have to start paying better attention.

"Nope. No Disney." He shook his head. "There's a twenty-five thousand square foot store full of M&Ms though."

"Y'all can pretend that you're being all educational. Statue of Liberty, Central Park, the Rockettes."

"Broadway." Lacey's voice was hungry. "Oh, Bryan. Can we go and see a show together?"

"Broadway like Vegas? They got girly bars?"

"Bryan!" Lacey looked horrified.

"Broadway, brother." Canaan sounded wise. "Singing and men dancing in tights and shit."

"Ugh!" Lacey stormed off.

"Wait. Hang on. You want to see a show, honey?" Bryan trailed after her. "I'll take you to a show."

"Oh, he's in trouble now."

"Be nice, Grainger." A heavily pregnant young lady

leaned against him. "I'd like to come, sometime." Her eyes went wide. "He's moving. Wanna feel, Banty?"

"Oh, Brandi, please!"

She took Hawk's hand and put it on her belly, and his lover's eyes went wide.

"That's so cool. Seriously, y'all. So damn cool."

The pregnant one is Brandi. Though with his luck the next time he saw them a different one would be pregnant. Jan smiled, watching them. They were so different from his family. Much warmer, more familiar, less stoic and serious... except where the matriarch was concerned. It was amusing as hell to watch these two hundred twenty-pound gorillas scared into silence by a woman not much taller than Hawk was.

"What do you do, Jan? When you're not following my brother-in-law around?" *Briana maybe?* And who did she go with? Canaan?

"I help nonprofits and charities get operational grants or grants for specific projects." Mostly from himself, but he always sounded so arrogant when he admitted that.

"That's cool. That's something that makes a difference." Grainger smiled at him. "We have a foundation deal to help rodeo kids with health problems." He dropped his voice. "Lacey and Bry lost their oldest boy to a weak aorta."

"Oh, I'm sorry. But we should talk. That sounds like a great thing. Maybe I can help." He absolutely could, he wanted to find out what specifically they might need. And he'd like to get involved with the family on a level that made him useful. "I mean that."

"Sure. Sure, the more people we can help, the better." Austin smiled at him, the look warm. "Briony is your contact there. She's a grant writer and brilliant. Seriously."

His eyebrow lifted with interest. "I'll make sure to do

that." He didn't know if it was a good thing or a bad one that he saw opportunity everywhere. Given an hour he could have Briony gainfully employed for the rest of the year.

And work wasn't something he'd expected to be thinking about over dinner with Hawk's family.

"Hey, you." He sat with Hawk and rested a hand on his lover's knee. "This turned out better than I expected."

"I told you, my people are good. Momma worries, but they've always had my back."

Charlene glanced over at them, and he saw her blush and nod once.

He nodded back to her. He understood her worry, even if they didn't completely agree on what was best for Hawk. He'd never had to let a child go, so what did he know about it? "They raised my favorite person in the world, so I'm not surprised."

Hawk blushed dark, but that smile? It lit up the room, and Lacey hummed. "Oh, that was sweet."

"He's learning to appreciate it.' Jan would have winked if he thought Hawk would see it, but instead he poked Hawk in the ribs, trying to tickle.

"I am. It's new, but I like that. New. And you. Us. You and me." Whoa. He'd flustered his lover.

"You and me are an us, yes. And I like it too. Us, I mean." He wasn't flustered; he was teasing. He gave Hawk a peck on the cheek that was completely chaste but felt utterly scandalous.

"You boys be good now." Momma Destry winked at him. "Tell us about you—what all do you do for fun? Are you a rodeo fan?"

"Well I wasn't. I don't know the first thing, honestly. I was out in Denver on business and ran into these cowboys... I'm learning about bull riding, I'm certainly a fan now." What else did they do for fun? "We cook. We... we spent some time exploring the city."

"Do you play cards?"

"Say no," Hawk stage-whispered. "She's a shark."

He looked at Hawk, then glanced sidelong at Charlene. "Some. Mostly... spades."

"Oh, we love that one, don't we, big daddy?" She grinned at Austin. "We all do."

"Your Yankee's going to be sorry he said that, boy." Austin's smile was smug as the cat that got the cream.

"I warned him." Hawk chuckled and shook his head. "He can't say I didn't."

"What can I say? New Yorkers like to live dangerously." He tried, but he couldn't quite get that out with a straight face, Live dangerously. Him? *Ha.*

"Lucky, lucky Hawk," Lacey teased, and his lover snorted.

"You have no idea, girlfriend."

Dammit. Now he was blushing. "Are we still talking about cards?"

"Y'all are going to give Momma the vapors." Eagle reappeared, pushing a cart full of food and followed by another. "Who's hungry?"

"Hawk!" The brothers cried. "Always!"

"Ha!" That had to be a joke as old as time. He leaned into his lover. "Always."

"Always." Hawk rolled his eyes, but laughed, so it couldn't be a bad joke.

This was good. Great, even. His cowboy was laughing, they were sitting with Charlene, and aside from Foley, who had been eyeballing him and hadn't said a word to him yet, the family didn't seem to hate him.

Maybe Hawk could relax now. That's what his lover

needed most. To relax and know everyone was on his side. It was one thing that Hawk knew he was loved, but it was good for the cowboy's confidence to know that everyone wanted him to be happy.

Jan did like his cowboy confident.

"One day I'm going to eat all these assholes under the table, you wait and see."

"All of them?" Charlene asked. "I'd pay to see that. Danny got banned from the all you can eat buffet at that casino in Shreveport..."

"Right on, Danny! That's a man after my own heart." And Jax's. Man, Jax could eat when he wanted to. "Speaking of..." He took a bite of his burger. "Mmm."

Hawk chuckled and began the process of playing with his chicken breast.

Jan wanted to stop at some of the little roadside oyster shacks along the coastal highway, but he wondered if that would be unfair. What was Hawk going to do? Split an oyster? Sniff a fried clam? And the view was going to be lovely, but he needed to find a way to help Hawk enjoy that too.

This was what he'd signed on for, so he was going to have to get creative.

Charlene glanced at him, and he swore she could read his thoughts. No doubts. Not in here.

Jan smiled and gave her a nod. *Got it.* He wasn't doubting, he was planning. But she was one very perceptive lady. A mother with eyes in the back of her head.

He poked Hawk in the knee. "How's that dinner you're not eating?"

"The broccoli is good. The chicken is awful. So it's okay."

"My chicken breasts are better." He chuckled so Hawk would hear him joking.

"Those ones made from cows are superior," Hawk shot back.

"Mm. Yes generally. Especially when topped with bacon." He leaned closer. "How long do we have to stay? Is there some family ritual about this?"

"We'll eat and visit for a bit, then we go." Hawk winked at him and managed a bite of chicken.

He ate his entire burger and an onion ring every time the enormous container of them was passed his way. "There's only like four left, Danny..." he said, peering into the bucket.

"We could split them, man. Two for you, one and a half for me, half for Banty?"

"Are you kidding? Hawk already had a bite of chicken, he's full." He held out the container toward Danny. "Come and get 'em."

"You sure?" Danny took the container from him with a grin. "Thanks. I love onion rings."

"Me too, but I have to watch my figure so I don't look six times as big as skinny here." He winked at Danny.

"Everyone's six times his size. Stunted little shit."

"I can still kick all y'all's asses." Oh, there was a hint of that temper. Was it wrong that he liked that little flash of electricity?

"No doubt. I imagine they call you 'Banty' for a reason."

"Yes. Because I'm tiny, but I'm an evil bastard."

"I guarantee you, son, I know who your daddy is."

Austin coughed and looked at Jan. "Never been in question."

He looked between Hawk's parents and started to laugh.

Suddenly the bunch of them cracked up, a joyous sound that filled the room.

Lacey perched on his knees, smiling. "Welcome to the family, Mister January."

He put an arm around her back. "Is Bryan going to beat me up now?"

"Nope, but if I'm lucky, he'll get puffy and I'll have a nice night..."

"Happy to help." He bounced her on his knees like a kid. "This is going better than I had expected, honestly. Thanks for breaking the ice earlier today."

"This is a weird, huge family. I was the first outsider to marry in. This is sort of a talent."

"Well, with any luck..." With any luck he'd be the last. Yeah, he was about to say that. Whoa. That would put him a few light-years ahead of where he should be yet. "With any luck, things will work out well for us."

"He's never introduced anyone to us. He's never defied Momma for anyone. He's never told anyone how bad his eyes are. You're special."

He looked at her seriously. "I appreciate that, thank you." He knew he was a handful of firsts for Hawk, he hadn't known exactly what it all meant. "He's special too. I've never known anyone like him." Brave, smart, beautiful, wild.

"Shit. There's no one like him." She grinned, so wicked. "Thank God."

"Thanks, indeed. I'm a lucky man."

"Are we telling secrets over here?" Bryan lifted Lacey off his lap like she weighed nothing.

Lacey grinned at Bryan. "I'd tell you, but it's a secret."

Bryan met his eyes, the signal clear as crystal. *I love her. Be good.* Then he turned to Lacey with a grin. "A secret?"

"He's in love, baby. You want the gooey details?"

"No." Bryan snorted. "I'm good."

Jan turned to Hawk. "You don't think Bryan was worried

I was hitting on Lacey, do you? I mean, even if I was straight, he's humongous."

"You're a stud, darlin'." There was no sarcasm, not a hint of doubt in Hawk's voice.

"Maybe not that much of a stud." He looped an arm around Hawk's back. "Lacey is very fond of you. Foley's not too sure of me, though. He's been watching me like... well, I can't tell if he thinks I'm going to pull a knife on someone or grow an extra head."

"He's not sure about the whole gay thing, darlin'. He doesn't know what to do."

The whole gay thing. Wow. But when Hawk called him "darlin'" everything was right with the world. "I wondered. He'll have to figure out you're happy." Hawk was the first man that had made him believe in a relationship. He knew that he was loved. He had no doubt at all.

"He's not trying to be mean, darlin'. He's unnerved, and he's shy as shit anyway." Hawk didn't seem worried, so Jan assumed he didn't have to either.

"I know. It's fine. He'll get it or he won't. He must love you, or it wouldn't worry him so much." He sighed. "My burger was really good. Are you full? Looks like you might have had *two* bites of chicken. Wow."

"It's not pizza, and it wasn't good." Hawk seemed to be more and more resentful of his self-imposed diet daily.

"I'm sorry. I'll give you good later." It couldn't be easy to sit in a room full of hungry family and pick at broccoli.

"Thank you, darlin'. You about ready to hit the road?"

"I love your family but yeah, I'm ready." He stood and ran a hand over Hawk's shoulder.

"You two going?"

Jan nodded, giving Austin a nod. "Yes, I think so. Hawk's had a big day."

"We're going to Disneyland tomorrow. Y'all want to come for half a day?" Bryan offered.

Hawk smiled and then leaned into January's arms. "Let us talk about it, and I'll text in a few. Promise."

Jan didn't hesitate to hold on, on arm tucking around Hawk's waist.

"Fair enough. We have some kind of pass, so the tickets won't be an issue."

He smiled at Charlene. "Thank you for dinner, and the company." By which he might mean the family, or he might mean Hawk, and he'd leave that to her to decide.

"You're welcome. If we don't get together tomorrow, breakfast Sunday?" Austin asked.

"Sounds perfect, Daddy. Love you, Momma."

Jan let his arm drop and took Hawk by the hand to lead him out, giving a wave. "Thanks. Bye everyone. See you tomorrow."

Everyone started wandering off, and Jan swore they took up the whole floor of the hotel. Thank god they were up on eight.

"They were waiting on us to go?" He laughed and stepped back, remembering to keep a friendly cowboy kind of distance from his lover as they waited for the elevator. "That was nice."

"Everybody did good. I'm happy, darlin'. I needed my lives to be connected." Hawk leaned back against the wall of the elevator. "You didn't want to go to Disney, did you?"

He shrugged. He'd never been to Disney. "I'd go. Or we could go to the beach. Or stay in and relax. I'm easy. But yeah, if you want to go, I'll go."

"I'd rather not. That's exhausting. And I may not ride, but I can't afford to get hurt."

"We can stay in, order room service. Enjoy the giant

shower. Watch—" *porn*. "Movies. Baking shows. Yeah." The elevator doors opened.

Hawk hooted. His lover had adored Jax and watching television together on Sunday. January had been stupidly grateful, because he wanted his lover and his best friend to get along. He didn't want to lose time with either one of them.

"Sounds good, right?" Jan led Hawk down the hall. They got around easily together now, he'd learned where to be so Hawk could follow, when to offer a warning about obstacles like stairs, it was starting to feel easy. Natural.

He pulled out his card and held the door. "This is us." Right next to the bull fighters.

"Sounds like Tommy and Mackey are crashed out already."

Shocking, given that the party had gone on 'til two, and Mackey was out of the room, singing and hunting coffee at six thirty.

"Guess we'll have to keep it down tonight." Jan had run into Mackey getting coffee and had gotten a very knowing wink and two thumbs up. They'd evidently been heard despite the music and the noise of the party. Jan had winked right back. He wasn't embarrassed.

"They're sound asleep. Tommy snores like a freight train. Mackey'll have earplugs in or he'll be listening to the TV."

Jan locked the door and reached for his lover. "I think your mother likes me."

"She didn't eat your face. I think so too."

"That would have been something to see. Did you think she might?"

"Not with Daddy watching. He liked you on sight." Hawk sat with him on the sofa. "Lord, they're loud. Not a single one of them, all of them together."

"Loud? Well, there are a lot of them. I guess you hear things I don't, I thought they were pretty quiet, until you mother and I struck a bargain anyway. Then they were a little more relaxed." They'd bring her to New York, take her to a show and Times Square, the top of the World Trade Center, feed her a fantastic dinner somewhere and send her home happy.

"Yeah, she rules with an iron fist. Seriously. She's not mean, she just— She's Momma, you know?"

He took Hawk's hand. "Is it true you've never brought anyone home before?"

"Never. Momma wants me home until the day I die, sitting on the porch of the ranch."

"I appreciate that you would defy your mother because of me. It can't be easy. But it definitely makes me feel loved." Lacey said he was special, and he felt it.

"You believe in me. Even though you know."

"I do. And I want to know everything. You're so much more than your mother is capable of envisioning you to be. I see amazing things in your future. Things I want to help make happen. Things just for us."

"See? You see shit about me that I can't yet. I want to, though. I don't want to be useless. I want to be real?"

He nodded, not sure whether Hawk could see it. "Yes. I hear what you're saying and you're not useless at all." Nobody had ever told Hawk that being independent was possible. "Like when you retire, I want to get you a service dog. You'll be able to do so much more."

"I want to learn Braille so I can read too." The words were whispered, almost ashamed.

He leaned closer. "Wouldn't that be great? I think you should too. Let's find a teacher when we get back to New York."

"They have teachers for that? I'd like that. I'm not stupid. I can figure things out." Hawk stared at him, so serious. "I've learned how to be basically independent. I know it's getting worse, but it's not the end of the earth."

Jan wasn't sure where to start unpacking all of that. He cupped Hawk's jaw in one hand and stared right back. "Baby, you are definitely not stupid. You have taught yourself coping skills no one even knows you've had to. You're one of the best in the world at what you do. You're *brave*." He smiled and gave Hawk a quick kiss. "You picked me out of a crowded bar. How brilliant was that? And honestly, I think your shoulder or your back will push retirement on you long before your sight does."

"Oh, you know it. I can ride with my eyes closed, but getting hurt—well, it *hurts* more than it used to."

"I guess eventually you'll get to the point that you're injured more than you're riding, right?" That's what happened to Olympic skiers and gymnasts and everyone else, right?

Hawk nodded. "Or there will be the big hit—like Charlie or Sky. One day I won't be able to get myself up off the arena floor."

Jesus.

"Sure. Or that." He sighed and leaned back in the couch. "We'll pretend like that's not going to happen."

"Works for me." Hawk cuddled right in, one hand on his thigh. "It's a hard call, though—when do you stop? Do you keep going until you can't no more? When is too early to retire? I mean, everyone knows when it's too late."

"I don't know, baby. I know it's not my call to make." He had no advice. He was new to this, and he wasn't— well, he wasn't Hawk.

"No. No, of course not. I was rambling. I don't mean

anything by it. I was thinking aloud." Hawk chuckled, and the sound was wry. "So, maybe we should go to Disneyland tomorrow, since you haven't been. It's worth experiencing. It's special."

"You should rest up for your ride. We'll save it for later. And I know you didn't mean... you'll have to forgive me. I don't know what the right thing to say is. I want you to ride right up until you don't want to anymore. And, I also don't want you to leave everything on the arena floor. Those are hard things to reconcile, that's all. I'm not sure it's possible. I'm not going to try to roll you up in bubble wrap."

"There's no right or wrong. I never talked to someone about this, 'cept Charlie. I don't know, I feel amazing to be able to talk to you."

He hugged Hawk against his side. "You can always talk. I'll listen. Sometimes you have to say things out loud to figure them out."

"You'd be surprised." Well, that was cryptic.

He rested his cheek against Hawk's forehead. "Why, because you've made a life out of keeping secrets?"

"No, because I talk to myself a lot. In hotel rooms, mostly. I hear my own voice all the time."

"Sounds lonely. Now you've got me, for what it's worth. I like hearing your voice. I'd like to hear you sing with that guitar sometime. Am I going to have to make you take me to visit Charlie and Ben?"

"I can't wait to introduce y'all!" Look at that smile. Hawk lit up. "They're going to love you. Seriously. We'll have a fuckton of fun at their ranch."

"I'm looking forward to that. I will look like a complete idiot on a ranch, but I'll learn." He still wasn't sure about riding a horse though.

"There's mostly singing and playing, really. Some cattle, but it's Nashville."

"Sounds like fun." He stretched and yawned. "Let's go to bed, baby."

"Yeah. It's been a day and a half. I'm wore."

Jan had grand plans to keep his lover up for a while, but maybe waking him up with the sun was a better idea. Then they could nap and have brunch. It was a plan.

"It was a good day. A really good day."

"It was. You met the ravening horde. Thank you." Hawk stood and held one hand out.

Jan took it and let Hawk haul him up and lead him into the bedroom. "They're not so scary once you get past Momma."

"The big boys didn't get to you, huh? You know, Momma's only little." Hawk fought to keep a straight face, but it wasn't working.

"Oh, they got to me, but not how you mean." Jan chuckled. "That's a horde of handsome men, I must say."

"Yeah—they're big motherfuckers, and they all look alike. Some people like that."

"Oh, ho!" Jan laughed happily. "*Some* do. I prefer what I've got, thank you."

"You get off on the wild, strong types. The uber macho." Hawk flexed, pumping his pecs.

"That's it. Uber macho." He squeezed one of Hawk's biceps, snickering. "Mmm. I might swoon."

"Damn right." Hawk's eyes lit up, and he pushed Jan onto the bed. "Starting now."

Well, this was fun. He liked that look in Hawk's eyes. "Are you going to take advantage of me?" Jan kind of thought they were off to nap like old people.

"I might, you never know with me." Hawk leaned down and kissed him, soft and lazy.

No, he really didn't. This was wonderful and new, Hawk taking some initiative, sure in Jan's willingness to play along. He returned the kiss, letting Hawk set the pace and the tone, enjoying every second, every gentle touch.

If this was his new normal, he could learn to love it.

27

Two rides out of four didn't suck, so by the time they all got together for supper Hawk was feeling pretty damned fine and ready for their vacation tomorrow.

"When y'all all heading home, Momma?"

"We're heading down to Santa Barbara tomorrow night in the RV. All the boys have different plans." She patted his hand. "Are y'all ready to hit the road too? I know your man's been chatting up Briony to work for him."

"With. Work *with* me. And I'm not pushing, I gave her my card and we set up an... informational call." Jan leaned in a bit to both of them, close enough Hawk could smell Jan's shampoo. "I got a good vibe though."

"She's excited. I haven't seen her so tickled since they got married." Momma chuckled. "Keep things in the family, right January?"

"When you can. That's what my father taught me." He could hear the smile in Jan's voice and Jan gave Momma a kiss on the cheek. "Thank you. It's been such a pleasure to meet you, and everyone."

"You're a good boy. You make Hawk smile. We'll have to plan a trip out to see y'all soon."

"Maybe we can come see y'all come Easter, Momma." He'd need some of his things, after all. And they wanted to go to Charlie's.

"That would be lovely. You go to church, January?"

"Oh. Uh…" Jan stammered. "I go anywhere Hawk wants me to."

Good lord and butter. She always pushed too far. "Momma, let it go. I want to enjoy the egg hunts and the brisket."

"When do you ride again, son?" Daddy cut in, changing the subject.

"Friday up in Oakland. Should be good. We'll have a nice drive up—we're going to the beach, and we're going to see all the neat things on the way up." He couldn't wait. He'd wanted something like this as long as he could remember. To be a couple, to be driving and free and tourists.

"Hawk planned the whole thing. All I have to do is drive. It should be great, right up the coast." Jan was finishing his supper, some kind of fish deal. It smelled great.

Oh, maybe he could steal a bite. He hadn't bothered to order this time. There was enough food in the dozens of plates from his family.

"It's salmon. You want a taste, baby? It's grilled, with a little soy. There are only a couple bites left." Jan waved a fork under his nose.

"Your momma and I spent a nice long weekend in Pebble Beach once. Your brother Bryan came along a little while after. Remember that weekend, Momma?"

"I do, you sly dog. It was quite the thunderstorm, wasn't it, my love?"

"Oh gag. Momma. Daddy. Stop." Okay, that was adorable. He did love how much they loved each other.

He took the fork and tried the salmon. He did love that soy flavor. What did they call it on Jax's shows? Ooo, mommy?

"A very, very memorable storm." Daddy laughed and put his arm around Momma's shoulders.

"I'm hoping for good weather, but if it has to rain, I'd take a nice loud storm. Coastal storms are powerful. How did you like the salmon? Tasty right?"

"I like it a lot. Fish is good for you, right?" Hawk forgot about that, getting fish. He stole another bite.

"It is. And not a lot of calories either, skinny. We can try lots on our trip. Have you tried oysters?"

"I haven't. I want to, though. I want to try—" His phone buzzed, "Don't Let Go" sounded. "Excuse me. Charlie's calling."

He stood and moved toward the edge of the room. "Hey stranger. How goes?"

"It goes. Got a headache. You still in New York?"

Christ, Charlie sounded exhausted.

"No. No, I'm fixin' to drive up the coast with Jan. We're in Anaheim today, Oakland Friday."

Charlie always, *always* watched the events.

"Oh. Yeah. I always liked Oakland. You came back pretty good, huh? Ben made sure I didn't miss you."

"I rode two. It didn't suck. You okay, man?" If they had to, they could fly to Nashville tomorrow...

"I'm fine, tired is all. You're taking your man on vacation you said?"

"We're driving up for the week, taking our time." He frowned, and he was developing a shit headache himself. "I'm wanting to bring him to you soon, have a visit."

"I'd like that, Bird. Can you come after Oakland? Do you have time?" Charlie swallowed so hard he heard it. "I... want to meet him, I want to see you happy."

"I'll make time. Even if Jan can't because of work, I'll come." Maybe they should go. Now. "Are you sure you don't want me to come on now?"

"Stop it, asshole. What difference does a week make?"

Hopefully not much.

"Everything okay?" Jan came up beside him.

"Yeah. Charlie was asking if we could come after Oakland, introduce you and him." He hoped Jan would understand.

Jan touched his elbow discreetly. "Sure. Tell him yes."

"We'll fly in Sunday night a week from now, okay? We'll hang out a few days."

"Great. Ben will come to the airport and get you, so text him your flights. Looking forward to seeing you, Bird. You enjoy your vacation. Say hello to Oakland for me."

"Will do. I'll be there in a week, and you can tell me all about the weird shit Ben's feeding you."

"Fuck off, Bird. Love you, man. Bye."

He tried to answer, but the phone went dead.

"All good?" January sounded worried. "Is Sunday soon enough?"

"He says so. He sounds tired. Like real tired." And he hated it. Still, it was hard to recover, and maybe Charlie was depressed, really down.

"Maybe call Ben in a couple of days and get a reality check. I'm sure he's overdoing it. That seems to be a bull rider thing." Jan socked him lightly in his good shoulder.

"Nonsense! I'm perfectly capable of taking it easy..." Asshole. Hawk adored the fine son of a bitch.

"Yeah, when you're asleep. We better get back to the table before you have to explain things to your mother."

"She knows that Charlie and Ben are my buds, but yeah." He nodded and made his way back to the table. "I did like the fish a lot. It was tasty."

"I haven't had a disappointing meal out here yet." Jan followed him back to the table. "I'm so ready to start driving. I kind of want to leave tonight."

"Yeah? Let's do it." They were adults and didn't answer to anyone. "We can pack up and go get the car."

"Really? We don't have to go too far. I want to be on our way, you know?"

"Let's do it." Hawk felt the weight that he hadn't even known he was carrying disappear.

Instead of sitting again, Jan walked around the table to Momma and Daddy. "We're going to get going, I think. Safe travels tomorrow."

"Everything all right?" Daddy was good to worry.

"Yes, fine. Hawk and I decided to get on the road a little early."

Hawk nodded, finding a grin for his momma. She knew about his need to move and go. "We're going to let the wind take us. It's our first vacation."

"Be safe then and have a good time."

"Are you leaving?" Word traveled around the room quickly and they got hugs and handshakes.

Lacey kissed his cheek. "Congratulations, Banty. He's amazing. You did good. Bry likes him."

"Thank you, sister. I appreciate it." He had done good.

"Hey." January was back at his side. "You get Bryan to bring you to New York, Lacey, and I'll get you into a show. Leave the kids with Charlene."

"Yeah? For real?" She squealed and hugged Jan hard.

"You rock. Really."

Oh, Jan had made her day.

"Careful, Lacey. Bryan will give me that look again." Jan laughed. "Ready, cowboy?"

"Let's go pack up." He nodded and forced himself not to grab Jan's hand. "I'm so ready."

Jan led the way out. "I don't know why I'm so anxious to go, but I'm glad you feel the same way."

"We're—I don't know." But he did, sort of. In New York there were no sponsors, no mommas, no fans or anything. It had been magic for three weeks.

He was ready to have more.

"It's real now, right? I met your parents. Maybe not the way you'd expected, but that's probably for the best. This was a good weekend I thought." Jan let them into their room and pulled out their suitcases.

"It was. It's time to get the hell out of Dodge, though. Explore the coastline." He wanted to smell the sea, walk on the sand.

"We can find some little place on the coast and get a room in a couple of hours." Jan sounded so excited. Happy. "Wake up tomorrow morning with a view of the ocean."

"Sounds perfect." Hopefully they could touch the water. He loved the sound of joy in January's voice, the lightness.

He arranged to pick up their car early as January got them packed and they were checking out in no time.

The rental company picked them up and after half an hour of paperwork, they were in the convertible and on the road.

"Do you like music when you drive?"

"I do. Go for it. Anything you want." Jan revved the engine. "This is a great car. We're going to have some fun."

"I'm ready." He figured the phone jack, got some random

playlist going, and leaned back. He let himself relax, swallowing hard at the sudden release of pressure.

"It'll be dark soon and we'll miss some of the view maybe, but I don't care. This is amazing. Have you done this drive before?"

"No. No, I've always flown. I've explored a lot of Anaheim." But not so much the coast.

"So this is new for both of us. That's cool. We can take our time and stop and see whatever we want. Where do you think we should try to stop tonight?" Jan rested a hand on his knee and gave it a squeeze. "It'll get chilly I bet when the sun is all the way down."

"Let's find somewhere we can hear the ocean. Do you think that's possible?" Somewhere they could sleep, where they could cuddle and see the sunshine in the morning.

"Sure. It's kind of late for a really nice place, but I bet we can find a motel near the beach."

"We don't need really nice. We need clean with a lock on the door and an ice maker." He did like his ice.

"Yeah, the lock is good. We could have some fun with the ice." Jan's fingers slipped higher on his thigh.

"Oh, ho! You got wicked ideas, don't you?" He cracked up, tickled shitless.

"Me? I have no idea what you... oh. Hang on." Jan swerved off the highway and onto a smaller road running along the beach. "Can you see the sun? All that color? Or do you want me to tell you about it?"

"I can see the light, the difference of it." He felt that it was a different animal, something new. "Tell me about it."

"Well..." Jan stopped the car and opened the door. "Get out. Come around here."

"I—Okay." He slipped out of his side and walked around the car. The sun was going down, he could see that.

"Okay." Jan leaned against the car so he could lean back against Jan and wrapped an arm around him. "All the yellow is turning bright orange and then red."

"I can see the yellow, the red. It's so big. The dark at the bottom is the ocean?"

"Yep. It's getting darker. Breathe in, you can smell the salt."

He closed his eyes and inhaled, sucking in a deep, deep breath. It was salty, humid, but different than back home. He could hear the cars, the splash of the water, the birds. "Is it amazing for you too?"

"It's not the east coast, right? The waves are bigger, louder, the wind is stronger. It's amazing, yes." Jan pulled him tight. "And it's been a long time since I stopped to watch the sun go down."

"I'm glad you did. This is our first beach, our first real sunset together." One day it would be the last one he saw, but he could live with that. He had this one.

"One of several this week, I hope. We'll have lots to remember." Jan chuckled. "Man, don't blink you'll miss it. The sun sets fast out here."

"That's cool. It's like the water puts out the ocean!" Lord, he made himself laugh.

Jan laughed with him. "Kind of looks like that, huh?" He got a quick kiss. "Okay. Back on the road. I bet we'll find a place to stay on this route."

He didn't want to go, but he guessed you couldn't stay out here, sleep on the ocean. He walked back around the car and got in, eyes closed as he buckled in.

"Don't worry, baby. We'll spend lots of time with the sand and the water. That's the point, right?"

"It is." Them. The sand. The road. The water. "That is totally the point."

28

"I 'm trying to figure out where to park." They'd pulled into Monterey a few minutes ago after a night in an amazing bed-and-breakfast, but Jan hadn't bothered with the GPS or thought to look at the map before they left. He was playing it by ear. They weren't in a hurry, and he'd been enjoying not being on a schedule. "You want to walk around first, or start at the aquarium? Oh. Cannery Row, right?"

"It sounds good. It all sounds good." Hawk was on a high, waking up to the barking of the sea lions. His lover was absolutely fascinated, those light blue eyes shining with happiness.

"It does sound good. I'll follow the signs for the aquarium." Not only was Hawk in a great mood, but so was he, and it was a beautiful day. The sky was so blue, the air fresh and clean and the ocean went on forever. "I see one. Go me."

"Can we see the water? I want to touch it." Did Hawk bounce?

"Yeah. Definitely." He scanned ahead, looking for a road

that would take them down to the water. "I need to figure out how to...ah." He made a left turn.

They went down a small hill and he turned onto a narrow road that led them right to a small parking lot near an entrance to the beach, almost like he'd done it on purpose. "Score."

"I want to do everything. Everything. Where do we start?"

"I don't know. I guess right here." Jan parked. "Ready?"

The place was ready made for tourists—from the bike rentals to the shore to the aquarium. It was a dream really.

Hawk moved forward toward the sidewalk separating the ocean from them, damn near hitting the railing. Jan jogged forward a step and caught his arm, steering him toward the sand. "You good?"

"Uh-huh." Hawk looked adorable—ballcap on, T-shirt with Ride 'Em Cowboy on it, paper-thin holey jeans, and flip-flops. "I'm great."

He watched Hawk, smiling. "Two more steps and we're in the sand, baby. Go ahead."

"Go ahead. Right on." Fearless. His lover was fucking fearless, charging ahead with a wild grin.

He laughed and followed, longer legs keeping up easily with the stride, though he didn't think he'd ever be that brave. "Keep going, cowboy, the water's coming!"

Hawk hit it, and his eyes went huge. "Cold! It's so cold!"

It didn't sound like a complaint at all.

"Yeah? Colder than the East Coast?" He shuffled in, kicking the water as he went. It was freezing, actually. He shivered, but he'd be damned if Hawk was going in farther than he did. "Fuck, that is really cold."

"It's amazing." Hawk bent down and scooped up the sand, touching it, rubbing it between his fingers.

"It's blue. Or... and green. Dark. And the waves break way out there and then roll all the way in here. I think the tide is going out... have you never been to the ocean?"

"Galveston. Padre. Corpus. A lot." So the Gulf. "This is way colder."

January laughed. "Yeah. I bet it is. It's the open ocean. There's nothing out there but... Hawaii. Or something."

"Hawaii. So if we got on a boat, we could go and go." Hawk kept walking, staying about ankle deep. "That's so cool."

"A big boat." He took Hawk's hand firmly in his and tugged Hawk to a stop. "That's another place I've never been. Hang on, smile for Jax." He held up his phone for a selfie with the open ocean at their back.

"Send it to Charlie too." Hawk smiled huge, and the picture was fabulous—lit up and happy.

"You got it. Oh, this is a keeper. I love it." He texted it to Charlie first and copied Hawk, then sent it to Jax.

Monterey! You're jealous, Jax. I know you are. I'll bring you a chef from San Francisco.

I hate you a little right now. Jax's reply made him laugh.

Charlie sent back, *U both look happy <3 go have a drink!*

That's a great idea. I think we will. CU soon.

"Charlie says we look happy and we should go have a drink. I totally agree. You think there's a place that overlooks the beach? I bet we can find one."

"I bet we can. That's what places like this are known for."

Sure enough, standing out there with bright flags, weird little shops, was Fisherman's Wharf. Bingo.

He laughed. "All I had to do was look past my own nose. There's like a whole boardwalk thing right up here. It looks great, come on." He tugged on Hawk's hand again. "I want crab. And chowder. And a margarita. Is it too early?"

"Nope. Breakfast was ages ago."

Breakfast. Right. The memory of that blowjob made his eyes cross.

"You're right. And damn, you deserve a margarita." He pulled Hawk onto the busy boardwalk and kept an arm around his cowboy's back. "It's a little crowded."

The restaurant was at the end, and they passed a half dozen or more goofy stalls selling cheap souvenirs and weird T-shirts and prayer flags.

"This is great, baby. It's the prettiest tourist trap I've ever seen." He squeezed Hawk's hand. "We're going to this place at the end of the boardwalk where we can sit at the bar and watch the waves."

"Sounds great. Are you having fun?" Hawk's cheek brushed his arm.

"Me? I could do this forever. Travel with you, see things, try new things... and you planned this so well. I loved that B and B last night. How did you find it?" Jan pulled Hawk over to a couple of open seats.

"It was cool and not, all at the same time. Because it was like a house, it was harder to learn. Hotels are pretty much alike."

Damn.

"Oh... right. I have to start thinking about things like that." Jan sighed. "Oh! But when we get your dog it won't be so bad, right?"

"It wasn't bad. Just new. I have to learn new things. It's important." That was one of the things he loved best about Hawk was his eagerness to learn.

"You've already taught yourself so much." He ordered them margaritas. "Do you want to eat anything?"

"I should. Is there something crunchy we can share?" Hawk asked the bartender.

"Fried oysters? We also have a lovely antipasto platter."

"Oysters. Definitely." He was hungry. And Hawk was only going to pick anyway. "Thank you."

"You got it."

Jan smiled at Hawk, still not really sure if his lover could see it. "Right on."

"So, we're going to the aquarium, and I want to try the two-seater bikes. They look fun."

"Yes, we're going to the aquarium. I heard they have a giant octopus. Are you sure about the bike? I mean..." Was that safe? God, he was such a chicken. "I guess maybe if I'm in front but..."

"I thought the website said they were side-by-side? Like paddle boats, but bikes."

"Oh yeah? That's wild. Let's do it." It sounded safer. Maybe. "What the hell, right?"

"Do you not like to ride bikes? I've done it my whole life, I think." Right, because that was how Hawk could move. That and horses.

"I haven't ridden one in forever, but I like it fine. I just..." Jan sighed. "Okay. I was worried about you on a bike. I'm sorry."

"Oh, because I can't see? I'd worry about you if I was on a bike. I mean, I can ride, but steering..." God, that grin.

He smiled back, a little embarrassed. "You forgive me way too easily. I'm going to take it though. And I'm steering. Your mother would kill me otherwise."

"Hey, I can be honest with you. That's all new and shit." Hawk winked at him. "You need to be honest with me too. It's important."

"Honestly, I think you're too comfortable taking risks, and I'm too comfortable not taking them. I have doubts sometimes, worries, but I don't want to offend you and it's not because I don't think you can do things." Hawk scared him, but mostly in a good way.

"You haven't ever been with a bull rider, darlin'. That's hard."

He shook his head. "No. No, it's not hard. It's a choice, it's something I thought about, but I made up my mind and now it's easy. The hard part was understanding what that bull rider needs. Sometimes it's tough to know for sure. But I think I've got this."

"I think you do. You make me happy, darlin'. You let me have fun, and I want to be around you, all the time."

Jan looked at Hawk, really looked at him because he wanted to remember this moment and those words. "I've been in a couple of serious relationships before you. The last one was years long. No one's ever planned a trip for me, taken care of arrangements and everything and said, 'Hey, we're doing this.' You make me happy too. And I want to spend all my time with you."

"No? That's a shame. I like giving you something special." Hawk's lips curved in a smile. "I mean, it's my special too, right?"

"I hope so. Yes, it is. Ooh. Drinks." They got margaritas and their oysters. "Oh, they look great."

Hawk found his glass and lifted it. "To us?"

A toast? Could Hawk be any sweeter? "Yes. To us." He touched his glass to Hawk's and then took a sip. The drink was strong, like his cowboy.

Hawk licked the salt off the rim, then he drank, humming softly.

Damn. That was a beautiful sight.

So good that Jan pulled out his phone again and took a picture of Hawk enjoying the margarita with the beach and the ocean behind him. He sent that one to Charlie as well.

He says he's happy.

He looks amazing. Relaxed.

He is. How are you? Hawk says you're having a good week.

Fine as frog hair. Tell that happy bastard to call 2nite.

I will. "Charlie wants you to call him tonight. He seems pretty good."

"Good deal. I'll give him a holler in between walking on the beach and wild monkey sex."

"Oh, wild monkey sex is on the agenda? Fantastic." He tangled his fingers with Hawk's. "Definitely call before, you won't have the strength after." Sex with Hawk was epic. All of it. From the quiet nights to the wild ones to their mornings in the shower.

"Yeah. I'd hate to get interrupted while we're banging away. It's awkward as fuck."

Jan laughed. "Like I would let you answer the phone. No way, Jose. You're all mine." His bull rider. His pocket cowboy.

Hawk's laughter filled the air, drawing smiles from all around them. He was having so much fun with his cowboy.

Jan held out a fried oyster in his fingers. "Open up, cowboy, I have fattening food."

Those lips opened like a baby bird's. Okay, that was hot as fuck. He fed Hawk the bite, and two more before they finished their margaritas.

The oysters were delicious, the aquarium was neat, and the double bikes were a great adventure. But holding Hawk's hand on the beach with the sand between his toes was better. The best.

He hadn't known Hawk long, but he had never seen his lover so relaxed, so happy, so engaged in everything.

"So, the bike wasn't as scary as I thought it would be." January actually felt weird saying it.

Hawk grinned at him, beaming. "You did great! I was

proud of you. I have a nice bike at home, but I haven't ridden in a while. Usually I go riding on Riddick."

"Riddick? Like Vin Diesel? I wouldn't mind a ride on Riddick..." It was a bad joke, but he cracked himself up anyway.

"When we go to the ranch, I can arrange that. He's beautiful, and such a good boy." Oh, that was a sweet expression on his lover's face.

"Baby, you're adorable. And I'll be happy to watch you ride, but I think I should keep my feet on the ground." Horses were big. And moved fast. And had their own minds.

"You could ride double with me. Riddick will love you."

"I'm sure he's wonderful." *No disappointing Hawk today.* "We'll see, okay? If anyone could convince me, it would be you."

"He is. I got his momma for my thirteenth birthday. She foaled three times, and Riddick is the one I kept."

"That's cool. Sounds like you miss him."

"Sure. He's my friend."

Huh. A horse can be a friend. Duly noted.

"Where do you want to watch sundown? Here on the beach? Up on the pier?"

"It's going to look basically the same to me—amazing colors. You choose."

"Okay." He pulled Hawk up higher on the beach where they wouldn't get wet. "Have a seat right here then. It's closer to the car and much quieter."

"Sounds like a deal. I love how the ocean seems endless." Hawk settled next to him. "Can you imagine being a Viking out in a boat?"

"I'd be a very seasick Viking. A very bad Viking. You, on the other hand, would be the hottest pocket Viking in a horned helmet."

"Dork!" Hawk busted out in a happy laugh. "No boats for you? I've been on a lot of boats. I was on a traditional canoe in Hawaii with Charlie once."

"Oh, how cool. A canoe would be okay, I think. The last time I was on a boat I was on a fishing trip with my dad and my brothers and I spent the whole time feeling green and leaning over one railing or another." He chuckled. "Of course, it's possible that was the company I was with."

"I've fished with my people a lot. And there's a party barge at Lake Travis too. I love hanging around all day in the sun."

"A party barge?" The sun was starting to set so he settled behind Hawk so that Hawk could lean back against him to watch.

"Yeah—a big flat boat on pontoons? Grill and coolers, great speaker system, diving platform off the back?"

"I have never seen one. But the coasts have lots of waves and surf... something like that would flip over, I think. You do that on the Gulf? Sounds like fun." He was trying to keep mental lists of the things that Hawk enjoyed that he knew nothing about. Things he could set up as surprises later.

"On the lake. We'll go out when you come to the ranch. We have four that we can attach together for..." Hawk smiled. "Oh, look at the colors."

"So pretty. And bright." He looked over Hawk's shoulder at the way the sun was reflecting on the water. "I'm not going to forget this you know, these sunsets with you."

"Good. This is special. This is ours."

It was theirs. And if one day Hawk couldn't see the sunset anymore, they'd always have this to talk about.

"The weather out here is better than in New York. The sun is brighter, even at sunset. The sky is more blue. I have nothing to complain about."

"Yeah, I love this. I love being here with *you*."

"Me too. I'm trying to keep my foot on the brakes. Oakland is a few days away, you know."

"Shh. I'm not ready." Hawk leaned a little harder.

He tucked his arms around his cowboy that much tighter. "Me neither. But I do love to watch you ride."

"I know. I'm not quitting today." Hawk's sigh was quiet. "I wish—"

He kissed Hawk's temple. He wanted to know how that thought ended. "What do you wish, angel?"

Hawk shook his head. "Nothing important. I was thinking out loud."

"Hm. Well, if it becomes important, you'll tell me." He hoped that was true. He thought it was, they were learning how to talk to each other about the important things. Hawk wasn't used to talking at *all*, so Jan would give him some time. "Almost dark."

"All dark for me. Tell me what you see right now, please?"

"Oh. Sure." He looked out over the water, really looked so he could describe it. "The sun is gone but there's still a glow right where it went down that looks like... kind of like a fire going out. It's reflecting across the tops of the waves, so there are these dark ridges in the water. And the sky is that twilight color. Dark blue here and there, clouds still lit by the sun striping the sky. It's pretty."

It *was* pretty, and Jan was sorry Hawk couldn't see it for himself.

"That's so fucking cool. Thanks."

He looked down and saw one single tear caught on Hawk's pale eyelashes.

"You're welcome." He felt like apologizing. Maybe it would be kinder not to comment on things Hawk couldn't see. He didn't know. It didn't seem fair, but this time Hawk had asked. "Can I have a kiss?"

"You can." Hawk lifted his face, and the smile seemed real, happy. "You can have two, even."

"All right. Score." He closed his eyes, so he could feel it like Hawk did, and pulled their mouths together. Jan could taste the salt spray on Hawk's lips as they kissed. He could hear the sound of their breathing and the waves rolling up on shore as the wind blew his hair around. He was totally tuned into Hawk, and he didn't feel like he was missing a damn thing.

Hawk's moan slid into his lips. It was less sexual than joyful, present. He hummed back, smiling inside, staying open to whatever Hawk needed. "The view is better over here."

"I wish you'd met me early on. I saw better, I had a longer career ahead, and I was prettier."

There it was, right? What Hawk couldn't say before. "I hear that. Part of me wishes that too. But younger me would probably have been terrified by you. And I told you before, this was fate. This happened right when it was supposed to. Maybe I missed your early career, but I get to see you retire, I get to help you build whatever's next. And I've been with pretty men. Pretty never lasts. This will."

"And Momma has footage of every ride, from the beginning. She can hook you up."

Oh, that could be fun. Asking her to show him her favorites.

"You know you're the hottest thing I've ever seen, right? On the back of a bull, on the beach, in my bed... anywhere you are, you're the hottest thing around."

"I know you like the swagger. It gets you off." Hawk winked at him, flirting like a mad thing.

"I do. I'm shallow like that." Hawk had that swagger in the arena, but he had it naturally too, when he was feeling good, confident, happy. Jan intended to keep Hawk happy.

"You ready to go find supper, darlin'? I want more fish. That's good stuff." His Hawk was having a love affair with fresh fish. It was adorable.

"I'm ready. Plus it's getting chilly on the beach, isn't it?" Jan got up and pulled Hawk to his feet. "Do you want to find a place on the pier or head back to the hotel?"

"Let's head back toward the hotel. If we see somewhere, we'll stop? Fair enough?" Hawk brushed the sand off his butt. "Nowhere fancy."

"Nowhere fancy." He helped Hawk, brushing the sand of his lover's ass, and giving one cheek a squeeze.

"Did you get it all?"

For a man that had been in the closet for so long, Hawk was relaxed as anything.

He laughed and took Hawk's hand, pulling him toward the car. "I got all the sand. I only got one cheek though."

"You can have both of them tonight." Hawk's voice dropped. "Over and over."

Jan unlocked the car. "You know, room service is starting to sound good."

"They have salmon and shrimp both. We could lick each other's fingers that way."

"You have the best ideas." They got in the car and he pulled up the GPS on his phone. "Seafood feast. You better call Charlie before we get distracted."

"I will." Hawk grabbed his phone and put it on speaker as he dialed.

"Bird." Jan could almost hear the smile. "How goes?"

"I have sand in my butt crack, buddy."

"What? Tell that asshole to get you a room!" Charlie laughed softly.

Jan snorted. "Hey, man, I'm easy but I'm not cheap."

"It's true. He's not cheap at all." Hawk's laughter filled the car. "But worth it? Oh my god."

"You guys sound so good. He better be getting you all pumped up for your weekend, Bird. I want to see you stay on this time."

"*Damn*." Jan laughed.

Ben joined in the fun. "Something in his meds is making him brutally honest, Hawk. It's been entertaining."

"Well, he can fuck the hell right off, dickmunch. I'm going to ride and when I win the event, you can grill jalapeno poppers for me."

The car filled with laughter. "Or save that until we get there because I have never had one!"

"You're dating a guy that's never had a jalapeno popper?" Charlie sighed. "You better get here quick. That Yankee has things to learn."

"I'm not sure he's had real brisket, either. It's a sorry state of affairs." Hawk's hand slid up his thigh, teasing him.

Jan shook his head. "Yeah, well... your bagels suck."

"Our biscuits are made of pillowy perfection, though," Charlie shot back.

Oh, snap. "You know what, Charlie? I'm going to let you win because you're Hawk's best friend."

"Chickenshit." Ben sang.

"Basically. Yes." He laughed.

"Y'all have to try the pizza though. Oh my god. The *pizza*." Hawk almost sounded like he was having sex.

"I have heard rumors about the pizza, for sure." Charlie agreed.

"You guys will come up and stay with us next. We can watch baking shows and eat pizza.'

"Sounds perfect. I can't wait. First, though, y'all come to me."

"Sunday. Right, cowboy?" He wasn't sure how he ended up so deep in this conversation between Hawk and his best friend.

"Sunday. Right. Y'all have a good one, Bird."

"Y'all too." Hawk's smile was a little bittersweet. "Night, you."

"Night."

He curled his fingers into the hand on his thigh. "He sounds good. Ben too."

"They do. I'm glad. I'm so excited to introduce y'all in person."

"Is this... I think this is the right hotel." Jan turned into the parking lot. "It's beautiful. Little."

"Perfect. It's getting cold, huh? It's damn chilly here at night."

"Don't worry, I know how to warm you right up. Let's go get our room." Jan opened the car door. "You promised me that perfect ass."

"I did. It's yours, however you want it." Hawk slipped out of the car, and there it was, that swagger.

"That's what I like to hear. Follow me, cowboy." He opened the trunk and pulled out their bags, then led the way into the lobby to check-in. "It's weird being places where people don't all know you." Hawk was a celebrity when they stayed near arenas.

"I love it. I can relax some." That was surprising. Not hugely, but a little.

"Some. Hopefully more than some." They checked in at the desk and crossed the quiet lobby to the elevators.

"What's the plan for tomorrow? Are we moving on first thing? Can we sleep in and have a nice brunch on the water somewhere?"

"Brunch sounds great. Lazy sounds fabulous. Let's do it." Hawk rocked on his toes. "This whole vacation has been perfect."

"Is. Is perfect. Don't end it on me yet." He pulled Hawk into the elevator. "We're on the fourth floor. The room is off the elevator to the right."

Hawk nodded and touched the buttons, tracing the Braille. "I want to learn about this."

"Yes. When we get back to New York. I promise." They got off the elevator and this time he let Hawk lead. "Right. Then right again."

Hawk whistled as he walked, head bobbing, gimme cap folded up and stuffed in his back pocket. The white-blond curls were a little too long, and they bounced as he moved.

"Two more doors on the left." Jan smiled, watching the way the bill of the ball cap twitched in Hawk's pocket as he walked. "Mmm. The beach was nice, but you are one of my favorite views."

"You can look at me whenever you want, darlin'." Someone wanted him, that drawl was thick as syrup.

"Move over, I've got the key." He hip checked Hawk playfully. The door beeped as he held the key card over it and he pushed inside.

The room was nice enough, with a huge balcony with a French door. Oh, that was worth the price of admission.

"Ooh. This is great, Hawk. We have a balcony!" He held the door for his lover and then dumped his bag on the floor. "I wonder if there's a view? I guess we'll find out in the morning."

"We can bundle up and drink coffee out there," Hawk

said. That, he'd discovered, was one of Hawk's joys—coffee el fresco.

"It's a plan." Jan locked the door. "Okay. Bathroom door is right here on the right. Dresser then the desk on the left, dead ahead are the doors to the balcony." He threaded his fingers into Hawk's and tugged on them. "And, over here on the right is an enormous, plush, comfortable looking, pillow-covered bed. And it's calling us."

"It is. It's whispering our names." Hawk shrugged off his shirt. "After we shower. Sand chafes."

"Mmm. Good thinking." He started to undress, eyes on his lover, drinking in the smooth and efficient way Hawk moved and the muscles that stretched and twisted with the effort. The scars shifted, highlighting the strong, compact body.

"Hottest thing I've ever seen," he whispered, fingers sliding down Hawk's side as he headed for the bathroom.

Hawk thanked him with a kiss that threatened to set him on fire.

Fucking sand. He wanted Hawk in bed right now.

Like *now*, now.

He pulled the shower curtain back and started the water, barely breaking the kiss.

Hawk's hands were hot on his ass, a burning kiss landing on the small of his back.

That was a spot that didn't get kisses often. "What are you up to, lover? Your hands are on fire."

Hawk encouraged him into the water, kneeling behind him as he leaned into the spray. More kisses brushed his back as Hawk spread him with gentle thumbs.

Then Hawk's blistering tongue dragged over his hole.

"Hawk!" Oh, fuck. *Fuck*. It had been a long, long time

since anyone had... "Hawk." He braced his hands on the tiled walls and pressed back into that tongue.

Hawk hummed and laved him, tracing his opening with the tip of his tongue, then pressed in, alternating between licking and fucking his ass.

"Jesus, baby." He didn't even know Hawk wanted to... would... *damn it*, he couldn't even think. He made some crazy, needy sound and curled his fist around his stiffening cock.

His entire body was on fire, his balls heavy, his prick throbbing in his touch. Hawk was relentless, determined to shove him over the edge.

And it felt so fucking good that Jan gave up thinking and let it happen. He spread his legs wider and arched to give Hawk all the access he could. He stroked himself just right —firm, long strokes, thumb gliding over the head—so practiced it needed no thought at all. "Fuck, baby. So good." So fucking good.

Hawk groaned for him, and he felt that sound, deep inside him, echoing in him.

"Oh. God." That set his fist flying and the sound of his own breathing echoed off the tiles and drowned out the drone of the shower. He gave right in, letting Hawk push him, loving every fucking second of it until the burning spiral finally overwhelmed him. He shot so hard it ripped the air from his lungs, from the entire room. He loosened his grip and worked his cock slowly, gently, moaning with his release. "Fuck, yes. God, baby."

Hawk nuzzled his ass, the small of his back, his spine as he stood. "So fucking hot."

He hung there a second and let Hawk hold him as he came back to earth. The touch felt amazing. "You surprised me."

"It felt good, loving on you." He could feel Hawk's smile against his shoulder. "Giving you something you needed."

"Exactly what I needed." He turned in Hawk's arms, gave Hawk a gentle kiss as a thank you and palmed his cowboy's heavy cock. "How about you? You still have too much sand here?"

Hawk arched into his hand, fingers digging into his shoulders hard enough that it proved Hawk's need. "Touch me, darlin'. I ache for you."

"You do. I love how you do." He could touch. But he could do better, like Hawk had for him. He put Hawk's back into the spray and dropped carefully to his knees, then took the beautiful prick right into his mouth. Right in deep to make his lover crazy.

Hawk cried out, bracing himself as he arched, sliding on Jan's tongue. He rocked in, eased out, panting beautifully.

He loved when Hawk needed him like this, he really did. He slid one hand around to Hawk's ass, then reached for Hawk's chest with the other to give the tiny little nub there a solid pinch.

"Jesus!" Hawk's cry rang out, echoing on the tile. "Do that again, darlin'. Please."

Your wish is my command, Champ. Even if the wish is mine too.

Jan slid his fingers to the other side of Hawk's solid chest and pinched. He hummed around his cowboy's full cock as well for good measure. Hawk's slow motions sped, his bull rider beginning to push hard, drive into him.

He loved this raw side of Hawk, so honest and unashamed. Jan held on, fingers digging into Hawk's skin, relaxing into it and letting his lover have everything he wanted.

Hawk's praise poured down over his head, the words

rough and raw, the cries growing more and more desperate. "Fixin' to. Need you."

Love you. Come on, baby. He pulled on Hawk's hips and swallowed.

The heavy cock swelled, spreading his lips a little bit more, and then Hawk stilled and shot, hot salt pouring into his mouth.

Fuck, yeah. He swallowed, fighting the grin that was getting in his way and losing. He let Hawk slide from him and stood, pulling his lover into a hard, happy kiss.

Hawk was shaking hard and they clung to each other, both of them panting. "Lord have mercy, darlin'. That was something else."

"It was. You just... make me burn." He took another kiss, finally starting to catch his breath. "I love you."

"Yeah. Yeah, I love you, so damn much." Hawk started to catch his breath, fingers trailing over January's face, exploring him.

He let Hawk touch all he wanted, kissing curious fingers as they slid over his skin and laughing. "Am I still handsome?"

"The most gorgeous bastard I've ever seen."

"Works for me." Jan searched through the little hotel bottles until he found the shampoo. "I think you might need a haircut, cowboy."

"Yeah? I'll find a barber in Oakland. I'll get them to cut it short."

"Well, how do you like it? The curls are nice, but to make that work you'd need to grow it longer." He worked the shampoo into Hawk's hair and pulled on a lock of hair.

"I usually let Momma hack at it. I like the way it feels, you know? Bouncy."

"Okay. So if it feels good, grow it out. Get a trim for some shape and let it go." He angled Hawk's head under the water and rinsed the soap out.

"Do you have a shop you normally go?" Hawk's hands were hot on his hips.

"In New York? Yes, I have a barber. You want to go to him?" He very happily scrubbed the rest of his lover down with soap, making very sure there was no more sand in Hawk's butt crack. He checked.

A couple of times.

"All clean. No sand to be found." Hawk shook it for him.

Jan laughed and showered off, enjoying the way Hawk helped, and the heated touches all over his skin. Hawk appreciated his body, made him feel sexy. That was something new and he liked it. A lot.

They finally shut the water off and he found soft towels and comfy robes in a little closet by the bathroom door.

"Oh, these are spiffy. I wonder if they'd notice if we took them."

"You're a bad cowboy. What would your mother say?" He hustled Hawk toward the bed, but stopped suddenly, spotting some fun. "Ooh. A minibar."

"Are you going to make a teeny tiny cosmo?" Hawk teased.

"Well you're a teeny tiny cowboy so..." Hawk left the opening, he had to tease.

"Oh dude. That was good. Low, but good." Hawk's chuckled started soft and low.

Jan grinned, pulled out a wee bottle of whiskey and tugged on Hawk's robe. "One sip and then we'll see how low I can really go, shall we?" He opened the bottle and waved it under his lover's nose.

"You got it, darlin'." Hawk took the bottle and twisted off the top, winking at him. "Then round two."

29

"Good lord, do we have to go back to real life, darlin'? Can't we be beach bums forever?" Hawk was teasing, but damn, he was sure having the time of his life.

They'd gone to the Winchester Mystery House, they'd laughed and played and kissed, and they'd torn up the sheets in a shit ton of hotels. He'd never been so happy.

"It's time to ride Champ, it's kind of your thing." Jan dug his NYU cap out of his suitcase.

"Kind of, yessir." He checked his gear, zipped up his bag. "Grab my shirt? I'll change when we get to the arena."

He grabbed his hat, checked his buckle, and slid his wallet into his back pocket.

"One shirt." Jan handed it to him. "Have I told you how much I like that tan on you? You've got some nicely toasted abs, baby."

He took the hanger and flexed. "I like baking my bones. I'm going to have to lay out on the roof—say in a month or two when it's warmer?"

"In a month or two it'll be really hot in the city. You won't have any trouble tanning up there. People lie out in Central

Park too. I'll go with you and hide under an umbrella." Jan laughed. His pale Yankee had lathered on sunscreen all week.

"Poor guy, staying pale to be my beacon in the darkness..." He grabbed his shit and shook his head. "Come on, darlin'. Let's go do this thing."

Jan gave his butt a squeeze and followed him out the door. "Right on, Champ."

He grinned, feeling good. He was going to ride tonight. He was going to ride all four bulls, win the money and the event, and he was going to rub Charlie's nose in it.

"There's that swagger," Jan whispered as they got on the elevator. "Ready to show those bulls who's boss?"

"You fucking know it. I got a good feeling tonight's going to be memorable." He was loose and relaxed, and he was ready.

"I can't wait to watch you kick ass and then get that buckle off you later." Jan took a step away as another couple got on the elevator.

Hawk nodded to the couple, smiling at the coiffed older lady with her league T-shirt on. "Y'all looking forward to the event?"

"Yes, sir." She beamed at him. "I'm glad to see you all healed up and looking solid."

He tipped his hat. "You and me both, ma'am."

"You think you can get the season back, cowboy?" The man's voice was rough and deep, the drawl familiar.

"I can sure try." He wasn't about to make any pie crust promises, but he intended to take another championship.

"Well, we'll be rooting for you."

"Good ride," the man said as they got off the elevator.

"Ah, back in the world where everyone knows you." January laughed, leading the way through the lobby.

"You know it." He was the champ, and that would be true forever. Always. He was a champion bull rider.

They rode in their usual limo, on their own this time. Jan stole a hard kiss as they pulled up to the arena. "That was for luck, Champ. Not that you need it. I'll be yelling the loudest, as usual."

He did love those kisses. "Enjoy your seats. Sky is doing a commercial, so you're sitting with him and Beck."

"Oh, cool. Thanks. Good ride, cowboy. I'm off to get my hot dog." Jan left him as they walked inside, giving him a wave.

He headed into the locker room, waving to different guys. He had signings tomorrow, but today he could bullshit with the boys and relax.

"Hey, Hawk! How's the shoulder treating you?" Danny came over and shook his hand.

"It's good, man. How's the mother-to-be?"

"Getting big. A little tired. I told her she could stay home or watch at the hotel, but she wouldn't have it. You look great, man."

"I've been outside playing like a fiend. It was a great drive up. Y'all ought to do it. It was—" Romantic. "—cool as fuck."

"Yeah? You did the coastal drive thing? Maybe we'll do it after the baby. Right now Nic isn't great at sitting in the car for too long, you know? Did I hear you guys are headed down to see Charlie after this? I think Nic said that was your plan."

"Yep. We fly out Sunday evening, get in Sunday night, and we're staying a week." He couldn't wait to introduce Jan to Charlie and Ben.

"Sounds like fun. January might be a little out of his

element, but if you can handle New York..." Danny laughed. "I still can't believe that. You in New York City."

"Yeah. It's—" He didn't have the words. It was the best thing that had ever happened to him, and his life hadn't been made of shit so far.

"Weird. Maybe good weird, but weird." Danny chuckled and pointed over at the lockers. 'I better get ready. I'll be around when it's your turn."

"Yeah, I'm in section two. You need me to pull your rope?"

"I'd love that, yeah. Cool." Danny took a step away and then looked back. "I'm really glad you're back. Hasn't been the same without you."

Oh, that was dear as all get out. "Come on, kid. Let's ride us some bulls."

They headed out to the line-up so they could get introduced. He climbed up onto the chutes, waiting for his spotlight at the end of introductions.

Every so often he looked at all this shit—the production, the lights, the livestock—and he couldn't believe it was all real. It had to be; it was his life, but if he was too quiet too long, it seemed like a dream.

Then everything started rolling fast—the anthem, the introductions, his trip into the spotlight. He listened for Jan and pretended he actually could hear his lover cheering louder than everyone else.

The bulls were doing their jobs, and he rode for an eighty-five, easy up, easy down.

He chest bumped with Mackey, then headed off the dirt to grab his shit.

"Great ride." Doc gave him a clap on the back as he headed toward the locker room. "Looks like the shoulder is holding up."

"Doing fine. You want another handstand?" He was pretty damn good at those, to be honest.

"Shut up, cowboy. You going to see Charlie?"

"Yes, Doc." The whole damn world knew his business.

"Good man. You make sure he knows we miss his face around here and give him my best."

"Yessir. I'm on it." His phone started to buzz, and he grabbed it, texting Jan's 'congrats' with a 'meet me in the back? I'm not staying'.

He changed his boots and grabbed his gear in short order, listening to the sounds of the crowds. "Someone had a good—"

His phone rang and he grinned at the sight of Charlie's face coming up. Someone saw him ride. Cool.

"Hey, buddy! You like that shit? It wasn't a ninety pointer, but it didn't suck, and—"

"Bird." That wasn't Charlie's voice. He didn't recognize it, but no one called him Bird but the guys.

"Yeah? What's up?" There was a silence, then a sob. "Ben? Ben, is that you?"

"Bird, man, it's Charlie." There was another long, heavy bit of quiet that made Hawk want to scream, before Ben shattered it. "He's dead."

30

J an picked up Hawk's phone and shut it off. It had been lighting up with condolences, but Hawk wasn't even talking to him right now and the constant buzzing was starting to grate on his last nerve. He went to the bathroom, wet a washcloth with cold water, and brought it to his lover who was sitting on the sofa, stiff as a board.

"Breathe, baby." He sat and draped the washcloth over Hawk's nape.

"I've changed our tickets. We fly out at six in the morning." Hawk didn't sound like himself, at all. Hawk sounded lifeless, so very still. "I sent the itinerary to Ben. I got us an AirBnB and a car."

Maybe he should have taken Hawk's phone away sooner.

"Anything you want. I'm right here for you." Here, yes, but at a loss as to what to do... what Hawk needed most. He leaned in and kissed Hawk's temple. "Maybe— do you want to lie down?"

"No. Thank you." He'd never seen his lover look so small, so still, like Hawk was scared to move, to breathe.

He took Hawk's hand and pulled it onto his knees. He

wanted to ask if Hawk had any idea how sick Charlie really had been. Their last conversation was good, Charlie had sounded strong and happy. This was such a shock. "I know how much this must hurt, baby. If you want to talk about it, I'm here."

Hawk's lips parted, but no words came out, so he closed them again, squeezing Jan's thigh.

All Hawk had managed to tell him was that it had been a brain bleed, it had been fast, that Charlie had laid down for a nap and never woken up again.

"It's okay. Maybe there aren't words yet. It's okay." He pulled the cloth away and rubbed Hawk's back with one hand. Maybe changing their flight plans was a good idea after all. This hotel was an awful place to be right now. It was probably going to be a long night. "Will you—" He knew Hawk wouldn't eat. "Are you thirsty? I can get you a Coke?"

"Diet Dr Pepper, if someone has one."

"Yeah. I'm sure I can find you one." Vending machines, the shop in the lobby... he got up and grabbed his wallet. "You'll be okay for a minute? I'll be quick."

"I'm good."

He grabbed his phone and headed out, running right into Skylar and Beck, who were heading up with a case of diet Dr Pepper.

"I know he drinks these. I do too. You want half?" Skylar's eyes were red, wet.

"I was just..." He nodded and sighed. "He asked for one. That would be great."

"We can put them in your fridge." Beckett had the case in one hand and a protective arm around Sky's back.

"Thanks." Jan nodded, then turned and led the way. "We're up the hall. I'm so sorry, Sky."

"Me too. It happens. It damn near happened to me. It's part of the job." Jesus, so matter-of-fact, so practical.

"Well, it sucks." He held the key to the door out and opened it. "Hey Hawk." He called out before letting them in. "I ran into Skylar and Beckett. They found Dr Pepper."

"Hey."

Skylar went to Hawk and sat. "Beck, can you go get ice with Jan? We'll toast to Charlie and make plans to meet up in Nashville tomorrow."

Beckett set the case of soda down. "Sure. Jan, where's your ice bucket?"

"Oh, uh..." Was he really being kicked out of his own room? "I got it. Ice is definitely important." He picked it up and Beckett followed him out.

"Sometimes ice needs to be a two-man job. They need a minute."

He nodded, but he wanted to know what he couldn't be there for. He didn't ask, though, he headed for the ice maker.

"I hope you don't mind. Sky's private with his tears, and we need to know who's coordinating things if Hawk can't."

Fair enough. "No, I don't mind. Thanks for clueing me in though." He filled the ice bucket, admitting defeat for the moment. "I didn't know what to say to Hawk anyway. I've never seen him like this."

"I know. I've been there."

Jan glanced at Beckett. He'd heard the story, how Sky had nearly died himself. "It's scary, right?"

"It's horrifying. I've never felt so helpless. I was..." Beck shrugged, cheeks reddening. "I can't say I was disappointed when they said he couldn't ride again."

Jan took a deep breath. "I don't even let myself go there. He's... I've accepted it's dangerous. I've accepted he is who he is, that he was a champion long before I met him. It's not up to me."

"Just stay honest. Keep talking. That's where we went wrong."

"Sound advice." That he could do. "Getting ice doesn't seem like a long enough errand."

"Nope, it's not. Sky will text me."

Jesus. "You've done this before, huh?"

Beck wandered over to the vending machines. "Split a candy bar? You like Milky Way?"

"I do." Jan shook his head. "So what does Hawk need to coordinate?"

"Whatever they need? Funeral stuff. Hotels. What we need to bring. What they need from us. There could be a couple hundred cowboys who show."

He blinked. "A couple of hundred? Seriously?"

"It's a big family. A... very big family."

"I was kind of expecting we'd go, chat with Ben some. You know, something quiet."

"That's why we're counting on Hawk. He'll let us know what Ben needs from us, right?"

Christ, that was a lot on the shoulders of a cowboy that didn't seem to be all that solid right now.

Beck handed him half of the Milky Way and he ate it in two big bites, hungrier than he'd realized. "Yeah. I need to help him with that. Has Sky texted you yet? I want... I need to be there for him."

"Let's go then. I hear you. If we leave, it's not personal, man, okay?"

"No, I get it. Thanks, Beck. I appreciate the talk. We'll see you in Nashville."

Beck gave him a nod. "You will."

They headed back to the room. He knocked before

opening the door and went right to the case of soda to take a couple cans out for Hawk so he could keep busy and out of Sky and Beck's business.

The guys didn't stay, Sky pressing a couple of pills into his hand on the way by. "To help him out if he needs, huh?"

"Thank you, Sky." He handed the rest of the soda to Beckett and saw them out. "You guys take care."

Once they were on their way, Jan closed the door quietly and locked it. He put the pills in a cup in the bathroom and stuck it up high where Hawk wouldn't take them by mistake.

"It was good of them to stop by." He moved slowly across the room toward Hawk, approaching him like Hawk might scream or bolt or something any minute.

"Yeah. I—I guess I'm the contact between the guys and the family. I got a lot to do. That's good." Hawk's eyes moved randomly, restlessly, like he couldn't focus on anything.

"You're the contact if you want to be. If you want someone else to handle things they will." He sat with Hawk and took his lover's hand. "But if you want to do it, I want to help."

"Thank you."

The two simple words felt huge, somehow, full of emotion, and Hawk leaned into him, the slightest pressure.

"It's you and me here, baby. All night. If you need to fall apart, I'm right here." It was probably better tonight than tomorrow when Ben... "Tomorrow there will be people around, and Ben will need you."

"Yeah. Yeah, there's so much." Hawk closed his eyes for a second. "So much."

Hawk's grief was heavy enough, but he hadn't done anything like this before, Jan could tell. He'd probably been one of those two hundred cowboys showing up to be supportive, but not the one running the show. "I know. We'll get started on it tomorrow. Tonight is for you."

Jan tucked an arm behind Hawk and pulled him closer. "I know it hurts, but listen to your heart, Hawk."

"I don't know what that means." It felt like Hawk was fighting to breathe, his chest tight.

"Hawk." He caught his lover's chin and turned it, his own heart aching to see Hawk this lost. "It means I know you loved him. Charlie was your best friend. It means it's okay to cry. I've got you."

"I wanted you to meet him. Day after tomorrow, I'd have been there."

"I know. I'm so sorry. I wanted to meet him too." God, the hollow look in Hawk's eyes— it was killing him. He wanted to wrap himself around Hawk and fix it. Make it okay.

But it wasn't even remotely okay.

"He told you to be where you were. He was happy you are riding again."

"Yeah. I—" Hawk closed his eyes. "He was one hell of a cowboy."

"How long had he been riding?"

"Damn near twenty years. He was the man when I started—rookie of the year already, won a bunch of events. I thought he was amazing—we trained together at the ranch, because he was madly in love with Bryan. Then I stopped being a weird little kid that wanted to be Charlie and started to be his friend."

"Sky told me that this is part of the job. I guess that's true, but it's not the part Charlie would want you to remember. That man you talked about, the one that was madly in love and happy, that's the man you need to hold on to. The friend you loved."

"I—" Hawk stood, damn near falling over the end table. "I need a shower."

Shit. "Easy, baby." He stood too, taking one of Hawk's elbows to steady him. Did Hawk mean alone? Should he ask if he could come?

Hawk answered him by taking his hand and pulling him along. Okay. That was clear.

"I want to go home and— but I can't. I owe this to Ben." Hawk wasn't talking to him, but Hawk was *talking*.

"After. We'll take care of Ben, we'll get everyone out of his hair after the service, and then we'll go home. It will be good for you to spend some time with Ben. You two were closest to him." Whichever home Hawk meant, he was game. They'd take care of Ben and then he'd take care of Hawk.

"We'll go home. You promise?"

"I promise. Anywhere you want, we'll go." He let Hawk pull him toward the bathroom where they undressed. He followed his lover's lead, in no rush, without an agenda... just in the moment. "Do you mean home to Texas, or home to New York?"

"Home to New—" Hawk stopped, frowning deeply. "Is that okay? That I want to go there?"

"It's our home, Hawk. It's more than okay." Jan was gratified that New York was the place Hawk was calling home now. "It's where you belong. Where we live. It *is* your home."

Hawk closed his eyes, and for a second Jan was sure he was going to collapse, but he didn't. "Okay. Shower."

"I got it." He stepped around Hawk and started the water. He'd stay close to Hawk, give his lover something to lean on. "Climb in."

"I'm sorry," Hawk whispered, slipping into the water.

"Shh." Jan frowned. What on earth... "For what?"

Hawk shook his head, shrugged. "I don't know."

"Your grief is real, baby. Don't apologize for it. I'm here for you." He smoothed his hands over Hawk's shoulders. He was here for all of it. Even the parts he didn't really understand yet. "I love you."

"I love you. I'll be okay. I'm just..." He shook his head and shrugged. "Hold me for a minute?"

"Forever." He pulled Hawk against him and hugged his lover close.

Hawk kissed his chest. "Amen."

31

F light. Check. Car. Check. Hotel. Check.

Now they were sitting in front of the big wrought iron gate that Charlie had given Ben for their fifth anniversary. "The code is 7610. It'll open.'

I'm here.

He texted, and Ben answered immediately with his, *Come in the kitchen door.*

"We're going to drive around the house and go in the back. I bet Charlie's folks are asleep. His daddy's not well."

"Damn. Okay." Jan drove slowly, following the path around to the back of the house. Ben was waiting on the back steps, face up to the sunlight like he hadn't seen it in days in a beat-up ball cap that was pulled down low.

"Ben." Hawk hurtled out of the car, his heart torn into pieces. He should have been here. He should have known. He should have been with them.

Ben stood and opened his arms. "Bird. Bird, he's gone. My Charlie is gone."

He nodded, because what was he supposed to say? What

the fuck did you say? He grabbed onto Ben and held on tight.

It took Ben a bit to react, he stood there like he was stunned or frozen, but then he swallowed back a sob and clung to Hawk like he was trying to keep his feet. "Sorry. Thank you for coming."

"I'm here. As long as y'all need me." Hawk held on, his eyes dry. He wasn't going to fall apart. He wasn't. This wasn't about him. It was about Ben and Charlie's folks.

Ben let him go suddenly and swiped at his eyes. "Sorry. I'm sorry. Why don't you... I haven't met your man yet. Come on in. Was it a good flight? Would you like some coffee?"

Jan was hanging back, still in the driveway getting their bags from the rental car.

"Jan, come meet Ben, and God yes, please." He waved to January, motioning him over.

"Hey there. I'm Jan." Jan shook Ben's hand. "It's good to meet you. I know it's not enough, but I'm very sorry for your loss."

"Me too." Ben gave Jan a watery smile. "He was looking forward to meeting you, so much."

"Hawk loves to tell stories. I feel like I knew him in a way."

Ben cleared his throat and opened the door. "Let's get you guys some coffee."

Hawk followed Ben in, the house familiar enough that he actually waited for Charlie to walk in, wave at him, and hand him a beer. His breath hitched, and for a horrifying second, he couldn't move.

"I know, right? It's like he's still here." Ben's sorrow sent shivers through him. "That's why I'm sitting outside."

"Whatever you want." *Whatever you need, man.*

"That's not possible. I want him back."

There was a long silence that hung heavily in the kitchen. Nobody knew what to say.

"Yeah. I know. I shouldn't say stuff like that. It freaks people out. Sorry. I'll make coffee " Ben filled the machine with water.

Jan came up behind him and rested a steady hand on his hip.

"You can say whatever the fuck you want, man. That's why I'm here. I want him back too, and I was his friend." Hawk got it. Ben needed someone to bash against a little; he was that man.

"Yeah. You were. Shit, you spent more time with him than I did, I think. I know he liked you more." Ben winked at him, the joke old and bittersweet.

"Yeah, but he swore you were better in bed."

Ben sat the coffee pot down. "How am I going to do this, Bird? How do people survive this?"

A thousand answers flitted through his head—you give it to God, one day at a time, lots of booze—but he ended up saying, "I don't know."

And he didn't. Hawk didn't know. He didn't want to know. He didn't know how he was supposed to do any of this, and he wasn't Charlie's husband. He was just the friend and his fucking soul felt like a car window that had a bird fly into it.

What he did know was how to make coffee, so he took over, everything right where it was supposed to be.

"We'd been talking about him retiring before this happened. Did he tell you? I don't think I'd totally convinced him yet, but I was working on it." Ben sat at the kitchen table. "I almost had him."

"Yeah, he said. He was looking forward to hanging out with you, running cattle, listening to you sing." Was that all right to say? Was that bad? "He was worried you'd be bored, once he wasn't a bull rider."

God, he wanted to go. He wanted to call Daddy and ask what was right, what he was supposed to do. He wanted to drink until it didn't hurt anymore.

What he did was make the coffee, get three mugs out. Get the sugar. The milk.

"He told me that a couple of times. He was such an idiot sometimes. I didn't love him because he was goddamn bull rider."

"They're a rare breed all right, those bull riders." Jan jumped in.

"Right? This one is as bad." Ben snorted, gesturing toward him.

"Every bit. Stubborn as the day is long." Jan chuckled softly. "Good men though."

Ben nodded. "Loyal."

"Hot."

"So hot." Ben agreed, sounding a little more like the man he knew.

He chuckled softly. He didn't feel hot. He felt old and broken. He felt like flying to Dallas and having Bryan pick him up and take him to the ranch so he could hide in his room.

He made up Ben and Jan's coffee and took it to the table, then poured his before he went to sit. "Charlie said he fell in love with you the second he saw you at that awards show. Said you were like a jewel to him."

"He thought I was handsome." Ben nodded. "But if you asked him in front of anyone, he'd tell you he had that first drink with me on a dare."

"You are sort of too pretty for words, Ben." He'd been there for that dare. That drink had ended in a wild case of sex and the beginnings of one of the great love affairs in history.

"Shut up. You only say that because you were taking odds on whether we'd end up in bed together."

"Scandalous." Jan laughed.

"I won three hundred dollars. I know Charlie."

"But you didn't know me."

Hawk shook his head. "Not then."

Ben sipped his coffee. "We're going to have the funeral Tuesday morning. Can you stay that long?"

"I'll be here. Sky and them are here in town. Lots will come in Sunday evening and Monday morning." He had over one hundred texts already, and he'd warned the hotel.

Ben peered at him from under the brim of the ball cap. "I don't know what to do with all those cowboys, Hawk. I don't know what to say. And all the noise in the house... I want to be kind, I appreciate they want to be here but—"

"I've got it. We'll be at the funeral, and then if you want, we'll have the feed somewhere else. I bet the hotel would let us." He would call home. Someone there would tell him what to do. Hell, Momma and Daddy were flying in Monday. "I got that part. I got whatever you need."

Ben's shoulders sagged. "Thank you. That's... yeah. Thank you." After a pause, Ben added, "You though... You're different. I want you around, okay? You guys are family."

"Whatever you need. I—" He was family. He was here for a reason. "You know I got your back."

"You make pretty good coffee." Ben held up his mug and took a sip. Ben looked at Jan. "My dad was born in Brooklyn."

"Yeah? Did he grow up there?"

"No. He grew up all over the place, but he started out a Yankee."

Jan laughed. "Have you forgiven him?"

"Mostly."

"Hell, Eddie Rabbitt was born there too, and he made a living singing, didn't he?" Hawk winked over. He wondered whether Ben would go back on the road now, whether that was even a thing. He sure as shit wasn't going to ask.

"Huh. Something else good came out of New York. Who knew?" Ben looked at Jan. "Maybe Hawk and I will play you a cover later, make you feel right at home."

Jan leaned toward Ben. "Hawk told me you were teaching him, but I haven't heard him play yet. He doesn't have a guitar at home."

"What? You haven't played for him, Bird? You've heard him sing though, right?"

"No, actually. Little snips here and there but not really singing."

"He don't need to hear me caterwaul, man."

"He's good, Jan. Really good." Ben shook his head, grinned. "Charlie loved to hear you sing, man. To hear us sing."

His cheeks burned, but he wasn't going to argue. Charlie would sit at the door of the studio for hours, listening, letting the music pour over him. He had to believe that Charlie's spirit was going to visit here, listen to Ben. Heaven had to allow that, right?

"If you're feeling up to it later, I'd love to hear you both. No pressure, though. Only if you want to."

"I'll play. I always play. Sad, happy, sick, tired. I played last night, sang to Charlie. He was listening, wherever his soul is. He heard me." Ben looked down into his coffee cup. "I need to believe that."

"Me too." Hawk swallowed hard, trying to dislodge the

sorrow that was building there, the pure agony. Thirty-five was too young.

Ben looked up at him, and although he couldn't make out every detail, he knew Ben was looking him right in the eyes. "He did, Bird. He can. We'll sing him a song later, okay?"

32

A fter today, if he ever needed a second career, Jan was pretty sure he could qualify as an event coordinator. Cowboys were coming in from the event in Oakland and elsewhere, their families joining them from Texas and Colorado and Oklahoma and everywhere. The hotel lobby was hopping.

"Sky and Beckett have a huge rental, they brought a bunch of guys with them, they should be here any minute."

He had made three trips to the airport today, picking up people who couldn't manage to get a ride or didn't want to rent a car. Hawk had stayed behind to make sure people had rooms and the arrangements for the funeral tomorrow. "Am I picking up your parents? I need to head back to the airport again. You want to wait here for Sky, right?"

"Daddy's renting a car. He doesn't like to be without." Hawk sighed softly. "Ben's going to want me back out at the house soon. He's been texting. They ended up sedating Charlie's momma."

Oh, shit. "Really? That's... wow." He couldn't imagine losing his best friend, let alone a son. He wouldn't even pretend to know that pain. "Have you eaten anything? You need to eat something. And then I'll drive you back to the house."

"I'm not hungry." Hawk shook his head, offered him a smile, but how many meals in a row had he heard those words?

"You're never hungry." And he was worried about the hollowed-out look in Hawk's eyes. "You need a protein shake or something at least. Come on." The hotel had a decent little food court; surely they could find something quick.

"Yeah, but I'm not." Hawk's phone never stopped beeping and ringing and booping. Jan was going to lose his mind.

He hooked an arm through Hawk's and moved them in the direction of the food court. "Listen, Champ. You're going to eat *something*. And I want you to put that phone in your pocket for five minutes. Okay? Let's focus on you for five minutes."

He was proud of how Hawk had tabled his own grief and held it together the last few days for Ben, managing people and logistics so Ben could breathe and grieve and have time with his family. And Jan had done anything Hawk asked. Random errands, trips to the airport, flowers for the funeral. Anything Hawk didn't have enough hands for. But he was tired, and anyone could see Hawk was beyond exhausted.

Hawk still had his nose in that phone, and Jan reached for it, lowering Hawk's arm. "Put it away for a few minutes. Please."

"I—" There was actual fear in Hawk's eyes, but he put it down. "I don't want to fuck this up. This may be the most important thing anyone's ever asked me to do."

"Baby. the most important thing is that you're here for Ben. There's no such thing as making this perfect. You've got this." And sooner or later—Jan had his money on the funeral—Hawk was going to have to work through his own grief too.

He pulled Hawk along with him, looking for something easy that Hawk could eat in the car and not have to think too hard about. "How about a protein bar?"

"I want a milkshake. Can we do that?" Okay, that was fair, reasonable.

"Yes. Let's find you a milkshake." In fact, it sounded so good he thought he would have one too. He looked around and sure enough there was a little ice cream counter across the way. "Look at that. They knew we were coming. What are you in the mood for?"

There weren't a ton of choices, but they did have milkshakes on the menu.

"Chocolate, please." Hawk closed his eyes, seeming almost asleep, right there, standing in line.

Jan ordered two of them and let Hawk lean on him as they waited for their order. "We're coming back to the hotel early tonight so you can get some sleep. You're going to need it for tomorrow." He knew he'd get an argument; Ben had kept Hawk up late the last two nights talking and playing music. It was great, but Hawk needed to say no tonight.

"If it's cool with Ben. I don't want to stress him out." Hawk sighed softly. "I hate this for him."

It would be cool with Ben. If he had to, he'd explain it to Ben himself. Gently.

"Two shakes!" The teenager working the ice cream counter set two tall cups with long straws out for them.

"Awesome." He carefully handed one to Hawk and then took the other for himself. "Do you need anything from the room before we go to Ben's?"

"I—I honestly don't know. I look okay? We have to find a western wear store and buy clothes for tomorrow. Thank God I brought my good boots. I should have asked Momma to bring my funeral shirt, but I didn't. It's okay. They'll have one."

"Jesus, I didn't even think about what I'd wear. I didn't bring anything either." And what was a funeral shirt? Black? He supposed he'd find out. He hadn't packed a suit, or anything appropriate to wear to a funeral. "I don't think I even have shoes."

"I'll take care of you, darlin'. No worries."

He'd never had anyone that said that so confidently, so sure.

"We'll stop by someplace before we go to Ben's." He pulled out his phone to look for a place, but Hawk was already on it. He led his lover slowly toward the elevator to the garage.

"Okay. That sounds good." Hawk sucked on his shake, blinking at it when he pulled the straw from his mouth. "It's good."

He smiled, ridiculously pleased to see Hawk happy about something. "It is. Also too cold to drink too fast. I have brain freeze after three sips."

"Yeah. Yeah, but it's good. I haven't had a milkshake in a long time."

"Probably not on your diet. But since you haven't eaten in two days, I think you're good." He led Hawk onto the elevator. "Did you figure out where we're going?" He could find a suit anywhere really. All he needed was a men's store or a department store.

"Yes. There's a Boot Barn on the way up north. It'll do for what we need."

"Boot Barn. Okay. Put the GPS on when we get out of the

parking garage." He drove out into a beautiful day that they really should be enjoying doing anything but this.

"I thought about moving out here, to prove to you I could live on my own. I like Nashville."

"Seriously?" He reached over and squeezed Hawk's hand. "You don't have to prove anything to me, Champ. You never have. I hope you know that now."

"I was worried. I've never lived all alone. I wanted you to know I could."

"It never occurred to me that you couldn't." He took a right turn following the GPS. Thank goodness because the only thing he'd memorized about Nashville was the drive to the airport. "You can do anything you set your mind to. You've proven that many times over."

"Yeah." Hawk sighed, the sound no more than a quiet exhale, but it felt so defeated.

He felt terrible that this happened in the middle of Hawk's comeback. Hawk could have ridden all weekend and reclaimed his place in the league... but none of that mattered right now. There would be another chance.

"This is one of the hardest things you'll ever do, and you're doing really well, baby. Breathe for a minute, it's just you and me."

"Breathing. Right. I'm on it." Hawk sat there, still and quiet. "I want to honor him."

Jan wasn't sure what that meant, but he thought Charlie would be pretty honored already. "I bet if Charlie could have asked you for something before he died it would have been to look after Ben. And you've done that. You're taking care of the person that meant the most to Charlie. That's honoring him."

"I hope so. I truly hope so." Hawk nodded so hard that

he shook. "I need to get a quick haircut too. I don't want no one to think I'm being disrespectful."

No one would. "We can do that. We'll ask if there's a place close to the... Boot... place. Barn? Boot Barn." The GPS told him to take a left to his destination and he found a place to park almost directly across the street. "Did you finish your milkshake?" He'd sucked his down until the straw made slurping noises.

"I did." Liar.

"A couple more sips, baby? Please?" *Come on, you stubborn bull rider.*

"Yeah. A couple more." Hawk took a couple of deep draws.

Jan watched him. It looked like Hawk had managed to drink half, which was something. Not enough, but something. Those last two sips were real though, Hawk wasn't humoring him.

"Thank you. You'll feel better with something in your stomach, I promise." *As long as you keep it down.* "Ready?"

"Let me have one more suck, and then yes. If I need to sign autographs or something, I will, but I'm hoping that they know what's up."

"Oh, shit. I didn't even think about that. Take your time and drink up. You want me to go in first and ask them to be cool?" Look at him running interference for a celebrity. Hard to believe this was his life sometimes.

"No. No, I'm going to go in and be straightforward. If they suck, I don't tell the guys to come get shirts here." Oh, that was hard and sure, Hawk's lips a straight line.

"Whatever you want, Champ." Jan shut the car off and climbed out, groaning as he unfolded like an old man. It had been a long couple of days, and he was feeling it.

"Yeah. We need a nap." Hawk stood too and waited for him to head into the store.

The entire place was like the west had exploded all over. Hats and boots, clothes and buckles and belts. It was insane and wonderful.

An older gentleman came up to them, face somber. "Mr. Destry, I'm sorry for your loss."

"Thank you. I need clothes for myself and Jan here, plus a recommendation for a haircut."

"Yes, sir. Do you need boots?"

"Jan does. I'm leading Charlie's horse, Peaches, in at the gravesite. I'll wear my worn-in boots."

There was no one crowding them, not a single person asking for an autograph. "I need boots?" He glanced at Hawk. "I mean... yes. I need boots." And a suit. Though now he wondered if Hawk had other plans.

Hawk nodded decisively. "Boots, black jeans, a gray shirt, the black suede jacket and a hat for him. I need dark jeans, a black shirt, and a leather vest. A bolo tie if y'all have one."

"Sounds good. You know your size I bet, why don't you work with Kyle here and I'll see what I can find for Mister..."

"Bell. You can call me January. What's your name?"

"Carson, sir."

"Great. Thank you, Carson."

Carson sized him up quickly. "That jacket is going to suit you well."

"Hawk knows what he's talking about."

"Yes, sir. I've met him before. Very sure of himself. No bull. We were all sorry to hear about Mr. McDaniels' passing." He was led to a dressing room, another employee pulling clothes and putting them on a rack. "What kind of leather do you like for your boots?"

"I have no idea. Comfortable. Simple I guess." He started

to undress, so he could try on the jeans. He was oddly nervous about this; he'd never imagined himself in cowboy boots.

The first shirt he tried on fit great, but the jeans took a couple of tries until he found a fit that Carson approved of. The jacket was good too, maybe a tiny bit long in the arms, but the fit everywhere else was good.

"You look good. If you'd like, get dressed and we'll deal with the boots. I'm assuming a black felt, simple?"

"Get him the 100X. It'll suit." Hawk's voice cut through the store.

"Yes, sir," Carson called back. "The Champ has good taste."

Jan smiled at Carson, getting dressed. "Whatever the man says. I'm just a New Yorker."

"Let him see the gray ostrich. I think he'll like them." Hawk came over, leaning against the wall. "I'm good to go."

"That's a nice jacket you picked out for me. I like it." He ignored the price tag. If Hawk wanted him in it, he'd buy it.

Carson measured his feet and brought out several pairs of boots for him to try on. He tried them all, because he didn't know the difference between one and another. "Which ones do you like, Hawk?"

"The ones that match your shirt. They're comfortable?"

"Yeah. More than the black. They fit pretty well. And you were right, I do like the ostrich.'

Kyle brought over a hatbox and opened it for him. "This is the 100X."

It was a beautiful hat, even from a few feet away. "Somebody better show me how to wear it."

"Just try it on. It'll fit or it won't.' Hawk nodded when he put it on, the hat settling on his head. "Perfect. That's it. Can you point me to a barber? I've texted around. There's lots of us coming, so y'all might pull out everything black."

"There's one up the street. I'll call and let them know you're coming." Carson bundled everything off to the register.

"Are you enjoying dressing me up, Champ?" Jan did like how sure of himself Hawk was. That confidence, like always, was hot as hell.

"You look amazing. Handsome as hell. They're packing it all up so we can get it in the car. Then I'll get my hair cut real quick."

"Sounds like a plan." Wait... did Hawk pay for everything?

The milkshake wasn't much, but it definitely had helped. Hawk's eyes were brighter, and he seemed less down. Or maybe he was enjoying being capable and in charge. Either way, things were better.

"Yeah." Hawk signed the ticket, and then grabbed the suit bag. "Can you grab the boots and hatbox, please sir?"

"I'm on it." He thanked everyone and then followed Hawk out with his arms full of goodies. If nothing else, dressing for the funeral would be fun. He popped the trunk of the rental car. "I have the directions to the barber, it's easy."

"Excellent. I don't want anyone to think I'm not at my best."

Jan let that go until they were in the car. "Hawk." He curled his fingers round the back of Hawk's neck. "You've lost your best friend. You're not at your best. No one is going to expect you to be." Most people would probably worry if Hawk were. "No one at that funeral tomorrow is going to be at their best."

"No, but I got to talk. Ben wants me to." Hawk sighed softly. "You look good in your finery."

He wondered what Hawk was going to say for Ben. "I felt good. I'm looking forward to wearing it tomorrow, and then we need to find an excuse for me to wear it. A much happier occasion."

"Yes. Maybe there's a place in New York where we can go and dance, all gussied up."

"I love that idea. There's always a place in New York. We'll find one." The drive to the barbershop wasn't even five minutes.

Hawk was getting those pretty curls hacked off, and he went to sit. He was glad he had, because about the time his butt hit the seat, his phone rang, the number a 903 area code.

He didn't recognize the number but with everything going on it could be anybody. "Hello? This is January."

"Hello, honey. It's Momma. How's he holding up?" The voice was instantly familiar.

"Hello, Momma—" Okay, that was weird. Good, but weird. "He took us shopping for something to wear tomorrow and is getting his hair cut right now. That might answer your question. I got him to eat a little."

"Good. Eating is good." She sighed softly. "I brought his funeral shirt, but new is better. I brought a suitcase of his favorite things from home too. And his pillow. I'm worried about him, son."

"I'll be honest, I am too. It'll be good to see you. I know he'll appreciate everything." Despite the worry, he had to smile a little. This was normal worried mom stuff, not obsessive, controlling, crazy Momma stress. And as much as he hated for her to worry, he knew it meant she trusted him.

He'd won her over. He was a little smug about that.

"Are you okay? Do you need anything while we're out? I'm fixin' to stop at the store."

"I bet Hawk would like some Dr Pepper and... maybe grab him something he'll eat?" Hawk wouldn't say no to his mother, right?

"Do y'all have a fridge in your room? If so, I'll grab him some popsicles. If not, he's never turned down a grape in his whole life."

"We do. It has a tiny freezer too." Grapes. Good to know. "Thanks, Momma. We're headed over to Ben's in a few. Are you stopping by there? Otherwise we'll be back at the hotel early. I want Hawk to get some sleep."

"No. No, I'll give my condolences tomorrow. I know how overwhelmed they have to be. Call me when you get in and we'll bring you groceries and stuff."

"I will. You okay?"

"Worried about y'all; my heart's breaking for Ben and Charlie's momma. He was a kid. I hate this. I know this is rodeoing, but I don't have to like it."

"They keep telling me it's part of the gig. That doesn't make me feel better. We're okay. Hawk's about done. We'll see you later for a hug." That was okay, right? He was allowed to commiserate a little.

"Yes, sir. Love y'all. Tell Ben we'll see him tomorrow." She hung up, and he sat there a second. Hawk was lucky—genuinely lucky. The huge family folded him in like he belonged.

He flipped through his phone and found a couple of texts from Ben, so he sent a quick note that they were on their way. "You all set, Champ? I think Ben is ready for company."

"I'm done." Hawk looked suddenly young without his curls, just these huge pale blue eyes behind thick glasses.

"Handsome. Come on, the car is this way." Jan unlocked the doors. "Your mother called me. They want to stop by for a quick visit when we get back to the hotel."

"She called you, did she? Impressive. She likes you, I can tell."

"Wait until she sees me tomorrow in that lavishly expensive hat you bought me. She'll be completely won over." That hat even felt sexy. "Thank you, by the way." He started to say "you didn't have to do that" but Hawk knew exactly what he'd wanted and bought it.

"You deserve a good hat. You don't have any." Hawk settled and then reached for him.

He took Hawk's hand and kissed it, careful to keep it quick. "You're a good man. I like how you take care of me. How we take care of each other."

"Let's go take care of Ben so we can go deal with everyone else." Hawk sighed softly. "We fly home Wednesday?"

"That's right, Wednesday." He hoped Hawk didn't change his mind about leaving Ben on his own. "Two more sleeps." This time he set up the GPS on his own phone and headed for Ben's ranch.

"Do you think that's too soon? I really want to go home." There was a desperation in Hawk's voice.

"No. I don't think so at all. I'm anxious to be home too." That was the truth. Funerals weren't Jan's thing. And Hawk needed to be somewhere he could let his guard down.

"Yeah. Yeah, okay. Good deal." Hawk sighed softly. "I want to help, but I need to go home."

"Deep breath, baby. We're in the home stretch. Why don't you put something on the radio? We've got satellite."

"I can do that." Hawk found the country music station and turned it up, singing along.

There. That was better. He leaned back in his seat and drove, relaxing, listening to his lover sing. Hawk's voice was so smooth and rich. It didn't matter whether Jan knew the words or not, Hawk's voice was beautiful, and it made him smile.

33

---

awk sat next to Ben in the front row, holding his best
friend's husband's hand. The whole world was here
—country music people, rodeo cowboys, family, friends—
and he was going to have to stard up there without falling
on his ass and say something.

He needed to say something important, something that
said how much Ben loved Charlie, what a good friend he
was, what a great cowboy he was. He needed to do it without
crying, without falling down, without passing out.

He wasn't smart enough for this. This wasn't riding bulls
or even being brave. This was saying goodbye to the best
friend he'd ever had.

*Please God, help me be able to do this. I'm scared like I ain't
never been, and I'm in Your house and I need Your hand on me to
make this happen. I want to give Ben comfort. I want to make my
folks proud. I want to stand before You and all my people and tell
them how much I loved him. Please, God. I need this. Please.
Amen.*

Ben squeezed his hand ther liked he'd heard the whole

thing. Jan sat on his other side, quiet and somber but steady. They believed he could do this, and maybe that was enough.

The preacher finally stopped talking, and Ben squeezed his hand again.

"That's your cue, Bird."

"Right on." Please God. Please, don't let me fall. Let me do this right. He stood up, heading carefully for the steps up to the stage. The preacher showed him to the podium, and he stood there.

This close, he could see Charlie, laying there in the coffin like a mannequin, and he could hear his momma, like she was whispering in his ear.

He ain't there, son. That's a shell. He's gone from this world; he knows no more pain.

He opened his mouth to speak, but—

"There ain't nothing I can say, y'all, that will make this right. Charlie, you were my good friend, and I'll miss you every day of my life." He took a shaky breath, and he wanted to say so much, but he couldn't. Charlie was gone, and it was bad.

So he closed his eyes, starting to sing "I'll Fly Away" because that was what Charlie always wanted to hear when he sang with Ben.

Slowly, he realized he wasn't singing alone. One by one, folks started in—famous voices, quiet voices, all singing to Charlie.

All sending him home where he belonged.

The silence that followed the song was full of love and truth, and then Jan was suddenly beside him, leading him slowly back to his seat.

Ben stood as he got there and hugged him hard, whispering "thank you" in his ear.

He hugged Ben back, then he sat, closing himself inside.

The graveside service with Peaches. The feed. Then they could go home tomorrow.

He could do this. He never had to say another word to anyone now.

Then suddenly the service was over. "It's time to go, baby." Jan took his arm. "To the burial."

He nodded. He was on it. Graveside service. Feed. Home. He could do this.

34

January picked up their bags from the sidewalk where the driver had left them. Hawk took his gear silently when Jan handed it to him, and they went inside.

This wasn't how he'd wanted this to go at all. He wanted to come home after a relaxing vacation with a Champ who was back in the saddle. He'd imagined them chattering and making plans on the plane ride home about Hawk's next event, watching a replay of one of Hawk's better rides or a movie, maybe deciding what to order for dinner.

Instead Hawk had his head down and his eyes closed most of the flight, face hidden under his hat. Jan tried to hold his hand but had run out of anything to say that might help. Nothing seemed to. Hawk was exhausted in every way possible—physically, emotionally—his lover needed sleep, and quiet, and time to process the loss of his dearest friend. Finally.

Jan understood, but it didn't stop his heart from breaking as they stepped into the apartment and the door closed quietly behind them. It was good to be home, but why did it have to feel like defeat?

Hawk's mother had sent a huge suitcase home with them, filled with things from Hawk's room in Texas, and his lover took it to the bedroom. "Where do you want my gear, darlin'?"

Jan followed him. "Anywhere. Everywhere. It's your place too, baby." He tossed his suitcase on the bed. "Welcome home."

"Thank you. I wanted—" Hawk trailed off, moving toward the window.

He watched Hawk for a second and then trailed after him, curling an arm around his cowboy, fingers resting on rigid abs. "I know. We'll get there."

"Okay." Hawk leaned into him, eyes closed. "I don't know what to do next, darlin'? Do you?"

Not really. Move on? What else could they do? "Rest, I guess. Give yourself a break. Be sad and angry and all those things you couldn't be around Ben." He kissed Hawk's shoulder. "And then we'll figure it out. Maybe we should start with ordering dinner."

"I'd say pizza, but I'm acidy. Maybe that ramen noodle stuff? I liked that."

Okay, that was first, not a fight, and second, an opinion. Third, Hawk had admitted he had an upset stomach.

"Sounds good to me." Ramen made him think of Jax, and that made him think of Charlie and gave him this weird pang of guilt. "You want to lie down until it gets here? There's no reason to get ambitious tonight. We can find great places for your things tomorrow."

"I think I will, yeah. It's been a long day."

Sure, let's eat. Sure, I'll have a nap...Okay was this agreeable thing good weird, or bad weird?

"I bet. We were up early in a different time zone. Let me

order, and then I'll join you, okay?" He pulled his phone out of his pocket.

"Yeah." Hawk sat on the edge of the bed and pulled off his boots. When Jan got back from ordering, he was still sitting in the same spot.

"Hey." Jan kicked off his shoes, and went to Hawk, taking Hawk's glasses and hat, a habit he did without thinking much about anymore. Then he sat on the bed, back in the pillows and tapped his hand on his thighs, "Come lie down, baby."

"I'm scared if I try to relax, I'll crack right down the center."

"I'm not scared." Jan was worried though. Worried that if Hawk didn't relax soon he'd snap and that seemed worse. "I've got you. Whatever happens, happens."

"Okay. Christ." Hawk stretched out next to him, muscles like rocks every place they touched.

"Oh, Champ. You're wound up tight. Take that shirt off for me." He rolled over and pulled out a bottle of oil from a drawer. "This is vanilla or almond or something. I don't know. It smells good."

"Can I?" Hawk's lips tightened. "Christ, this is my place too, I can be naked if I want to."

"I approve. I'm a fan of you naked. You can be naked all the time." He approved of naked, and he approved of Hawk's tone, too. It was their place now.

As long as Hawk was stripping, he figured he would too. He set the bottle down and hopped up to pull off his jeans.

Hawk pulled his clothes off and settled on the bed. "Where do you want me, darlin'?"

He hummed. "Mmm. That's a great view right there. But you better roll on your stomach, anywhere that's comfy."

"It is stupid to say I've forgotten how to be comfortable?"

"I'll remind you." He put a hand on Hawk's shoulder and leaned on it, flattening his lover into the mattress and moved to straddle Hawk's hips.

"Mmm..." Oh. Oh, that was a happy little sound. Seriously. That was joy, and he needed to believe that he could find more of it.

He took a second to remind himself which was Hawk's bad shoulder because cleared to ride didn't mean fully healed and he didn't want anything to hurt. He oiled up his hands and started in, gently at first so he could find the really bad spots. "You tell me if I go too hard anywhere, okay?"

"You got it. Thank you." Hawk wiggled, teasing him and settling deeper into the sheets at the same time.

Okay. That was hot and adorable, and much more like his Champ. He got his fingers and his thumbs in everywhere, kneading the big muscles with both hands and working the smaller hot spots with a more careful touch. It was like he'd forgotten in all of the stress and the sadness how much Hawk craved touch.

And honestly, it made him feel better too; both the warmth of Hawk's skin and the fact that he was helping.

Hawk's silence didn't seem so heavy like this either. It felt like his lover was losing himself to the sensations. That was good and he let it be what it was. It was better than words, so he didn't speak, he let the touch be enough.

And he kept one ear out for their delivery.

By the time the door buzzed, Hawk was melted, snoring softly, sleeping hard.

Jan slid away reluctantly, grabbed his robe and tucked his phone into the pocket before going to the door to get the food. He decided to go ahead and eat. With any luck, Hawk would stay asleep until morning and be more rested and ready to deal when he woke up. He'd climb back into bed after a snack.

We're home. He fired off a quick text to Jax and pulled the noodles and the garlic sauce out of the bag.

How did everything go? Do you want company? Fresh bagels? Another pie?

Jax must have missed him. *Nashville was rough. Hawk is devastated and exhausted. Maybe this weekend. I bet he'd love a pie. How are you?*

Okay. Working. Worried about you guys.

You're always working. I've missed you—Sunday work? We're home, that's the best thing. Sunday would give Hawk a few days to get his bearings, and for both of them to catch up on their sleep.

Just tell me when and I'll be there with bells on. That was his Jax. He didn't know what he'd do without him.

He guessed the same thing Hawk was going to do without Charlie.

I'll get back to you. This sucks. You're not allowed to die until you're 90.

Fair enough. I'll put that on my calendar.

Good. Thank you. Oh, and don't ride bulls. Wait. No. He wasn't going there. He told himself he wasn't going to go there. There was no point. Hawk was a bull rider. End of story.

That didn't stop a sick feeling from settling into his stomach.

Charlie had ridden the wrong one. That's what Ben had said. He'd almost retired and then he'd ridden the wrong one.

No. No bulls for me.

The wrong one wrecked Hawk's shoulder. He wasn't going to think about the next wrong one.

Good. Gotta run. I'll text you tomorrow about Sunday.

He put the food back into the delivery bag and stuck the whole thing in the fridge. He wanted Hawk. All of a sudden, Jan needed to see him and know he was okay.

As soon as he sat on the bed, Hawk moved, sliding close and wrapping around him. "Darlin'. Hold me."

"I got you, Champ." That was exactly what he wanted. He stretched out and pulled Hawk against him, breathing in the warm almond oil and raw cowboy. "Yeah, that's better."

"Mmhmm. Cold without you." Hawk kissed his collarbone and settled. "Love you."

"I love you too, baby. It's good to be in our own bed." He planned to stay here a long while. As long as Hawk would stay with him.

"It is. It's all I wanted. To be home."

He combed his fingers through Hawk's freshly cut hair, missing the curls a little. "Tomorrow will be a better day. And it's warmer here now than when we left. Maybe we can get some sun." Maybe. If they got out of bed for more than five minutes. If not, the city would be there when they decided to come up for air.

35

Hawk felt like he was drowning. He couldn't climb up out of the waves of tired, the dreams that called him back, the dozens of phone calls and hundreds of texts that were waiting on him.

He wanted to, but he couldn't.

"Coffee." Jan's voice sounded miles away, but Jan was right there, pressing a cup of hot coffee into his hands. "Do you think you're up to opening up that suitcase of things Momma sent back with us today? I think we should."

"Yeah? I don't know what's in there. Probably clothes." It felt odd, having bits of him there and bits of him here.

"Let's find out. Maybe it's more than that. It seemed important to Momma that you have it. And anyway, I don't like living out of suitcases. It's a weird thing with me. I need to have them put away when I'm home." Jan sat close and tucked an arm over his shoulders.

"Okay. I get that. Can I stow my riding gear somewhere out of the way?"

"We can clear you a spot for it in the closet for when you're home. Obviously you took this weekend off but you'll be heading out again in a few days, right? Where is the show next weekend?"

"I don't know." He ought to look, he guessed. Jan had to be tired of him being here. "Oklahoma City, I think? Possibly Houston." If it was Houston or Oklahoma, his people would come.

"Well, let me know when you figure it out. I want to see if I can hook up with Briony while we're on the road and talk business." Jan was planning on traveling with him?

"Anytime you want to. She'd love it—she's a smart one."

Remember, he's into you because you're a bull rider. Nothing's fixin' to change that. Maybe he could see how Sky did it, retired and had lots to do.

"She's interested too. She's called me twice. Strike while the iron is hot, right?" Jan shifted. "Oh! Speaking of... yesterday, I did some searching, and I found you a braille tutor. A potential one. If you want to contact them. Which is totally up to you because you don't need me doing all your homework for you. Sorry-not-sorry?"

"Yeah? Is that how it works? I'd try." Hawk swallowed hard, because dammit, he wanted to learn something. Something important and that he fucking needed.

"I think so. It's a school. They have classes and private tutors. I guess you could do either one, but I figured with the traveling that a tutor would be better. They'd know better than I do. I'll text you the info." Jan kissed his cheek. "Let's go look at that suitcase."

"Okay."

Jan sure seemed busy. Maybe curious. He wasn't sure. Of course, there wasn't anything in the suitcase that he hadn't seen before.

"You're going to be disappointed when it's all tighty-whities and my spare jeans."

"You're right, I will be. I feel like Momma would have sent a few gems along from your room. If not, I guess we'll be able to put away the suitcase at least." He put the suitcase on the bed and Jan sat next to it.

"God, I can only imagine." He rolled his eyes and opened the case. The smell shocked him, because it was home—Momma's laundry detergent and leather, a hint of grass and then something he only knew as home.

The first thing he pulled out was his robe—dark and soft and patched at the pocket because he didn't want a new one. Then his comb, his first buckle, the pocketknife his pa-paw'd given him for his eighth birthday.

"I don't see any tighty-whities." Jan touched the pocketknife in his hand. "What's this?"

"My pa-paw gave it to me for Christmas. He told me I was a man now, and it was time to learn how to use a knife. Momma damn near died." He touched the handle, every bit familiar. "I have a few knives, but this one's the first. I whittled..." He searched around in the case, his fingers finding his little leather jewelry box, his stuffed cowboy he came home with, a pile of movies. "Do you see some wood? A fish?"

"Hang on, Champ, quit digging and let me look." Jan moved his hands out of the way. "Uh... wait. Yes. This?" Jan put a little figure in his fingers.

"I made this. I've made a bunch, but this was the first one. There should be a box of tools and carvings. I can smell it, I think." He'd spent hours whittling with it.

"There's all kinds of stuff. There's... this looks like a jewelry box. And there's another box that's bigger. Is this it? With the carved lid? Wow, this is beautiful work."

"That's it. That's my carving box. The jewelry box—we all have exactly the same one. You want to see?" It had Uncle

Frank's dog tags, the pocket watch he'd bought in Cheyenne. His class ring was in there, the puka necklace he'd bought when he was sixteen, the earring he'd worn for about seven seconds.

Jan took each thing he offered, admiring and asking questions, genuinely interested in these random objects that marked moments in time, pieces of his past.

They went through the suitcase slowly, and then they found places for everything, weaving them in and among Jan's things so the apartment started to feel like he lived there.

"See? Only two pairs of jeans and no tighty-whites at all." Jan laughed, a real laugh not one colored by the sorrow of the last week.

"I know! I bet she was scared to go into that drawer." He didn't think he had any porn in there. Not anymore, but maybe…

"I would be too." Jan was still chuckling as he put the suitcase away. "Your carving box looks great on that ledge with that little statue I brought back from my vacation in Mexico. It's so pretty. How long did that take you? Were you seeing better back then or did you do it by feel?"

"I was seeing better when I started, I guess. It doesn't go by fits and starts. It leaks away, like a bucket with a little hole." He guessed he needed to get a doctor up here at some point.

"Got it. Well, it's a beautiful box and it looks great there. I like having your things around." Jan tugged him by his hand and stepped close. "I like having you around too. This is the part where I kiss you."

"Is it? I think that part's important." He lifted his face for the kiss, letting Jan soothe the raw parts for a second.

Jan's kiss was warm and gentle with the usual familiar heat lingering beyond the moment. "Very important."

Hawk wanted to wake up. He did. But he couldn't seem to manage.

"Is it okay if Jax comes by tomorrow? He said he'd bring an apple pie. I know you're probably back on your diet, but he'll bring a small one like last time" Jaz squeezed his hand. "He wants to do something, you know?"

"Sure. I'd like to see him." Was he on his diet? Was he going back? He didn't have to. Maybe he could just...All the stressed thoughts came rushing back.

"Cool. We can watch some stupid TV and—hey, are you okay, baby? Is something wrong?"

Is something wrong? My things are here, not in my room. My best friend is gone. I have to leave in a few days to go to an event that I don't want to ride. Nothing is okay. Nothing feels normal. "Yeah. I'm good."

"You went pale for a second is all. Is it Jax? I can ask him not to come..." Jan touched his face, stroking fingers along his jaw.

"No. No, he's got to be missing you, and he's a good guy, a good friend." And Hawk wasn't a bad guy, dammit. He was a white hat. He needed some time to figure out which of his ends was up.

"Okay. I'm listening any time you want to talk." Jan gave him another quick kiss and headed toward the kitchen. "You want more coffee?"

"No, thank you." Talk? What was he supposed to say? What needed to be said? He hurt—but saying so wasn't going to help it. He wanted to talk to Charlie. Charlie was the one that he talked to when he needed to.

He grabbed his phone and sent a text to Charlie's phone. *I miss you, man.*

I can't turn his phone off, Bird.

He stared at his phone, horrified, and he dropped it and ran, making it to the bathroom before he lost every bit of bile in his belly.

"Hawk!" Jan was suddenly standing behind him, one hand rubbing his back. "Breathe. Shhh. Easy, baby."

"I—" He'd fucked up. Bad. Oh God. He emptied himself out, leaving himself broken on the floor.

Jan knelt with him, cradling his head and... talking. "I've got you. You're okay, I'm here."

"I'm sorry. I'm so sorry." He couldn't stop leaking from the eyes, couldn't stop apologizing, because that had to hurt Ben so much.

"You're fine. Shhh. Don't apologize. It's okay." Jan's fingers brushed his hair, stroked his cheek.

He shook his head. It wasn't. It wasn't okay. It wasn't. The pain was eating him alive, and he was little.

"Shhh." Jan pulled him into his lap, holding Hawk close. "Okay. Breathe. Deep breath." Jan took a big breath and let it out. "Breathe," Jan told him, before doing it again.

He sucked in a breath, trying not to shake apart. He didn't know what to do. He didn't.

"Hawk?" Jan's fingers touched his forehead, his neck. "Jesus, you're burning up, baby. On your feet, come on. I want to get you... come to bed." Jan stood, hauling him to his feet, taking his weight on the way out of the bathroom.

He stumbled, eyes closed. "I didn't mean to. I didn't know. I wouldn't have sent the text."

"What? Who did you text?" Jan stripped him quickly.

"Charlie. I wanted to tell him I missed him." He almost lost his knees.

"Whoa. Sit. You...?" Jan caught him and sat him on the bed. "It's okay. I'm sure you're not the first person to do something like that. I want to cool you down. I'll get a cloth for now... maybe a bath in a bit? Tylenol maybe..."

"I—" His eyes filled with tears. "I'm broke dick. I'm so sorry. I wasn't trying to be evil."

Jan came back, curled a cool cloth around his neck and put two pills in his palm and held a glass to his other hand without letting it go. "Swallow those. No one thinks you're evil, baby."

"There's something wrong with me," he confessed. Something broke in his soul.

"No. I mean, yes, you're grieving. But there's no normal for this. Whatever it is, it's okay. It takes some time, baby. Take the Tylenol."

He took it without looking, drank deep, and he could swear to God that he heard the water splashing in his empty belly. "Jan."

It was all he could say. That was it. Everything else hurt too much.

"Right here, love. Lie down. You're making yourself sick. You need to rest." Jan sat beside him, one arm over him. "That's it. Close your eyes. I'm here."

"I'm sorry. I'm so sorry." Tears slid from his eyes and slipped down his cheeks.

Jan didn't move, only sat with him, stayed with him. "I love you. I'm here. I love you no matter what."

"I wanted to tell him I missed his face. He was my...I could call him, anytime. I could text, and he'd talk to me." Even when neither of them knew what to say.

"He was your friend. He knew you. Saw you. I know, I get it. Of course you miss him, baby. You can't turn your feelings on and off with a switch. You need some time." Jan's words started to slur, and he wondered if his lover was as tired as he was.

"Yeah." He blinked, nice and slow. "Love. I—I can't go. I don't want to."

"You don't have to go. You don't have to do anything. It's okay. Just relax and sleep. I've got you."

"Okay." He grabbed Jan's fingers and held on. "I swear, I didn't know Ben would see it."

"That Ben..." Jan squeezed his fingers. "Oh. I'll uh... I'll text Ben and make sure he's okay. Don't you worry."

"Promise? Tell him I'm so sorry. So sorry." He tried to breathe, but he couldn't for a second, then Jan was holding him, and he sighed.

"I promise... trust me. Just give it to me. Go to sleep."

"Thank you. I love you, darlin'." He let himself trust, let himself believe, and let himself sleep.

36

*J*esus Christ.

Hawk was asleep. Finally, thank God. That was horrific, Hawk had scared the hell out of him, and it was getting hard to hide how his hands were shaking.

Jan untangled himself from his lover and slid carefully off the bed, hoping whatever Sky had given him would keep Hawk out for a while. He needed to think. He needed to... he had no idea what he needed to do.

Fuck.

The first thing he did was try to look at Hawk's phone, heading right for where it was still lying face down on the living room floor. He stared at it when it asked for Hawk's passcode—how was he supposed to know that?—and sighed.

"Shit."

Should he know his lover's passcode? Ben obviously knew Charlie's... The things he didn't know were starting to pile up and make his stomach hurt.

He put the phone on the coffee table and shot off a quick text to Ben. He'd promised.

Hey, Ben. I'm not really clear on what happened, but Hawk says he's sorry. We're thinking about you. Talk soon.

He had no idea what he should do with his hysterical cowboy.

The next thing he did was text Skylar. *Hey Sky. Hawk's a fucking wreck. What did you give me? How long will he be out?*

He needed help.

Calling. The phone rang almost immediately. "Hey, man."

Jan didn't know if he was relieved or more worried that Sky dropped everything to call, but it was good to hear a familiar voice. "Hey. He lost it. He texted Charlie's phone—which is weird, but I get it, and I think Ben replied and he spun out."

"Oh, poor guy. He's hit overload. He'll sleep a few hours, maybe longer if he's real tired. At some point it had to happen." Sky sighed softly. "He's not going to try and ride this weekend, is he?"

"No. Not this weekend. We're in New York and I don't think he wants to ride next weekend either. Is that... is that okay? Should I let it go? Should I be pushing him to ride? I don't know what to do. He's been so... disengaged."

"Jesus." Sky blew out a sharp breath. "Don't let him ride if he's not with it. He'll hurt himself. Let him be home and whole. He's got money enough."

"Okay." Jan didn't care about money, but home and whole sounded good. "I've been trying to get him to let it out, I knew eventually it had to happen, but I didn't expect this. Who else did he talk to besides Charlie? If not me, who's next?" If Hawk wouldn't talk to him, there had to be someone. "He doesn't... I don't know why he won't talk to me."

He swallowed hard and shook his head at himself. *Just hang up. Sky is not your fucking therapist, Jan.*

"I do." Sky's voice was soft. "He loves you, man. It's hard, to be weak in front of the one man you need to impress. He's moved to New York City, for fuck's sake. The man's damn near blind, has lived in the same room for thirty years, he's wanting to retire, he lost his best buddy—he wants you to believe he's not terrified, but I guaran-damn-tee you he's out of his mind with it. I would be, and I ain't got the sense to be scared of shit."

Well, fuck. "Great. Well, I don't know what to say about that. Should I take him home? Is New York too much? I asked him if—" Jan made an exasperated sound. Hawk was at a low point maybe, but he wasn't a quitter and neither was January. Hawk told him he wanted to be in New York. "No. You know what? There's no cure for any of that but to put one foot in front of the other."

"You know it. He trusts you enough to fight through this. You let him love you as best he can. He's a cowboy; he can do this."

He didn't really know what "he's a cowboy" meant, honestly, but he knew Hawk.

"Of course he can do this. He can do anything." Hawk was blind bull rider. He was a fucking stud. Still... "He didn't tell me he wants to retire."

"He didn't tell me. You can see it on him like a shadow. It's like—every hurt lasts longer, every event you're waiting to be over, something's bigger than riding. He might not announce this year, but his heart's tired. He's rooting for Danny to win."

Moments like this were a tough reminder that as much as he loved Hawk, he was still an outsider when it came to the show. He had no idea that— "I guess we'll see. I'm behind him no matter what." In the end it really was that simple.

"Good. That's the whole thing."

"Thanks, Sky. Sorry to panic text. I wanted to make sure I knew what I'd given him. I guess you've seen this a few times." Probably more than a few

"A couple. It's been me, more than once." Sky's laugh rang out. "He'll find his way out. No worries."

"Yeah, you don't know me very well yet." Jan couldn't help the rueful laugh. "I worry about everything. But I've got this." Maybe. Probably. It wasn't the first time he'd helped Hawk find his confidence anyway. "Thanks for the talk."

"Anytime. Talk at you later." The phone line went dead.

Bye. And then he was on his own again.

He looked at his phone but didn't see a return text from Ben yet, so he stuck it in his pocket. Hawk had scared the hell out of him. His heart was still aching for Hawk. He was worried, but he needed to get it together before his Champ woke up. Hawk didn't need him worried, Hawk needed to know who he could lean on, and that it was okay to do it.

What Jan really needed right now though, was some strong coffee. Coffee and some kind of plan. Even if the plan was not to make one.

37

Hawk woke up with stupid brain, but there was a calm inside him, and he grabbed onto that peace with both hands.

He stumbled into the shower and let the sick sweat and gross sluice off his skin. Lord have mercy, he'd had a damn fit. Just a damn hissy. Jan was probably scared out of his mind.

He didn't remember Jan sounding scared though, not that he really remembered much. Jan being there and then not being able to fight his eyes closing.

He stretched up tall as he could, humming under his breath as he felt all his backbones crack and pop. Oh yeah. That felt good.

"Look who's up." Jan's voice floated in with the steam, deep and gentle.

"Yeah. I slept hard. You coming in, darlin'?" He wouldn't mind that at all.

"I was hoping you'd ask." It only took Jan a minute to undress. "Make room for a tall Yankee."

"*My* tall Yankee." He wanted that clear.

"Damn right. Every inch." Jan stepped in crowding him playfully. "I do like this big shower."

"I do too. I like how the water pours down on us." And he needed this—the feel-good part.

"I'm glad you got some rest." Jan's hand landed solidly on his ass. "You look better."

"Yeah. I'm sorry, huh? I just..." Suck. "I'm sorry."

Jan kissed his forehead. "Why do you feel like you need to apologize?"

"Because I acted like a moron and pitched a fit?" Surely that was a good reason.

"You acted like my sweet lover, my cowboy, who cares about people and misses his best friend. I hate to see you in pain, baby, but your heart is the reason I love you."

"I feel bad that we didn't go see him sooner. Maybe I could have helped somehow, at least said goodbye. I wanted you to know him. He was a good guy. He was a lot like you—he didn't care that I couldn't hardly see. We did things anyway."

"I'm sad I didn't get to meet him. I know I would have liked him. And I'm sorry you didn't get to say goodbye." Jan hands were strong and gentle, sliding over slippery skin and working into his muscles. "I keep thinking about how he told you—told us—to keep enjoying our vacation. He wanted you to ride and be confident. You were doing what he wanted for you. You were making him happy."

"I hope so." He wasn't sure he was happy anymore—not about the work. Maybe he needed a couple more weekends off. He could ride the Finals even if he didn't do another event. He couldn't be the champ, but that thought didn't hurt too bad.

"Hope is fine. We'll hope." Jan picked up his hand and kissed his fingers.

"Thank you. Love you, huh? A lot. You've been good to me."

"That's my job. You're good to me too. That vacation was the best I've ever had. Truthfully. It was perfect."

"It was. I had a ball." And he sort of felt guilty about that. Charlie had been dying, and he'd been wandering along the coast.

"If our vacations are that good, imagine what our real life is going to be like? I'm looking forward to every minute." Jan fingers were naughty, circling his nipples, rolling them and tugging. "Every single second, starting with this one."

"Oh..." It was like he'd forgotten that he could feel good. He stretched and pushed up into Jan's touch. He'd forgotten, but he was more than willing to remember.

"Mhm." Jan kissed him, tongue sliding along his, the tug turning to a pinch. He gasped and opened up, and his cry was muffled between them.

Oh fuck yes. Yes. More. "Jan."

Jan grunted and leaned on him until his shoulders hit the chilly tiled wall. "I didn't plan... you're just..." Jan pressed their hips together. "Beautiful."

"I need you. It feels like it's been eons." Maybe longer. Who the fuck knew how long an eon was?

"Forever." Jan's finger curled behind his balls and stroked the sensitive skin there.

He spread like someone had pushed a button. "Uh-huh. Forever and ever."

Don't stop.

"Yours, baby. Right? I want to make you feel good." Jan's tricky tongue tasted and teased over his jaw, behind his ear, down to his shoulder.

He was feeling good, and he needed that, didn't he? He needed to know Jan wanted him. That he wasn't alone.

Jan knew his body well, expertly finding his sensitive spots. Knowing fingers played up and down the length of his cock, exploring and admiring.

"Yes. God, I need you, darlin'. My soul's been aching, and you're a goddamn balm."

"I didn't want to ask. I didn't want you to think this was all I needed from you." Jan's grip grew firm and purposeful, stroking as Jan's words filled his ears.

"But we need it. Both of us." He loved fucking, craved the sensation, but he needed to be loved on.

"Yes." Jan nodded against his temple where he could feel it.

He smiled, and it damn near hurt. Like his face had frozen in sadness.

"We'll focus on each other for a while. You and me." Jan slid gracefully to his knees and a second later his lover's tongue found his slit and tasted it gently. "Mmm. I missed that."

"Oh." Talk about pure, unadulterated sensation. It flooded him, like he'd been dipped in boiling water.

Jan licked and teased, tasted and touched but didn't take him in, giving him plenty to feel, and the finger that had been stroking slid back far enough to tease his hole. His lover was in no hurry, despite the running water.

He let himself feel every second of it—from the heavy weight of Jan's wet hair, to that burning tongue, to the way relaxing his jaw actually felt odd.

"Feeling good, cowboy? You look good." Jan lips closed over the head of his hungry cock, tongue driving back through his slit, pressing hard and deep.

"Feel—" He arched, his hands slapping behind him on the tile. "Please!"

Jan swallowed him in, stroking and sucking, not giving

him time to breathe, to move, to think. The teasing was over, Jan wasn't letting up for a second. He may have babbled; he may have cursed—he had no fucking idea. All he knew was that Jan was sending him to the moon.

Jan made hungry sounds when he took a breath. The finger that had been tapping at Hawk's entrance pressed hard and popped inside, surprising him, and Jan swallowed around him.

"Fuck yes!" His balls drew up, and he shot with a rough groan that came from his fucking soul.

"Mmm." Jan's hands splayed out over his thighs and took everything he gave up, humming and moaning for him. He blinked slowly, watching Jan's profile swim.

"Damn, darlin'."

"I really can't tell you how satisfying that was." Jan chuckled getting to his feet. "I can't resist you."

"You don't have to. Come to bed. I want to feel you inside me." He figured that was clear as crystal. He wanted the pressure, the physical proof they were together.

"Let me think about that a second. Yes." Jan reached past him and shut the water off.

"I don't think that was a whole second..." he teased, grabbing a towel from the bar.

"I tried?" Jan toweled off too, and backed out of the bathroom, gaze so hot Hawk swore he could feel it.

His answer was to make a beeline for the bed, snuggling into the blankets, his ass in the air. He knew what he wanted, what Jan wanted.

"Jesus, cowboy. That's a beautiful view." Jan hurried to the nightstand, and the sound of tearing foil and the pop of the bottle of lube was unmistakable. He could feel Jan's heat as his lover moved in behind him. The lube was cool, but Jan's hands were hot on his ass.

The sheets smelled like them—warm and male and perfect—and he let the scent fill him, relax his muscles and let him spread that much wider.

Jan's cock stretched him, his lover not waiting another moment to take what he offered, hips rocking them together. "Fuck, I need you."

"I'm yours. Like all the way."

Jan knew him, had seen him hit the bottom, and loved him anyway. This was it for him.

"I like the sound of that, angel." Jan took Hawk's hips in both hands and pulled hard, taking what he needed. "A lot."

"Y-yeah. Fuck. Fuck, yeah." His body clenched around Jan's cock, trying to keep Jan in deep.

"Jesus, tight." Jan humped wildly, driving him into the bed. His lover's breath was rough and shallow, and he knew that sound. It meant Jan was close.

He squeezed his lover tight, adding to the sensation, forcing Jan higher.

"Fuck." Jan gasped and bucked, his powerful climax rushing through them both.

Hawk groaned, his body feeling stretched and warm and like he lived in it, finally.

Jan ditched the condom and flopped into the sheets, pulling him in, both of them still coming down, catching their breath. "I'm yours all the way, too, baby. Everything."

"Good. I'm—I'm thinking we need to talk about the rest of the season, about things, but not now. Now I want to be with you."

"I'd love to talk. To listen. Any time you like." Jan kissed his forehead. "But yes, right now is just this. This is perfect."

"Okay. After this peace is done. I want our afterglow, dammit." He chuckled at himself, because he was a dork. He was a happy dork, though.

"Mmm. Me too. We earned it." Jan sighed, the sound totally content and at ease. "I'm glad you're feeling better."

"I'm sure it'll hurt again, but right now, I'm okay." That was fair, he thought.

He felt Jan's smile against his skin. "Right now keeps getting better."

"Yeah. Right now is good, and I want to stay." He knew Jan was hearing him. He knew it.

"Your hair is super soft. I kind of miss those curls." Jan combed through his hair, fluffing it, giving him more *now*.

"It'll grow. It'll come back all curly. It always does." Things always came back around, somehow.

Always.

38

It was really early. Jan left Hawk sleeping, marveling at how hard they'd both crashed after last night's fun. Coffee was definitely in order so, while the morning was still cool, he pulled on sweats and slipped out to buy bagels and some fruit for breakfast, hoping to tempt Hawk into eating. That would be like icing on the cake.

He dropped Sky a text while he was in line to let him know Hawk was okay and to say thank you. He'd been a little hysterical, and he was grateful for Sky's level head. He'd happened to pick the right voice to reset his compass.

Jan felt great. He felt like he was breathing for the first time in days, like he and Hawk had punched through a wall and finally found some air yesterday.

He carried the bag of bagels and tray of coffee back up the street, smiling at the good weather and the reasonably quiet New York morning. He loved to travel, and he loved his city too. He wondered if part of what Hawk wanted to talk about was living here, but he pushed that away. It was a talk. They'd figure it out. He wasn't going to start speculating before he'd had his coffee, that never went well.

And Hawk needed him to meet whatever he needed to say with calm, peace, and—

Hawk was in the shower. Singing. At the top of his lungs, and he was lovely.

Jan smiled, the sound making him happy on so many levels. He set the food down in the kitchen and carried both coffees into the bedroom, but he didn't go into the bathroom right away. He listened. Singing like that was something Hawk hadn't indulged in for as long as they'd been together, and he didn't want to interrupt the simple joy of it.

One country song melted into another, and then the water turned off, his very clean cowboy emerging from the steam.

He poked his head in, trying not to startle his lover. "Good morning, handsome. I brought you coffee from the bagel place. I'll set it on the counter for you, right of the sink."

"Hey, thanks." Hawk smiled toward him. "Did you bring me an everything bagel?"

Score. The Champ was hungry. "I did. And I got cream cheese as well as some of that whipped butter. I couldn't decide which I wanted more." He'd gotten half a dozen so there'd be more for tomorrow. "I bought a cinnamon raisin for you to try too. I was listening to you sing..."

"Yeah, I'm sorry, I was caterwauling. I woke up this morning, and I felt, well, you know."

"Stop. It was beautiful." He sipped his coffee, watching Hawk towel off, totally unashamed for enjoying it. "You know what? We need to go buy you a guitar."

"Yeah? I'd like that. Ben's taught me pretty good, and I like to practice."

Bingo. Something to help fill Hawk's time here. Something worthwhile that his lover enjoyed. "I walk by this place in Midtown all the time, we should go check it out." He followed Hawk out of the bathroom. "It's going to be hot out there today, but the weather looks great the rest of the week."

"Good deal. What's your plan for today?" Hawk threw on a tiny, tiny worn pair of soft shorts that made his mouth dry, then went back to grab his coffee.

You mean other than watch your ass walk around in those shorts? "I need to make a phone call for work, but that won't take long. I thought we could get out and get some air after breakfast. Jax is coming by tonight for dinner."

"I could do that. I bet Jax is nervous to come."

"I don't know. That's possible. Jax is a little high-strung anyway. He'll feel better if he knows we want to see him. Kitchen?" Jan led the way, heading for the bag of bagels. "I got some fruit too, like a mixed thing. Berries and melon."

"Uhn. You know how I feel about berries. I'd be nervous too. He has to know I'm low from Charlie passing."

"He does, he wants to see you though, and he's good with stuff like this. You know how he chatters. He takes your mind right off things." Jan cut an everything bagel for Hawk and put it on a plate. "Bagel, baby. You want cream cheese?"

"I think so. Is that how yours is? I like yours. I want a half of my own, I think." Someone was happy to be home, Jan thought.

"You got it." He spread the top half where all the yummy spices were with cream cheese, and slid the plate over to Hawk. Half a bagel. That was real food. "Here you go. That's the tasty half. Did you know they only put the stuff on the top?" He put a few berries in a bowl and handed that over too.

"I didn't, no. The other half will be yummy tomorrow

with butter." Hawk took a big bite, seeming somehow settled in his soul.

"Yeah, I like them toasted the second day." He sat with Hawk, munching on his bagel and loving the cantaloupe. He'd had a craving for something fresh. "What did you want to accomplish today?"

"I think we need to have a talk about stuff. Life stuff. We've been playing house, and it's been fun, but I like to have a plan." Well, okay. That was sure.

He nodded. "I knew that was on your mind. Can we talk and walk? Or do we need to sit and write things down?"

"I think we can walk. If we need to, we can stop and make notes on our phones." Hawk nodded and licked cream cheese off his lips. "We're smart dogs, you and me."

"Cool. Sometimes I think better moving, you know? I thought we could try the park." He sipped his coffee. Hawk was right, they'd been playing house, and that had been good. But "all the way" meant more than take out and sharing a bed. This was long term. And some of who they were going forward, together and separate, was going to be complicated.

It felt good that Hawk not only knew that but seemed more than willing to work at it to make things, well, work. "I like parks. I like being outside a lot under the sun."

"Great. So we need more than threadbare shorts and stretched out sweats, and then we can talk about the future." He took Hawk's hand and gave it a squeeze. "I like the sound of that, by the way."

"Me too. I never— well, that's one of the things we'll talk about, right? About how glad I am to be with you."

"I'm looking forward to talking about that." And returning the sentiment. "But let's not have it all here at the table. How's your coffee?"

"Perfect. Not as good as the bagel, but pretty damn good." Hawk chuckled, and the soft sound turned into a real laughter. "I'll have to brush my teeth though, or I'll be breathing fire on folks. All hail Hawk the Mighty Dragon!"

"Yeah, me too. I'd race you, but I ate a lot of bagel." He stood and took their plates to the sink to put them in the dishwasher.

Hawk brushed off the crumbs from the table, threw them away, then headed to the bedroom. By the time he got in there, Hawk was naked and brushed and picking out a pair of jeans.

"Hello. There's a hot cowboy in my bedroom." He dragged his hand over Hawk's abs as he walked by, heading for the bathroom to brush his teeth.

"Is there? Where?" Hawk snorted, turning around and turning.

"Ha. The little guy!" Jan cracked up and stuck his toothbrush in his mouth.

"Ah, the little ones are firecrackers. You gotta watch for them." Hawk picked out a T-shirt, tucked it in, and did up his belt.

"Trust me, I know," he said around his toothbrush. "I already have one of my very own."

"Lucky bastard." Hawk came to him, hands sliding around his belly in a hug.

He rinsed his mouth and turned around to return the hug, breathing his cowboy in, fingers sliding over a worn-in T-shirt. "You're dressed. I'm not."

"I promise not to chafe you, darlin'. Fair enough?" Hawk pinched his butt.

"Ow!" Jan laughed and danced away to look for his jeans. "Brat." He got dressed and found his NYU ballcap.

"You know where your sunglasses are? It's a good day for them." His were in the dish on the table by the front door.

"Yeah. I'll get them." Hawk popped a battered straw on his head and switched out his glasses.

"You ready, Champ? Did you want your coffee?" He stuffed his phone in his pocket, grabbed his keys and what was left of his morning coffee.

"I'll finish it here and grab me a Coke while we're out and about."

"Works for me." Jan handed what was left of Hawk's coffee to him. "A little sun will do us some good, right?"

"Yes. I like wandering with you, darlin'. I like you."

"That's handy, since you're stuck with me." He waited for Hawk to finish his coffee and then they were out the door. The street was less crowded now that it was a reasonable hour of the morning, but the humidity was low, so it wasn't too sticky.

"We can walk right into the park this time. Do you remember doing this before? Before we went to the subway, which is left, but this time we're going to the corner and we're going to head east. It's a short walk."

"Right. I'm ready. Short walk it is." Hawk bounced a little. "Let's go."

He took Hawk's hand, not because Hawk couldn't walk alongside him fine without help, but because he wanted to, and because here in New York he *could*, dammit. They waited for the light at the corner and headed two lengthy avenue blocks east until they hit the Central Park. "I thought we'd wander, see where our feet take us." By then he'd finished his coffee too, and he chucked the cup in a can by the park entrance.

"Sure. Totally. I—I have so much to say, and I don't know how to start."

That made Jan smile. For Hawk to have a lot to say it all had to be very important to him. "Okay... so what made you decide we needed the talk? What were you thinking about? Was it Charlie? Was it before that on vacation?"

"I—all of them. I mean, I want to talk about riding, but that's the hardest, and the biggest, and I think the one we have to start with."

He thought about what Sky had said—not to push him, not to let Hawk ride unless his head was right. But he didn't want to express any opinion at all until he heard what Hawk had to say. "It's maybe the elephant in the room right now, yeah. So... I'm listening."

"I don't know if I want to retire, but I'm tired, Jan. I know that's one reason you got with me, but..." Hawk frowned deeply. "And it's not because Charlie died, but it was one hit. One. And I've taken lots of hits and every time you get up it takes longer to feel better. I'm tired of pretending I can see everything. I'm tired of missing out because I can't read or I can't get around as well as before. I want to be able to use the things made for folks like me."

Shit, that was a dissertation from his cowboy.

He squeezed Hawk's hand so his lover knew he'd heard but he took a minute to decide which part of all of that to respond to first.

"You were riding when I met you. It was definitely part of what drew me to you, sure. And the decisions about your career are ultimately yours to make. I accepted that it was risky because riding was about everything you were then. But if I'm being honest, I love the cowboy more than the bull rider. I'll support any decision you make or decide not to make right up until you retire. But I'm looking past the riding because that's where we're headed."

"So you're good with me taking off at least until the

Finals? I have to attend, one way or the other, but this way I can take the whole summer off and think." Hawk's voice dropped to a whisper. "Right now, I'd think about Charlie, but more than that, I'd think about Ben, and about how his heart is gone, and—and how—before I would think, I'll be blind, let the fucking bull have me. Now, I've got a good man that loves me, and I don't want to hurt you like that."

Jan stopped them. It didn't matter whether Hawk could really see him or not, he wanted to look into those eyes. He hurt for Hawk, a deep kind of ache he couldn't put words to. But there was something he could say.

"I don't want to be Ben. The next bull scares me, that's the truth. I think maybe I also need the summer off, if you know what I mean. If you decide not to retire, I need to have my head in that game too. Ben had Charlie retired in his head even before Charlie got hurt. If you're riding, I want to be in it with you."

If Hawk decided to ride it would be because he loved it, not because he had to. And if he loved it, then Jan wanted to be able to handle whatever happened.

"I do know. I have enough money to pay my half, you know that." Hawk saw him, stared at him. Jan knew it. "You're important. You're more important than the rush, than the cash, than the fans. I've given my life to riding. I want—us. I want to be us, give my life to being us."

"I'm yours, whatever happens." He would never ask Hawk to retire. Hawk needed to make that decision for himself so he never regretted it. Hawk heard him, understood what he was saying. "We have a limitless future, baby. We can do whatever we want, anywhere we want."

"Right. So, what I want is to take the summer off. I may ride the Finals; I may not. I have to show up and sign things.

I want to take you to the ranch, and I want the rest of my things to bring home. Fair?"

"Sounds great to me. Is New York where we want to stay? I mean... whenever you do retire, is this where you want to be? Should we talk about that?"

Hawk shrugged, that frown coming again. "I can't answer that. I haven't lived here long enough, you know? Maybe I won't be able to go out anywhere, but in the country, I go out and I'm in the middle of nowhere. Can we decide later? Together? Next year or the year after?"

"Of course. One thing at a time is fine. And you'll be able to go out. We'll get you a service dog, you'll learn your way around... I'm totally confident you can manage here. I was thinking about what you'd said about Nashville and it sounded nice. Anyway, it's all on the table as far as I'm concerned. I'd love to go visit your family's place." It would be good for Hawk to be there for a bit, somewhere he knew so well, didn't have to think too hard about. Somewhere he could show off a little.

"I love Nashville. Love it. And Ben and Ch—" Hawk stopped, swallowed hard, and closed his eyes before continuing. "Ben is there. I got friends there. Maybe we'll buy us a condo there, something little to stay at when we visit."

That was settled. Hawk loved it, so they'd do something. A condo, a little house, split their time. Something. A discussion for another time.

Jan took Hawk's hand again and turned off on a path leading deeper into the park. "That was the hard part, right? That was the big, looming issue and we're good. So what's next?"

"I want to learn to get around here. I need that. I want to know places to go for music, groceries, food. I want to— I don't know how to make money now. I need help figuring it out. I can. I'm not dumb. I can so do things, but I need a little help."

"You're brilliant. You're resourceful and self-reliant. If you want to work, we'll find something." He didn't need Hawk to work, but he understood the need to have a purpose better than most. He got creative with his line of work, so did Jax... he was sure they could do the same for Hawk.

"As for the rest, I'm excited to show you my city. We'll figure that out too. I think it would be easier with a cane or a dog, but if you're not ready for that, you have me."

"Can you have a dog in your place? Because I'd love that. A cane will help, I guess. I got to figure out the hows on getting a dog."

"Service dogs are allowed. And I'm way ahead of you, I researched how to get a dog. There's an application process that includes some paperwork and a home visit, and then you get matched up with a dog and go through a training course." He bumped shoulders with Hawk as they walked. "But... what if someone sees you with a dog?"

"Then they see me. And if the league bitches, fuck 'em. I carried this whole thing, me and my family. Now I don't want to." Hawk shrugged a little bit. "Do you think that's wrong?"

"I think you're the bravest man I've ever met." Jan hooked an arm behind Hawk and tugged him close for a kiss. "Fuck 'em."

"That's it." Hawk's laugh rang out, making the birds fly up. "You got anything you want to talk to me about?"

"Well...I want you to keep talking. I want you to speak up. I want you to take some ownership in the apartment and make sure it suits what you need. Don't feel like you're asking for too much, or too often. It should really be *home*. Not my place that you moved into. And if it doesn't work in the long run, we can find a different place that does." He'd never lived with anyone in the city; he'd never known another blind person. He was well-intentioned and fundamentally clueless.

"Huh." Hawk nodded, a wicked smile on his face. "Maybe we could get a wood coffee table? That glass one is murder on the knees."

"But the bruised knees are so hot." Jan laughed. "I'd thought about that. I did pull up the throw rugs in the foyer and the hall. I guess we better dog-proof the place too."

"Yeah. Yeah, that would be cool. If you love the glass table, I'll learn. It's so hard to catch sight of."

"I like it. I don't love it like I love your knees. We'll shop for something we both like." Jan felt better right now than he'd felt since vacation. Lighter, relaxed. "This was good. This was really good, right?"

"It is. I needed to say things to you, you know? I worried that you only thought I was fine because of the bull riding." Hawk squeezed his hand. "I mean, I knew better, but I needed to know it more. I needed to say it out loud so I couldn't believe it. Brains lie. Hearts, not so much."

"Hey." He stopped them again and pressed the hand he was holding to his chest. "Do you feel that? Thumping in there? That's yours, no matter whether you ride or don't, no matter what you do next. No matter where we go. No matter what."

And he wasn't afraid of it.

"No matter what. And I will love you with all of me. You're mine, darlin', and I intend to keep you and make you happy."

"Good." And if those promises didn't warrant a certain

conversation with Hawk's father, nothing did. Handy that Hawk had planned a trip to the ranch. There were so many good things in their future. He was even looking forward to the challenges. "How about some ice cream?"

"You'll tell me if you think I'm getting too heavy, right? Because I want to try everything. Everything."

"It's ice cream, baby." Jan chuckled. "Are you trying to keep weight all summer?"

"No. I'll stop eating in October for the Finals if I need to." Hawk grinned, looking so young, so damn happy. "I'll get strawberry, for Charlie."

Jan smiled, leading Hawk back toward the street. "And you'll tell me if I'm... babying you too much? I want to be helpful, help you learn, but I don't want to overstep and I'm never sure exactly where the line is."

"Fair enough. I'm pretty straightforward, and right now, this is wild and fucking new. Exciting, though. I love wild and new."

His fearless lover.

He could try to be. He'd jump right on that bandwagon. "I think I'll have strawberry too."

EPILOGUE

"Bird, can you help me with my bolo tie?"

Hawk went to Ben, straightened his tie. "You ready for this?"

Ben shook his head. Hawk got it. It wasn't a memorial, but Ben was going to sing at the opening, and they were all gonna honor Charlie. It was going to be horrible and wonderful, all at the same time.

"You'll start folks singing with me after the first chorus okay? I don't want to do it all alone. You get the guys to join in, then everybody will."

"No problem. We have plants in the audience too. We'll be solid." He had this. He'd ridden three bulls, won two rounds, and tonight was it. "How do I look?"

He knew he looked good; Jan said so all the time, but he needed someone that wasn't in love with him.

"You look good, Bird. Handsome. Happy. Charlie would be proud of you." Ben chuckled. "He might even like your hair."

"Shut up." He was all curly, but he got it trimmed and it

felt good when Jan's fingers tangled in it. "It's like my freedom beard."

"It looks good, man. Honestly." Ben looked around. "Where's my guitar? Jesus, I'm nervous."

"Don't be. You're amazing." He sighed softly, suddenly missing Charlie like a sore tooth. It got better, but sometimes, he wanted to talk to the bastard. Fortunately for him, he had Jan.

"Thanks. I get nervous before I perform all the time. I'd worry more if I wasn't." He gave Hawk's shoulder a tap. "You ready for this? I mean, not just *this*, but... all of it?"

"Yeah. I'm ready. One more bull. For Charlie. Then we're going to Hawaii for three weeks. We're taking surfing lessons." And he was going to eat all the sushi he wanted, dammit.

"Hawaii! You're serious? That's great." The hand on his shoulder tightened up a bit. "Don't try to be a hero on that last one."

"No. It'll be what it is. My last bull. You hold Jan's hand for me." He wasn't worried. He was riding fine.

"Jan's seemed pretty laid back this weekend. Is he worried?"

"Superstitious." And he didn't blame January one bit. He got it. Momma and Daddy were here, Danny was riding great, he was riding great. It was driving Jan nuts.

"I'll sit with him. I'm not worried," Ben said, a smile in his tone. There was a confidence in Ben's voice that actually made Hawk believe him.

"We're a go, Mister Starnes. Two minutes."

"Right on." Ben straightened his hat, grabbed his guitar.

"I'll be singing with you, man. For Charlie." He wished he could see Jan right now. He needed it.

"For Charlie. And for you too, Bird." Ben pulled him in for a quick hug.

He swallowed hard, trying to remember how to breathe. "Love you, man."

Ben let him go. "We've got this." Someone took Ben by the arm and steered him into the arena.

Hawk stood there, the lights flashing and moving and keeping things dizzying, so he closed his eyes.

His cell phone vibrated in his pocket and he pulled it out to find a text from January.

I love you, Champ. I'm still the one yelling the loudest.

Thank you, darlin'. He smiled. He had to. *Flying out at midnight.*

Can't wait. Beach. Sand. Sun. Water. I'm ready.

Me too. For everything.

Ben began to sing, and he grinned, singing along. One more bull, and it was done.

One more. For Charlie.

Then him and Jan? They were gone.

**If you enjoyed Flying Blind,
check out Tending Tyler!**

Tending Tyler
**another East Meets Western
By Jodi Payne and BA Tortuga**

Bartender, Tyler McKeehan, feels like his whole life is on hold. All he does is work and sleep, because he just doesn't know how to move on with his day to day after the shocking loss of his best friend. When he meets Matt at Les's Bar where he works in New York, though, he thinks he might have found someone who can nudge him out of his rut. The cowboy seems to live on fast forward, but at the same time, this kind, generous man makes Tyler feel wanted and safe.

Ranch owner, Matthew Whitehead, is just in New York for a visit. But when he runs into Tyler at Les's Bar, he can tell right away that Tyler is special. Matt's family thinks he makes snap decisions, and they worry about him, but he knows what he wants, and even after just a few days, he's willing to fight to keep Tyler in his life. When Matt has to head back to Texas, he tells Tyler to come visit him and meet his kids. Soon.

Tyler doesn't know if he can just pick up and go to Texas, but he misses Matt's affection and calming presence, so when life gets too overwhelming, he makes the call. Between Matt's huge, boisterous family, his children, his busy ranch, and the vast differences between New York City and Texas, Tyler wonders if he should go back to his old life every day. Matt is determined to keep Tyler right where he is, but can they overcome the odds against them and make a new life together?

FIND OUT MORE
or Buy on Amazon

ABOUT JODI

JODI takes herself way too seriously and has been known to randomly break out in song. Her men are imperfect but genuine, stubborn but likable, often kinky, and frequently their own worst enemies. They are characters you can't help but fall in love with while they stumble along the path to their happily ever after. For those looking to get on her good side, Jodi's addictions include nonfat lattes, Malbec and tequila any way you pour it.

Website: jodipayne.net
Newsletter: http://bit.ly/whatsupjodi
All Jodi's Social Links: linktr.ee/jodipayne

ABOUT BA

Texan to the bone and an unrepentant Daddy's Girl, BA Tortuga spends her days with her basset hounds, getting tattooed, texting her grandbabies, and eating Mexican food. When she's not doing that, she's writing. She spends her days off watching rodeo, knitting and surfing Pinterest in the name of research. BA's personal saviors include her wife, Julia Talbot, her best friends, and coffee. Lots of coffee. Really good coffee.

Having written everything from fist-fighting rednecks to hard-core cowboys to werewolves, BA does her damnedest to tell the stories of her heart, which was raised in Northeast Texas, but has heard the call of the high desert and lives in the Sandias. With books ranging from hard-hitting GLBT romance, to fiery ménages, to the most traditional of love stories, BA refuses to be pigeon-holed by anyone but the voices in her head.

BA loves to talk to her readers and can be found at http://batortuga.com/ and her newsletter signup link is http://bit.ly/BAJulianews

AVAILABLE FROM JODI & BA

The Cowboy and the Dom Trilogy

First Rodeo, Book One

Razor's Edge, Book Two

No Ghosts, Book Three

The Soldier and the Angel, a Cowboy and Dom Novel

Sin Deep, a Cowboy and Dom Novel

East Meets Westerns

(single titles)

Wrecked

Window Dressing

Flying Blind

Special Delivery, A Wrecked Holiday Novel

Temptation Ranch

The Higher Elevation Series

Heart of a Cowboy

Land of Enchantment

Keeping Promises

Bigger Than Us

The Triskelion Series

Breaking the Rules

Making a Mark

Making the Rules

Les's Bar Series

Just Dex

Hide Bound

The Lone Star Series

Tending Tyler

Roped In

The Collaborations Series

Refraction

Syncopation

Puzzles Series

Cryptic

Interested in learning more about BA's cowboys and Jodi's gentlemen? Want free fiction and news? Join our newsletters!

What's Up with Jodi
http://bit.ly/whatsupjodi

Spurs and Shifters
https://lp.constantcontact.com/su/A9CRUzp/baandjulia